The fiery brilliance of the Zebra Hologram Heart which you see on the cover is created by "laser holography." This is the revolutionary process in which a powerful laser beam records light waves in diamond-like facets so tiny that 9,000,000 fit in a square inch. No print or photograph can match the vibrant colors and radiant glow of a hologram.

So look for the Zebra Hologram Heart whenever you buy a historical romance. It is a shimmering reflection of our guarantee that you'll find consistent quality between the covers!

C0-APP-834

A LESSON OF LOVE

"Teach me, Nick. I want to know how to please you."

Morgan's fingers entwined in Nick's sun-streaked hair as she pressed herself into him, feeling the slight pressure of his belt buckle against her stomach, his leather breeches clinging to her bare thighs. Impatient now, her hands moved inside his shirt, enjoying the feel of his coarse curly hair beneath her fingertips. She wanted . . . she didn't know what, but every nerve ending was acutely sensitive to the touch of his calloused fingers, his manly scent.

Aware of her impatience, Nicholas scooped her into his arms, her hair falling across his shoulders in a cascade of silken loveliness. As he nuzzled her neck, he could see the tiny goose bumps along her arms. His voice husky, Nick said, "I want to teach you the finer points of lovemaking, beauty. Trust me, Morgan. I will not hurt you."

Before she could utter a protest, Nicholas enveloped her mouth with a kiss that erased any fear or doubts she might have had. All she wanted, all she ever wanted was Nick. . . .

PASSION'S PIRATE
VICTORIA LONDON

ZEBRA BOOKS
KENSINGTON PUBLISHING CORP.

ZEBRA BOOKS

are published by

Kensington Publishing Corp.
475 Park Avenue South
New York, NY 10016

First printing: March 1986

Printed in the United States of America

TO H.I.L.
MY BEST FRIEND, MY HERO, MY HUSBAND

Prologue

PHILADELPHIA—APRIL, 1808

"Gentlemen of the jury, have you reached a verdict?"

"Yes we have Your Honor. We find the defendant, Samuel Rhinehart, guilty of treason."

The once hushed courtroom erupted. Hands bound by rope, his gray head and shoulders slumped in utter defeat, Samuel Rhinehart no longer cared what happened to him. It was his family that he was concerned about . . . had always worried about. What would his wife and daughters do now? They were vulnerable, dependent on him. How would they manage when he was not there to protect them?

Slowly he turned his thin body to meet the loyal gaze of his eldest daughter, Morgan. She was standing alone in the corner of the room, her golden eyes drowning in tears. Thank God his wife was home with little Elizabeth who still suffered from a bad chill. At least they were spared this day's horror. But Morgan insisted on being in the courtroom, making her daily presence felt, intuitively knowing that Samuel found tranquility from her strength. Well, as long as his family believed that he was not guilty of stealing the copper currency plates, Samuel was content. Morgan and his wife Charlotte never once doubted his innocence. They believed his story about the "journalist" who had spent so much time with Samuel and his bank assistants because he wanted to write about the U.S. banks and the printing of U.S. currency.

In fact, Samuel thought he was such a nice young chap that he wanted to introduce Mr. Andrews to Morgan. But then Andrews abruptly left. And Samuel never did read the article. It wasn't until two weeks later when Samuel was accused of stealing the plates that he realized Andrews might have had something to do with this theft, leaving all the incriminating evidence at Samuel's doorstep.

His assistant had verified the presence of this writer at the trial, but the prosecutor dismissed the whole idea.

As soon as this line of questioning had begun, friends and allies disappeared. No one wanted to be the friend of an accused traitor.

But his family remained loyal. Not in these long months of imprisonment did they once question his innocence.

Suddenly, as if in a silent nightmare, he saw Morgan clutch her throat, her eyes reflecting her astonishment.

"Since the plates have not been recovered, the jurors have recommended this sentence." The judge was shouting above the din.

What sentence?

". . . sentenced to spend the rest of your life in prison." Samuel heard the words but could not comprehend them. Not a death sentence? Well, perhaps there was hope. Yes, he smiled, this must be God's way.

Morgan continued to believe that the traitor would come back to Philadelphia; that he would confess and hand the copper plates back to the bank authorities.

Still, how could his family get by without him? Morgan trusted too easily. What would this spirited eighteen-year-old do with her life? The daughter of a traitor! Who would marry her? Could she support her mother and sister? Samuel knew the family exhausted its savings months ago.

The noise in the courtroom penetrated his tired mind once more. Hands reached out to touch him, people cursed him as he was led out of the courtroom back to his cell. All Samuel saw was Morgan's lovely face, her chin proudly lifted, her determined gaze focusing directly at him. Then he heard her whisper, "I love you, Papa. There is still hope," before she disappeared. Yes, he thought, there is always hope.

It was strange but Samuel was glad it was almost over. Yet he could not shake the uneasy feeling that he must have overlooked some clues; perhaps the associates of Andrews and other unusual occurrences, anything that would help him identify the traitor. Was Andrews his real name? There was one thing that could help identify the man if the opportunity ever presented itself: Andrews had a strange red mark on his left cheek—a birthmark or scar.

Well, I will have plenty of time Samuel decided. Yes, too much time.

They were almost outside of the dimly lit courtroom. A small group of persistent gawkers remained, almost encircling Samuel. Looking up, he saw a face lurking behind the crowd. He was wearing a dark brown hat and cape, which partially obscured his face and medium frame. It was him! Andrews!

"Wait!" he shouted. "I must talk to you." Desperately turning to the jailor, he tried explaining about the man. His voice was barely heard among the people, but Samuel knew that Andrews heard him.

Slowly turning, he doffed his brown hat and smiled. It was a bloodless smile.

"Wait," Samuel struggled with his bonds, then implored the jailor. "I must see that man. That's Andrews!"

"Of course Rhinehart. Mayhap the old lady in the corner is the one ye're looking for. Come along," he tugged at the rope bindings, pulling Samuel past Andrews.

"No. You do not understand. I must . . . ahh."

The jailor suddenly felt himself being pulled down by the weight of his prisoner. People were standing so close to them. As the jailor fell to his knees, he quickly looked to his left, and recognized death in the glazed eyes of Samuel Rhinehart. A knife protruded from his back.

Bending to the prisoner, the jailor heard Rhinehart's last words. "He . . . is the . . . traitor." His bony hands partially lifted pointing at his assassin. But with all the pandemonium Andrews easily escaped.

The stunned onlookers spread out staring at one another in horror and fear. "Who killed the traitor?" they asked.

It was a question no one could answer.

Chapter 1

NEW YORK—JUNE, 1808

"Nicholas, for the last time, I am telling you . . . no I am ordering you to stop your activities or they will be the death of your mother and me."

"Why?" the tall man queried. "Are you concerned for my well-being, Father, or for your public reputation?"

"Nicholas, you are twenty-seven years old. You have had your fun, the experience of pirating your own ship, of being shot at by the British and the Americans. It is enough!"

Warren Rhodes looked at his younger son and sighed. Why couldn't Nicholas be more like his older brother, who happily shared the success of the family's law firm. Jonathan was married—his wife was nice, albeit a little plain—but the perfect mate for Jonathan. They both wanted the same things: respectability and a place in New York's society.

Not Nicholas. He had always been different: independent, oftentimes defiant, and determined to make his own fortune while having a damn good time of it.

"Stop staring out the window Nick. The scenery hasn't changed. There is just more traffic on the street nowadays. All these matrons parading their eligible and often very unattractive daughters along Broadway."

"Father you never take the time to appreciate the good things in life. You are too concerned with politics, making money, and being respectable."

11

Nicholas moved away from the window, seating himself in the deep red leather sofa. He was bored and very restless. Whenever these feelings possessed him, Nicholas knew it was time to go back to work. Whether Warren Rhodes approved or not, sailing the *Anastasia* across the American border—buying and selling American and British goods—was his occupation. Quite a profitable one too.

Looking at his father's stern expression, Nicholas repressed a smile. Instead, his light gray eyes focused on the portraits along the panelled walls of the study. There they were, neatly lined up—the Rhodes family—all reputable New Yorkers, the men well-known lawyers or politicians and the women somehow distinguishable from each other. Hair piled high on their heads, expressionless eyes—all in assorted colors— diamonds around their necks, gowns in whatever were the most stylish designs of the time. He looked further down, locating his mother's portrait. It just did not do her justice. The gray eyes and blond hair—so like his—were there. But her spirit, the laughter, and her love of life were missing. She never liked that portrait. In fact, she had insisted it be put in the darkest corner of the room.

There were two portraits missing: his own, since he steadfastly refused to be among the group, and his Uncle Eric's, who was a rogue no better than himself. Apparently Uncle Eric had the good sense to leave the family at an early age to move west, shunning the Rhodes name and fortune. Of course, it was said that Nicholas took after Uncle Eric.

"Son, you are not listening to me." Warren's voice intruded on his thoughts.

"Father," Nicholas turned to face him, "why don't you let me be. Each time I come home for a visit, we go through the same charade. You tell me about the merits of your wealth, power, and law firm; how important the family is; how important it is to marry and join you and Jonathan in the firm. Well," his gray eyes turned to steel, "I do not want it. Thank you but no! I do not need it. I will make my own name and my own money."

"Illegally," his father replied. "Really Nick, this whole thing is ridiculous. How much longer can you avoid the

12

authorities?" Seeing that his son was angry enough to stalk out of the house, Warren softened his tone. "All right, we will not talk of this anymore today."

"Not today, not tomorrow," Nicholas snapped.

Deciding it was time to change the topic for now, Warren calmly said, "Sit down son. Please. I have something I need to talk to you about." Noting the hesitant look in Nick's eyes, Warren smiled. "Since you are so disinclined to have anything to do with the Rhodes law firm, perhaps you can assist me in another way."

Instead of fully complying with his father's request, Nicholas leaned against his father's large teak desk, crossing his booted feet over one another. Hands lightly gripping the edge of the desk, Nicholas waited for his father to pour the brandy before sitting in the Sheraton armchair to his left. The fading rays of the sun filtered through the shuttered windows, catching the golden highlights of Nicholas's sun-bleached hair, settling on the oddly shaped ring on his left hand. The ring, meticulously carved in gold, was in the shape of a ship's anchor. What made it appear more unusual was the horizontal center of the anchor—a pirate's sword. The hilt, facing his knuckle, was made up of alternating rows of diamonds and sapphires. An ornate object on any other man, but on Nicholas the odd ring symbolized his love of the sea and his profession. For Nicholas was a smuggler, free-spirited and untamed. This was the life he chose to lead.

"Nick, I want to ask a favor of you."

"I told you . . ." he began to move.

"Just wait a minute." Warren's blue eyes darkened. "It is not what you think."

"Go on."

Nicholas took the glass his father offered, resuming his former stance.

"Since you are so accustomed to danger, I have an assignment for you. Do you remember the little scandal of a few months ago, concerning the theft of some currency plates from the U.S. Bank of Philadelphia?"

"I thought they were found, and the bank supervisor tried as a traitor."

13

"Samuel Rhinehart was sentenced, but not to die. Before he left the courtroom, some fanatic murdered him. No one knows who killed Rhinehart. Nevertheless, the story the Treasury Department gave to everyone was that the plates were found. . . . But they were not. Our government does not want anyone to believe otherwise. You know as well as I do Nick, that the whole economy of our nation could collapse. The paper dollar is printed from these plates."

Somewhat intrigued by this story, Nicholas moved toward the desk chair, arrogantly propping his legs up on the desk, amused by his father's scowl.

"What does any of this have to do with you, Father?"

"Come now Nick. You know how many friends I have in the government. You know that if I wanted to be appointed a state judge, I could arrange it at any time."

Nicholas loved the way his father proudly announced his friendship with the leading Democratic-Republicans—including Thomas Jefferson and the soon-to-be new President, James Madison. It was, however, all true. From as far back as he could remember, there was always some politician in the Rhodes home asking for—sometimes pleading for—Warren Rhodes's advice and support.

"The Secretary of the Treasury, Albert Gallatin, has quietly asked some of his closest friends to cooperate in this matter."

"I see." Nicholas drained his glass, helping himself to another.

"As I previously said, the copper plates have not been found. Rhinehart, until the day he was murdered, insisted he was innocent, that he knew nothing of the stolen plates. But many of us think differently."

Warren looked up into his son's suntanned features, dispassionately admiring his handsome face and strong, lean body. His coloring was so like his darling mother's that Warren felt a softening of his attitude toward his younger son. True, Nick was different from him and his brother, but he was still his flesh and blood; stronger, more determined, and far more courageous than Jonathan could ever hope to be.

"Nicholas, are you listening to me?"

"Of course, Father. But," he glanced at the large French

14

mantle clock and added, "I uh . . . have an engagement this evening. One I uh . . . cannot cancel."

"Certainly. I will try to be brief. Heaven knows I shall not be the one to keep you from your latest female friend. What is this one's name?"

"Margaret."

"Nicholas, not Margaret Lawson, the daughter of the largest merchant family in New York!" He smiled broadly. "Why son, you are more socially minded than I thought."

"Hardly. You do not know Margaret Lawson." Nicholas felt a tightening in his loins, remembering their previous evening and morning together.

Before Warren had time to consider his son's words, Nicholas insisted he continue his story about the currency plates.

"Rhinehart had a family you know. A wife and two daughters. They have left Philadelphia. The last I heard, they settled in Boston—using different names."

"It must be difficult for them."

"Don't get maudlin now. Nick, we have reason to believe that Rhinehart's oldest daughter—her name is Morgan, an odd name for a female—knows exactly where the plates are. She probably has them in her possession and is waiting for a propitious moment to sell them to the highest bidder. French or English—it does not matter to a traitor. Can you imagine what would happen if they printed dollars from those plates— or if they tried to blackmail us, threatening to wreck our currency if we do not comply with their demands. Both countries can only profit by our economic failure."

"What does any of this have to do with me?" A note of suspicion crept into Nicholas's voice.

"I want you to find the Rhinehart family. Find the girl and the plates. I don't care how you manage this, but Nicholas, I am asking this one favor of you. I am asking you to demonstrate your patriotism, your loyalty to your family and country." He sighed loudly, "This is the least you can do to atone for your other . . . shall we say, less legal activities."

Nicholas was out of the chair in an instant. "Me?" he bellowed. "Why me?"

"Because you are more familiar with those, ahem, questionable people who would know about this kind of skullduggery. And," he rushed on as his son was about to interrupt, "you still have a good name to get you into the best social circles. I also heard that you have an honorable reputation as a smuggler—if there is such a thing."

"Pray continue." Nick grinned, acknowledging his father's odd compliment.

"If you find these plates, I promise you I shall not harass you too much about changing your profession. Nick," his father's tone became conciliatory, "I would really appreciate this and surely you owe me this much."

"Perhaps I do." Nicholas walked behind his father. For the first time he noticed the slightly hunched shoulders, the gray hair—almost completely white now. Warren Rhodes was not a young man; if this little assignment could bring his father some measure of confidence, then so be it.

"What else do I need to know?"

Chapter 2

BOSTON—SEPTEMBER, 1808

An old beggar woman shuffled down the dark cobblestoned street toward the harbor, the moonless night hindering her journey. Slouched shoulders, thick chest, and grizzled gray hair, mostly hidden by a tattered black shawl, made more than one sailor turn away. The old woman did not seem to care or notice the people along the streets. Nor did the chilly, damp air seem to affect her weary bones. Slowly, she made her way.

The middle-aged man seated in the worn leather chair was about to leave his office. The *Anastasia* had docked early this evening, and from all the stories George heard this day, the ship—thanks to her arrogant but clever captain—barely escaped capture by the American authorities. There would be so much activity tomorrow when the hordes of merchants and residents descended the docks for a glimpse of the cargo containing the tea, silks, and manufactured goods from England. Then there would be the other merchants, hauling their goods onto the slick three-masted schooner, to be sold to equally eager British merchants across the American border.

The Embargo Act of 1807 did not win support in most New England homes. There was no reason in the world why these two countries should not trade with one another, regardless of what Thomas Jefferson thought about the British. The whole episode was absurd, and most New Englanders recognized that to be a fact.

A soft knocking at the door interrupted George's angry thoughts.

"Come back tomorrow!" he answered. "It is too late. The office is closed."

"Mr. Taggart," a soft yet insistent voice called, "you must let me in. It's Morgan Rhinehart."

The man cursed before getting out of his chair. He opened the door with one quick move.

"What are you doing out so late in the evening, Missy? Come in. Come in."

He liked his newest client. Soft-spoken, obviously well-educated and refined, there was an unmistakable air of mystery and sorrow about her. When he first met her, he was touched by the sad story. He had heard the rumors before he met Miss Rhinehart, but after hearing her version of the terrible story, it confirmed his instinctive belief that her father was innocent. And when she began to cry, her tawny eyes filling with tears, George felt so moved as to reduce his usual fee to half. His wife always scolded him for being such a good-hearted fool. It was no small wonder that they still lived with her mother.

"You cannot walk about the harbor alone, Miss Rhinehart, especially at night. I insist upon walking you home."

The young woman smiled. "I can assure you sir, no one would accost me looking like this."

Closing the door, she reached for the rags stuffed into a battered straw bag. Within minutes, the lovely dark-haired beauty who had proudly stood before him turned into an arthritic looking hag!

"Impressive Miss Rhinehart."

"Sir," she removed the ugly black shawl, "I am not naive. I do know how to protect myself. See?" She pulled a tiny pistol out of the huge gray cloak. "I know how to use it." Her cultured voice was so grim that George Taggart wondered what this young creature must have experienced to sound so bitter.

"Yes, well, ahem . . . why don't you transform into your original self and have a cup of tea with me?"

Without smiling, she did as he asked.

18

"Well," he began, "I still do not have the information you seek. A man fitting this fellow Andrews' description was seen in Baltimore a few weeks past. He was not alone. There were two other people with him—a young man and woman."

"Their names?"

"Anderson."

"It is close, I suppose." Morgan sat stiffly on the edge of the seat, her erect spine making no contact with the high-backed chair. "Did he have the birthmark?"

"Don't know. This fellow was sporting a full beard and his hair was reddish, not the dark brown you described. But," he waved his hand, "that could be because of a wig or some artificial coloring. He might have been wearing a wig when your father met him."

"How will I ever find him, Mr. Taggart?" Morgan was at the end of her wits and money. The sewing she and her mother were doing for Madame Flournay could not support them and pay Mr. Taggart too. Nor could they continue to live off the charity of Charlotte's brother and his family. They had to find a home of their own.

"If he is the one you are looking for, Missy, and if he still has those plates, I am sure that he will try to sell them. Now, there are not too many people who could handle that kind of transaction," he paused, offering Morgan another cup of tea.

"How will I know about that?"

"That is what you are paying me for. I know the right sort of people who are willing to sell that kind of information."

"When did the Andersons leave Baltimore?" Her voice sounded weary with frustration.

"About a fortnight ago. They will appear soon. I don't believe he has left this country, for if he did, my friends who know the Baltimore ships would have written me. No," he leaned back in his battered chair, "I feel it here," he pressed his heart. "That traitor will reappear and I will find him for you, Miss Rhinehart."

A slight smile appeared on her face. "I wish I had your confidence, Mr. Taggart. I am tired of living this fraudulent life—the poor relation who makes her money as a seamstress. I am proud of my father's name. I hate using the name Maryann

Richards in public."

George patted her trembling hand in a paternal gesture, his eyes showing his sympathy. "It must be a terrible strain on you and your family."

Holding back the familiar tears, Morgan nodded and sighed. "Well, I guess I should make my way home now." She rose from the chair reaching once more for the worn straw bag. Transforming herself into the old hag with the tattered black shawl, she shuffled down the dark street successfully avoiding the people hurrying toward a ship docked further down the wharf.

She would have made it home without incident if a horse and its rider that came thundering around the corner had seen her crossing the road. Recognizing the sound, Morgan tried to scramble away from the horse and rider. But her foot caught on a loose cobblestone and she crashed to the ground, bumping her head. When she looked up, she saw the rider, pulling back on the animal's rein as it approached her. She screamed as the horse reared, its front hooves scratching the air. Morgan tried desperately to rise just as the horse descended. Something hit her temple, and she unconsciously crumpled onto the damp street.

"Why didn't that stupid old woman see me?" the deep voice complained to no one in particular. Rushing to the old woman's side, he cursed himself for not paying attention. So eager to be off the *Anastasia* and into Cynthia's waiting arms, Nicholas left the unloading of the cargo to the hands of his first mate.

Now this! "Damn my luck! I hope the hag is alive." He bent down to examine the woman, unmindful of his snowy white breeches in the mud. Turning her around, he placed his finger to the pulse in her neck. She was alive. Slowly removing the shawl from her injured head, he tried not to touch her. The light was so dim, he failed to recognize her youthful face, stained now with blood and mud. As he lifted the black rag from her head, Nicholas was shocked to see the gray wig lift with the shawl.

20

Not until the midnight hair spilled onto his hand, did he fully realize that this was not an old woman in his arms. Fingers gently probing her temple, Nicholas stiffened when the woman groaned. A large bump continued to grow as he felt her temple. But it was the stickiness in his fingers that concerned him. She was bleeding and there was no possibility of finding the wound in this dingy street. Cursing once again, Nicholas gingerly lifted the still form, surprised by how little she weighed. Placing her on the horse, he slowly mounted the animal, cushioning her frail body with his much taller frame. Realizing there was nowhere else he could take her, Nicholas turned the horse to slowly make their way back to the *Anastasia*. With luck, the ship's surgeon would still be aboard.

Morgan's eyes fought to open but the sharp pain in her head made it nearly impossible to do anything but groan. Lifting her hand to touch her temple, she cried aloud when she felt the outline of the large bump.

"It is all right. Don't worry angel, you will be fine."

The voice was so reassuring and very masculine. It was an educated voice . . . like her father's.

"Papa. Is that you?" She struggled to open her eyes to see her father once more. "Papa?" she whispered, lifting her hand to his face. But the chin was much firmer than her father's and the nose longer and straighter.

He could sense the young woman's rising panic. Nicholas crooned, "You are safe. No one will hurt you. My name is Nicholas Rhodes and you are on my ship. I will send someone for your father. Who are you beautiful lady?" He wanted to ask many more questions, but Casey had told him she would not fully comprehend very much in the next few hours. Thank God the injury was not as severe as Nicholas first thought.

"Dead," she cried. "He is dead. Oh Papa, I miss you so much." Tears ran down her temple onto the fluffy pillows.

"Open your eyes, sweetheart. Come on, try." The voice sounded so kind. Struggling against the sharp pain, Morgan forced her eyes to open.

If Nicholas thought the unconscious mysterious woman in

his bed was attractive, he was completely taken in by the golden eyes staring at him. She was beautiful and so fragile lying on his big wooden-framed bed, covered to her neck with a heavy down quilt.

Observing her opulent surroundings and finally comprehending the gravity of her situation, Morgan vainly tried to sit up. "I must go home. My family will worry about me."

His strong arms caught her shoulders. "You are in no condition to go anywhere. I will send a sailor with a note explaining everything. Perhaps your mother will want to return with him so she may spend the night here with you."

"No. She cannot. Lizzie is sick again."

"Who is Lizzie?"

"My sister. She is only seven. No," she struggled again, but was too weak to continue, "I really must leave. Thank you Captain." A wave of dizziness overcame her as Morgan whimpered.

"Please. Let me help you. I am completely responsible for your accident. I was the rider."

Strange, he did not sound very remorseful, she thought. Vaguely, she remembered how strong he felt when she was in his arms. His voice was that of a young man. If she ever stopped seeing double, perhaps she could see his face.

"What is your name, angel?" he coaxed, realizing she was losing consciousness once more.

"Morgan."

Nicholas stiffened. Could this lovely weakened creature be the same Morgan Rhinehart he was looking for? How many young women named Morgan could there be in Boston? Could his luck be this good?

"No, it's Maryann," she hastily corrected. "Maryann Richards. Please, my head hurts so, I don't know what I am saying any longer. You can send a message to my mother. We are living with my uncle Benjamin Driscoll on Beacon Street."

After she gave him the address, Nicholas carefully penned a note to "Mrs. Richards" about her daughter. Assuring the family of her safety, Nicholas asked if she wanted to send a maid to spend the night with Maryann. He personally offered to escort Mrs. Richards to the ship in the morning. Not knowing how much her family knew of her late night escapade, Nicholas made no mention of her being so near the Boston wharf. Instead he fabricated a "safer" area where the accident had occurred.

Looking down at the unconscious young woman, Nicholas felt his body stir. Such a beautiful creature, he mused. Her long black hair—now neatly spread out on his white pillow—invited his touch. Her pert nose, with just a slight sprinkling of freckles, high cheekbones, and heart-shaped mouth reminded him of how many weeks he had been without a woman. But those round tawny eyes with dark irises and black-fringed lashes made him wonder. Could she be a traitor, a calculating witch who fully knows her effect on men, who uses them until she gets what she wants?

But she seemed so vulnerable lying on his bed. His large hands could almost encircle her tiny waist. And the dark circles under the catlike eyes revealed that she had known deep sorrow. When she cried in her stupor, "Papa, I miss you," Nicholas's heart fluttered. Would this woman use him too—make a fool out of him? Or was she innocent, in life and in love?

Gently brushing a lock of hair off her bruised temple, Nicholas raised it to his lips and asked, "Who are you Maryann/Morgan?"

Knowing there would be time to speak with her, Nicholas relaxed, kissed her forehead, then sought a sailor to deliver his message.

Chapter 3

"Morgan, can you hear me?" Charlotte placed her cool hand on her daughter's warm brow, hoping her fever would not rise. For two days, Morgan lay motionless on the captain's large oak-framed bed. Charlotte tried not to worry. Lord, if anything happened to Morgan, she too would die, knowing that she could not take any more heartache. Morgan was only doing what *she* should have done, Charlotte told herself for the hundredth time. It was my duty to hire Mr. Taggart, my duty to find my husband's murderer, not my child's responsibility. Overnight, Morgan had lost her vivaciousness, her quick smile, her silvery laughter, that took pleasure in being alive and loved by her parents.

Charlotte could not let Morgan carry this burden alone any longer. Pursing her thin lips, Charlotte ran her hand through her dark hair—streaked with gray. No more, she promised Morgan.

As she placed a cold wet cloth on her daughter's temple, she listened to the sounds aboard this ship. A large schooner, the captain told her. When she had been escorted aboard two days ago, she could not help but notice the neatly stacked wooden crates with various markings and suspected Captain Rhodes of dealing in illegal contraband. But he was such a nice young man—and obviously a gentleman—his occupation was irrelevant, Charlotte decided.

From the moment he had shown up at her brother's door, Charlotte knew that this young man was kind—and very solicitous of her needs. More importantly, Captain Rhodes felt such remorse over the accident and worried about Morgan's health that he often remained in the room with them. Nevertheless, as soon as her daughter was able, they would leave his ship.

In the last year, Charlotte Rhinehart had learned to be cautious. Even though this man offered to help them, Charlotte could not reveal the truth. In spite of her nightmares the last two nights, Morgan revealed little of the past year. She seemed to block out this real nightmare, going back to a time when the only concern she had was which beau she would allow to visit with her family.

"Mrs. Richards," the captain's rich voice intruded on her thoughts, "you did not hear me knocking. May I come in?"

"Oh, I apologize Captain. I was thinking about Maryann and her sister." Charlotte watched the man bend his head and shoulders before entering the doorway.

"The previous owner of the *Anastasia* did not concern himself with doorways that were higher than six feet two inches. He was barely five feet tall." His deep rumble of insouciant laughter made her smile in response.

"How is she?" His concerned gray eyes focused on the lovely patient. His desire to bed Cynthia was now forgotten. Nicholas only left the ship during the day to see the broker who was handling the sale of his lucrative cargo and to share a drink or two with his crew.

Looking at the mother, Nicholas could see why the daughter was such a beauty, although she too wore a look of dismay and pain. When he had escorted "Mrs. Richards" to the ship two days ago, he tried to comfort her when she cried over her almost lifeless daughter. And when the mother whispered, "I cannot lose you too," Nicholas wanted to forget about his father's request and offer his services to the distressed widow. But Mrs. Richards was too cautious or probably too afraid to trust anyone, let alone a smuggler. Undaunted, he offered to help them each time he visited the cabin. He was politely refused, yet Nicholas sensed that Mrs. Richards would eventually—if given enough time—confide in him.

It was different for her beautiful daughter. Underneath that lovely exterior beat a heart of steel. The ugly bruise on her right temple told him she was in a good deal of pain, much more than she admitted. Watching her unconsciously bite her sore lip to prevent the moan from escaping, Nicholas recognized her inner strength. She was a stubborn fighter.

More than once he cursed himself for imagining his arms wrapped around her curvacious body. How would she respond to me? he wondered. Was she still an untried virgin? Nicholas was almost ready to give up his ship for the chance to intimately explore the body of the mysterious woman in his bed.

"Captain, I do not think we can impose on your generosity much longer. Perhaps I should ask my brother to bring a litter so that we could bring Maryann to his house."

"Nonsense. I will not hear of this. I am responsible and I will not let your daughter leave until she can walk out on her own." Nicholas reached for Charlotte's hand, wanting to reassure her. "Please, Mrs. Richards. Say," he brightened, "why don't you bring your daughter Lizzie to the ship. She must be well by now and I have never known a child who would miss an opportunity to explore a ship."

She hesitated, but Nicholas knew she would relent. Promising to watch Maryann, Nicholas sent his first mate with Mrs. Richards to collect Lizzie.

There was a shining light—blinding her now with its intensity. Annoyed, Morgan lifted her hand to protect her eyes, then opened them. Looking around the strange room, she found nothing familiar. Almost everything, from the dark cherry wood-panelled walls, to the matching desk and table, even the brightly colored Persian carpet, bespoke of a masculine touch. The room was very large and quite comfortable. But where was she? And whose bed was she in?

Struggling to rise, Morgan fought the dizziness that had formerly overcome her. Only when she thought she saw a man—the familiar face in her dreams—did she remember what had happened.

Nicholas was reclining in a high-backed uncushioned chair.

His long muscular legs in tight fawn leather breeches and knee-high black leather boots were propped up on another equally uncomfortable looking chair. The man appeared to be dozing. But his squirming body shifted so often, Morgan wondered how he could possibly be asleep after squeezing himself into that chair.

Fighting a losing battle, Morgan's eyes roamed over the stranger's face and form. He was incredibly handsome. Morgan could almost believe that this was not a mortal but a god before her. His blond hair was streaked with white highlights. It was long—to the middle of his thick neck—and slightly wavy with unruly locks folding across his forehead and ears. His golden skin showed the many hours he must spend out of doors. An aristocratic nose and firm, almost square, chin reminded Morgan of his masculine beauty. Only the slight scar slashing across his brow—very near his left eye—marred his perfection.

Her eyes lowered to his mouth, which quivered as he lightly snored. She wondered what it might be like to be kissed by this Adonis. Instinctively, Morgan knew that this man could bring forth a passionate response in a woman.

It wasn't until her eyes focused on the lower regions of his body that she realized he was lying perfectly still. A deep red blush crept up her face. Morgan was afraid to look up. When she finally gave in to the temptation, his smoky gray eyes—creased in the corners with obvious amusement—met her surprised look.

"Do you like what you see, sweetheart?"

"I . . . uh . . . I . . . am not sure," she stammered. "I . . . uh . . . who are you?"

He was instantly at her side, seating himself on the edge of the bed.

"Do you remember what happened?" She nodded. "That was two days ago, my beauty."

"Two days! Mother, Lizzie, they must be frantic. I must leave now." Her eyes rounded and her complexion paled as she struggled to rise. She swung her feet off the bed, digging her hands into the deep mattress. She stood for a few seconds before her head and limbs refused to obey her brain.

"Ooh." Morgan sagged into the strong embrace of the captain.

"Easy beauty," his voice was comforting. "You are not well. Your mother and sister are fine. In fact, your mother was here most of the time. She went home to bring your sister here for a visit."

He was still standing with Morgan leaning against his body, his hand smoothing her hair in a gesture that seemed familiar to her. Her head fell against his chest, blond curly hairs tickling her nose. But she felt at ease. Unthinkingly, her hand reached up to feel his smooth linen shirt and touched his skin. She could hear the steady thumping of his heart against her ear, and Morgan closed her eyes. What did it matter that nothing in her life was normal anymore? She wanted to forget her misery. This man's strength, clean masculine scent, and gentle stroking hands were all part of her fantasy. Nothing was real.

Her compliance surprised Nicholas. His urge to feel her skin was pronounced by the late morning light passing through her white lawn nightgown. Large, calloused hands lowered to her shoulders, continuing a slow downward path along the curve of her slender spine, then lower, to her rounded derrière. The girl sighed seconds before Nicholas pressed her into his hardened caress.

Before she could voice a protest, his mouth found hers, delighting in the feel of her warm, smooth lips. The tender kiss deepened when Nicholas sensed that she had no idea of what it meant to be kissed by a man. His tongue moistened her soft lips, easing them open and gaining entrance to her mouth and tongue. The heightened sensation reminded him of the experienced woman he had forsaken two nights ago.

Morgan was in a trance. Chills and heat simultaneously assaulted her body, weakening her to this stranger's touch. It was as if she had entered her home, seated at the warm hearth after suffering from the bone chilling cold of the outdoors. His hand slid around to her narrow waist, moving higher, resting on her left breast, caressing the contours then teasing her nipple to heightened exhilaration. This must stop, she thought, but she could not find her voice.

"You are a rare treasure, Morgan."

She froze.

Pulling herself out of his embrace, she whispered, "Why did you call me Morgan?" She should have felt enraged. She should have accused him of forcing the information out of her—a captive of her unconscious ramblings—or perhaps forcing her mother to confess, but she lacked the emotion. Of course she was surprised, but more than that she was relieved. There was no need to pretend with this man, for she thought she would never see him once she left his ship.

"Did I tell you or my mother?"

Expecting a heated denial, he was perplexed by how resigned she was to the use of her real name.

"You did when I first brought you aboard," he responded, studying her face, looking for some signs of anger or fear. "Who are you hiding from?" Leading her over to his armchair, Nicholas pulled her onto his lap. He stroked her long black hair, feeling the rest of her muscles relax as she moved into his embrace. "You can tell me if you want. I am no fool, Morgan. I know that you and your mother are suffering. Perhaps you simply need someone to talk to."

His genuine smile, strong voice, and comforting touch undid her. Before she could stop them, crystal tears trickled down her still-bruised face.

Nicholas let her bury her face in his chest, soaking the front of his white linen shirt. Her sobs were so deep that Nicholas wondered if she had ever truly expressed her emotions during the long months of her family's ordeal. When the sobs seemed to lessen, he offered his silk handkerchief to wipe her nose.

"Now tell me your troubles, my sweet."

"It would only shock you," she replied in a small voice.

Placing his finger under her chin, Nicholas lifted her face to his. Smoky gray eyes stared down into her topaz gaze. Sensing her shame, he said, "Do you know what I do, Morgan? I am a smuggler. Most people would not consider it a very noble profession. But I do. Frankly, I am not concerned about people's thoughts."

Her eyes caught the gold glint of his oddly shaped ring, and she realized he was more than likely an unconventional sort.

"What I am trying to tell you, beauty, is that there is nothing you could say or do that would shock me. I have seen it all. I could not be any more jaded." His smile lifted the corners of his mouth. Morgan noticed the tiny creases about his eyes. In spite of her distressed state, she still managed to admire his handsome face and smiled at the realization of her predicament.

"Ah, you can smile. If it's possible, I think you are lovelier when you smile." His index finger traced the curve of her mouth. Nicholas quickly reminded himself that this was not the time to renew his desire for her.

"My name is Morgan Rhinehart." There was a defiant tilt to her chin. When he did not appear to recognize the name, she continued. "My father, Samuel Rhinehart, was falsely accused of being a traitor. He was arrested and charged with stealing four currency plates from the United States Bank in Philadelphia. It was believed that he was trying to sell these plates to either England or France. My father was found guilty." She angrily brushed aside a tear from her cheek. "He was not sentenced to hang, as we all thought. His life was spared because the plates were not recovered. On the day of his sentencing, just as he was leaving the courtroom, he was murdered."

"Were you or your mother there?"

"No. But if I had been there, I would have seen that man Andrews. My father saw him, even shouted after him. The jailor did not pay attention to my father. *I* would have! I would have prevented Andrews from . . . from . . . stabbing him. Even though many were in the courtroom, no one paid attention to this assassin." Nicholas saw she was losing control again. Holding her tighter in his comforting embrace, he asked, "Are you blaming yourself for your father's death?"

"Yes! I should have stayed with him that day. I could have . . . I could have stopped Andrews. But I didn't. And," she choked on her tears, "my father died alone. No one was there to comfort him, to tell him how much he was loved. Oh, Captain, he was such a good man."

"You loved him very much. Tell me about him and your family," he said, taking the silk handkerchief from her hand, tenderly wiping her eyes, then helping her to blow her nose. "Don't you think, after sharing this intimacy, you could call me Nicholas?"

For more than one hour, Nicholas listened to Morgan's tale. She told him about her generous, loving father who for many years was the supervisor in the Philadelphia bank. Samuel was a very meticulous man, and according to Morgan, was an extremely loyal employee. There was never any reason to be dissatisfied with his employers. Money was not a serious problem for the Rhinehart family. Samuel was earning a good salary. In addition, Charlotte had some property and income from her family estate.

There was, as far as Nicholas could tell from the girl's teary recital, no reason why Samuel Rhinehart would suddenly turn traitor. He was highly respected in his community, the family had resided in Philadelphia for many years, plus the Rhinehart family had many friends, until the trial that is. . . .

It was as if a summer storm had descended upon the Rhineharts: rapid, fierce, carelessly uprooting anything in its awesome path. Within weeks, the family was torn apart, Samuel was arrested, their income decimated. Charlotte's property had to be sold to pay off the growing debts.

When Morgan described her father's encounter with the mysterious Andrews, Nicholas found it hard to believe that Samuel had allowed the man into the bank's vault. But, as Morgan pointed out, Andrews had so much documentation, including letters of introduction from some very well-known politicians and journalists, that there was no reason to deny him access to the bank for his story.

"You say you never met Andrews?"

"No, Captain, I mean Nicholas. Papa had invited him to our home, but Andrews declined. Once, when I met my father at the bank, Andrews had just left."

"Why did your family leave Philadelphia?" Nicholas needed to stretch his cramping legs, but did not want to let go of the wounded doe nestled in his lap.

Eyes studiously examining the ribbons on her nightdress, Morgan answered, "We had no choice. Mother and I could not find any positions. We certainly would not impose on anyone's

32

charity. Only my Uncle Benjamin would not hear of my mother remaining in Philadelphia, and insisted we come to live with him in Boston."

"It has not been easy for you, I know. But what are your plans now?" It was clear to him that she had no idea what he was leading up to. Nicholas wanted to make absolutely sure Morgan knew nothing about the missing plates.

"I must find Andrews, Anderson, or whatever his name is. And I swear I will not give up until my father's name is cleared," she vehemently replied. Her clear eyes met his, her expression resolute.

This young tigress was determined to try everything, of that he was sure. Still, he admired her for it, recognizing a kindred soul. More importantly, Nicholas believed her. The girl was innocent, as was her father. Samuel's name would have been cleared eventually, had he remained alive. Andrews must surely have known that, but why did he ruthlessly murder Rhinehart? What was Andrews afraid of? Nicholas dismissed the idea, concerning himself more with the beautiful waif comfortably resting in his arms. Why did he ever promise his father he would help? Suddenly, Nicholas didn't give a damn about the currency plates.

"Nicholas? What's wrong? Please let go of my arm."

"I am sorry, my pet. I did not mean to hurt you. Here," he stood up, still holding her in his arms, "you must be tired. Let me help you."

He only meant to put her back in his bed, but when her arms circled his neck, he felt the slight pressure of her breasts against his chest. Looking down into the trusting face, Nicholas felt the desire for her flare up once again. He lips captured hers in a slow, sensual kiss that would not appease him.

"I want you, beauty."

Feeling her own blood surge, Morgan responded by bringing her fingers to outline the full curve of his mouth.

"Kiss me again."

Nicholas lowered her onto the bed, leaning against her. He could not let go. Forgetting everything else, Nicholas's hand slid under the lawn nightgown, slowly tracing the path of the

33

material that he held aloft. Her smooth white skin invited his caress. As his hand moved higher, his tongue explored her mouth, searching for her tongue. Unable to catch her breath, Morgan groaned. She was without judgment in the arms of this blond god.

It wasn't until his fingers tickled her inner thigh that she boldly lowered her hand to feel his firm buttocks, the fine, smooth leather breeches becoming coarse to her touch. She needed to feel him, and wished that they could be free of their clothes.

Nicholas softly touched her moist center, and Morgan could not believe that another's touch could be so inviting.

"Morgan," he nuzzled her neck, "you must stop me. Your mother and sister are returning. I do not want to cause you embarrassment."

There was no need to reply, for in her hazy state she could still recognize Lizzie's insistent chatter, becoming clearer with her approach. With unusual strength born out of fear, Morgan pushed Nicholas off her and the bed.

Unaware of her sudden strength, Nicholas fell to the floor. The astonished look on his face caught Morgan's attention, even as she hastily smoothed her nightgown and adjusted the bedcovers. A soft, hesitant giggle emerged. But when he remained on his behind, legs and feet sprawled before him, Morgan's throaty laughter rang out.

"You look ridiculous!" Her face was an unusual shade of pink.

Nicholas should have been furious. No woman had ever pushed him out of bed. It was *his* bed. But she looked so carefree, it disarmed him. He reasoned that once she realized how close she came to losing her virginity, her good humor might end. He also realized how foolish he must look, as his deep hearty laughter mingled with hers.

That was how Charlotte and Lizzie found them.

Chapter 4

By the time the day ended, Lizzie Rhinehart had become the unofficial mascot of the schooner *Anastasia*.

Except for her hair, Lizzie had the same features as Morgan. Unruly, tiny corkscrew curls in a deep shade of brown with occasional red highlights could not be tamed by a multitude of hairpins. Long hair fell about her face, gold-flecked eyes, and neck. Because of her recent bouts with illness, Lizzie's coloring was quite pale. Only two red spots adorned her cheeks. But the crew of the *Anastasia* vowed to remedy that. Taking the burly hands of two sailors in hers, Lizzie allowed them to give her a thorough tour of the schooner, from the hold in the bowels of the ship to the furled sails of the mainmast.

The captain was also quite taken with the child. Perhaps her older sister was once as carefree and spontaneous. Nicholas was now more confused than ever. His gut reaction to Morgan's story was that she was not lying. Samuel Rhinehart's mistake was in believing that journalist—the real traitor—and for that he was falsely accused by his peers . . . then ruthlessly murdered. And the currency plates? Those, he was positive, were not in Morgan's possession.

However, believing Morgan Rhinehart would complicate Nicholas's life, possibly forcing him to break his promise to his father. Should he disassociate himself from the bloody mess? What would his father think? Would his father assume that his son was so involved in his smuggling enterprise that there was no time for keeping his word? It was the word of a gentleman, but then Warren Rhodes no longer—perhaps never did—think Nicholas was a gentleman. Warren and his associates believed that the Rhineharts were guilty of treason. How much would it take for Nicholas to prove otherwise? Did Nicholas have to prove otherwise?

"Yes, dammit," he said aloud. "Why did the Fates throw that beauty in front of me?"

Nicholas stalked around the main deck, barking at the first mate who had the misfortune of being in his path. He had to get off the ship, away from Morgan and her family. As soon as she was well—hopefully tomorrow—he would escort them home and be done with them.

"No, Nick," he scolded himself. "That is no longer possible, not if you want to keep your word to your father." He angrily kicked his booted foot at a wooden bucket, its contents now spreading across the wooden deck.

"Mr. McNeil!" he shouted to the first mate, "get this filthy mess cleaned up, now!" Once the tirade was unleashed, Nicholas found dozens of things suddenly wrong with the crew of the *Anastasia*.

The men grumbled, yet reluctantly did as bid, knowing the captain had a fearsome temper when crossed or when the mood struck him. When they saw the little girl fly across the deck, heading straight for the dour-faced captain, they tensed. Oh no, they mumbled, the poor little lamb is surely in for a spanking, or worse.

Arms outstretched, skirts and petticoats flying above her knees, Lizzie saw the tall, rigid back of the captain. In her opinion, he was a combination of Zeus and Adonis, no matter what Morgan said.

"Captain Nick," she called, "wait for me!"

Nicholas turned scant seconds before she bounded into him, her short arms trying to enfold his waist. Lizzie did not see the dark scowl on the man's face nor the quicksilver gleam in his eyes. All she heard was a soft "whoosh."

"Oh Captain Nick, you must come. The cat had kittens last night. Come," she pulled his arm, "I will show you. Cook said I can help care for them," her large golden eyes beseeched him, "if it is all right with you, that is."

Nicholas's frown disappeared. Lifting the child in his arms, he ruffled her curly hair. Lizzie's chubby arms wrapped around his neck in an affectionate hug before she kissed his stubby cheek.

"Ah," he laughed, his mood completely reversed, "now what sort of a response will I get, my pet, when I tell you that you may pick a kitten for yourself—if your mother and sister agree, of course."

Lizzie did not reply. She merely dragged him below to his quarters and charged into the room, landing on the bed. "Mama, Morgan, Captain Nick said I can have a kitten!"

Both Morgan and Charlotte appeared imperturbable. But the amusement in Morgan's eyes temporarily brightened Nicholas's attitude toward the Rhineharts.

"Captain, this is most generous of you. I feel that we are always thanking you for something." Morgan's smile affected him in a way he was reluctant to identify.

"No need."

To Morgan, the captain seemed cold and remote. The very idea of being in anyone's debt rankled her. But what was really troubling, was the ease with which she surrendered herself to him this morning. If it weren't for the timely interruption of her sister, Morgan knew that she would have complied with his every whim. Now, he appeared quite indifferent to her. This was unsettling. As much as she disliked being in her uncle's house, it was preferable to being coldly analyzed by this man. Despite a woolen shawl draped around her shoulders and the bedcovers pulled high over her, Morgan felt that the captain could see right through the thick material. A light pink flush warmed her cheeks and neck as Morgan met the captain's experienced gaze.

"Captain Rhodes, I am feeling well enough to leave this afternoon."

"Tomorrow morning will be fine," he curtly stated, suddenly miffed by her eagerness to depart.

His statement answered her unspoken question. Captain Rhodes was an anxious to be rid of her as she was to be rid of him.

Meanwhile, Charlotte watched the curious byplay between

the captain and her daughter. She smiled. She had a strong premonition that Nicholas Rhodes would not be out of her daughter's life as quickly as he might wish.

There was no time for a private good-bye. After dawn, Morgan's uncle Benjamin arrived to escort her off the ship. When Benjamin graciously thanked the captain, he hastily added that Nicholas must come to his home for dinner, for it was the least he could do to repay Captain Rhodes.

Preferring not to accept the invitation, Nicholas stole one look at Morgan's downcast eyes and immediately changed his mind.

"Why thank you, Mr. Driscoll, I accept."

"When are you due to leave Boston?"

The question was innocent enough, but once again Nicholas watched Morgan, who was valiantly trying to maintain a stony expression. But he noticed the way she twisted and untwisted a lace handkerchief in her hands. What was she thinking? he wondered. Was she waiting for me to offer my assistance in her quest for her father's murderer? He thought she had wanted to ask him something moments before her uncle's dawn arrival, but he was no longer sure. He needed time to sort this predicament out before committing himself to her investigation.

"We will remain in port for two more weeks." Was that relief he saw in her amber eyes, or was it merely his imagination waiting for some sign of her affirmation.

"Splendid. Let's say one week from Thursday then, shall we?"

The days of the week seemed like months to Morgan. Her face had not completely healed and she was reluctant to leave her uncle's Beacon Street house. She was still not able to accept any sewing assignments from Madame Flournay, for Morgan's left eye was slightly swollen and gave her some discomfort.

As long as Lizzie and the kitten "Cookie" were around,

Morgan felt some relief from her boredom. In Lizzie's eyes, however, Captain Rhodes was the embodiment of goodness and near sainthood. On more than one occasion, Morgan fought the desire to shut her ears to the wonderful exploits of the captain. "Oh Morgan, you should have heard what Cook said about the captain. He is the bravest man alive! Why do you know that he was once a private?"

"A what?"

"You know, a private. He used to sail his ship searching for and fighting the Spanish."

"Oh Lizzie." Morgan pulled her sister into a fond embrace. "You mean a privateer."

"Yes, and he was the bravest. Cook said the captain, all by himself, killed a dozen Spanish pirates who had tortured two captured seamen. And then another time, Captain Nick gallantly rescued a beautiful French countess who had been kidnapped and brought her back to France."

"Isn't he wonderful?" Morgan's sarcastic tone was lost on her sister. Beautiful indeed, Morgan thought, positive that the lady did not remain alone in the captain's cabin while they sailed across the Atlantic. These tales of triumph about this sainted seaman were beginning to irk her.

It also seemed that each time Lizzie discussed her hero, Cousin Alice was not far behind.

Alice Driscoll was a year younger than Morgan. Being the only child of the wealthy Benjamin Driscoll led to a very pampered and spoiled existence. Alice was pretty, but shorter than Morgan and slightly plump—her cousin adored sweetmeats. Her red hair perfectly matched her temper, for whenever Alice did not get her way—which was rare—she let everyone know. The house servants found many things to do when Alice was in a snit. Most of all, Alice Driscoll hated competition. Her dark brown eyes glared venomously at any young lady who vied with her for some young man's attention.

As one would guess, Alice Driscoll hated her cousin Morgan. It did not matter that Morgan had no desire to be involved in her cousin's social circle; nor did it matter that Morgan found all of Alice's friends—including the men—immature and self-centered. Since her cousin's unfortunate arrival, the number of young men suddenly calling on the Driscoll's during tea had multiplied . . . all of them anxiously waiting, not for Alice's arrival, but for Morgan's. Yet Morgan often declined, pleading a headache. Alice hated her for that too, because the callers found some reason to depart early.

If only Alice did not swear to her parents that she would not reveal Morgan's father was a traitor! Oh, how quickly the ardent beaus would run away. But then, she selfishly thought, these same people might also shun Alice for being the niece of a traitor. Alice did not want to take a chance. Her social position was too important to her.

Upon hearing Lizzie's glowing account of the dashing Captain Rhodes, Alice became fascinated. Could such a dream exist? Certainly her skinny cousin would not give her any information. She was always so circumspect. Alice wondered what really happened aboard that ship; what she would give to be alone with a handsome sea captain. She eagerly awaited Thursday's dinner. If this man were a fraction of what Lizzie claimed, Alice would throw herself at his feet.

From the way Alice and everyone else was behaving, one would have thought that the President was coming to dinner and not the mortal Captain Rhodes. The preparation had begun days ago, and it was more than Morgan could tolerate. Her aunt Nancy had decided to make this the event of the season. After all, how many Bostonians could boast of having the famous smuggler Nicholas Rhodes as a dinner guest? At least a dozen other people were invited: some of Boston's most eligible bachelors, some old friends of the Driscoll's and their equally eligible daughters. Alice was so excited about the arrival of the guest of honor that she didn't even complain to her mother about the other invited women.

Wishing she could pretend illness, Morgan prayed she did not have to see him again. The events of the previous week were almost a forgotten dream. Did he really hold her so protectively in his strong embrace? Were his lips as firm and warm as she dreamt? And his hands, were the long fingers as gentle as she remembered when they roamed along her back and up her sides to caress her breasts? Did his gray eyes turn to molten silver when he explored her eager form? Did his sun-kissed hair fall onto his forehead when he bent to claim her lips? The memories brought an uncomfortable feeling, threatening to suffocate her.

Unfortunately, Morgan remembered much more. Did she really lose control of her emotions? Was she wanton? What would happen when she saw him again? And oh, how she had trusted him, telling him all about the horrible events of the last few months. Why did she allow herself to trust him? He was a rogue, a stranger, little more than a pirate. She practically told him her life's story, and if that were not enough, threw herself at him, offering her maidenhead.

How could she face him again?

Dressed in a deep rose cotton gown, her long black hair curling freely down her back and secured on each side by tortoiseshell combs, she felt out of place among these elegantly attired people.

Morgan had no idea that the very simplicity of her empire gown provocatively accented her figure. The low-cut front, with the high bodice and short capped sleeves, revealed her slim neck while outlining her breasts. When she walked, the thin cotton material softly clung to her trim waist. She was too inexperienced to know the effect she had on the young men, overlooking the eagerness in their eyes. In her mind the dress was plain . . . just like me, she decided. . . . Well, perhaps Nicholas will never notice me among the well-dressed women who have the sophistication that I lack, thought Morgan.

Nicholas arrived early. Alice had not finished dressing—she was planning a late entrance—and to her annoyance some of the guests had not arrived. As soon as he walked through the doorway, Morgan felt his presence. She was standing to the side of the parlor, talking with two of Alice's male friends, not really paying attention to their prattle. His entrance into the room was like a shooting star from which no eye could turn. Nicholas was superbly dressed in the latest fashion: dark blue breeches, buff colored jacket, satin quilted waistcoat in muted colors, a snowy white pleated silk shirt and cravat. His muscular legs settled easily into deep mahogany knee boots

41

that seemed to be molded to his calves. He was splendid looking, and Morgan did not miss a detail.

The candlelight toyed with the pale yellow highlights of his hair and when he lifted his hand to smooth an unruly lock, the light also caught the strange gleam of his gold and sapphire ring.

Thank goodness for Lizzie. Allowed to stay up well past her bedtime to greet her hero, she pulled him away from Morgan's path. Kneeling down, he returned her loving hug.

"Hello precious. How have you been?" His white teeth were perfectly even, a sight rarely seen among sailors saddled with the physical blight of scurvy.

"You should see Cookie. She is the most lovable kitten. Can I show her to you after you've paid your respects?"

"Anything I should know about them?" he nodded at a group of guests.

"No," she honestly replied. "Aunt Nancy has been excited though. Oh, and wait until you meet my cousin Alice. She's been dying to meet you."

With some reluctance, Nicholas sheepishly asked, "How is your sister? Is she feeling well?"

"Her eye bothers her a bit, but that is all. The bruise is almost gone. But come," she brightened, "see for yourself."

The moment he was anticipating and Morgan was dreading arrived.

"Look Morgan, here he is."

Morgan politely introduced Nicholas to her friends who remained a few minutes before excusing themselves.

"Hello beauty. You look as if you've prepared for this occasion."

She tried to fight the blush building in her cheeks, but lost. "Hello Captain." Her voice was low and husky.

Reaching for her hand, Nicholas entwined his fingers in hers, then brought them to his lips for a polite kiss. But Morgan felt the heat of his intense gaze, his eyes never leaving her face.

"I am happy to see you again. My entire crew sends its regards to both you and Lizzie. Actually, I have something I would like to discuss with you. I have been giving some

42

serious consideration to your problem and believe . . ."

"Well," a cultured voice interrupted, "Cousin Morgan, are you keeping our guest of honor to yourself?"

Having no idea what Nicholas was about to say, Morgan felt more anxious than before. Perhaps he was going to ask . . . what? More questions about her father, how the kitten was, her hand in marriage? All of this seemed so ridiculous, she giggled without an apparent reason. Moreover, Lizzie was not around to rescue her from the embarrassment.

Her laughing face was a puzzle, although Nicholas wished to put the pieces in place. Unfortunately, Alice Driscoll was demanding his complete attention. Nicholas had no time to talk to Morgan again until the dinner was served.

To Morgan's dismay, she was sitting directly across from him. Alice, of course, was seated next to Nicholas, appearing to be completely enthralled with each word he uttered.

Next to Morgan, was a young man who spent the evening making overtures that she rejected while displaying his disenchantment with the venerated sea captain. "Why he is no more than a pirate," Marcus sneered loud enough for Morgan and the young lady on his other side to hear. "Imagine, he is buying and selling illegal merchandise and making a profit, no less."

"Not everyone feels the same as you do," his companion replied. It was obvious that she too could not take her eyes off the handsome captain.

"Well, I think he should be arrested and his cargo confiscated." The young man's voice became shrill, making Morgan uncomfortable. Turning to address Nicholas, Marcus asked, "Tell me Captain Rhodes, do you think you should be treated like a local hero or a pirate?"

Nicholas had digested each word spoken to Morgan as if it were a bitter herb he was forced to devour. He was not unprepared for this verbal assault. Now was his chance to respond. Slightly drunk, Marcus was hardly an appropriate antagonist for Nicholas's wrath. The dinner guests were hushed; only the sound of the tinkling crystal goblets nervously being raised by some of them could be heard.

"I am neither. I strongly believe in my government as I am

43

sure you do, sir. However, I also strongly believe that this Embargo Act is hurting the American people, particularly the merchants and shipbuilders and not the British or French as was its intent."

"Aye," agreed an elderly gentleman at the other end of the long rosewood table. "My business is nearly ruined. I cannot sell the raw materials—like lumber, whale oil, cotton—to the foreigners, nor can I buy the finished products. Tell me, Marcus, how much did tea cost two years ago? You do not know; well I do. And if you can find any tea these days, I can guarantee that the price is five times what it was."

"Have you been to Mystic, Connecticut, Marcus?" asked another. "It was once a booming seaport and shipbuilding center. But since this Embargo Act of Jefferson's, the town is slowly dying. Men are out of work, goods are scarce. Tell me, what will they do?"

Marcus was feeling less brave, but was undaunted. "You are making a profit, Captain Rhodes, from the misfortune of others."

"Nonsense," Nicholas replied. "Perhaps you can enlighten me on what it is you are doing about this Embargo Act, sir. Until the law is changed—and I have friends who are working very hard at doing just that—I shall continue to buy and sell cargoes from the British, French, and the Americans. We are the ones who are truly suffering. Do you think the British are overly concerned about not being able to buy our cotton, or our tobacco, for example? No." He calmly raised his champagne glass to his lips, took a long sip, then continued, "They will buy those goods elsewhere. But what do we do? Can we only trade with ourselves? President Jefferson says that we should not trade with the French and the British who are trying to involve our country in their war. That is undoubtedly true, but I ask you, did he have to deny us our livelihood in the hope of remaining a neutral country?"

"Well said my boy," Benjamin proudly looked upon the captain. "We are all loyal Americans, but I must confess feeling somewhat outraged by the President's Embargo Act. And surely you must realize, Marcus, that it is not accomplishing what was intended."

44

"Father, I think we have heard enough." Alice was completely bored by this conversation, although she did not miss the looks that passed between the captain and her cousin. What really happened aboard his ship? she wondered again. As soon as the dinner guests resumed normal conversation, she turned her most gracious smile on the guest of honor, placed her hand over his, and said, "Captain Rhodes, perhaps I can show you the gardens later?"

Not mistaking her intent, Nicholas replied, "I would be pleased if you and your charming cousin would show me about."

"Oh," her smile instantly disappeared. "Morgan does not really belong. Wouldn't you agree, Captain? Just look at her, she is hopelessly out of place, as bland as a country mouse. The only reason she is with us this evening is because my father insisted on doing something for you. Besides," she added, her voice becoming louder and shrewish, "my father feels sorry for her."

If he could throttle the little bitch here and now, he would have cheerfully done so. More than one pair of eyes focused on Alice's cousin. Nicholas saw her quivering lip, the unsteady rising of her chest. Yet Morgan continued to stare at her plate, pretending to ignore Alice's remarks. His eyes beseeched her for attention, in the hope that he could demonstrate his support. When she finally looked up, her expression was transparent. Nicholas sensed her unease, her frustration at being unable to defend herself. He eagerly wanted to defend her, to shout down this unrelenting detractor. But he could not, for it was not his place to do so. Silence governed his actions the way diplomats respond to protocol. It was out of character for Nicholas to behave this way. But any forthright defense of Morgan would, under these circumstances, be unsuitable.

And so he helplessly watched. The flames from the dining table's candelabra flickered, as if there was insufficient oxygen to sustain them. Nicholas was breathing fitfully, torn by the need for decorous behavior and his emotions. For a moment, he was at one with the flames.

Nicholas's emotions were entangled: He felt pride in

45

Morgan's unshakable constitution and fear that he was being enveloped into Cupid's vortex. Tearing his eyes away from Morgan's face, he realized that the pudgy, bejeweled fingers still possessively rested on his arm. "My dear, perhaps you would like to see the *Anastasia?* I can arrange for you to visit tomorrow afternoon."

Too enthralled with his invitation and his undivided attention, Alice failed to notice the captain's forced smile and rigid posture.

Morgan, however, could stand no more. She would not remain in the same room as her cousin and that scoundrel! They were both obnoxious, probably deserving of each other. If the notion of destiny exists, then surely Nicholas Rhodes had found his mirror image in Alice.

As soon as the dinner ended, Morgan pleaded a recurring headache, brought on by the accident, and then quickly fled to the tranquility of her room on the upper floor.

Chapter 5

Good fortune, however, was not with her. Over the next two days, Morgan was haunted by Alice's presence and her cheerful, lovesick stories about her newest beau. Convinced that the captain reciprocated her feelings, Alice nauseated Morgan with her future plans. No matter where Morgan sought to hide, Alice invariably found her, going so far as to remain with Morgan in the kitchen behind the house. She was an impossible gnat, that even when quickly flicked away, returned to buzz in her ear.

"Nicky is so wonderful. Did you know, cousin, that he comes from a very wealthy family?" Alice rushed on, delighted to see the surprised look on Morgan's face. So, she thought triumphantly, my perfect cousin does not know everything about the captain. "His father is a very wealthy New York lawyer. Nicky could have it all anytime he wants."

Alice followed a silent Morgan out of the kitchen, down a long passageway that eventually led into the library—another room she rarely saw. "I do not understand why he continues to work so hard and live so dangerously. Why, he could be arrested or killed."

"No, I don't suppose you would understand why any person may hate to accept another's riches or generosity. Not everyone prefers living as a pampered lapdog, Alice. It must be awfully tiresome waiting for the scrap of meat, no matter how fine the cut."

Reaching for the first leather-bound book she could see on

the second shelf, Morgan hastily left the room, assuming Alice would never follow her to the stables. She did not wait to hear Alice's sharp intake of breath or her mutterings about some people living off of other's charity.

Much later the same day, Morgan received a neatly penned note from George Taggart:

"I will not take the chance of finding you running through the streets like a hoyden. Since you refuse to let me come to your uncle's home, I decided to write this note and include everything I was told by my contact. It appears as if a gentleman fitting Andrews's description, and that of his two friends from Baltimore, has been seen in New York. Andrews is using the name Armstrong and he says he is a journalist!

"I advise you not to do anything, Miss Rhinehart, until you hear from me again. I am expecting more information by the week's end."

There was more information but Morgan could no longer concentrate! Andrews was in New York! How was she going to get to New York City? What's more, would Andrews be there long enough for her to catch up to him? Crumbling the missive, Morgan grabbed her pale blue wool cloak to protect her from the cool September air. More than ever, Morgan felt a sense of urgency to accomplish her mission. She had to see Mr. Taggart. He must have more information than he was willing to put on paper. Certainly, she reasoned, he would help her find passage to New York.

It would be faster, she decided, if she went out the back way, past the gardens. Unaware of the couple rounding the perfectly manicured tall green hedges, she raced down the same pebble path they were on, crashing into Nicholas. His strong arms reached to steady Morgan, who was winded by the headlong collision.

"Going somewhere, Miss Rhinehart?"

The familiar deep voice startled her. Why, she asked herself, did she have to run into him, of all people? "I am so sorry Captain Rhodes, and of course, Alice," she noted her cousin's scowl, "but I am in a terrible hurry. I just received some very important news." Looking into his metallic eyes, Morgan again felt the loss of breath.

He was nattily dressed in a dark blue woolen jacket and nankeen breeches. His beige silk shirt was open at the neck, revealing the curly hairs on his chest.

"I am sure, beauty, that it can wait a few more moments. In fact," he looked over at Alice, "I was just taking my leave. I would be honored to escort you."

Alice did not miss the affectionate name he used, nor the way he still held Morgan in his arms. Her jealousy overcame her cool demeanor, and like a snake moving to devour its prey through instinct, Alice said, "Nicky, you really do not know my cousin."

There was something about her voice, perhaps the acidic tone, that made Nicholas turn his appreciative gaze away from Morgan and toward Alice.

"No, I do not, but I hope to." The hidden meaning was lost on a still-dazed Morgan, who remained motionless, allowing Nicholas to support her with his arm. However, Alice's malicious intent was too obvious to go unnoticed by Morgan, who was quickly losing her patience.

"I am really in quite a hurry, Alice. Can we continue this conversation another time? Say, next week?" Morgan adjusted her cloak after she reluctantly pulled away from Nicholas. "If you will excuse me?"

"Well," Alice snorted, "I never. Who are you to act so uppity, Miss Rhinehart? You do forget your place."

"What place is that, Alice?"

"That you are no better than a servant. You are living off of my family's charity, as you well know Cousin Morgan." Alice was aware of the discomfort she was causing her cousin. As soon as Nicky heard the real truth about the Rhineharts, he would not look so favorably upon Miss Purity. Allowing her green shawl to slide open, Alice took a deep breath, now that Nicky's eyes were fastened on her bodice.

"Hello, out there," Marcus and another friend called. "Your servant said you were all outside. I hope you don't mind that we decided to call on you lovely ladies. We thought we could take you for a stroll around the Common." Still smarting from the captain's rebuke at the dinner party, he barely nodded to Nicholas.

"Oh, I am so happy to see you Marcus, John." The appearance of the young men reminded Alice that she was supposed to behave like the well-bred young lady she was. Indeed, she was seriously considering apologizing to Morgan for her behavior. But as soon as the young men surrounded Morgan, Alice's pudgy cheeks reddened in anger and her desire to be avenged prevailed.

"Oh, you missed the most interesting conversation. We were just talking about Morgan's family." Alice noticed that she finally had everyone's attention. She made an elaborate scene out of seating herself on the marble bench near the rosebushes, while the others remained standing around her.

"We know about Morgan's family, Alice," said one.

"Not about her father." There! She said it, relishing the look of dread on her cousin's face. Even Nicky gave her his full attention now, although she did not see him moving closer to Morgan, searching for her hand beneath the folds of her cloak, lacing their fingers.

"Alice, I have no time for your petty quarrels. Captain," she turned her gold-flecked eyes to Nicholas, "I think I would very much appreciate your offer to escort me."

Nicholas was anxious to get her away from this group. Morgan had not let go of his hand, despite her outwardly calm demeanor. Again, he felt the frustrating knot building within his chest. He would not allow Alice to humiliate Morgan this time.

The two young men had no idea of what they innocently walked in on. Marcus stupidly thought that this whole conversation was a silly joke.

"Come now, Alice. What are we supposed to know about Morgan's father that you are obviously dying to tell us? What about the skeleton in the family's closet?"

"Did you know," Alice's honeyed voice lowered, "that her father was Samuel Rhinehart? You know, the traitor from Philadelphia who was murdered before he went to prison." Enthralled by the shocked expressions of the two men next to her, Alice decided to tell the whole story, no longer caring how her own reputation would be compromised by this admission. But one quick glance at Nicholas almost made her falter. He was livid! His bronze skin was taut with rage, while the silver sparks shooting from his eyes made her catch her breath. Who was he glowering at? Certainly not her. His fury had to be directed toward Morgan.

"Alice dear," Nicholas finally interrupted her, "I am surprised by your behavior. I find it most disconcerting that you would reveal this information to strangers." Standing as stiffly as a soldier awaiting orders, his cold gray eyes bore into her. For the first time in months, Alice wondered about her own actions. Yet, causing her cousin's downfall would make it all worthwhile.

"Nicky, didn't you hear me?" She stood up, her foot impatiently stomping on the gravel. "I said that Morgan's father was a traitor!"

"Alice, I know all about that terrible mishap of justice." Nicholas ignored the others, while he leisurely withdrew his jacket. "I am afraid that you are unaware of certain facts. Really my dear," he admonished her, "if I had known earlier that you were wont to spread rumors, I certainly would have informed you of my offer to assist Morgan in her search for her father's murderer and the real traitor."

All eyes were on him now, but Nicholas did not care. It was Morgan's warm smile and amber eyes nearly brimming with tears of gratitude that gladdened his heart.

"You did not have to make a public declaration on my behalf, Nicholas."

They were walking away from a flabbergasted Alice, Nicholas's hand firmly securing her elbow, leading her toward his rented carriage.

"Morgan, I owe you an apology." He was quite serious. "I did not know your cousin could be such a viper. Spoiled and empty-headed was what I previously labeled her. But I was wrong." He paused, long enough to face her, pulling her cold hand into his warm ones.

"You have no idea how I have been feeling these last two meetings when she viciously attacked you. I wanted so much to assist you, but unless I was your betrothed," he smiled warmly at her open mouth, "there was nothing I could do. After that dinner, I vowed not to let it happen to you again. So, I hope Alice fully understands what I think of her viciousness."

"Hardly, Nick. She is probably telling Marcus and John the whole story again." Morgan's brows arched in dismay. "I honestly do not care what they say about me. But it is awfully hard on Mother and Lizzie."

"I am going to help you. You have my word. When Nick Rhodes gives his word, it is the word of a gentleman." He chuckled, crossing his hand over his heart in an effort to lighten her mood, forgetting that these very words were similar to the promise previously given to his father.

Chapter 6

How he regretted his promise to help Morgan. Now Nicholas was irrevocably involved in this god-awful situation. Like steering a course between Scylla and Charybdis, Nicholas had to find a way to keep his word to two people, one of whom was becoming too important to him. The goal was the same, but Morgan and her family could be destroyed in the process.

Nicholas had escorted Morgan to meet with the somewhat unkempt but very sincere George Taggart. He took an immediate liking to this balding man, who treated Morgan more like a relative than a paying client. Taggart would do what he could, Nicholas surmised, but in order to find Andrews, someone had to be free to move about as quickly as Andrews evidently did. Moreover, it would be crucial to discover if there were some pattern to Andrews's movements. Philadelphia, Baltimore, New York; there was a reason that eluded Nicholas and a baffled Taggart.

Upon discovering that Miss Rhinehart's escort was none other than Captain Nicholas Rhodes, George Taggart had been willing to share all his information. The captain asked some pointed questions about Andrews and his two traveling companions, requesting complete physical descriptions of each. The captain was serious and businesslike. Only when his flinty eyes looked upon Miss Rhinehart, did George notice a softening in his manner. Despite his sloppy appearance, George Taggart was extremely good in his line of work. It only took ten minutes for him to determine that something was troubling the handsome captain—something to do with Miss Rhinehart, yet going deeper than the obvious physical attraction to the lady. Well, he was not being paid for that, George decided, dismissing his train of thought.

George was sure of one thing. The captain was not going to allow Miss Rhinehart to jeopardize herself in this search for her father's murderer. Promising to notify Miss Rhinehart and the captain as soon as he received more information from his contact in New York, George bade them good-bye. But not before giving the captain a firm handshake and a few parting words. "Watch over her, Captain Rhodes. I would not like to see the young miss hurt any more. Don't you agree?"

Nicholas had no chance to reply, for Morgan quickly joined them. The sky was turning a deep shade of purple, and the air was cooling. But Nicholas needed to feel the clear air fill his lungs and suggested they walk a bit before climbing into the cramped carriage that would follow them. No one would dare accost them on the street, and Nicholas had no doubt that he could easily protect them if necessary. Perhaps, he wondered, he merely desired to steal some more moments alone with the bewitching woman beside him, her small-boned hand delicately resting on his arm.

He was at least half a foot taller than she, and from his vantage point, Nicholas stole the opportunity to study her. The hood of her woolen cloak obscured her raven curls. Nicholas decided she would look enchanting with a pure white Venetian lace shawl covering those thick locks of hair. He mentally added it to the list of items he would love to buy her—if ever given the opportunity. In the fading light, her complexion became a dusky rose, slightly contrasting with the long, sooty lashes that veiled her amber eyes, which he knew could widen with pleasure when he kissed her ripe and expectant lips. The slanted cheekbones made her face appear angular, but the spray of freckles across her pert nose still had the ability to make him smile. He wanted to pull her into his arms, to slide his hand inside her cloak, to stroke her warm, lush body before capturing her mouth with his. Never before had he felt such uncontrolled desire for a woman—an innocent one at that.

She was trouble.

"Nicholas," her soft voice interrupted his lascivious thoughts, "I need to know your plans."

"My what?"

They were leisurely strolling along Dock Square. Morgan was looking up at him now, causing Nicholas's mind to wander again.

"Nick. Are you listening?"

"What? . . . Oh yes, Morgan, my plans. Are you so interested in my whereabouts?"

His teasing smile produced an answering one in her. "I am merely asking because I want to know if you are truly going to assist me."

"I said I was, did I not? In front of your cousin, those two fops, and George Taggart. Is there anyone else you want me to announce it to?"

"No, I did not mean it that way, Nicholas. I apologize. Nor am I interested in your amorous comings and goings, as you seem to have implied." She was having difficulty repressing her anger.

"I did no such thing Morgan. I merely stated . . ."

"Oh, I don't care what you have said," she snapped, glaring up at him, refusing to take another step. "Are you going to New York or not?"

"Morgan," he turned to face her, placing his large hands on her shoulders. "Let's try this again, shall we?" He forced a smile, "I will be sailing the *Anastasia* to New York shortly after . . ."

"Good," she cut off his next sentence, "I shall be ready whenever you sail."

The light of comprehension was finally struck. "No Morgan, you misunderstand me. I am sailing the ship to New York and," he rushed on placing his index finger on her mouth, "I am going to do everything I can to find out about Andrews. But I am going with my crew and not, my beauty, with you."

"No! You promised," she shouted, twisting out of his gentle hold. "I must go with you Nick. Don't you understand? I have to go! I have to do something. Besides, I know what I am looking for."

"Do you? Tell me Morgan, did you ever see Andrews? Do

you know how to use a knife—like the one used to stab your father? Have you ever felt a man's hands about your neck," his hands moved up to lightly touch her neck, his fingers slowly tracing the slender column, stopping at her throat, "cruelly choking the breath and life out of you? Have you? He shook her, causing the hood to fall back a bit. A stray curl escaped the confines as Nicholas reached for it, twining it about his fingers. He knew he was frightening her, but it had to be done.

Shaking her head in denial, she whispered, "No, but I must do something."

Suddenly, she was in his arms, his warm mouth kissing the top of her head. "I will go alone, Morgan. If I have no luck, I promise to take you with me the next time. I will not abandon you. You have my word."

He decided not to tell her that he had to sail elsewhere first. Nor did Morgan give her word that she would wait for his return.

Upon returning to the large three-storied house on Beacon Street, Morgan took pleasure in learning that Alice's behavior did not go unnoticed by her father. He raved for hours, ultimately promising to cancel her trip to the Continent. Nevertheless, over the next few days Morgan skillfully avoided her cousin, making plans for her imminent departure.

Whether Captain Rhodes knew it or not, there would be one more sailor aboard the *Anastasia* when it sailed. Nicholas had already informed her that he would be sailing on the next Saturday morning. It was now Tuesday, and Morgan had more than enough time to set her plan into motion. She could not, however, avoid the curious knowing eyes of her younger sister. With the wisdom of an adult, Lizzie let Morgan explain her plan, initially trying to discourage her, then reluctantly accepting Morgan's decision.

It was raining outside. Despite the steady rhythm of the raindrops against the window, the sisters sitting on the window seat inside the warm room almost felt the security they once knew in their Philadelphia home. Their parents would have been sitting by the warm fire in the parlor, reading or talking to one another. The sisters would have been in bed upstairs, the older one telling a story to the younger, lulling her to sleep. . . . But that was a long time ago.

Once Morgan had obtained Lizzie's promise not to tell anyone until after the *Anastasia* sailed, she confided her scheme to depart the house unnoticed, making her way to the harbor where she would sneak aboard the ship. Only after the *Anastasia* was out to sea, would she reveal herself to the captain.

Lizzie would give Morgan's letter to Charlotte after the ship sailed. At the same time she would try to convince their mother that this adventure was absolutely necessary, that Morgan would be safe with Captain Rhodes, who was above all else, a gentleman. Of course, Morgan would contact her family as soon as she was able.

"Morgan, what will Captain Nick say when he finds out you tricked him?"

Nicholas' reaction was the one thing she could not predict. In fact, the more Morgan thought about his fury, the more apprehensive she became. But her mind was made up, and damn him for not letting her join him as he had promised.

Morgan had only seen him once since that day. Nicholas had insisted upon taking the Rhineharts to a farewell lunch at a quaint inn just outside Boston, near Dorchester Neck. He was utterly charming and such pleasant company that Morgan almost forget her scheme to deceive him. It was one of the rare times since Samuel's arrest that they all enjoyed a family outing.

Morgan wore a deep wine velvet dress, trimmed under the bodice with pale pink satin ribbons. The high neck and tight fitting sleeves accented the graceful lines of her body. Judging from Nicholas's admiring look, Morgan knew that she had chosen the right dress from Madame Flournay's beautiful collection. The Frenchwoman had insisted that Morgan select a dress as payment for the extra work she recently had done; not the usual everyday woolen dresses, but one more suitable for tea or theater. Only her hair remained unadorned. The long, thick black curls hung loosely down her back. Morgan was unaware that Nicholas mentally added a set of pearl combs to his gift chest.

It was during this lunch that Morgan learned more about the captain and his family. Nicholas spoke warmly about his mother, whose family was one of the early colonial inhabitants of New York. His spoke less of his father, but from what he did not say, Morgan concluded that Warren Rhodes was an upstanding citizen, as arrogant and proud as his son, but disappointed in Nicholas's profession.

"Then there is Jonathan and his docile wife, Sally. Jonathan is five years older than I, yet I often feel that the age difference is similar to the one between my father and myself. We never saw eye to eye. Jonathan is everything my father wanted in the perfect son." His smile held a hint of sadness.

"Lastly," he seemed to brighten, "there is my father's brother, Eric. My father could never understand him. Eric preferred the untamed wilds of the west to the sedate, opulent New York society. In fact, my first sea experience was with Eric, who was once a sea captain. I was a tall, awkward lad of twelve," he paused leaning back into the chair, savoring the fond memory. "Eric, against my father's wishes, insisted I go along on the voyage to France, then on to Spain. I remember everything about the voyage and our stay on the Continent."

"Is that when you decided to be a captain too?" asked a wide-eyed Lizzie.

Nicholas patted his lap, motioning for her to join him. The main meal was over. They were lingering over dessert: freshly baked apple and cherry pies, tea for the ladies, a glass of port for Nicholas.

"From the moment I saw my first sunset, on a deep gray-blue sea, the clear sky slowly turning a burnt orange, the sun gradually making way for a full moon and thousands of stars . . . Aye, my sweet Lizzie, that was when I knew I was going to have my own ship someday."

The child was comfortably curled in his lap, her lids slowly drooping as Nicholas continued to stroke her curly hair. Morgan looked at the peaceful, trusting expression on her sister's face. For the first time, she fantasized about a life with his enigmatic man. Was he capable of loving a woman? More importantly, could he love me, she wondered? Would he want

58

to father children? Could he settle down in one place and call it home?

As if reading her mind, Nicholas looked up into her tawny eyes, then kissed the top of Lizzie's head.

Morgan's own deep sigh intruded upon her fond memories of their lunch. What difference did it make if he were capable of caring for her? As soon as he discovered her ruse, Morgan doubted that Nicholas would forgive and forget. Besides, she had a mission to accomplish and no one was going to prevent her from finding her father's murderer.

The following evening, after midnight, Morgan slipped out of her uncle's home. Wearing a pair of old gray woolen breeches that were "borrowed" from the stable boy, a heavy linsey-woolsey dark blue shirt, and a black seaman's cap, Morgan slowly made her way toward Long Wharf. She carried a small canvas bag that contained another shirt and food that she and Lizzie had pilfered from the kitchen. Her adventure was only beginning.

The cold, moonless night aided the street urchin possessively clutching a canvas bag to his chest. Few people were on the dark streets. As he got closer to the harbor, the wind picked up, becoming cool and damp. Yet his nose filled with the combined smells of rotting fish and brine, typical for a busy harbor but not common to him. Impatiently, he tucked in a damp dark curl that was threatening to escape the confines of his cap. The streets were almost familiar now. It had been so easy up to this point that he could not help but marvel at his own daring abilities. Confidently hoisting the canvas bag over his shoulder, he strutted around the street corner toward the *Anastasia*.

There she was, proudly sitting in the water, her white sails contrasting against the black sky, her outline illuminated by the torches set along the wooden planks, easing the path for the sailors who struggled with the heavy cargo barrels.

It was a beautiful but alarming sight. For how was he going

to sneak aboard the ship this night? It was just as obvious that a late night cargo loading meant an early morning departure. How much time did he have? The longer he stood on the wharf with his canvas bag, the greater the chance of his being noticed and chased away.

Then the one voice he prayed he would not hear bellowed across the wharf.

"Come on lads, hurry. We do not have all night. The tide will not wait for us. . . . No, McNeil, over there! Mr. Simpson, help those men. . . . No, not that way; here I'll show you."

Obviously, the captain had to be involved in everything. But how long would he remain in the center of the pier?

Someone must have answered the urchin's prayer, for the captain was called over to the other side of the ship. It was time to act. The lad boldly strode up the plank, between two seamen who were hauling crates of vegetables and squawking chickens.

"Here boy," shouted one, "you the new cabin boy?" He did not wait for the reply. "You look a bit scrawny, but here," he shoved a canvas bag at him, "take this aboard for me. That's a good mate."

The boy managed to get the items aboard. Being familiar with the ship and Lizzie's description of the cargo hold, he made his way below. Despite the cool air, tiny beads of perspiration dotted his brow and neck. It's almost over, he decided. Just find a safe place to hide, only for two nights.

His "room" became the raised wooden beam along the port side of the ship. Three barrels already surrounded the area. It was a natural hiding spot. Taking off the jacket and sweater, he spread them on the deck as a cushion and pillow.

Pulling the cap off, she delighted in the clean scent of her hair as it fell about her face and shoulders. Feeling quite pleased with herself, Morgan stifled a giggle as she settled into her niche and took out a small piece of cheese, finally relaxing for the first time in days.

The sounds of creaking timber and the slight bobbing motion of the ship awoke her some time later. The only light and fresh air came from the open hatch—the only entrance or exit from the hold that she could see. However, Morgan was prepared. Digging deep into the canvas bag, she withdrew a man's gold timepiece—her father's, she thought fondly. Clicking it open, Morgan checked the time. It was three A.M.; soon they would be at sea. Then she wistfully gazed at the smiling painted family portrait before her. Samuel had the miniature portraits made a little over a year ago.

"No, Morgan, you cannot cry. You must be strong. Now, find that candle you packed and you will have all that you need for now. Stop talking to yourself too," she laughed softly. If only Lizzie could see her. They would burst into hysterics.

"Captain Nick," she imitated her sister, "I hope you have a sense of humor."

"Which damn fool left the hatch open?" a sailor shouted. "I damn near could've tripped and broke me leg. The cap'n sure wouldn't like it neither!"

There were more words, but the loud slamming of the hatch door abruptly shut off all light, sound and, Morgan thought miserably, air. She would manage, adjusting to the meager light of the candle. She must. Yet without the comforting noise of the sailors scurrying about above her, even Nicholas's deep voice, and the smell of the sea air, Morgan felt lonely and more than a little frightened.

Some time later, she could feel a different motion of the ship. The rocking motion could only mean that they were out at sea. It was much stuffier in the hold. The odor of rotting wood mingled with the obvious smells of tobacco, animal skins, and other goods stocked in the neatly arranged barrels made her feel queasy. It was becoming more unpleasant with each passing hour. Morgan could think of nothing else but the relief of the cool sea air on her face. Just the opportunity to smell it would suffice for the time being.

Another hour passed, the movement of the ship becoming more pronounced. The awful smell worsened. Morgan had to try it! Leaving her alcove, she cautiously made her way to the wooden ladder. So eager was she to get to the hatch that she stumbled on the bottom rung, banging her shoulder against the ladder. With a muffled curse, she gently rubbed the bruised area, then moved her arm. This was not the time for an injury.

Slowly making her way up the ladder, Morgan reached up to open the hatch.

It would not budge.

Now what would she do? Suddenly a more frightening thought occurred to her. How was she going to get out of the hold tomorrow? If she banged on the door, would someone hear? Should she try it today? No, she decided, she could not risk being discovered this early in the voyage.

"Calm yourself, Morgan. It will be all right."

Chapter 7

Nicholas's foul mood worsened with the weather. The ship was at sea for only two days, but Nicholas knew they would not make Halifax within the week. Not with the brewing storm.

"Damn my luck," he cursed. "First that impossible black-haired beauty crosses my path, complicates my life, and now this blasted storm."

He had to be near Halifax before Friday, otherwise the American patrol ships would be sailing in the same area that the *Anastasia* must cross. His associate, Peter Mackenzie, had obtained the patrol schedules and planned Nick's shipments around them. Nick rarely saw the American ships, but when he did, the *Anastasia* easily lost them. But this time, the *Anastasia* might sail directly into their trap.

Their late departure had been Nicholas's decision—all because he wanted to delay his stay in Boston, to be near Morgan and her family. The oncoming storm could only add to the time they would lose, making this a very unprofitable trip.

"Damn!" he cursed again. He would have to wait and see. Perhaps the schedule of the patrol ships would also be affected by the storm. If not, well, it wouldn't be the first time he had to rely on his instincts.

The storm hit that afternoon, but the crew of the *Anastasia* was prepared. The captain stood on the raised quarterdeck surveying the scene before him, firmly holding the wheel, ordering the crew to maintain their posts. It was a fierce and long storm. By nightfall, Nicholas knew that the worst was over. They would assess the damage and hope that they could make up the lost sailing time.

"Mr. McNeil!" he called to the first mate, "check the cargo hold. Report the damage to me immediately."

"Aye, Captain Rhodes."

Within ten minutes, Mr. McNeil was standing before the captain, his face a mask of concern.

"Captain, you better come quick. There's something you better see."

"Mr. Morrow, take the helm," he ordered.

A terrible odor assailed his nostrils as soon as he reached the bottom of the ladder. Something must have spoiled. Lowering his head, Nicholas walked along the darkened cargo hold.

"Over there." McNeil pointed to the port side where the smell was more pungent.

Nicholas heard the mewling sounds. An awful premonition suddenly made him move quickly. "What the hell . . ." He was too furious and shocked to say any more.

Morgan was curled in a tight ball, clutching her stomach and moaning. Bending on one knee, Nicholas swept the dirty, tangled hair away from her perspiring face, turning her toward him. It was obvious what was ailing her: The worst case of seasickness he had seen in some time. He could have laughed, for certainly the minx deserved this fate, but her distressful moans reminded him that she needed help.

"Morgan." His cool hand touched her cheek, but his voice was surprisingly warm and tender. "Wake up, beauty. I am going to help you."

"Nick, I . . . don't feel . . . very well." She forced her eyes to open even though she could not focus.

Shifting her body so he could lift her, he ordered the very curious first mate to have his cabin prepared for her.

"Oh, and Mr. McNeil, have someone bring me a tub with hot water and plenty of scented soap." He lifted his head and smiled. "She needs it."

"Captain, how did she get aboard?"

"I have no idea, but believe me, as soon as she recovers, she will wish she had never come aboard this ship."

As he lifted her, she again moaned. "My shoulder, I hurt it."

64

"Put your arms around me Morgan, I am taking you to your old cabin." He wrinkled his nose. "I think I am going to need a bath as well." He felt the object she was clutching in her left hand. "Morgan, what is in your hand?"

"My father's watch."

"Here, let me hold it for you."

"Nick?" Her voice was raspy. "I think you better hurry. I am going to be ill again. And then," she groaned as the cramps began anew, "I am going to die. Please give the watch to my mother."

He wanted to throttle her for putting him in such a position. Why couldn't she let him handle the situation? Looking down at the pathetic woman in his bed, lost among the quilts, he felt a portion of his anger abate. At least, she was clean again.

Morgan was so weak, she had barely protested when he stripped her of the foul-smelling clothes, placing her in the hot-scented tub. She vaguely heard him ordering someone to burn the clothing, but it did not matter now.

"So good," she murmured resting her head along the side of the copper tub. "Nick, I cannot . . . I mean I do not think I um can . . . wash myself."

"I know, sweetheart. I am going to do it for you. Just relax. Trust me."

For two more days, Morgan drifted in and out of slumber, which was punctuated by bouts of seasickness. She would not allow the ship's surgeon near her. Only Nicholas.

Meanwhile, the crew was amazed that Miss Rhinehart had managed to sneak past them all, once again ending up on the *Anastasia*, in the captain's cabin with him nursing her. They could also see his fury mounting in the last couple of days, fearing he would unleash his temper on them and the girl. Their captain had a ship to run, a cargo to smuggle past the American ships, and now the sick woman in his bunk.

"Poor miss," they murmured, feeling more sympathy than resentment toward her. "What will Captain Rhodes do to her when she gets well?"

By the afternoon of the third day since her discovery,

Morgan was comfortably settled in Nicholas's huge bed, wearing one of his fine white linen shirts as a nightdress. Her health had dramatically improved since the previous day, making her more than anxious to be out of his room and his bed. She wanted to postpone the inevitable confrontation with him. But Nicholas charged into the room without knocking, his face taut with unleashed anger.

"I should have tied you to your bed in Boston! I should have known you were too agreeable that day after we left Taggart's office. Do you have any idea what kind of position you have put me in? Do you Morgan?" He raved on, alternately pacing across the fine Persian rug in the cabin and shaking his fist at her.

"Nicholas," she calmly tried to answer each of his questions, "I promise not to bother you again once we reach New York. Furthermore," she looked directly into his face, her expression showing no trace of her fear, "I release you from your promise."

"My promise!" He stopped pacing to stand at the foot of the bed, towering over her. He was so formidable looking, and so angry. "Are you daft, woman? Do you have any idea what you got yourself into this time? I cannot turn this ship around to take you back to Boston." His metallic eyes were piercing her now. "Neither are we going to New York."

"But Nick, you said . . ."

"I know what I said Morgan," he interrupted her. "We are going to Halifax *first*. I thought you understood that."

"How could I?" Her own anger was rapidly reaching his level of fury. Throwing the covers aside, she marched over to him, meeting his flinty gaze with her own fiery one.

"Why didn't you tell me, Captain Rhodes? Now look what you have done!"

"What I have done?" he bellowed loud enough for the sailor who was about to knock on the captain's door to scurry away from the captain's temper.

"Yes!" she shouted back, her arms resting on her hips, her chest heaving. "It is all your fault! Now I'll never find Andrews."

"Damn you, Morgan. Is that all you can think about? Do

you know the danger you are in? I cannot turn back. We may have to fight our way to Halifax. Do you think I care anything about your concerns at this moment? Tell me madam, what am I going to do with you when cannon fire strikes us?"

"Let go of me, Captain."

In his state of uncontrollable anger, Nicholas had no idea that he had grabbed her shoulders. The feel of her fragile body beneath his hands, the memory of her naked body glistening with sweetly scented water, suddenly affected him, turning his molten anger into an equally explosive state of desire.

Not bothering to examine his feelings, Nicholas swept her into his hard embrace, claiming her soft lips in a punishing kiss.

"Morgan, you are driving me mad!" he hoarsely whispered. Loosening his grip, Nicholas's hands reached up along the slender column of her neck to her hair. Lifting the heavy mass in his hands, inhaling the sweet fragrance that was Morgan, Nicholas felt the need to possess her completely, to make her his. Nibbling her neck, he felt her stiff body begin to relax, but when her arms came about his neck, he resisted the urge to laugh in triumph.

"Say it, beauty. Tell me that you need me me." His mouth found hers again, his tongue outlining her soft lips, gradually seeking hers then plunging inside, causing her to gasp with delight.

"Nicholas, we can't. I mean I can't." It was a very weak protest and they both knew it.

"Why not?" His hands moved to capture her lovely face. "This is my cabin, my ship. If we escape the patrols we will be together for weeks, perhaps months. I cannot postpone the inevitable." He paused to claim her mouth again, then moved across her cheek to her ear. He felt her body strain against his, searching for yet not knowing what it was she wanted.

"Neither can you, Morgan. You want me as much as I want you. Say it!" he ordered softly, looking down into her golden gaze. "For I swear to you I shall walk out of here leaving you to long for me. I know what that pain can do."

Flinging herself into his embrace, she offered her mouth to him in response. Nicholas was not satisfied.

"Tell me, love." His hand slid along her neck then lower, his fingers toying with the top button of the shirt she wore.

"All right Nick. I want to know . . . to feel . . . to belong to you. Don't punish me."

He should have felt greater satisfaction at her surrender, but the tiny tear that fell from her eye onto his finger scalded his heart.

"You are so beautiful," he murmured. The metallic glint in his eyes disappeared, replaced now by a warm, smoky gray, which deepened when he smiled at her.

"I wish I could give you more, but that is not possible. I only know how much I want to please you."

Again his fingers toyed with her shirt button, slowly undoing it and each one beneath, finally opening the garment and exposing her firm breasts to him. As his hands fondled each soft mound, he gently played with the rosy nipples, teasing them to hardness. Her expression told him what a delightful experience it was. Her tawny eyes were half closed, her mouth slightly parted in anticipation of the unknown. No matter how much restraint it would take, he vowed to go slowly. Her first experience would be remembered forever. Nicholas suddenly wished he could be with her each time she recalled her first glorious night of love.

His dark silver eyes never leaving her face, Nicholas pulled the oversized shift off her shoulders, down her arms, dropping it on the wooden floor and quickly kicking it away from her feet. Her smooth, pale body was fully exposed to his view. Although it was not the first time he had seen her naked, it was the first time her body called to him, begging him to touch the rounded curves, to intensify its already aroused state. Everything about her was perfection.

Not quite sure of what she was expected to do, Morgan shyly stood before him, mesmerized by his compelling gaze. Her heartbeat quickened, she felt a nervous fluttering in her stomach, her breathing became more laborious. But not for one minute would she back down. His ship, this cabin with the oak-framed bed, was where her destiny lay. There was no one else, nothing else more important at this moment than Nicholas Rhodes. Wanting to feel his mouth and hands explore every inch of her body, Morgan shamelessly thought that she wanted to remember every glistening part of him, to touch and arouse in him the same feeling he was instilling in her.

"Teach me, Nick. I want to know."

Her fingers entwined in his sun-streaked hair as she pressed herself into him, feeling the slight pressure of his belt buckle against her stomach, his leather breeches clinging to her bare thighs. Impatient now, her hands moved inside his shirt, enjoying the feel of his coarse curly hair beneath her fingertips, finding his taut nipples. She wanted to rub her body against his. She wanted . . . she didn't know what, but every nerve ending was acutely sensitive to the touch of his calloused fingers, his manly scent. Even the salty taste of his skin stimulated her.

Aware of her impatience, Nicholas scooped her into his arms, her hair falling across his shoulders in a cascade of silken loveliness. As he nuzzled her neck, he could see the tiny goose bumps along her arms. His voice husky now, Nick said, "I want to teach you the finer points of lovemaking, which you so eagerly seek. Trust me, Morgan. I will not hurt you."

Carrying her over to the large bed, Nicholas gently placed her on the soft mattress, his own body half reclining across her chest while his long legs touched the floor.

Raising her eyes to his face, Morgan could only concentrate on his mouth, his full lips that were slightly open. She wanted to taste him again, but he stopped her.

"Take off my shirt," he instructed.

Her clumsy fingers had difficulty with the buttons. Eventually, she needed his assistance. His eyes did not leave her face as he slowly removed the shirt, carelessly flinging it across the room.

Morgan's tremulous smile let him know that she liked what she saw. There was not an inch of excessive fat on his broad, muscular frame. Once again his bronze body reminded her of a Greek god. His masculine beauty intoxicated her. Still, a voice deep within cautioned that this was wrong: He was too worldly for her; he was a rogue who collected women's hearts the way others collected coins. Nicholas was not capable of loving her.

Pushing her hands against his chest, she protested, "No, I

can't Nick. I shouldn't."

Capturing her wrists in his hand, he responded, "It is too late, love. You desire me as much as I want you. And I shall prove it to you."

His golden head moved to kiss her, a kiss so deep, so exciting, that Morgan lost the will to think, let alone resist him.

"I must be wanton."

"Look at me, Morgan." He lifted his head to gaze directly into her worried face. "You are beautiful. You were made for love. You were made for me. Don't fight me."

Within the space of a heartbeat, Nicholas stood, taking his time as he removed his breeches. When she saw him proudly standing before her, so obviously ready for her, Morgan gasped in wonder.

"You must not be afraid, love," his smile and gentle touch made her quiver. "Here," he guided her hand, "touch me, feel how much I want you."

Eyes closed, Morgan thought she must have hurt him when he groaned. How could she ever describe the heady thrill of feeling him respond to her touch, of growing larger in her small hand? Yet still she hesitated.

Nicholas knew and said, "Don't stop, sweetheart. Here, let me show you." His hand quickly taught her the motion. "That's it, beauty. Ah, you are so good. Now, I want you to feel the same desire."

Lowering his body onto hers, his expert hands traced a fiery path along her softly rounded curves. Then running up her silken thighs, he found her moist center, awakening the tiny bud to hardness. His fingers played havoc with her senses, making her cry out in pleasure when his stroking prepared her for him. At the same time, his mouth tantalized her neck, tracing a path from her earlobe to her shoulder then up to her face, placing tiny kisses on her cheeks, eyes, nose, nipping her mouth, but not giving her the full satisfaction of his mouth melding to hers, stealing her breath.

It was more than she could bear. Morgan clutched his shoulders, not really knowing what kind of release she sought. Tiny tremors assailed her, making her tense and frustrated.

"Nick, please," she moaned, closing her eyes in rapture.

70

Positioning himself above her, Nicholas's molten eyes bore into hers, dissolving all of her doubts with his tender smile. His knees gently parted her creamy thighs while he placed his hands beside her head. Slowly, he lowered himself into her, hoping that the pain would not be too great. He could feel her muscles stiffen in response to his gentle probing.

Before she could utter a protest, Nicholas enveloped her mouth, his tongue plunging between her lips as he entered her, breaking the barrier of her innocence.

Her soft cry of pain hurt him more than a knife wound. "No more, beauty," he softly said, his hand smoothing her face and hair, then lowering to fondle her breast. "I swear to you I will never hurt you again."

The rhythm was new to her, but Nicholas's hips taught her how to respond. It was as if the pain had never existed. All that existed were his stroking hands, his breathtaking kisses, his words of love.

"You stir me as no one ever has, my beauty."

She wanted more. Having lost her inhibitions, Morgan gripped his back, enjoying the feel of his rippling muscles as they responded to her touch. But it still was not enough. Finally, she lowered her hands to caress his buttocks, pushing him deeper into her, raising her hips higher for his hands to grasp her as she met each one of his powerful thrusts.

"I don't want to stop," she moaned, the passion driving her over the edge of sanity. She wanted to feel him, to be one with him.

"Let yourself go. Don't hold back, Morgan love."

They were swallowed up in a passionate storm of desire. The rippling stream of emotion carried them along a path of ecstasy. There was no longer any limit to their mutual desire. She was his in the way the stars are part of a constellation. They could no longer resist nature's demands.

"I never knew," she sighed minutes later. Wrapped in his comforting embrace, her head resting on his chest listening to the steady beat of his heart, Morgan finally understood.

"You know, sweetheart, it will never be the same again. No

matter what happens, how many lovers you take, how many times you give me the opportunity to teach you, you will never forget your first time." Nicholas's face was shadowed by the dying rays of the sun. His tone was melancholy and his mood was oddly philosophical.

"What does that mean?" she inquired in an offended voice. How dare he assume she would take lovers? Didn't he know that she only wanted, would only want, him?

"Ah," he chuckled, "don't attack me yet, kitten." He straightened up to lean against the headboard, taking her with him, letting the sheet fall below their waists. Looking down at her, he saw the expression of a fulfilled woman; an expression she was too inexperienced to recognize. Her exposed breasts gently pressed against his chest. Nicholas could not keep his hands off her.

"What I mean, love, is that a woman always remembers the time she lost her virginity. It means," he smiled, greatly pleased with the thought, "that you can never forget me. And I dearly hope that you will always think wonderful, kind thoughts of the wicked smuggler who awoke your passions, who taught you how to love."

"And you wicked smuggler, do you always remember the trusting virgins who were lured into your bed? Perhaps you make a habit of finding and seducing the most innocent ones." If she was trying to hide her bitter tone, she did not succeed.

"Now, now, Morgan. I did not exactly seek you out. As I recall," he laughed, "you stepped onto my path the first time we met. Nor did I abduct you, stealing you away from your uncle's house in the middle of the night."

The monster was ridiculing her! How could he after this!

"How dare you mock me!" Angrily pulling back the covers, Morgan scrambled off the bed, unmindful of her nudity. "How could you be so, so damn arrogant, Nicholas?"

Her unruly black hair fell about her face and shoulders, the tawny eyes glaring venomously at him. She did, he decided, look like a lioness about to attack her prey.

Chapter 8

AT SEA—OCTOBER, 1808

"Where do you think you're going?" he calmly inquired, observing her from his still-comfortable position in the large bed. "Are you planning to stroll along the deck, with nothing more than my shirt to hide your body from my lusty crew?"

She picked up the discarded shirt to cover herself, hastily buttoning it. Unfortunately, she missed the top button, and one side was longer than the other. When he laughed at her uneven appearance, she wanted to strike him. Her fingers curled around the first object in her reach without caring what it was, then aimed for his grinning face.

"There! I hope you can still laugh, Captain Rhodes."

It was his inkwell. Stealing a look at him, Morgan wished she could have remained in the stinking hold.

Nicholas was covered with black ink! His hair, chest, and sheets, were smeared with black ink. He was definitely not grinning now.

"Come here," he growled.

"I will not!"

"I could have you whipped for this. Now I said come here!"

She took three hesitant steps toward him, then thought better. Nicholas saw her standing in the center of the cabin, clad only in the unevenly buttoned shirt, warily eyeing him. She was afraid, yes, but she held her ground.

Unexpectedly, his temper evaporated.

"I won't hurt you, Morgan, just help me clean up this mess, will you? Perhaps I did anger you." Wrapping a towel around his torso, Nicholas walked over to the washstand.

Grateful that he was not going to beat her, Morgan accepted his half apology, withholding her own.

Nicholas did not realize she had a temper or that she could be so stubborn. In the past, Morgan often appeared fragile, her will and independence not quite defined. Perhaps he did not know her or, as he preferred to think, a new woman might be emerging.

After they cleaned up the mess, Nicholas did the best he could to clean the ink off his hair and body.

A small giggle caught his attention.

"I suppose I do look a trifle odd."

"Oh Nick," she laughed aloud. "You look ridiculous!"

"My dear girl," he resumed toweling his hair, "have you had the chance to look at yourself in the mirror yet?"

She almost cried. The linen shirt splattered with ink still hung unevenly from her body, while black smudges decorated one cheek and her forehead.

"What I wouldn't give for another hot bath in your copper tub," she moaned.

"If I could perform such a miracle, will you promise not to throw anything at me? Will you stay in this cabin until I find suitable clothing for you?"

"Oh yes!"

He walked over to her, pulling her into his arms. "Then your wish is my command, my love."

Only when she smiled did he take the chance of tasting her ripe lips, making them both forget everything else but the heat of each other's response.

Perhaps, Nicholas thought as he lowered Morgan onto the bed, having her aboard would not be so bad after all.

Nicholas was beginning to feel confident that they would sail into Halifax Harbor without trouble. They had been at sea for five days now, and as long as the weather held they would arrive in two more days. No other ship had been sighted. Just maybe, the captain smiled, we might escape the American patrols.

Still, he realized his troubles were far from over. What was he going to do with the comely girl in his cabin?

Nicholas strode along the quarterdeck, slapping his thigh with his spyglass. That she had been compromised was obvious. Yet he had no intention of marrying her for the sake of her honor, or his. Although he could trust the crew of the *Anastasia* not to reveal anything about Morgan, how could he keep her hidden while they were in Halifax? By all accounts, Nicholas knew he'd have to stay for at least four weeks. Selling the cargo and loading the new merchandise would take some time. Then he and his associate, Peter Mackenzie, had some other business to settle. He could not keep Morgan aboard his ship for one month, even though she deserved it for tricking him the way she did.

No, he would have to think of something. Just this morning, Morgan had shyly asked what he had in mind for her. Despite the suspicious tears that filled her eyes, Nicholas had not been able to check his sharp response.

"Dammit Morgan, I've got other things to worry about," he had answered. "But I'll take care of it. All right?"

"I don't seem to have a choice," was her haughty reply.

Yet Nicholas knew she was as unhappy as he about this new situation. It would serve her right if he introduced her as his mistress. Why not? he considered. He could keep her in his house. What difference would it make if people whispered about them? Certainly he didn't give a damn, nor did he care much about Morgan's feelings. She would never see these people again.

"I owe you nothing, Morgan Rhinehart!"

The more Nicholas thought about her, the less considerate he became. He was prepared to tell her so, when he once again looked out across the vast ocean.

He tensed. Lifting the spyglass, he could make out a black shape, then another.

"McNeil!" he shouted. "Sail ho! Prepare for a chase! Trim the sails. I want to catch all the wind we can get!"

"Sir. Is it the patrol?"

"Indeed. I don't want to fight them. We must outrun them. Come on man, move!"

There was no need to explain further. Having experienced this before, each crew member knew exactly what he was assigned to do. The *Anastasia* carried cannon, but they would not compare to the heavier ones of the other ships. Besides, Nicholas knew he would never fight an American ship, even if they were fired upon. Speed was his weapon and best defense. The *Anastasia* could outrun the ships. She was sleeker, and even with the heavy cargo, lighter than the converted merchantmen that were now threatening to cross her path.

"Captain, one of them is coming about. If she closes in any more, she'll be able to fire one at us," the second mate shouted.

"The *Anastasia* can outrun anything. Look at those luggers. They're old ships, too heavy from the cannon aboard. Aye, we can outrun them if the wind stays with us."

Unwilling to leave his post on the quarterdeck, Nicholas was startled when a small hand tentatively landed on his shoulder.

"Nick," Morgan called above the noise created by the scurrying sailors, "what is happening?" Wearing another of his shirts belted over an oversized pair of breeches, her black hair blowing across her face, her femininity could not be hidden.

At any other time, Nicholas might have noticed her small body shivering against the cold, her sickly pallor, the strange look in her amber gaze. But his anger at seeing her above deck, endangering herself—and his piece of mind over her safety—erased all rational thought. When the warning shot from the other ship loudly whizzed across the bow, Nicholas lost control.

"What in damnation do you think you're doing here woman?" he bellowed. "Who gave you permission to leave my cabin?"

Roughly grabbing her arm, he whirled her about, shoving her toward the steps of the raised quarterdeck.

"I have enough on my mind right now. I don't need any more of your childishness!"

"But, I only . . ."

"Enough!" Silver daggers sparked from his eyes. The wind ruffled his hair, pushing it off his forehead, while his face stiffened with his fury. When he raised his hand, Morgan was sure he was going to strike her. Desperately, she tried to free herself from his brutal grip.

"Nick! Stop! You're hurting me!"

"Get out of my sight Morgan. Now! I've had more than I can take from you. This wouldn't have happened if we never met." Shoving her down the steps, he cursed himself for ever agreeing to help her.

"McNeil!" he called to the first mate. "Get her out of my sight."

Before she could catch her breath, she was forcefully pushed into the arms of the first mate.

"Captain Rhodes, sir." Recognizing the captain's uncontrolled rage, yet seeing the trembling lass in his arms, McNeil tried to loosen the tension. "She meant no harm, Captain."

"She can endanger us all. Do you think they won't fire on us again because they see her standing at the rail? The first was a warning shot. The second, I assure you, will not be. Make haste man. Lock her in or I'll have you both keelhauled!"

"No!" She whirled, her hair whipping about her face like the rain that foreshadows a hurricane. "I refuse to leave."

Grasping her shoulders, Nicholas began to shake her. "Listen to me you little fool. It's because of you that we are in this mess. Get below now, or I swear you will feel the back of my hand!"

The demonic gleam in his eyes convinced her to retreat.

"I hate you Nicholas!" she spat. But her words were lost on him for he was making his way back up the steps to the bow.

"He does not mean it, Miss. You just startled him. He does not want to see you hurt." McNeil had seen the two tears slide down her cheek before she hastily brushed them away.

"I doubt that, Mr. McNeil. I am sure he blames me for all of his problems. But I promise not to give you any trouble. I will remain in the cabin."

Minutes later, she heard Nicholas's deep voice booming above the din. He seemed to be everywhere, cursing, shouting orders, even encouraging the men. When she felt the ship

77

sharply lurch after hearing the cheers of the crew, she rushed over to the porthole. The two American merchantmen were obviously losing the wind, falling behind the quicker *Anastasia*. Morgan, though, was not completely ignorant of sailing, realizing that the nautical skills of the captain had much to do with their escaping the merchantmen.

Her pleasure over their escape was short-lived. How many more minutes would it take before he charged into the cabin, before he carried out his threat to beat her?

But he did not come. In fact, he stayed away for the remainder of the day, and well into the night. The meals were brought in by Cook, who told her that the men were enjoying the two extra rounds of drink the captain had ordered for them. She did not ask where he was, but Cook volunteered that someone had to stay sober and keep watch.

"Captain Rhodes thought the men deserved it. That's why they'd follow him anywhere. He's a good man, Miss."

Why were they telling her how nice he was when she obviously knew differently? Eating her meal in silence, Morgan again wondered what his plans for her were once they reached Halifax. Perhaps she should try to find another ship bound for New York or back to Boston. She must continue her search for Andrews. Or, a tiny voice asked, was it that she had to get away from Nicholas?

A terrible wave of doubt assailed her. What's wrong with me? Pushing the tray of food aside, she rose from the table, pacing about the large cabin, yet finding the room closing in on her. The pants Nicholas had secured for her were too big and baggy despite the leather thong tied about her narrow waist. With each step, she felt the breeches slip lower, tripping her.

Searching the room for something to occupy her time, Morgan grinned when she found the crystal brandy decanter on a shelf in the corner of the room.

"Well, why not?" she asked aloud.

Unable to find the snifter, she settled on Nicholas's mug, filling it almost to the brim. By the fourth gulp, the burning in her chest was gone, as was any feeling in her legs.

"Thish is good," she mumbled. "Why haven't I tried thish before?"

The warm glow continued to spread through her body. Everything was good, she decided. She had no problems, nothing hurt. But it was getting too warm in the cabin. For at least ten minutes, Morgan struggled with the leather tie on the breeches, wanting to be free of the scratchy wool.

"Success!" she cried with glee when the stubborn knot finally loosened, the breeches dropping to the floor. She found it funny when she tried to get them away from her ankles, howling with laughter as they were kicked across the room and landed on top of Nicholas's sea chest.

Another two gulps of the golden liquid made Morgan quite brave. Weaving over to the chest, she felt no qualms about sitting on the floor and opening the heavy lid to explore the treasures within. The mug rested next to her bare thigh.

There wasn't very much inside, she thought disappointedly. A few trinkets, leather breeches, a silver comb, some shirts, soap that clearly reminded her of his scent. She kept digging anyhow. Finally, her hands fell across a beautiful blue silk shirt, obviously a dress shirt. The texture was so smooth that Morgan carelessly yanked the shirt out of the chest, rubbing the cool material against her flushed skin. Two buttons fell across her lap.

"Uh oh!"

Another sip made her forget what she was worried about. All Morgan wanted was to feel the rich material of the sky-blue shirt against her skin. Quickly removing her linen shirt, she donned the silk one, loving the sensation against her warm skin.

"Mmmm, so good." It took a little effort to stand now, but she safely made it back to the desk where the decanter was now placed.

"How would you like a dress made out of that material?" A deep, rich voice floated over her.

Nicholas was casually leaning against the closed door, arms folded across his chest, his feet planted slightly apart. It was obvious he had been there for some time now.

"Ooh, I'd love it Nick. Could I?"

Then she realized something was wrong. After all, she was supposed to be angry with him for the horrible way he had treated her above deck.

"I just remembered that I don't like you. Go away," she frowned.

It took some effort to remain standing still while he and everything else in the cabin was moving.

"I cannot do that Morgan, this is my cabin."

"Then I will leave."

Trying to summon the strength, Morgan awkwardly staggered to the door. But he was blocking the way.

"Out of my way, sir."

He had been prepared to scold her, to tell her exactly how careless she had been. Allowing his temper to cool, he deliberately stayed away from the cabin. Yet, when he heard her talking to herself as he opened the door, he became curious. Slowly easing the door open, he was dismayed to find her perched near his sea chest, holding up his blue shirt for inspection. Scanning the room, Nicholas finally located the source of her peculiar behavior. My God, he thought, she must have consumed half the contents of the brandy decanter.

Certainly, her current state of mind would make any chance of reasoning with her impossible. So, he merely watched her as she babbled to herself, caressing the shirt in a way that made Nicholas wish he could have been wearing the damn thing. This minx was full of surprises.

Of course Nicholas knew that his temper could often disarm the most stalwart person. Hadn't his parents warned him that his temper was something that needed to be controlled? However, his anger never lasted long. Most of his friends, even his crew, knew as much. Yet this half-dressed, inebriated woman, who was now trying to stare him down, had no way of knowing that more than once his temper had quickly disappeared when she had confronted him. Once or twice, he even felt more like holding her than ranting at her antics. No one had ever had that kind of effect on him.

"Well? Are you getting out of my way?"

"No," he smiled down at her, "I am not, and you, my dear, need some sobering up. You are drunk, Morgan."

"Me? Thas ridicul . . . ridic . . . stupid."

"Here." He reached for her arm, intending to guide her to

the desk chair. "Let me assist you."

"No." She pulled away from him, the motion making her dizzy. "I do not want your help. Ever. I can do it myself."

It took a little more time, but she managed to seat herself. The cabin was still too warm for her. Finding the discarded leather thong alongside the table, Morgan vainly tried to pull the heavy mass of raven hair off her shoulders.

Nicholas wanted to offer his help, but her quelling look prevented him from speaking. When she finally succeeded, he wondered how he was going to summon the strength to keep his hands off her exquisite face.

"Morgan," he began, moving toward her.

"Stay where you are. I think you are mean and surly, Captain Nick. Not at all a Greek god; not even my romantic knight."

Reaching for the mug, Morgan raised it to her lips, still glaring at Nicholas. Unfortunately, the mug was empty. Undaunted, she located the decanter, but as her hand closed about the base, Nicholas's hand stayed hers.

"You've had enough."

"I thought I told you to stay over there, Nicholash." She looked up at him, taking her time examining him. "You're so tall . . . so many muscles. And you have no right to be so handsome. And," she dramatically waved her hand, "you are not going to make me fall in love with you." Her hand covered her mouth in an effort to hold back further confessions. "Oops."

"Well, I think you are very beautiful, Morgan." His broad smile was so nice to see for a change.

"Am I, Nick? I never thought of myself as being beautiful. Prettier than Alice, but never beautiful."

Cupping her chin in his large hand, Nicholas lowered to sit on his haunches. "You are the most desirable woman I have known."

His voice sounded so sincere, she was tempted to believe him, then remembered how abusive he was earlier in the day.

"Hah! You're just saying that Captain, so you can have a willing wench in your bunk. I," she summoned her haughtiest voice while trying to stand, "am not interested."

"Oh? What do you intend to do when we reach Halifax?" He stood up, but did not even move close to Morgan, who was beginnnig to weave.

"Why, I'll find another ship to take me back to Boston or New York."

"Truly? How do you intend to pay for your passage? Or would you like me to find you another set of boy's clothes so you can stow aboard? You will have more experience this time."

He knew he should not be arguing with her now; she had no idea of what she was saying. Hopefully, she would not remember tomorrow. Otherwise, Nick realized she would be furious with him all over again for blurting out things she would never reveal if sober.

"It will not be your problem. Who knows, maybe the captain will find me beautiful."

Forgetting everything else, Nicholas closed the distance between them, spinning her around to face him.

Wanting to rail at him some more, Morgan opened her mouth, but upon seeing two angry faces before her, she had no idea to whom she would speak. Then he and everything else in the cabin began spinning.

"Nick, stand still. I can't tell you what I want to say if . . ." she paused, losing her train of thought, watching both faces grin at her, "if you're moving. . . ."

"Sweetheart, here." He bent down, raising her small body into his arms. "I think you should be put to bed."

Her arms limply hung over his shoulders, while her messy hair—no longer secured by the leather strip—obscured her vision and part of his.

Trying to lift her heavy head from his neck, she said, "I am not tired, Nick. I have more to tell you . . . I think."

"Fine. After I put you to bed."

It did feel so nice to stretch out on the large, soft bed. The silk shirt rose above her shapely legs, soothing and exposing her warm skin along its slow path.

"Come, sit with me."

"Morgan, I don't think . . ."

"Please Nicholas." Her eyes implored him. "I feel so happy.

82

So comfortable."

After he gingerly sat beside her, she pouted, "Why don't you kiss me?"

How was he going to explain this to her in the morning? he wondered. Yet, why should he be so foolish to decline such an invitation? Gathering her pliant body into a tender embrace, Nicholas held her head in his hands, then captured her sweet, brandied lips with his.

The kiss was so pleasant, so sweet, that Morgan wanted to feel much more.

"Take your clothes off, Nicholas."

As her limpid golden pools looked up at him, Nicholas felt an overpowering desire for her. He stood up, turned his back, and hastily removed his clothes, placing them on the nearest chair.

Only when he turned back to her, completely ready for her, did he notice that Morgan was sound asleep!

Nicholas Rhodes slowly reached for the brandy decanter.

She was back in the courtroom. The room was stuffy, and the stale odor from the sweaty, grimy bodies seated all around her assailed her nose. It was unbearably warm. Strange, she thought, there was so little light in the room, yet she could see that one side of the room was strewn with barrels. Why were all those barrels in this court of law?

Nicholas was there too. He was seated on top of one of the barrels, roguishly grinning at her. Wearing his dark leather breeches and a flowing white cotton shirt, Morgan thought he looked more like a pirate than a gentleman. Seated next to him, her hand offensively resting on his muscular thigh, was her cousin Alice. There was no mistaking her seductive pose, her breasts daringly exposed by the low-cut dress. Alice, too, was looking at Morgan, but it was not a friendly smile.

Hearing a loud commotion near the back of the room, Morgan quickly looked away. A man in tattered clothes was being pulled up the aisle. Around his waist was a heavy chain, which was held by the man leading him. This man was better dressed than the other, his black-hooded cloak being of the finest wool. But Morgan strained to see him, sensing something urgent, something she should know. Each time she turned her head, an old beggar woman seated next to her also moved, completely obscuring Morgan's vision.

The man in chains stopped near her. It was her father.

"Papa! Wait, I will help you!"

"Come to me Morgan." He lifted his bound hands. "Help me."

"Yes." She tried to rise, but the smelly bodies nearby prevented her by placing their grimy hands on her shoulders, holding her down.

"No," she shouted, "I must go! Nicholas," she called to the laughing pirate, "help me. My father needs me."

He was still staring at her, so why did he ignore her pleas? Then he turned to Alice, whose hands began to boldly roam his bronze body.

Morgan's thoughts were interrupted by the loud banging, like a hammer or a gavel. It must be the judge, she decided. But the noise was so loud that Morgan had to cover her ears.

The crowd again pressed close against her, making it difficult to move. But she had to reach her father. The man in the black cloak ruthlessly tugged at the chain, making Samuel trip, then fall. She could no longer see her father.

"Papa? I will help you."

Before she could move, the man in the black cloak turned around, lifting his hand high above his head. The light gleaming off the large dagger blinded her for a moment. But Morgan knew what he was going to do.

"Don't! Don't kill my father!"

His hand rapidly moved to the prone, helpless prisoner. The blade disappeared. She heard a man scream. Fighting her way out of the crowd, she finally reached her father. It was too late.

"Don't die, Papa. Someone help me. Please!" she implored the blank faces surrounding her.

Looking around the crowd, she spotted the man in the black cloak. He moved to stand in front of her. As he turned his head, she saw a big red mark on his cheek, but she still could not see his face, for his hood effectively hid the rest of his features.

"Nicholas!" she screamed. "Where are you? It's him! It's Andrews! He killed my father. Help me," she sobbed, cradling her father's head in her lap, ignoring the sticky blood that saturated her clothing.

"Nicholas!"

"I am here Morgan. Morgan wake up! Morgan," he held her thrashing body, anxiously trying to awaken her from her nightmare. "Open your eyes, my love." She was trembling, struggling with the demons. "You were having a nightmare."

"Oh, Nick," she finally looked up at him, as reality helped clear her foggy brain. "It was terrible," she whispered. "Please, just hold me." Her tongue felt so thick that she found it difficult to speak clearly. She also had a terrible bitter taste in her mouth. The hammering in her dream was still going on in her head.

"I feel awful."

"No doubt, my dear, considering the quantity of brandy you consumed." His hands moved under the silk shirt to stroke her back. "Do you want tell me about your dream? Although, judging from your ravings, I have a very good idea of what you were reliving."

His deep voice was a balm to her. The cabin was still shrouded in darkness. Looking at the gallery window, she could barely see the faint pink streaks in the sky.

"What time is it?"

"Almost five A.M. Come sweetheart, tell me."

She told him as much as she could recall. It all sounded so silly to her now, particularly the part about him and Alice. Nicholas chuckled when he heard that, reinforcing Morgan's discomfort. Stealing a glance, she realized that he was barely clothed, wearing only his breeches, his bronze upper torso inviting her to touch his muscular chest after she smoothed his tousled hair from his forehead.

"Nicholas?" He did not stop rubbing her back.

"What?"

"What is going to happen to me when we reach Halifax? How will I get to New York?"

"I told you not to worry, didn't I?"

"You did?"

Obviously she remembered nothing of the last few hours.

He smiled, settling his long legs on the bed before pulling Morgan into the protective circle of his embrace. Kissing the top of her head, he murmured, "I will take care of you . . . somehow, my love."

She must not have heard the last few words, for her head dropped onto his chest. Her soft, relaxed breathing told him she was sleeping again.

This time, her hand was confidently resting across his stomach. How odd, he thought, seconds before he too fell asleep, it was all that he wanted from her this night.

Chapter 9

HALIFAX, NOVA SCOTIA

The welcome sound of dozens of sea gulls circling the ship awoke Nicholas. Quickly yet gently disengaging himself from Morgan—who was still in a deep, trouble-free sleep—Nicholas walked over to the wired gallery window that Morgan still referred to as a port hole. It was a sunny, brisk day, the seas not too choppy. If the wind held, they would make port within a few hours.

Although he had slept in a somewhat cramped position—he did not shift his body all night, firmly holding Morgan against his chest—Nicholas felt rested. Casting a whimsical look at the source of his comfort, or lack of it, he smiled. She was a handful, but in sleep, Morgan Rhinehart looked no older than a sixteen-year-old maiden who has yet to learn of life's hardships and pain. She lay on her side, her black hair scattered across one pillow, her hand holding the other, perhaps assuming he was still in bed with her. If only she could look this peaceful when awake, he thought, briefly wishing that he would become the source of her future contentment.

But that could not be, he decided. He had neither the time nor the desire to devote to her. Morgan would only be in his way. Besides, his promise to both his father and Morgan must somehow be kept. When this matter of the missing currency plates was finally settled, Miss Morgan Rhinehart would be escorted home, placed once and for all into her mother's care.

*   *   *

The irony of sailing into Halifax Harbor was not lost on Nicholas. Halifax was primarily a British military base. Yet the British did not discourage the American smugglers from using the harbor, needing their trade as much as the Americans valued the goods of the Haligonians.

Halifax had become Nicholas's main port of entry for his smuggled goods. Together with his business associate, Peter Mackenzie, Nicholas Rhodes had built up a lucrative enterprise—without the assistance of Warren Rhodes.

Expertly guiding the *Anastasia* into its berth, Nicholas failed to notice Morgan's approach.

Upon waking and finding one side of the bed empty, Morgan hurriedly dressed in the wool breeches and clean white linen shirt that Nicholas had thoughtfully placed on the chair for her. How could a man be so cruel one moment, and thoughtful, even tender, seconds later? Lately, he was monopolizing her thoughts, she realized. The warm sensation in the pit of her stomach whenever she thought of their passionate times together, unsettled her more than last night's brandy did.

"He's a rogue, Morgan," she had told her image in the looking glass. "You cannot completely trust him."

Yet she had tried to make herself look as presentable as possible under the circumstances. Using her brush to smooth out last night's tangles, she loosely braided her hair to one side, then hastily washed with the scented soap, rinsing her mouth. Although the covers did not seem as messy as previous nights, Morgan still straightened the bed. Glancing about the room to assess the damage of her night's bout with brandy, she was pleased to see that little needed to be done. Quickly looking at her image once more, Morgan winked to herself, smoothed an unruly side curl, reached for a blanket to use as a shawl, then went topside. It would be good to be on land again.

He was standing at the wheel, his legs molded into dark brown leather breeches and high black boots, a billowing white silk shirt open at the neck, his dark blond hair mussed by the wind. But it was the way he pursed his lips in concentration, his gray eyes sharply focusing on the port ahead, which made that funny quiver again heat her body. Was it possible, she wondered, for her to lust after him? If so, how different was she from dozens of women who must fall to pieces at the sight of his inviting smile?

"Nicholas," she began hesitantly, her soft voice finally reaching his ears, "what is Halifax like?"

When he looked at her and smiled, Morgan did not care what he said just as long as he continued smiling at her.

"Come here, Morgan. Would you like to hold the wheel?"

Positioning her directly in front of him, Nicholas placed her hands on the large wooden wheel, letting her get the feel of the ship and his own firmer guiding hands. He suddenly missed the sight of her unbound hair flowing in the wind, tickling his face. Nicholas had to content himself with the few errant locks that intermittently touched his chin. Lost in the memory of her, he did not realize she was again asking him a question.

"I'm sorry, sweetheart. You were asking me about Halifax?"

At the moment, Morgan just wanted to hear the melody of his rich voice near her, feel his muscular body moving against her back. Afraid he would leave her side, she decided to keep him talking.

"Is it, um, is Halifax similar to Boston?"

"In some ways, yes. Halifax is a busy port town, thriving on the mercantile trade. Did you know that the Province of Nova Scotia was the fourteenth colony before the Revolutionary War? If the Nova Scotians had thrown in with the Americans, the British might have been forced out of this entire area."

"What happened?"

"I am afraid that the Americans did not fully grasp the significance of this area. The colony was not easily accessible to the other thirteen colonies. Also, it was hard to keep Nova Scotia supplied with military support and ammunition when the rest of the colonies were in more serious need of weaponry."

"The colony was sacrificed, wasn't it?" she asked, leaning into him.

"In a way, yes. That's quite astute, Morgan. I had no idea you were interested in history."

Neither did I, she wanted to reply, but instead half turned to him, giving him a view of her near-perfect profile.

"You don't know everything about me."

"Well," he chuckled, "I think we shall have plenty of time for that."

Mr. McNeil was loathe to interrupt the pleasant picture of his captain kissing the top of the lady's head, but . . .

"Captain Rhodes, excuse me sir."

There was a sudden chill when he left her, after politely disengaging himself. "I guess I should go below," she said, turning to leave before they could see the dull red stain in her cheeks.

Morgan patiently waited for someone to claim her. After one hour of sitting by the captain's desk, she slowly lost her resolve. Finally, the unmistakable sound of Nicholas's booted feet descending the stairs relieved her.

"I thought you had forgot about me." She stood to greet him.

"That would be impossible. But . . . there is much to do." He walked over to his sea chest, searching for something.

"Here," he withdrew a woolen jacket and cap. "I think you will need these. It gets quite cool this time of year. Besides, until I get you some decent clothing, I think it would be best if I let you resume your role as my cabin boy." He saw that she was about to protest. "Please understand, Morgan. There will be too much activity when we disembark, and I do not want any of the scum who frequent the docks to see you."

She should have been angry, but when Nicholas pulled her close, lifting her chin, allowing her to gaze into the smoky depths of his eyes, she lost her determination. Instead, standing on the tips of her toes, Morgan pulled his head down to meet her moistly parted lips. It was her tongue that softly invaded his mouth, searching for then dueling with his. But it was his hands that began a slow exploration of her body.

"Witch," he murmured, "you make me forget all of my good intentions."

Allowing him to lead her toward the bed, Morgan had the uneasy feeling that she would miss the captain's cabin.

Ignoring the knowing looks of the crew when they finally emerged, Nicholas led Morgan to the stern, placing her in the care of the ship's surgeon and ordering them to remain on board until he returned.

Morgan was mesmerized by the activity on the docks. With the exception of the red-coated soldiers, the scene below reminded her of the bustling activity along the Boston wharves.

Among the scurrying sailors, she spotted a finely dressed young man in dark woolen breeches and matching cloak. His auburn hair attracted her attention, since he was one of the few men—aside from Nicholas—whose head was bare.

It was early afternoon, yet the fall air was turning much colder. Morgan was glad now that Nicholas had insisted she wear one of his heavy white wool sweaters underneath the jacket. The dark blue cap was settled down low on her forehead, only her topaz eyes betraying her excitement at the scene below. With her hands dug deep into the pants pockets, Morgan could have been mistaken for one of the crew. When the young man on the wharf called out to Nicholas, she moved toward the deck rail.

"Ahoy there Captain Rhodes! Welcome back, my friend. It's about time too." He agilely sauntered up the plank to greet Nicholas, patting him none too gently on the back.

"Mackenzie, it is good to see you too. Although for a while, I was sure we would have lost our cargo to the patrols."

"Why in blazes are you so late Nick?"

Morgan saw Nicholas look her way before hastily responding. "I had a little unexpected business to attend to in Boston."

"Hah! What was her name, old chap? Seems to me that happened once or twice before. Wait until I tell Catherine. She suggested as much."

If the deck could have opened to let her fall through, Morgan would have welcomed it.

Nicholas said something, but it was too low for her to hear. Whatever it was, the fellow called Mackenzie appeared more serious. Remembering now that Nicholas had told her about his associate, the cargo agent, Morgan wondered if Nicholas would tell this man of her identity.

All of a sudden, Morgan felt an impish desire to surprise both of them. With the surgeon engaged in conversation with a sailor, Morgan slowly moved away toward the port side of the ship—not far from Nick and Mackenzie. Lifting one of the small canvas bags conveniently left nearby, she called in her deepest voice, "Captain Rhodes, sir. Where shall I put this?"

Nicholas swore, attracting Peter's attention.

"Not now," he growled.

"Why sir, I thought you needed this bundle. Isn't this the one with all of the gifts for your whores, I mean lady friends?"

Morgan sauntered up to Peter, then dumped the bundle on his feet.

"Oh, I am sorry sir. I hope I didn't hurt you."

"Nick, what is this?" Peter was obviously taken aback by the audacious behavior of the lad with the peculiar voice. His friend, however, appeared to be gritting his teeth. Surely, Peter thought, Nick was going to throttle the lad.

"It's all right lad. Here," Peter lifted the bag, "let me help you."

"Don't Peter. I'll handle this. Come on Morgan, I'll show you where this goes." He almost ripped her arm from its socket.

"No need Captain." She twisted away from him agilely. "Mr. Mackenzie here has been downright decent. Sorry again guv'nor," she grabbed the bundle. "Here Captain Rhodes, you may need this."

The bundle was shoved into Nicholas's stomach, and his soft "whoosh" caught Peter's attention. Amused now by the curious byplay between the captain and the lad, Peter said, "Stay a moment lad. What's your name?"

Eyes downcast, she replied, "Morgan, sir. Morgan Rhinehart from Philadelphia. Nice to meet you sir," she extended her hand.

Peter immediately realized something was very wrong. The lad was small, but brawny, yet the hand was very soft, almost feminine.

"Uh, Nick . . ."

"Not now Peter," he snapped. "Please excuse us. You!" he finally caught her at the elbow, "I have work for you below." When they were out of Peter's earshot, he growled, "Get below right now Morgan, for I swear I shall put you over my knee.

Believe me you have earned it."

She should have been upset or angry, but as soon as Nicholas had slammed the door and she heard him stomp away, Morgan dissolved into laughter.

"Have you had your fun, Morgan?" he asked much later when he returned with a package tucked under his arm. He had been furious with her outrageous behavior, but after a few minutes, he saw a bit of humor in it.

Peter was aghast when Nicholas had explained that the cabin boy was a well-bred young lady. Peter's expression was almost worth his embarrassment.

"Not a word to anyone, Mackenzie, or I vow I shall run you through. If you do as I ask, I will explain it all to you at another time."

Nicholas had explained what he needed. Peter, now the eager accomplice, was glad to be away from the mercurial Nicholas Rhodes.

"I cannot wait to see what is beneath that cap," Peter said before departing.

Nicholas now stood before her. He was in no mood to do battle with her again. Morgan, still clad in the boy's clothing—including the cap—eyed him warily.

"Please," he held up his left hand, the sunlight catching the golden glint of his ring. "You, madam, have sapped my strength for now. Here," he offered her the package, "perhaps this might help."

Morgan eagerly opened the paper wrapper, softly exclaiming when she saw the pale yellow dress before her.

"It's . . . why it is lovely, Nick. I don't know what to say."

"Good," he laughed, "that's different for you. But don't thank me yet. It was Mackenzie who picked it out for you. I only told him what I thought to be your size."

"Oh. I assume you are quite skillful in estimating a lady's size."

"I have had some experience. Just put the dress on Morgan. We can argue later. I am waiting for two more packages: shoes and a cloak. You have very small feet." He looked down, "I

93

hope the slippers will not be too large. I've never concentrated on ladies' feet," he grinned, enjoying her rising anger.

"Please turn around," her voice was cool.

"Morgan, don't you think we are being a bit too formal under the . . . uh . . . circumstances?"

He watched her remove the cap and lift off the bulky sweater. When she slowly undid the buttons of the breeches, he groaned. "Perhaps I should not watch this display."

"Nicholas, where the devil are you taking me?" she asked, completely changing or ignoring the subject.

"To my home on Oakland Road. Peter and his fiancée will be joining us for dinner."

"Oh."

The dress was almost a perfect fit—a bit tight across the bodice, but after a week of wearing boy's breeches and Nick's shirts, Morgan thought it was the most beautiful dress she had ever possessed.

Nicholas must have thought so too, for his eyes did not leave the swell of her breasts above the material. With a muffled oath, he led her out of the cabin to the carriage waiting on the wharf.

It was too dark for Morgan to see everything about her. Nicholas scurried her into a waiting closed carriage, settling a blanket about her legs. Trying to view the scenery as they swiftly traveled along the cobblestoned streets, Morgan's squirming body rubbed against Nicholas.

"Morgan, I will take you about the town tomorrow. Now sit back and relax," he gently ordered, pulling her into him. "I see you are still squinting. Are your eyes bothering you again?"

"Not really. Although I do not see so clearly at night. Things become a bit blurry."

"I should have had the surgeon examine your eyes. But I will take you to a physician in town. Perhaps tomorrow."

"Why do you care Nick?" she turned to look at him. He appeared so serious, so concerned about her welfare. "One minute you rave on about how miserable I make you, then the next you bundle me up against the cold, and worry about my eyesight."

"I am responsible for you Morgan. That's all. After all, it was my horse that struck your lovely head."

"That's not exactly what I mean Nick, and I think you know it. Well," she straightened herself, glancing out the window again, "I suppose I have no right to ask you a question that I cannot truthfully answer."

He reached for her hand, remembering her revelations when she was drunk, wishing she would repeat those words when completely sober.

"Do you care Morgan?" His voice was barely a whisper.

"Sometimes. Oh Nick, I've never known anyone like you. And, I've never known these feelings, such as," she hesitated, thankful that the darkened coach hid her face, "how pleasant it is to be made love to. Is that caring Nick? Is that what you feel each time you make love to your women?"

"Jealous, my love?"

"No, not really. I just want to know what you feel, what you think. Like now."

"Ah, you are unique Morgan Rhinehart." He leaned over to kiss her temple. "I'll tell you something. When we make love, my only concern is for you; that you enjoy it, that you want me more than anything else in your life, my love. More than wanting to run away to find Andrews."

"Enough to marry me?"

He stiffened, silently contemplating how to answer without hurting her any more than he already had. "If I ever were to marry, sweetheart, you would be the one that comes closest to my ideal of the perfect mate," he smiled, thinking about the stubborn side of her personality. "But you see, Morgan, at the moment I have no intention of marrying. There is too much I have to do. My work is dangerous. I cannot ask someone to share that kind of uncertainty."

"Well," she laughed, the sound a bit tinny to her ears, "you are an honest rogue. Remind me, sir, never to fall in love with you."

"You deserve better than me."

"Yes I do, don't I? Well," she sighed, "I suppose I should worry about each day as it comes. The way you do, Captain."

Her complete acceptance of the situation rankled him. But there was no time to question it, for they pulled up into the short drive leading to his house.

From what she could see, the house looked like a miniature estate.

"Nicholas, it is quite lovely."

"I know. Unfortunately, I hardly use it. Tomorrow I will show you the grounds. I do not have much land, but then I have no use for it. I was spending so much time in Halifax that I was tired of staying in the Blue Bell Inn or in Peter's home. So, I decided to purchase my own."

Helping her out of the carriage, Nicholas led Morgan up the stairs to the double doors in front. They were greeted by a kindly-looking older man, his hair mostly white, who hobbled toward them.

"Nick, me boy. Glad to see ya back. How was it? You were due back much earlier. What happened lad?"

When he saw the lovely woman emerge from behind Nick, the man broadly smiled. "Oh, I see. Finally got hitched, have ye boy? Well, congratulations. Yes sir, it's about time too!"

"Arthur, stop chattering for a moment, will you? The lady is not my wife."

The man's rheumy eyes hardened. "Oh? Then what is such an obvious lady—I said lady me boy—be doing in your company?"

Wanting to get into the house and not spend the night explaining himself to Arthur, Nicholas snapped, "Listen, you old salt. She's my . . . she is, uh . . . she's my fiancée! Now are you satisfied?"

Noticing the shocked expression on both Nicholas and the beautiful woman, Arthur replied, "No I am not. But I can see that the lady must be tired. So here," he reached for one of the bags, "I'll help ye now. Ye'll explain to me later."

"Morgan Rhinehart," Nicholas's hand rested on her back, "this nosy busybody is my butler and occasional manservant, Arthur Gleason."

"I used to be his first mate. He's the finest and the best cap'n ye'd want ta sail with. But the sea air was getting to me old bones. So the cap'n brought me to this house and retired me." Arthur's lopsided grin was infectious.

"It is a pleasure to meet you Mr. Gleason. I see you know the

96

captain better than most."

"He's like my son. Which also means I can tell him exactly what I think. I don't give a hoot if he don't like it. He can't be smuggling forever, though. He needs a good woman to settle down with." Arthur pulled her into the lighted hallway and looked her over, studying her face. "You just might be the right one."

"Why thank you Mr. Gleason. I hope I live up to your standards," she softly laughed, enjoying the discomfort of the tall man shuffling his feet beside her. "I think I need a friend."

"I'll take good care of ye Miss Rhinehart. And heaven help him," Arthur threw a harsh look at Nick, "if he's lying to me."

"Arthur, do you think you can stop scolding me and tell Agatha to prepare dinner for four. Peter and Catherine will be joining us this evening."

"Agatha's me wife, Miss. A good woman she is. Come, I'll take you to her."

Morgan helplessly looked at Nicholas and smiled, seconds before she allowed Arthur to lead her toward the kitchen.

"Agatha, I don't give a damn what you and Arthur think. The lady will have the room adjoining mine!"

Agatha Gleason wanted to hit him over the head with the largest copper pot she could find. She was chubby and not very tall, with short, curly gray hair. But what she lacked in height, she made up for in determination and nerve. Not sure what the captain was doing with such a fine young woman, Agatha decided that the lass needed her protection—especially from him.

"But Captain, you're not married yet. It isn't decent."

"Decency be damned! This is my house, Agatha, and if I want Morgan to sleep in my room it is my business, not yours. Now which is it? My room or the one adjoining it?"

"I am going to pray for you Captain. And the lady."

"Good. Now, have her room made up and finish dinner. You know how prompt Peter is."

Morgan would have loved to laugh, but Nicholas was too angry and she did not want him to vent his anger on her. No, she reasoned, as long as she had the Gleasons to protect her, what else could she want? Now that she was Nick's "fiancée," she was tempted to ask him if this was a marriage proposal, but thought that he would not see the humor in it. Not at this time.

The Gleasons loved Nicholas as their son. Morgan also saw that he deeply cared for the retired seaman and his wife. As she walked up the wide staircase to the second floor, Morgan again marveled at the complicated personality of Nicholas Rhodes.

Chapter 10

Before the evening had ended, Morgan decided that she did not like Peter Mackenzie's fiancée, Miss Catherine Stevens . . . for more than one reason. First, Miss Stevens's petite blond features, dark brown eyes, and impeccably good manners irritated Morgan. She supposed it was caused by the young woman's complete state of helplessness, a trait that Morgan believed was not quite sincere. Still, Morgan could have overlooked it, for she dearly wanted a friend of her own age, someone to confide in, to share her fears, her secrets, her feelings about people, particularly one tall, sun-streaked blond man. But after the first two hours of light dinner conversation, Morgan knew the second, more important reason why she did not like Miss Catherine Stevens.

Catherine was in love with Nicholas Rhodes.

So why was she engaged to Peter Mackenzie? Peter was such a warm, friendly man, who openly adored his fiancée and enjoyed his friendship as well as his business relationship with Nicholas.

Was it possible that both Nicholas and Peter could not see through Catherine Stevens?

"Morgan dear, you must tell me how you and Nicky met."

The third reason for disliking Catherine crystallized: Using the endearment "Nicky" reminded Morgan of her cousin Alice.

"Is something wrong dear? Why are you looking at me that way?" Her syrupy voice sickened Morgan as if she had eaten too many chocolates.

"Oh, you remind me of someone I know."

"Really? Who is that?"

"My cousin, Alice Driscoll."

Nicholas choked on the wine.

"Nicky! Are you all right?" she asked, raising her soft bejeweled hand to his.

"No, no. I am fine," he responded in a hoarse voice, but his knowing look told Morgan that he had understood.

"Well, how did you meet?" Peter asked, wondering when or if Nick would tell him a truthful story.

"We met in Boston. Quite by accident, really." Morgan answered for him, enjoying the piercing look in Catherine's eyes when Nicholas affectionately placed his arm on Morgan's arm.

"Yes, indeed. My horse knocked her down."

"He was so kind, so chivalrous, so solicitous, that by the time I recovered, I swear I was half in love with him."

Morgan winked at Nicholas before she raised another forkful of roast beef to her mouth.

"That I was," he laughed, beginning to enjoy himself for the first time in weeks. "You could say I felt a certain pull toward Morgan. Besides, she really wasn't my first choice." He did not see the triumphant look in Catherine's eyes, but Morgan did. However, it was short-lived, for Nicholas quickly added, "Her sister Lizzie is too young for me."

"So Morgan, your family approves?" Catherine persisted.

"Of course. Why Catherine, whose mother would not approve of such a handsome young man?"

"What about your father?"

Nicholas seemed to notice the slight flicker in the topaz eyes. "He died. It was a sudden illness. It is still hard for Morgan to talk about it."

"But how did your mother allow you to leave with him before you married?"

It was obvious to Morgan that Catherine was not giving up, not until she knew every detail.

"It's quite simple. Darling," she turned to Nicholas, taking his hand in hers and ignoring his raised brow, "don't you think your closest friends should be the first to know the truth? What difference will it make? The whole town will know soon enough."

"Why certainly," he answered, having no idea of where this would lead to, but feeling too good to protest. What could the minx possibly say to extricate herself? Nicholas was more interested in her imaginative response than any reaction it would cause.

"We were married in Boston! Please Nick, I know we can confide in them," she hurried on, looking into his surprised face and squeezing his hand. "We did not tell many people in Boston. Our marriage had to be kept secret." Her head swung back to look at Peter and Catherine."

"Why?"

"Well . . . you see . . ."

"It's a matter of her inheritance," he quickly interjected.

"My what?"

"Cherie, we have told them this much, we might as well tell them the rest." He returned her painful squeeze.

"You see, Morgan will inherit a good deal of money from her father's estate—provided that she does not marry until her nineteenth birthday. It was a stipulation her father wanted to change, but his sudden death altered a great many things. Morgan's birthday is on, ah, precisely, ah . . ."

"The eighteenth of November."

"Of course. Next month. So we thought this little deception would not really hurt anyone but Morgan's solicitors. Her mother completely agrees with us."

"As does my uncle and his family."

"So," Nicholas raised his wineglass, "here's to my beautiful bride, to our American secret, and to friendship."

"Here, here," joined Peter.

Morgan smiled at Nicholas, then glanced at Catherine. Somehow, her smile did not quite reach her glaring brown eyes.

After Agatha's delicious dinner, Nicholas and Peter politely excused themselves for half an hour to discuss some business matters that Peter said could no longer wait. The two women decided to have tea in the parlor. Catherine said she was dying

101

to know about Boston.

"My family was originally from Maine. After the Revolutionary War, there was not much sympathy for Loyalists, so my family—like many others—moved further north."

"That must have been difficult for them. Starting anew, pulling up one's roots is a difficult experience, but under such conditions . . ." Morgan's voice held the memory of her own hasty departure from Philadelphia. How dearly she knew what it felt like to be forced to leave one's only home.

"It was well before my time. It did not bother me." Catherine coolly pointed out. "My father managed quite well, in fact. He is of noble birth."

Raising the hot tea cup to her mouth, Morgan deliberately took a big swallow, hoping the burning in her throat would cool her raging impulse to slap Miss Stevens's smug face. What could Peter Mackenzie see in this viper? Morgan hoped she would find out.

"Catherine, tell me about your wedding plans."

"My wedding?" She absently looked at the open doorway.

"Have you set a date yet?"

"Well no, we were waiting for the best man to return from the sea."

"Oh, I hope Nicholas and I did not upset your plans." Morgan lied, dearly hoping that this wedding would not take place in her presence.

"No, you won't." Catherine absently smoothed her pink satin skirt. "Tell me Morgan, are you with child? Is that why he married you so suddenly?"

"Why Catherine, of course not." Her reply was surprisingly calm. The possibility that she could be pregnant was unsettling. It was the first time Morgan seriously considered the thought. But never, never would she confide in Catherine.

"I don't really believe he would marry you so swiftly. Nicky is not the besotted fool that Peter is. You won't keep him, you know."

"Do I?" Morgan settled the cup and saucer on the table in front of her. Rising from the gold-cushioned settee, she deliberately walked to the other side of the room, pretending to admire the papered walls and brightly colored rugs.

102

"Nicky is mine!" The shrill voice irritated Morgan.

"Why Miss Stevens," she turned to face the witch, "I think you are overlooking some essential facts. You are affianced to Mr. Mackenzie. If you so desired my hus . . . Nicholas, then why have you waited all this time to declare yourself?"

"Because I met Peter first. Two months after he began courting me, I met his mysterious business partner, the sea captain. Nicky is a proud man and a loyal friend. He would never hurt Peter. Perhaps," she brightened, "he married you to spite me! Or," she appeared to delight in another train of thought, "Nicky decided to take a wife so he could settle here in Halifax and be close to me."

"I am sure my husband would be delighted to hear all of this. Shall we tell him together?"

"You can tell him and Peter all you want about me. They will never believe you. I am quite positive of that."

Was it possible that Catherine believed such drivel? Morgan did not have the chance to pursue the conversation, for Agatha Gleason marched into the room to gather the dishes.

"Agatha dear, don't you ever knock? Really," Catherine looked at Morgan again, "I do not understand why Nick puts up with these common folks. Please leave."

"Miss Stevens, I am not sure why the captain puts up with the likes of you, except that you're Peter's fiancée. Besides, I don't take orders from you. I only answer to the captain and his lady wife."

The walls were thinner than Morgan realized. That, or Agatha must have left the doorway leading to the dining room slightly ajar.

"Mrs. Rhodes, would you like some more tea?"

"I think not Agatha. I am very tired." Her hand dramatically lifted to her brow. "It's been such a long, difficult day. Perhaps I should tell Nick, I mean my husband," she paused, archly looking at Catherine, taking pleasure in her discomfort, "that I must excuse myself. You do understand, Catherine."

"Understand what?" his deep voice startled her for a moment.

"Oh Nicholas," Morgan ran into his arms, enjoying the feel of his body against hers and the aromatic scent of tobacco that followed him into the room. "I am exhausted. I apologize for being so rude to your best friends. Would you forgive me if I bade you all a good night?"

"Of course not," he replied, looking down into her earnest, almost loving gaze. "It is I who must beg your forgiveness for tiring you so. Why don't you go upstairs to our bedroom? I will see to our guests."

When she stood on her toes to kiss him, Nicholas decided not to let such an opportunity escape. His mouth swooped down on hers, kissing her so rapturously that they both forgot there were people still in the room.

Peter's cough quickly remedied that. Nicholas sheepishly smiled, then lowered his head to whisper something that only Morgan could hear.

"Wait up for me."

After changing into the most unrevealing nightgown and bed jacket she could find, Morgan unsuccessfully tried to take out her fury on her long black curls. Not even the electric sound of bristling hair could calm her nerves. Never in her life had she met such a calculating, loathsome woman! To think that she would have to spend more time with that person infuriated her.

"Men!" she muttered aloud. "How can they be so dull-witted?"

"You know that love is often blind."

Nicholas was casually leaning in the doorway that separated their rooms. Still dressed in his evening clothes, he began tugging at the perfectly knotted cravat, finally pulling it off his neck. Morgan was quite calm when he removed his deep blue velvet jacket, then the embroidered waistcoat. But when he slowly opened the buttons of his shirt, she decided it was time to stop him.

"Nicholas, don't you think, uh, that you are taking too many liberties?"

"I beg your pardon *wife?* Are you addressing your newly wedded husband—the man you are so passionately in love with?" He did not appear at all perturbed.

"Oh, please," she started to laugh. "I do apologize. I just became so involved in our charade that when Catherine began asking all those rude questions . . . well I don't know what overcame me. But it was such fun. Don't you think so?"

"I have no idea where this charade will lead us, but it seems as if I no longer have control." He started moving toward her, reminding Morgan of his state of undress.

"Nick," she began as she stood up, walking farther away from him toward the large window, "I think you and I need to come to a private agreement."

"Indeed?" he inquired in an odd voice.

What Morgan did not realize was that her body was perfectly silhouetted by the candlelight directly behind her. As she reached up to close the brocade curtains, Nicholas had an unobstructed view of her tantalizing body. The nightgown was cut low in the back. Her straight spine, curvy waist, small hips, and well-rounded derrière reminded him of how much he would enjoy their charade. She would not, he knew, prevent him from making the most of this ridiculous situation.

"Nick, do you understand?"

"I think it's time you understood me, my love." In three long strides, he was at her side, his warm breath tickling her slim neck.

"As long as we are together, telling the world we are man and wife, we shall live as such," his hand rested on her hip, slowly moving lower, "in the true sense of the word."

"How dare you!" she exclaimed indignantly. But as she turned, she found herself caught between his hands, feeling him pull her close, pressing his hard length against hers.

"Stop playing the coy maiden. Morgan, when I take you to New York or back to Boston, you can resume the virtuous part, but not," he suggestively rubbed against her, "here, not with me. You want me to be the devoted spouse. Well, there is only one way you can do that."

His sudden implacable mood change, his stern but sensuous voice laced with determination, alarmed her. Nicholas would not show her any mercy. Why had he become so selfish, so ruthless? Was it because of the way she had spoken to Catherine? Could it be that Nicholas was really aware of

Catherine's lust, had even impetuously accepted what that witch was offering? Could it be that Morgan's announcement militated against his true sexual desire? Perhaps he had been enjoying Catherine's favors all along.

Her power of concentration quickly diminished with each tiny nibble Nicholas placed on her exposed neck. She did not stop him when he relieved her of her bed jacket, exploring her now-bared shoulders. I must be insane, she wildly thought, or I must be as immoral as he.

"You are mine Morgan. Remember that. You will share my bed because you cannot deny your passions any more than I."

All will to protest disappeared as his mouth forcefully claimed hers, his warm lips moving over hers, his tongue probing and parting her mouth.

Instead of protesting, Morgan wrapped her slender arms around his neck, returning the kiss with a passion that astounded him.

Wanting to prolong the moment, Nicholas roughly lifted her into his arms, then walked into his master bedroom. The large four-poster bed was partially hidden in the shadows created by the embers in the white marble fireplace. Nevertheless, it beckoned them.

Not once did he lift his mouth from hers. For Morgan Rhinehart, there was no escape from his sensual onslaught. She was his woman!

As she lay on the bed waiting for him, Nicholas leaned over her, still half dressed in his nankeen breeches. His hand slowly roamed up her thigh, taking the satin nightdress with him. Sliding his hand underneath the material, his calloused fingertips slowly inched along the sensitive area of her inner thighs.

His hand was like the water flowing through a stream, cutting a path through the soft curves of her body. When she tensed, expecting Nicholas to touch her most sensuous area, he did the unexpected by moving his hand up. Untying the tiny ribbons along the bodice of the nightdress, his mouth briefly left hers to kiss her rounded breast over the material. Opening her eyes, Morgan saw the golden anchor on his ring pointing to the next area he would claim with his sensuous mouth and hands. The material of the gown seemed to spread without his assistance, her rosy nipples straining to greet his tongue.

When he groaned, Morgan realized in the dimmest corner of her mind that her hand was charting its own course along his body. Playing with his chest hairs, then imitating his hand movements, she gently pinched his nipples. Still, her hand wandered lower.

Not really knowing what to do, Morgan wanted to feel his hardened body. Were her hands that clumsy? Was it her voice, moaning in frustration when she could not unbutton the breeches so she could feel his flesh grow in the palm of her hand?

"Here, my love, let me help you," he murmured, staring into her half-lidded eyes. He was smiling, yet it was not a self-satisfied grin; rather a knowing half smile, promising much more to come.

Within a fraction of time, Nicholas quickly stood over her, his proud manhood inviting her touch. How she wanted all of him! Morgan did not think there could be any man on earth who looked like her god. Leaning on her side, she gropingly reached out and instinctively stroked him like a furry cat.

"Am I doing this correctly?" she huskily inquired, not the least bit self-conscious about her bold behavior.

"Oh God, Morgan, don't stop," he managed to reply, unable to say another word for fear she would lose her concentration.

Brazenly, her mouth replaced her hand. As if she had provided pleasure for men many times before, she seemed to know exactly how to torture him.

Nicholas groaned, gently placing his hands along the sides of her head, creating a new rhythm with his body as he moved in and out of her moist mouth. It was more than he could bear. The woman was a born courtesan.

"Morgan, let me please you!"

He was alongside her now, his hands urgently seeking her moist center, promising much more. He saw conflicting emotions across her lovely face; the look of sublime pleasure combined with the growing frustration of desperately needing him.

Time and again he brought her close to the edge—but not

yet, not when her hands dug into his shoulders. Not when her soft lips parted, wetting her tongue along the contours. But when she begged, "Please Nick, I want—no I need—to feel you inside me," he relented.

Moving her above him, he slowly lowered her pliant, moist body over his, teaching her the movement. Each time she threw her head back, her black hair fell down her spine, onto his thighs. She was on fire. She saw nothing, heard only her rasping breath mingle with his passionate groans. Her hands splayed across his golden chest. His hands captured each of her rounded globes, teasing them unmercifully.

Proudly, she rode him as if she were the most accomplished horsewoman in the world. Nicholas moved up into her, not knowing how much more he could wait.

Seconds before they exploded in volcanic fury, she thought she heard him say, "You are mine and I shall never want another."

Much later when he was sleeping, his head lying across her breast and his left hand possessively draping her stomach, Morgan fleetingly wondered how she could ever be free of him. Forgotten now was his earlier mistreatment of her. Tomorrow, she decided, she would ask about Catherine Stevens.

Chapter 11

The bright morning sun peeked through the frosted windows. The fire had gone out many hours ago, allowing the cold air to fill the room. Morgan was buried deep under the heavy quilts, which were pulled high up to her pert nose. Leaning on her side, curled into a tight ball, her legs were tucked under his. One arm was folded across his chest, her cheek rested on his shoulder, the glorious silky black hair spread behind and underneath her body.

Nicholas had been awake for some time. Because he did not want to awaken her, he remained motionless. She was snuggled so closely to him, seeking his warmth, his comfort. He did not have the heart to leave her in a cold, empty bed.

Seemingly impervious to the chill, Nicholas tucked one arm under his head, then smiled. Their passion of the previous night had been sublime. Morgan had completely given herself to him, something he found rare even among the most experienced women. To think that only a few weeks ago she had been a total innocent! How much more could he teach her?

Nicholas closed his eyes, allowing his mind to wander, imagining future months, even years together. Being with her, pretending to be her loving husband, was going to have a deleterious effect on him. Furrowing his brow in concentration and dismay, Nicholas wondered when, no if, he corrected himself, he could give her up.

If he kept her with him, certainly his mother would be thrilled, since she would love Morgan as a daughter. She would think that Morgan could cause her son to finally settle down. But not his father! To Warren, Morgan would only be seen as the daughter of a traitor, and that she was probably one as well. Warren Rhodes would surely have a stroke. Besides, his father not only wanted Nicholas to settle in New York and take up law, he wanted his son to marry the wealthy Margaret Lawson, thereby combining the two powerful families.

No, he smugly thought, Warren would not win this time. Over the years, Nicholas had successfully built a barrier between them. For as long as he could remember, Warren could not, would not, grace his youngest son with a compliment. Words of encouragement and words of pride were never given. No; Jonathan was the perfect son. Why, there were times when Nicholas could close his eyes during a conversation with his brother and swear that his father, not Jon, was speaking.

Jonathan did not seem to know any better. As youngsters, Jon was unable to shake off Warren's overbearing hand. Warren chose Jon's friends, his schools, even his wife. Many times Nicholas had felt that *he,* not his brother, was the elder by five years. Nicholas wanted to reach Jonathan, physically trying to separate his brother's dependency on his father, verbally battling with Warren, insisting that Jon be given the chance to make up his own mind. His brother had no idea what Nicholas was trying to do. Often he had said, "I don't understand you Nick. I like everything I have." The tone of voice, even the mannerisms, were Warren's.

Gradually, Nicholas had pulled away, realizing that he did not have the words or the power to change his brother. Jon would forever remain in a state of contented ignorance. At times, though, Nicholas felt empty, wishing his big brother would be his best friend, his partner. He had seen brothers enjoy a special friendship. Even the easy, loving relationship between Morgan and Lizzie was a pleasure to observe.

"Nick, why are you scowling?"

Her voice, husky with sleep, brought him back to the present. Looking down at her, Nicholas's expression quickly changed. This woman made him feel less lonely. It would be difficult to let her go, but there was no doubt he would leave her after their blissful stay in Halifax.

"So 'Mrs. Rhodes,' would you like me to show you about town today? You could use some warm clothing."

"Nick," she tried to uncurl her body, but the air was so cold that as soon as his weight shifted, she felt goose bumps on her arm. "Oh, is it always this cold? I may never leave this bed." She gathered the covers over her once more.

"Excellent idea. Then I could have you all to myself, keeping you warm every night."

"I do not think Catherine would be very pleased." She hadn't meant to bring up the topic so soon, but the word slipped out before her sleepy mind could caution her.

"I can't understand why you don't like Catherine. She's such a sweet young woman."

They could not be talking about the same person, Morgan decided.

Afraid to start an argument, yet strangely curious about his perceptions—or lack of them—Morgan chose to press on. Rolling onto her stomach, her hand still resting across his chest, she raised her head to study his face. He was devastatingly handsome, even after—no, she corrected herself—especially after last night.

"You're not still angry with me, are you? It's just that Catherine would not stop questioning everything we said. I am not sure she believes us, even now."

"Oh, I am sure she does. She is very trusting. Did you notice how she idolizes Peter? How she embraces everything he says?"

"She did, she does? Nick," Morgan raised herself onto her forearms, ignoring the chill, "don't you think Catherine is a trifle insincere?"

"Definitely not. She's a lovely, honest creature. Perfect for Peter."

"Did you know that she, um, how shall I say this, that she looks at you quite a bit?"

"Of course. Often she tells me I am like a brother to her. Morgan," his hand gently massaged the area between her shoulders, "I want you to be friends with Catherine. It would mean so much to her."

"Are you quite sure you know what you are saying?"

"Of course I am. Give her time. Get to know her better. It wouldn't hurt you to have a friend either."

"I cannot believe what I am hearing." She raised her mutinous face to his, but he began to notice a subtle softening around her eyes. "Oh, all right, Captain. I will try once more. But I do not have much faith in becoming fast friends with her."

"Thank you." He pulled her up to him, ignoring her complaint about his trying to freeze her into submission. "Give me a minute to warm you."

Having decided not to enlighten the Gleasons as to their true marital status, Morgan noticed the warm greeting Agatha gave the captain when they appeared for a late morning breakfast.

"Never slept this long before, Captain," she knowingly grinned at Morgan. "You needed the rest, traipsing about on the high seas the way you do. That ship's cook canna properly feed you. I bet you havna had a good meal since the last time you were here."

Turning from the mahogany sideboard, his plate filled with ham, eggs, and muffins, he replied, "Believe it or not Agatha, there are other people who cook as well as you do. I know of at least two such persons in New York and . . ."

"Mrs. Rhodes, you have to take better care of him," Agatha declared, ignoring Nicholas's words. "Ah, it is good to have such a fine lady for my Nick."

A faint blush rose along her slender neck. Yet Morgan was getting used to her new situation. Amazing, she thought, I am beginning to engage in deception as well as a fox who knows the ways of the forest. So much had happened so quickly that Morgan doubted if she would ever again be the same person.

Gone was the innocent Philadelphia girl whose primary concern was which hair ribbon she would wear with which dress. Gone was the dependent, loving daughter and sister. Gone was the young girl who valued honesty and morality above all else. Within six months, Morgan had undergone a major metamorphosis. Was she not as immoral as some

112

common tavern wench? Was she not a deceitful woman, unwilling to tell the Gleasons, Peter, and even her own mother the truth?

Morgan was living in a sinful arrangement with Nicholas; why didn't she at least admit as much to the people who so obviously cared about her? Was she a coward, afraid to acknowledge her lustful tendencies?

But, she reasoned, wasn't it also true that she was determined to accomplish an important mission—the clearing of her father's name as well as recovering the missing currency plates? Did it matter how she set about achieving her goal? If Nicholas hadn't agreed to help her, who would? Since she and Nicholas had already been thrown together—her fault, she reluctantly admitted, for stowing aboard the *Anastasia*—then was she not a victim of circumstance? Perhaps Nicholas would never have made her his mistress if she had gone directly to New York, or if she never had gone aboard that ship.

Who was really responsible? In all fairness, could she blame Nicholas? Morgan had truly given herself to him; could she now deny their attraction for one another?

Morgan did not have an answer. Her spirit was troubled and she knew, as the days progressed, it would not improve.

Nicholas took her into town in the early afternoon. The carriage left them near Citadel Hill. A tall clock, which unerringly chimed each hour, was in the center, but like Québec City the Citadel was a plateau; built around it was a rectangular earthen fort with four bastions, all surrounded by a wide dry ditch, at least ten feet deep.

To Morgan, everything about Halifax had military overtones. As she looked up at the loud clock, she could not help but notice the fort's heavy cannon, which were aimed at the harbor. Scarlet coats were everywhere; so were military barracks. Nicholas again explained the importance of Halifax to the rest of the British-held provinces in the North. The sight of the scarlet coats and the sound of the clipped accents made Morgan wonder what life might have been had the Americans not won the Revolutionary War.

"I don't understand how you can get used to them," she stated, allowing him to hold her by the elbow as they made

113

their way along the wooden walkway on the side of the street.

"It was not easy at first, but we are not at war with the British—not yet. Besides, I find it easier to work with and understand the British than I do the French. It is all a part of my business."

"Nicholas, your family would not approve."

"After all the things I told you about my father, do you think he would approve?" he chuckled. "Oh no, my love, I can assure you that there must be times that my father is tempted to disown me."

Nicholas led her to a dressmaker's shop on Sackville Street.

"Hello Captain Rhodes. It is good to see you back in Halifax." The proprietress greeted them with warmth. Morgan wryly wondered how many women Nicholas had brought to this establishment. In fact, she was sorely tempted to ask, but Nicholas promptly intervened.

"Mrs. Simpson, may I introduce my wife, Morgan? We left Boston quite unexpectedly, and I am afraid that I did not allow her to bring much clothing with her. So," he made an elaborate show of raising her hand to his warm lips, "I promised Morgan a complete new wardrobe. From underthings, to shoes, to hats. Morgan, my love, Mrs. Simpson has talents those stuffy Bostonians would never dream of."

Morgan saw the plump dark-haired woman grin with pleasure. Nicholas must be one of her favorite clients.

"What a beautiful young woman, Captain. You have waited long, but I think she was well worth the wait."

"Mmm, I agree," he lovingly gazed into Morgan's sweet face. "I have never known anyone like my Morgan."

Morgan was touched by Nicholas's soft words and his generosity. Remaining with her for the next two hours, he assisted in the selection of day dresses, evening gowns—items Morgan did not dare to think she would have any need for—woolen shawls, riding habits. The chemises were of the finest silks; the dress materials were warm, heavy brocades, velvets, and satins in bright colors. Morgan was surprised when Nicholas insisted she have an evening gown made out of a rich gold satin material shot through with brighter golden threads. It was magnificent.

"It will match your eyes to perfection," he announced, "and your moods, because the candlelight will catch the various shades of gold as you gracefully glide across the ballroom floor. And I had better be the one partnering you."

She was exhausted by the time they left Mrs. Simpson's. The fittings were strenuous, more because Nicholas stood so close, scrutinizing each style as the material was draped over her. She knew when his eyes lingered on her lips and then lowered to the soft swell above the bodice that Nicholas was remembering last night. His gray eyes glistened with promise of nights that have yet to be experienced.

The streets were busy with an odd combination of businessmen, soldiers, sailors, and ladies of various ages. But the captain and his lady could not walk more than five steps before they were stopped by people Nicholas knew. Each time he dutifully introduced his wife, he was amused by the surprised looks of the mamas who sadly realized that the most eligible bachelor was no longer available for their girls. He was heartily patted on the back by some of the properly dressed gentlemen who reluctantly let go of the lady's hand when Nicholas continued to stare at them.

It was a pleasant experience and a delightful walk. The air was cold but Morgan had a new beautiful off-white woolen cloak to warm her.

Nicholas led her to the area in Halifax noted for its bustling merchant activity. The merchants, well-dressed gentlemen and gentry, freely mingled on Granville Street. Each day, between eleven o'clock and twelve noon, men gathered to buy and sell merchandise almost as quickly as the wardrobe Nicholas had just purchased.

Eyes turned to the captain, many a voice calling out a friendly greeting. They knew that when Captain Nicholas Rhodes was in Halifax, a superior cargo had been smuggled in. They were also quite anxious to sell the captain and Mackenzie their goods. Morgan had quickly noted the respectful yet friendly voices welcoming Nicholas. Obviously, he was a clever seaman and smuggler, and a better-than-average businessman.

However, Morgan soon discovered that not everyone was

impressed with Captain Rhodes.

Nicholas had decided to take Morgan to a nearby restaurant for a light lunch. Again, people greeted them, wishing them well—except one. Seated in a corner, toying with a glass of port, was another gentleman who stared at Nicholas. It was not a welcoming look; rather, it was as if the man were surprised to see him in town.

While Nicholas assisted Morgan in removing her cloak, she had one more chance to look at the man. He was almost handsome and could not have been much older than Nicholas. He was very well dressed in a tailored woolen jacket and waistcoat of dark colors, his white cravat being perfectly tied. His thin, dark hair contrasted sharply against his pale skin. But Morgan was most disturbed by his dark, fathomless eyes, which were first riveted on Nicholas's back, and then slowly turned to gaze at her. He did not smile; in fact, she could have sworn that he did not look *at* her, but *through* her.

"Sweetheart, who are you staring at?"

"Nick, who is that man in the corner? He keeps staring at you, but it doesn't seem to me that he's giving you a friendly greeting."

"How right you are. Here," he pulled out the high-backed armchair for her. When she was comfortably settled at the window side table, he sat down across from her. Taking her hand in his, Nicholas looked about the room, locating the man who made Morgan feel uncomfortable.

"That charming creature is Bennett Williams. He is from a titled family. His father is a duke or something. But Bennett was one of five sons, so now he is forced to soil his hands in the merchant trade, although he has not given up trying for his own title."

"Nick, that fellow does not like you, does he?"

"That is an understatement." Nicholas did not appear concerned. "I suppose you could call it a feud that has been going on for a few years now." He paused to wave at a group of men who were passing by the window. "Bennett Williams would prefer not to have any competition. Especially one who is better than he. You see, four years ago, he too had a rather profitable business in shipping and smuggling. Over the next

116

year or so, Williams lost his three ships—one in a terrible storm, two to the patrols. At first he blamed the Americans. Then, as my luck held and my runs became more profitable, rumors spread that I had been bribing both the Americans and the British. Williams apparently decided that I was the one responsible for his financial loss. He's never abandoned that absurd notion."

"Surely no one believes him?"

"No, of course not. But it does not mean that Williams had learned to forget. If he could find a way to ruin me, he would gladly do so."

"Oh. What will you do Nick?"

"Why nothing," he laughed. "You do not think I am going to let that insignificant brooder bother me?" His left hand reached across the table to touch her cheek. "I appreciate your concern, my love."

Morgan swiveled to her left, trying to catch one quick glance at Mr. Williams. His dark gaze encompassed both of them.

A buxom serving girl made her way to his table, blocking Morgan's vision. Nicholas seemed to know where she was looking but merely smiled. A pleasant lunch of black bean soup, freshly baked him, vegetables, and baked bread was promptly served. Nicholas's delightful banter almost made her forget that Bennett Williams was still in the same room.

They were eating dessert when he made his way toward their table.

"I was sure you would not make it back this time, Captain Rhodes," he sneered in a gravelly voice that unnerved Morgan. Wanting to avoid his leering stare, she suddenly took great interest in her tea cup.

"I heard you were married recently. May I offer your bride my congratulations?"

Bennett Williams had seen the black-haired beauty the moment she walked into the room on the arm of that bastard Rhodes. He could not remember a time when he had not hated Nicholas Rhodes. That man had the golden touch, something Bennett sorely lacked. When he had heard that Rhodes's ship was overdo, he joyously thought that the vessel was finally caught or sunk. Bennett felt that his luck was about to change;

he had even found the backers to help him buy a new ship—the same backers who had an interest in the *Anastasia*'s cargo.

No sooner had the ship been sighted, then the backers changed their greedy minds. It was Rhodes's fault; it always was. Bennett was nursing his anger for the last two days. Then he saw the ship safely anchored, comfortably bobbing against the ropes that held it in place. He also saw the barrels and crates that were unloaded and knew the profits from the sale would be enormous. Next time, he vowed, he would assist the patrols in finding the *Anastasia*, any way he could.

Upon seeing the beautiful woman by the captain's side, Bennett again felt contempt for the man. The once aromatic food no longer appealed to him. When the woman laughed at something Rhodes said, Bennett's fingers grasped the wineglass, nearly breaking off the stem. Nicholas Rhodes had everything, he jealously thought, but if the woman could be taken away from him, that might be a deliciously vengeful blow to his overblown masculinity.

When the serving girl brought his dessert, Bennett could not resist asking her who the woman was. As soon as her name was mentioned, he broke the stem of the glass in his hands. Married her! He sat back in his chair, observing the handsome couple, frowning as Rhodes's hand smoothly slid over hers.

But Bennett could learn to be patient. If he could not steal the woman away from the captain, then he could at least compromise her. Yes, he decided, folding his napkin before he rose, the captain's wife was just what he needed to change his luck. Bennett headed for the captain's table.

"This is my wife, Morgan Rhodes. Morgan, this is *Sir* Bennett Williams. It is 'Sir,' is it not?" Nick innocently asked.

"No. It never was, but things can change. I think you colonists forgot quite a bit," he replied, turning to Morgan. "Mrs. Rhodes, I am sorry you met him before giving the rest of the Haligonians a decent chance to capture your heart."

His accent was clipped and, Morgan reluctantly admitted, Bennett Williams was appealing in a strange sort of way. But no man could favorably compare to Nicholas.

"It is nice to meet you, sir."

"No, no," he smiled, "not 'sir' to you, dear lady. I hope I see

118

you again, Mrs. Rhodes. Perhaps we will have a chance to chat.

"Never alone, Williams. I will always be close by," Nick admonished.

"Is that so?" he laughed, his dark eyes absorbing the muted glow of the sunlight. He politely half bowed, then turned on his heel as he greeted another acquaintance.

"Likable chap, is he not?"

"Oh, he seems harmless."

"He's about as harmless as a cobra. Don't let his charming British accent deceive you. You know, I think he'd kill me if he could. Especially if it meant getting close to you."

"Nick," she flashed him a brilliant smile. "Are you concerned about my well-being or yours?"

"Yours, sweetheart, always yours. If you keep smiling at me like that, I might forget that we are in a public room and ravish you right here."

She blushed so becomingly that he lost the will to tease her further. "Now to prove how concerned I am about you, I am taking you to the doctor." At her confused look, he continued, "Your beautiful golden eyes, remember? Your blurry vision?"

"Oh, it's nothing serious. I told you . . ."

"No," he raised his hand, cutting off her protest, "I insist." Then his tone softened, "Do it for me, will you. Please?" He thought he would choke on that word, but surprisingly it did not hurt at all.

Much later, with a small pair of wire-rimmed glasses in one hand, Morgan tearfully marched out of the physician's office, his words ringing in her ears.

"Only a corrective measure," Dr. Craig had said. "Nothing serious. No damage as far as I can see but you will need to see another physician. Someone with a little more knowledge of this matter. Perhaps in Boston."

He droned on, but Morgan would hear no more, suddenly needing to feel the cold air against her heated cheeks. Unsure of her destination, she resolutely walked down Hollis Street, not knowing when Nicholas stepped beside her, holding his left hand out in a gesture of comfort and support. Morgan clutched his hand as if it were the axis around which her universe revolved.

Chapter 12

The next few weeks were a strange combination of pleasurable activities, social obligations, and frustrations for both Nicholas and Morgan, albeit for different reasons.

Morgan was growing accustomed to her life as Mrs. Nicholas Rhodes. With each new introduction, each loving pat from her husband mixed with kind words, she began to feel a sense of security. But it was a facade. She was not his wife! No matter how many times she pretended or ignored the truth, she would be reminded of it each night as she lay entwined in his hard embrace, the candlelight catching the glow of her wedding band—the false wedding band that Nicholas had insisted she wear, casually handing it to her one night after dinner.

"I think you should wear this ring for now," had been his casual words.

She had met most of his Haligonian friends, business associates, and the society notables. They had gone to many soirees, the theater, and one elaborate ball. She had worn her golden sparkling gown. For the rest of the evening, she felt like a fairy-tale princess on a flying carpet of gossamer silk. Each time Bennett Williams approached her, Nicholas hovered close by, never giving Williams the chance to steal Morgan away.

It would have been so nice, if only. . . . Her heart ached each time she thought of those two formidable words.

Gradually, she began to withdraw from the man who was the source of both her pain and her pleasure. It did not take long for Nicholas to notice the change. His frustration became evident when he realized she was unhappy, but he did not know the source of her discontent.

She found it impossible to form her usual furtive smile. Their routinely animated dinner conversation lost a bit of its playful banter. Morgan did not look directly at him when he asked about her eyesight. But the real proof of her withdrawal was revealed at night.

Last night, she had pretended to be asleep when he entered the room. Nicholas knew enough about her sleeping habits to realize that her body was stiff, her eyes almost squeezed shut. On this morning, bringing her a pot of hot chocolate, he finally asked if anything was wrong. Morgan rolled over to her side, complaining of a mild stomach ailment.

"Morgan," he inquired gently, "do you think, I mean is it possible you are. Have you missed your monthly? . . ." he stammered.

"No!" she snapped.

"Oh." He felt foolish, but Nicholas did not know what to say. Yet, he blindly continued. "Then what is it sweetheart? I know something is troubling you. I'd be happy to listen." The bed sagged beneath his weight, but Morgan moved away.

"Tell me Nicholas," she asked the wall, "what would you do if I were carrying your child?"

"I'd marry you."

"Is that what it would take to salvage my reputation?"

"I don't understand, I thought you . . ."

"You could marry me," she whispered, her words spoken into the pillow.

"Is that what you want?" Nicholas's brows lifted in confusion. She had become a puzzle to him.

"Don't answer me with a question. I want to know."

Slowly she turned to face him. It did not take an astute man to see the pain in her mournful gaze. It baffled him, for he had no idea that she could have become this unhappy so quickly.

"Answer me," she persisted.

"For Christ's sake, Morgan, I can't keep up with your moods!" He jumped off the bed, angrily stomping across the fine Aubusson rug. "How am I supposed to know that you've changed your mind? So now you want to marry me? Will you still want to marry me tomorrow, or will you run away?" He tunneled his hand through his hair, pushing the wavy locks off his forehead. In a quick mood reversal of his own, Nicholas's voice suddenly mellowed. Turning to face her, a soft smile on his handsome face, he said, "Hell, I don't know Morgan. This whole situation is as bizarre to me as it is to you."

Pulling herself up to lean against the cushioned headboard, she began in a low but determined voice, "Perhaps I am not being very fair. This situation is as much my fault as it is yours." At his quick start, she amended, "Well, I should take most of the blame."

"How generous of you," he drawled. Still, he moved to sit on the edge of the bed near her feet, leaning against the wooden post, one booted foot crossed over the other. He looked so handsome, informally dressed in a cambric shirt, which was loosely laced at his neck, and tight black riding breeches.

"Morgan, I want to understand. So tell me."

"I am not sure if I can."

"Woman," he sighed heavily, "you just might make me crazy. Now all I ask is that you tell me whatever is on your mind. I no longer care if it makes sense or not, but for heaven's sake, speak to me."

Was he really so concerned about her? she wondered. Nicholas seemed to be making an effort to understand her.

"I feel immoral Nick. I know I put myself in this situation by stowing aboard the *Anastasia*. I suppose, in my innocence, that I had no idea of what our being together would mean. Nick," she paused, trying to find the right words, "I don't know how or if I can face my mother after this. She'll obviously know the truth. Even you say I don't hide secrets very well; my blush gives me away." She nervously twisted a long curl around her finger but continued, desperately wanting him to understand what she was trying to say.

"I feel ashamed, but then again, I don't. I enjoy being with you. I . . . dammit, I can feel my face glow. . . . I enjoy being here in this bed with you. But tell me, when you leave me in Boston, or New York, or wherever my search for Andrews leads me, can I pretend this time never existed? Can I deny my lust for you? If I ever met another man—I am not saying that I will or that I even want to—but if I did, what do I say to him? 'Oh, you want to know about my loss of virginity? That happened when I was masquerading as the wife of the notorious sea captain, Nicholas Rhodes. It was nothing really.'" Her voice rose a bit, "How can I explain it? Do I have to explain? Do I, Nick?"

"No. You do not owe anyone an explanation. Not even me. Morgan, I should have known better." Again, he began pacing, walking from one end of the bedroom to the other and back again in four long paces.

"Why? How often do you pose as a woman's husband? You know you never did tell me, was there—I mean is there—someone special in New York?"

"No," he said, not considering Margaret Lawson. "Don't tell me that would make a difference to you now, my love. But I've told you before, I am not the ideal husband, for reasons you've experienced at sea."

"What about love?" she persisted.

"What about it?"

"Do you love me?"

"Do you love me?" he countered.

"You're doing it again, Captain," she couldn't hide the smile.

"In answer to your last question, I am not sure if I can love any woman. Morgan, in all my twenty-seven years, I've never given love much thought. Never had to, I guess."

"Actually," she admitted, "neither have I—in all my soon-to-be nineteen years. You know you really are a very nice man, when you want to be. But I won't tell anyone. Let them think you are the carefree smuggler who thrives on danger as much as he thrives on Agatha's pies. Here," she patted the bed, "sit next to me."

"Do you feel better now?" He gently massaged her neck. His shirt lace tickled her bare shoulder when he moved closer to her side.

"Oh, I have never been so confused in my life. Not even when I decided to go find my father's murderer."

"Do you think we can postpone the topic of marriage and

morality for a short while? At least a few more days. Then you can tell me if you think marriage to me is the answer to your problems. Also, let me think about what you've said today. No, I am not deliberately avoiding the issue. But I must admit that you confuse the hell out of me too."

His wide grin made her stomach flip. When it made funny noises, she sheepishly looked at him.

"May I have my breakfast now?"

The following evening, Morgan and Nicholas were invited to a formal dinner party. Dressed in a dark blue-black velvet gown that was the same color as her hair, Morgan radiated a sophistication she did not feel. The "Empire" style suited her to perfection. It had a wide, bare neck with puffed shoulders, and long wide sleeves that tapered down to tighten at the wrist. The skirt flared only slightly beneath the high bodice. It was beautiful in its simplicity.

Nicholas had known it would perfectly enhance Morgan's beauty. When she laughingly twirled in front of him, he sat down on the sofa near the fireplace to watch her trifle with her long hair. At that moment, he decided to present her with a set of pearl combs that he knew would gracefully hold back the sides of her hair.

But there was still more. Artfully arranging the curls around her combs, Morgan did not notice his slow, pantherlike strides. Nicholas stood behind her, his mouth set in a straight line. Morgan caught the look through the mirror, immediately thinking that something was amiss.

"What are you angry about?"

"I am not angry, only thoughtful," he replied, placing his left hand on her bare shoulder. "It's just that I think you are not properly dressed." He stayed her shoulder before she had a chance to turn around to differ with him.

"I think," his finger traced a path along the column of her slender neck, "that your neck is too bare." Reaching into his waistcoat, he withdrew a velvet box, slowly opening the lid.

"For you, beauty."

Her breath caught in her throat when Nicholas placed a

double strand of perfectly matched pearls about her neck. A tiny diamond clasp held the choker in place.

"I believe it suits you perfectly."

"Nicholas," she sighed, "it's so lovely. I really shouldn't accept this."

"Why?" his eyebrow rose in mock confusion.

"It must be expensive. I don't think . . ."

"Did you not say you would stop worrying about our situation for a few more days?" He sat beside her on the cushioned seat, turning her to face him.

"I want you to have it. It belongs on your exquisite neck," he kissed the soft area. "I bought it the moment I helped you pick out the velvet material at the dressmaker's. Along with the combs, of course."

"Ah, you do spoil me," she shyly smiled, secretly pleased that he noticed so much about her. There were times like these when she truly believed he cared a great deal about her.

"I enjoy spoiling you."

She looked into his liquid silver eyes, watching them darken in anticipation of a more thorough kiss. Lifting her oval face to his, she placed a tiny kiss on his patrician nose. Before she could pull away, Nicholas locked his arms around her, inhaling the rose scent on her skin, ready to take more.

"You madam, are spoiling me. I don't think I could ever hold another after feeling the fit of your body in mine. You are an anodyne for my senses. I think, however, we must—much to my chagrin—leave for the Tuckers' home."

Reluctantly disengaging himself from her voluptuous body, he walked into his dressing room, locating his dove-gray jacket and shrugging his broad shoulders into the well-tailored garment. Everything he wore fit perfectly: the sky-blue silk shirt—she thought it was the same one she had worn that night aboard his ship—embroidered waistcoat, and snug black breeches. Nicholas wore his clothes with a casual grace that would put most men, regardless of age or breeding, to shame.

For this night, he was hers.

Moments before they left the house, Morgan sought her off-white woolen cloak. Nicholas offered to get it, but he returned with another surprise. It was a sable-lined black hooded cape, which made Morgan and Agatha gasp.

"Lordy, Captain. You have the finest taste in clothing and wives."

Slowly, he settled the sable cloak about her shoulders, taking sublime pleasure in her loving expression as he solicitously lifted the fur hood over her hair. For one brief moment, his hands rested on her bright cheeks. In the dim light of the foyer, he became lost in the glow of her golden gaze.

"Thank you," she whispered in an emotion-filled voice, "I think you . . ."

"No." His fingers on her lips cut off her next words. "I do not want to hear your gratitude. It is I who should be thanking you."

They were not the last to arrive at the Tuckers. Catherine and Peter were. During the last fortnight, Nicholas had continued to maintain to Morgan that Catherine was the friend she sorely needed. Yet Morgan was beginning to rely on her own instincts. The only friends she needed or wanted in Halifax—aside from Nicholas—were the Gleasons and Peter Mackenzie.

Catherine Stevens was more difficult to take than sour milk. Each time the couples were together, Morgan became more convinced of Catherine's deception. Catherine wanted her husband. . . . No, Morgan admonished herself, he is not my husband. . . . Nevertheless, Catherine wanted Nicholas as her own. Each time Catherine tenaciously clung to Nicholas's arm, Morgan made a genuine effort to distract Peter from that woman's treachery. Since Nick was as blind as a bat when it came to Miss Stevens, Morgan did not expect Peter to be any more astute. Her heart went out to dear Peter.

Rachel Tucker led her guests into a large salon where the others had gathered. Among the dozen elegantly attired guests was Bennett Williams. Attached to his arm was a pretty little red-haired girl who giggled each time Bennett spoke. At first it appeared as if he did not notice their arrival, but Nicholas knew better.

Bennett Williams was aware of each movement. In the last two weeks, Nicholas had heard that Bennett was discreetly inquiring about Nicholas's business activities. That in itself was not surprising. However, Bennett's inquiries about Morgan were what infuriated Nicholas. Obviously Williams was up to something, but Nicholas swore he would kill Bennett before he harmed Morgan.

After discussing the matter with Peter, Nicholas had decided not to tell Morgan about Mr. Williams. It was senseless to add another problem to her growing list. No, he would watch Williams and thwart his every move, any way he could.

Watching Morgan converse with different people, Nicholas felt a great deal of pride. More than one man had complimented him on his superb choice of a bride, but it was more than that. Morgan was becoming a part of him. She was the other half, perhaps his better half. She was the reason he quickly and efficiently completed each business day, so he could rush home to see her, to spend an evening alone with her. Those were the evenings he most enjoyed. She was the reason his nights were filled with utter bliss. Nicholas was by no means an inexperienced lover, but with Morgan, he eagerly anticipated each passionate moment, the chance to teach her some loving gesture, to give her pleasure, which in turn heightened his.

Something else was happening to the charming smuggler: He was beginning to accept the idea of marrying her. After all, could he do much worse? Was there any other woman with whom he wanted to spend his time? Not wanting to go as far as to admit he loved her—for he never gave credence to that absurd possibility—Nicholas thought that Morgan was better suited for him than any other woman.

Becoming accustomed to the idea, Nicholas spent the balance of the evening admiring his woman.

Catherine noticed his lovesick look. As soon as she was able, she made her way to Nicholas's side. His presence filled the room. Somehow, Catherine had to make Nick understand that she was his one true love. Tonight, she would try.

"Nicky, did Mrs. Tucker show you her newest collection of paintings? Would you believe she claims she purchased a Gainsborough. You know so much about art. Let me show you."

Like a sheep being led to slaughter, he allowed her to lead him to the library. Studying the painting, Nicholas concluded that it was indeed a genuine work of art. Anxious to return to Morgan, he failed to notice Catherine's ploy.

"Nicky," she seductively moved against him, "I was wondering about something." Both arms captured his in a surprisingly strong grip. "Do you think it is pretty?"

"Well," he began, still looking at the lovely landscape in the painting, "pretty is not one of the words I would choose to describe this painting."

"I wasn't referring to the painting. I was referring to me," she batted her lashes.

This time he did look at her. Only a blind man could miss that look. It was the look of a woman whose sights were set on a very specific goal.

"My, you are brash Catherine."

"Only when I know what I want."

"What should that be?" he asked, thinking he could brazenly snub her. Catherine's full mouth quivered in anticipation.

"I'd love to be kissed by a smuggler."

"Doesn't Peter kiss you?"

"You know what I mean, Nicky. I think you are the most handsome creature I have ever seen. So why won't you kiss me?"

Feeling utterly ridiculous, then angry, he gently tried to disengage himself from her grip. What was wrong with her tonight? Did she consume more wine than he had realized?

"Please Nicky."

It was meant to be a chaste peck on the cheek. But she must have known his intent. Swiftly turning her face, Nicholas met her lips instead. Her lips were warm, moist, parted to give him the opportunity to discover her mouth.

Although his hands remained at his sides, Catherine entwined her arms around his neck. But Nicholas pulled his head away.

"Catherine, I apologize if I misled you by coming in here." He sought to apologize for a blatant act that was in no way his fault. For Peter's sake, though, Nicholas felt he had to set the matter straight.

"Catherine, we need to talk."

129

"I know. I have so much to tell you."

Finally extricating himself from her grip, he moved toward another group of paintings, painfully trying to put the words together.

"Ah hah! There you are. Morgan and I set out to look for you. She found you first. Supper will be served soon."

Both Morgan and Peter stood in the doorway. How much they saw—or heard—he did not know. Judging from the mutinous look on Morgan's face, he could surmise that if she did not see anything, she had an uncanny imagination.

"Oh, Nicky and I were just looking at the Gainsborough. Weren't we?" Again, Catherine hooked her arm through his.

"Well I do not know about the rest of you, but I am famished." Peter extended his arm to Morgan, who had not moved from the doorway.

"I would like the pleasure of escorting your bride, Captain. With your permission, of course."

"Oh, we don't mind. Nicky and I can finish our conversation. We were talking about pretty things."

Since Morgan had not said a word upon finding them in the room, Nicholas could only assume that she was angry. That, or she was smugly thinking how right she had been in her assessment of Catherine. Morgan allowed Peter to lead her out of the room.

Unwilling to continue Catherine's conversation, Nicholas began an inane discourse on art. Catherine began to say something, but he would not give her a chance. Instead he deposited her in her seat, which he soon discovered was next to his! If he could get through this night without being compromised by his best friend's fiancée, it would be a supreme accomplishment.

In his dismayed state, Nicholas failed to notice that Morgan was seated at the opposite end of the long dining table, next to Bennett Williams. But when he did, the glass of champagne in front of Nicholas plus many others were consumed.

All of Morgan's previous suspicions about Catherine were confirmed. When she had seen Catherine in Nicholas's embrace—she was too angry to notice that his arms were disengaging hers—Morgan wanted to scream. Catherine *did* want Nicholas, and damn him for betraying both Peter and herself. He was such an indiscriminate lecher, she decided. Even as Peter spoke, Morgan could only see Catherine in Nicholas's arm. He had looked uncomfortable when he saw her enter the room, but that must have been more because they were discovered. Morgan doubted that Nick felt any remorse.

Desperately, she too wondered how she would survive the evening. Her first glass of champagne was not nearly enough to cloud the memory of Catherine's smug face.

Bennett Williams could not believe his good fortune in finding Mrs. Rhodes next to him. Without question, her dark ethereal beauty outshone every woman in the room. The stab of pleasure he felt was more powerful than the thirst for vengeance against Rhodes.

As soon as Morgan sat down, he gallantly rose to assist her, starting a clever conversation about life in Halifax, deliberately including the people around him.

"Oh, Mrs. Rhodes, you should have been here during the time of the Prince Regent. It was only a few years ago that he was here, and we shall never forget him."

"It was a gay time," said another. "Prince Edward loved a good time more than his military commitment."

"Actually," Bennett fixed the cuff on his white-frilled shirt, "Prince Edward did much for the military. Why, we now can boast of the strongest military fortress outside Europe. He had supervised the building of the Royal Artillery Park and barracks on Sackville Street. He even invented a telegraph system for Halifax."

After her second glass of champagne, Morgan became quite interested in everything Bennett Williams was saying. It was that, or watch Nick enjoy himself with Catherine.

"Was his wife with him?" she asked.

"Oh no. His mistress, Julie. Loyal woman. I think she loved him a great deal. You know the prince built a new country house on the wooded shore of Bedford Basin. It's a lovely house, Italian style. That, of course, set the pace for many other country homes that were built along the Basin. My home is there too. It is quite lovely. I would very much like you to see it."

131

"That is most kind of you, Mr. Williams. My husband and I would be delighted to visit."

"I did not invite your husband," he said in a quiet voice, his dark eyes devouring her.

No one heard his invitation, but Morgan was troubled nonetheless. "I think you are mistaken, sir."

"I never make mistakes, my lovely. Especially not with beautiful women. And you are the most beautiful I have met."

Surreptitiously looking about, she realized that the people who were once involved in their friendly chatter were turned elsewhere in conversation. There was a mild reprieve when the next course was served. Bennett Williams was obviously trying to seduce her with his words. But what did it matter? She was in a crowded dining room, with Nicholas and Peter close by. What could the man possibly do? Besides, Morgan calmly reasoned, he was a rather engaging conversationalist.

"Now where was I," he began, turning his full attention to her once more.

Nicholas saw the man leaning close to Morgan. Williams was definitely leering at his wife. If that were not enough, she actually smiled back at him, shyly looking at Williams, her glass raised again to her lips. Remembering how liquor could affect her, Nicholas tried to catch her eye, but Morgan did not look his way.

Peter was seated across from them, oblivious to the intrigue around him. Nicholas was totally unprepared for what happened next.

Catherine's hand was suddenly on his muscular thigh. Before he could move, her hand moved to his inner thigh, making small circular motions with her hand. And still going higher.

This had gone too far. Certainly women had made advances before. Some of those advances were unwarranted. Always, Nicholas was able to either put a stop to them, or to encourage them. Honor among friends meant something to Nicholas. If he had known Catherine as anything other than Peter's fiancée, he might have welcomed her advances. That was before Peter and, God help him, before Morgan Rhinehart. Could his judgment have been so poor? He had thought

132

Catherine such a fine, virtuous young woman. Now, within the span of one hour, he saw her differently—the same way Morgan must have seen Catherine when she first met her. Concerned that he could make such a grave mistake in assessing another's character, Nicholas wondered if he could make the same error in judgment again.

He looked at Catherine. She was staring at him, smiling, then she winked! Nicholas could not take it. Grabbing her hand underneath the table, he removed it unhesitatingly. Smiling tightly, he whispered, "I think you are gravely mistaken, Catherine. I would hate to tell Peter about this indiscretion. Don't make me do it, Catherine," he warned, still smiling. When she placed her hand on the table, he raised it to his lips. "Don't ever do this again."

Nicholas's bright smile and gallant kiss on Catherine's hand was the only act Morgan saw. Having little experience in dealing with men—particularly one as rakish as Nicholas or one as devious as Williams—Morgan turned her full attention to her dinner partner.

It was the worst move she could have made. By the end of the evening, Bennett was convinced that Morgan Rhodes could be compromised. Ever so lightly, his leg pressed against her velvet one. It was his most fervent desire to have her now, this minute. If he could whisk her away, keep her with him for a few months, he would gladly do so. Perhaps he would never let her go. She should be his possession. Soon, Bennett could no longer tell which was sweeter, his vengeance or his lust.

Plans were set in motion that evening, plans that would consistently clash with one another, as would the individuals. More than once that night, the four protagonists in this unfolding drama experienced passion, love, jealousy, frustration, and hatred. Only Nicholas and Morgan fervently hoped that the evening would end with minimal damage to their relationship.

Rachel Tucker had arranged the after-dinner entertainment. The guests were taken into the grand salon to the neat rows of cushioned chairs. Bennett had not left Morgan's side. As he was holding the chair to comfortably seat her, Nicholas appeared.

"I thank you for escorting my wife here for me, Williams. I must remember this gesture the next time you speak to my financiers."

There was no room in that row for Bennett. Rather than make a scene, he moved to an empty seat in the last row.

A rather plump woman, accompanying herself on the harp, sang a series of love ballads. Between sets, Nicholas politely managed to ask Morgan about her evening.

"I am surprised you took the time to notice. Catherine must have been looking elsewhere for three seconds."

Her words had an effect on him, but it was not anger. Rather, it was a quiet elation. Could Morgan be jealous?

"I would suggest, darling, that the next time that snake Williams puts his leg against yours, you might want to stab him with your fork."

"I beg your pardon?"

"Don't play the innocent with me. Not this time, Morgan. You have learned too much, too soon."

"One assimilates a wealth of information around Catherine." She cast a meaningful glance at the blond woman behind them.

The next musical set began, cutting off any response Nicholas might have had. Determined not to let the guests think the Rhodeses were anything less than a happy couple, Nicholas held Morgan's slender hand between both of his, rubbing his thumb along her palm. He leaned over to whisper in her ear, "Shall we leave early, my love? I am sure our hosts will understand how anxious I am to get you home."

As Catherine watched Nicholas whisper something to his wife, she wondered why it couldn't have been her instead of that black-haired country bumpkin. Stealing a glance at Peter, Catherine wondered how much longer she could stall their marriage. On the other hand, perhaps she should not postpone the wedding after all. If she and Peter set a date, maybe Nicky would finally come to the crushing realization that he might lose her. Yes, she smiled to herself, that's the answer. Catherine wove an intricate fantasy, convincing herself that Captain Rhodes was desperately in love with her.

"Peter, darling, I think we should set a date for our

134

marriage, don't you?" she announced.

Startled by her sudden about-face, Peter beamed with delight. For an astute businessman, Peter Mackenzie was very obtuse when it came to Catherine Stevens.

From the rear of the room, Bennett Williams had observed more than he could stomach. Out of necessity, Bennett had learned to form alliances with people who could serve his specific goals. There would be no harm in learning a little more about Miss Catherine Stevens. Engaged to one man but seemingly interested in another, she just might be of assistance in ending the marriage of Nicholas and Morgan Rhodes. Sitting back in his seat, Bennett concluded that he had several visits to make in the next few days.

Morgan was tired. The evening had drained her. Helping her into the coach, Nicholas was oblivious to her silence. She couldn't believe that he was not aware of how upset she felt. Unable to stand the silence, Morgan had finally said in a rather cool tone, "Nick, when are you going to tell Peter about your special 'friendship' with Catherine?"

"My what?"

"Oh stop it," she snapped. "You don't think you can fool me? I may not be as intelligent as some people, but I can see more than you are giving me credit for."

"Is that so?"

"Nick, if you don't tell Peter about you and Catherine, I swear I will." Morgan really had no idea of what she was saying. She was too furious; she simply wanted to strike back at him.

"Be quiet, Morgan. You are beginning to sound like a shrew."

"I mean it."

"Say one word to Peter before I do and your backside will be sore for one month. I mean it."

"Before you do what?"

"I will talk to Peter."

"About you and Catherine?"

"Dammit Morgan! I don't know what you are talking about.

135

There is nothing between me and Catherine to talk about. If you must know, you were right about her. She is not the fine young woman I thought she was."

It was a small blessing that it was so dark in the coach. Morgan could not see Nicholas's frustrated look, nor could he see her elation.

"Well it's about time. What did she do, seduce you underneath the table?"

"Very close to it," he laughed, finally seeing the humor in it. "Morgan you better be a good sport, for I am about to tell you exactly what she did. And if you tell Peter, or anyone, my threat still holds. Besides, I am not sure I should tell Peter the whole thing."

They arrived at the house before he could finish his tale. But she was not about to let him go, not without his complete confession. Following him into his dressing room, she insisted he tell her every detail of the incident.

When he finished, Morgan thought she would die of laughter.

"You let her do that to you! Since when are you such an easy target? My goodness, Nick, I might try the same thing at the next dinner party we attend."

"I knew I shouldn't have told you. I thought I could confide in you." He looked so forlorn that Morgan instantly felt contrite.

"I am sorry, Nick. In fact I should be thanking you. It is nice to think that you trust me."

She started to say more, but Nicholas had other thoughts in mind.

"Tomorrow, we can continue this conversation, if you really want to. At this moment, I'd prefer another far more satisfying activity."

Turning her around to undo the tiny buttons in the back of the dress, Nicholas's mouth followed his hands, sending delightful chills along her bare spine.

The evening's accumulation of anger and jealousy had flared into a heated passion for one another.

"I do not care about anything else tonight, but feeling your naked body against mine; I thought of nothing else all evening."

He began to slowly strip Morgan of her garments, leaving her in the pale yellow silk chemise and stockings. His hands, his mouth, transmitted a sense of urgency.

"Let me help you," she whispered in a desire-filled voice. "I want to feel you—now." She helped him undo the buttons of his breeches until he proudly stood before her.

They could not refrain from touching one another, their frenzy consuming them. Nicholas tried to undo the ribbons of her chemise, but became clumsy and impatient. Grabbing the front of the garment, he tore it off her, flinging it aside. His hands groped for her naked skin. Their mouths searched for fulfillment. Nicholas lowered his head to take her rosy nipple in his mouth, nipping it with his teeth while his hand freely roamed her body. It was heavenly. She wanted him to take her, not slowly, not tenderly, but with all of the uncontrolled, unleashed passion that she had decorously contained. Their desire reached their temples like a flame bringing water to a boil.

In this fevered state, Nicholas lowered her onto the floor.

"Morgan, my God how I want you." His mouth possessed her, his tongue dueling with hers, making her every vessel pound in his ears.

"Nicholas, I can't wait. Take me now."

He entered her forcefully. But she was ready, matching his powerful thrusts with her equally powerful response. Consumed by their intense appetite, they lost track of time and space. Desire directed their every movement. Together they rose to a new plane, a place that neither had ever been to before. They were as one.

Later, Nicholas carried her to their bed, settling in beside her. Pulling her into his arms, he softly kissed her face. Morgan looked into his smiling eyes.

"Do you think we can try it again, more slowly this time?" she boldly suggested.

"With pleasure."

Chapter 13

"I tell you, Nick, this has been the most profitable sale yet. The merchants are lining up, begging us to take on their goods. Your next trip will be even more profitable."

"Just keep depositing the money in the bank, Peter, and I'll be content."

Nicholas lit a cheroot, enjoying the pattern created by the blue swirls of smoke. They were comfortably seated in Peter's office, calculating the profits from the cargo's sale.

After the completion of their latest business transactions, Nicholas decided to open another topic—one that had been bothering him since the night of the Tuckers' party.

"Say, Peter," he propped his booted feet on Peter's oak desk. "Are you quite sure you want to marry Catherine in two months?"

"Of course," he waved the papers in his hand. "I am delighted by the sudden change in events."

"Hmmm," he puffed on the cheroot, deep in thought. "I think there is something you should know, Peter." Nicholas had rehearsed what he wanted to say, but now that the moment was before him, he could not recall the proper phrases. "I mean, are you sure you really want to marry?"

"Hah! I would have asked the same thing of you, if you hadn't decided to marry Morgan on a whim."

"It wasn't a whim, I assure you. However, we are talking about you not me."

A quill pen in his fingers, the lit cheroot burning in the

ashtray, Nicholas still looked for another object with which to toy—anything rather than look directly into Peter's trusting face.

"Sit down, will you Mackenzie?" He motioned to the armchair near the window. "You are more than my business agent. I think you know that," he began, although he still felt quite uncomfortable with what he knew had to be said. "Therefore, I feel it my duty to tell you . . ."

"What? How much more time do you need Nick?" Peter smiled, his handsome face aglow with delight. Never had he seen Nick this uncomfortable with any subject.

"I don't believe Catherine is for you."

The smile instantly disappeared. Peter looked again at Nicholas, hoping to see some sign that this was just another prank. "I, uh, I don't know what I am expected to say, Nick. What kind of mischief are you up to now?"

Once more, Nicholas took a deep breath. He lowered his legs to the wooden floor, bracing himself for what was yet to come.

"How well do you know Catherine?"

"Very. After all, I have known her family for years. I was courting her for four months before asking for her hand."

"I mean, Peter, have you ever been intimate?"

"Have I what? Good God man," he bellowed, "I should call you out for this!" He shot out of his chair, taking a menacing step toward Nicholas, who remained quite still, his elbows resting on his knees and the cheroot between his fingers.

"Peter, I have a point to make. Please, I mean you no harm. I doubt you realize that at this moment. Have you and Catherine been intimate?" he repeated his shocking question.

"No. Does that satisfy you? Were you intimate with Morgan before you married her?"

"Yes. Does that satisfy you?" he countered, looking up at Peter, who was so shocked by the conversation, that he had no idea he lit up a cheroot—something he had never done before.

"We will talk about Morgan and me later. Now, I thought you were going to let me finish," he said, failing to force a smile. "Oh hell, Mackenzie. I'm not good at this either. I was trying to help you understand, but I am not very convincing. What I have been trying to tell you is that I do not believe

Catherine loves you. In fact, I am sure of it. No," he raised his hand, cutting off Peter's retort, "there is more. Three nights ago, Catherine practically offered herself to me! In front of Morgan and you and everyone else at the party."

"You're lying, Rhodes!"

"I have never lied to you before, Peter. It is the truth, the hard, difficult truth." He rose from the chair to face his friend. "If you were to tell me something shattering about someone or something I believed in, I think I would strike you. So," Nicholas slowly placed his hands at his sides, "go ahead."

"Don't be absurd. It is just that I find it hard to accept." His face crumpled in despair. His dream evaporated like a drifting cloud. It seemed odd that he was willing to accept Nicholas's contentions. Then, looking back to that evening, he remembered finding Catherine's arms linked with Nick's. Morgan was strangely silent that night. Had it been anger at seeing her husband with Catherine?

Dragging his body to the desk, Peter dropped into the wing chair, his hands rummaging through his auburn hair, his dark eyes mirroring confusion. He thought of all the times that Nicholas had sailed into Halifax, invigorating Catherine. Usually, she would suggest an evening where the three of them could be together. She always seemed to dislike Nick's women—especially Morgan. Like a man who had suddenly broken through the dark maze of a forest into a clearing, Peter knew why Catherine had reacted so violently to Morgan. Catherine did not want a rival.

Little incidents, previously forgotten, floated in and out of Peter's head: Catherine's postponement of their wedding; her sudden reversal the other day; her lukewarm kisses; her self-absorption.

"Nick," his voice broke. "This is hard to accept. How can you suddenly realize that the one person who had filled your heart and mind for months is a fraud?"

"I think," Nicholas said, placing his hand on Peter's slumped shoulder, "that this calls for some serious talking. And some very serious drinking. If we are still coherent after two hours, remind me to tell you about my woman."

Six hours later, they were feeling quite good about

141

everything—except Catherine. They agreed she was a witch. Tomorrow, Peter would send her a terse note, breaking off their engagement. Later, when he felt more compassionate, he would return the dowry to her father.

Weaving their way down the dark cobblestoned street away from the Blue Bell Tavern, their arms supporting one another, they failed to notice the two brawny sailors behind them.

"Hey mate!" One of them shouted, "Have ye got any coins?"

Still laughing over something they could not really recall, Peter absently reached into his pocket for some shillings.

"Here you go chums."

Normally, a warning bell would have gone off in Nicholas's head. Danger was not an unfamiliar experience. But his senses were dulled by more than one bottle of whiskey. Something was not quite right about these two oafs. Only when the third appeared out of nowhere, did Nicholas realize what was about to occur.

"Get out of here, Peter! Now!" he shouted, shaking the fumes from his head.

It was too late. The three men brutally pounced on them. Effectively landing some solid punches, the two were still unable to overcome their attackers. Seconds before the lights dimmed, Nicholas felt a hard sharp kick to his ribs. He also though he heard the largest sailor say to him, "Be warned, there's more to come, Captain."

"Nick, Nick," Peter's voice finally broke through his stupor, "Are you all right man?"

Nicholas opened one swollen eye to focus on Peter, who was on his hands and knees beside him. Peter's shirt was torn in half, his head was bloody, and his lip was swollen.

"Seems like we ran into a hurricane, mate," Peter tried to grin, but it became a pained grimace.

Slowly struggling to his knees, Nicholas sucked in his breath at the first stab of pain in his side. "Seems our friends left me with a couple of broken ribs."

"Oh you look a sight, Captain," Peter said, trying to ignore Nick's battered state. Of the two, Nicholas had surely received the worst of the beatings. A deep gash marred his brow, his nose was bloody, his lip cut, his ribs broken.

After they managed to help each other stand upright, Peter expressed that which was clearly on Nicholas's mind.

"This was not a mere robbery," he breathed heavily, leaning against a brick wall. "They knew us. I heard one of them call you 'Captain.'"

"I know. Now the question is, why, or rather who was behind this?" His limbs felt so sore from the beating. He was exhausted from their struggle. Yet Nicholas could only imagine how much worse they'd feel tomorrow.

"Come on. Do you think we can make it back to the office? My carriage is there. If this was your way of keeping my mind off of my troubles, I think you overextended yourself, Captain Rhodes."

Spitting blood from his mouth, Nicholas could manage only a slight wave of his hand. There would be time to figure this out, for he already had a good idea who was behind the attack . . . Bennett Williams.

"Peter, come to my house. Arthur can tend to our wounds. Besides, I don't want Morgan to worry if I don't come home tonight. She'd never believe—until she saw my face—that I had spent the night with you and not some beautiful blond. . . . Oh, damn. Excuse me. I didn't mean that."

"Catherine is beautiful—just dishonest. But you know Nick," he slapped his friend's back, then stopped when he heard his friend's loud groan, "I rather think I'd prefer to be in my shoes than yours. Unless, of course, you do the sensible thing and marry Morgan as soon as possible."

"Why did I have to tell you everything? Now you will never let me be."

They practically crawled into Peter's carriage, taking twice as long as usual to ride to the house on Oakland Road.

Morgan had been standing at the bedroom window for the last two hours. It simply wasn't like Nick to be this late without having some message delivered. Twice, she had asked Agatha and Arthur if they had heard any sounds, and twice she returned to the lonely bedroom.

"Where are you?" she pressed her hand to the chilled windowpane, beckoning him to come home. She hated this helpless feeling—worrying over another's well-being and becoming fidgety and waspish. He was quite capable of taking care of himself, wasn't he?

Pulling the Chinese shawl tightly around her, Morgan tried to ward off her morbid thoughts. But to no avail. Only when Nicholas walked through that door, would she find some surcease.

Finally, she heard a carriage slowly make its way up the drive. Then she saw Nick's horse tied to the rear of the coach. Flying down the stairs with renewed spirit, she was at the front door before Arthur, pulling it open. The frigid night air rushed in but she did not seem to feel it. When Nicholas did not jump out of the coach, she ran down the stone steps.

The door opened. The hand that held the door was wrapped in a linen handkerchief.

"What? Agatha, Arthur! Come quickly!"

A weakened voice called from inside. "I'm fine Morgan. Just help old Peter here."

"Not me, my dear, help him," Peter managed to say.

When they emerged from the coach moving as slowly as snails, she thought she might collpase or scream or both. Arthur had joined them, a lantern held high. The dim light and the night shadows magnified their injuries. They were such a deplorable sight!

Peter definitely had one blackened eye, maybe two. His cheek seemed cut, his clothes muddy and torn. When he stood, with Arthur's assistance, he seemed to favor his right leg.

But Nicholas looked worse.

Judging from his reluctance to step down from the coach, she knew he was hiding something.

"Nick," she whispered frantically, "can I help you?"

"I think so, thanks."

She stood on the carriage step, extending her right arm to his. His low groan followed by a muttered curse made her shudder.

"Give me your hand, Nick." It, too, had been hastily bandaged. Leaning heavily on her shoulder, he tried not to cry out when she wrapped her arms around his waist.

"Not that hard, Morgan! I'm afraid I am not in one piece. A couple of broken ribs can do that to a person." He tried to smile, but it was a bit labored. Morgan looked so frail with the wind whipping through her nightdress and hair. Yet she gallantly tried to support him as he made his way into the house.

"Oh my God! Nick, you look frightful!" she declared. "And you smell like dried seaweed after it's been submerged in a barrel of whiskey."

His dark blond hair was streaked with mud and matted with dried blood from a cut that still oozed on his scalp. The left eye was swelling, his cheek already swollen. That was only above his neck.

"It looks worse than it is—really, my beauty. Help me upstairs, I'll be fine. Right, Arthur?"

"If ye says so, Cap'n. But I have seen ye lookin worse. What happened?"

"Not so fast, Arthur. Take slower steps, will you? Morgan," he wrinkled his nose, "I think you are wrong. I smell like a barnyard animal. Peter? Where is he?"

"Agatha already took hold of me," he called from another room. "Ouch, woman. Stop that!"

"Peter," Morgan called over her shoulder as she helped Nicholas up the stairs, "I think you had better stay the night."

Sighing heavily as he lowered his bruised body into his leather armchair, Nicholas watched Arthur hobble into the next room for medical supplies. Meanwhile, Morgan placed her shawl around his shoulders, ran to the wash basin, and quickly returned with a damp cloth. Heedless of the cold and her state of undress, she placed the cloth in the water, gently wiping the grime off his face.

Recognizing her look of concern, he smiled, then closed his eyes as the night's whiskey-laden activities began to claim him. When Arthur returned to begin his ministrations, Nicholas stirred.

"Morgan, I know you think I'm mad, but could you get me a brandy? I left the decanter in the library." His eyes turned to a dull silver. Yet he was pleased that Morgan did as he asked, for

145

as soon as she departed, he turned to Arthur. "Hurry man, bind me quickly. Before she returns. I don't want her to hear my complaints."

"Cap'n, when are ye gonna tell me what happened?"

"Tomorrow. My God man, since when did your hands turn to lead?" he accused. "Time for talk tomorrow, if I can bear your gentleness."

By the time Morgan returned with his brandy, he was tightly bound by neat linen strips.

"Morgan," he took a full swallow of the amber liquid, "remember the time we struck a bargian over a copper tub? What could I bargain with?"

"Same as I did, mate," she said cheekily. "But I am not sure you are quite up to it tonight."

"Don't push me, woman." He tried to sound harsh while he gestured with his snifter. But his eyes became heavy and his breathing became labored.

"Arthur," she asked in a worried voice, "do you think we could help him into the bed?"

"He'll be fine, Mrs. I guarantee it. Here," they helped a protesting Nicholas onto the high bed. "Now, his boots."

That took much longer than they expected. Nicholas was too weak to assist them, so they slowly removed the high black leather boots, trying to cause minimal pain to his ribs. His two loud groans made Morgan cast a frightened look at Arthur.

It told him exactly what he needed to know. The lady deeply cared for her husband.

"I think I will check on Peter. Then I'll return to Nick," she announced, sounding very much like the lady of the house. She pulled the armchair toward the bed in preparation for her return.

When Morgan reached the library, she insisted that Peter be moved to one of the guest suites. He did not protest, preferring the comfortable bed to the less roomy couch. Propped up against two pillows, still fully clothed, a large woolen blanket spread over him, he generously allowed the others to attend to his needs. Peter was in a chatty mood, the quantity of brandy recently consumed having loosened his tongue. He told Morgan and the Gleasons as much as he could recall about their "ambush."

"We were outnumbered. But," he grinned lopsidedly, "considering our celebratory state, we gave them a good show."

"What were you celebrating?" Agatha asked.

"My pledge to remain an unmarried, eligible bachelor. I am going to end it tomorrow. I think you know why." He looked into Morgan's face. Such a beauty. If Nicholas did not marry her quickly, Peter decided to renege his new pledge.

Morgan's hair loosely fell about her shoulders. She was still wearing a nightdress, but a long white robe and colorful shawl were worn over it. "She doesn't deserve you, Peter," Morgan correctly interpreted his fragile state of mind. "Perhaps that was why you did not protest very much when she postponed your wedding date."

The Gleasons had excused themselves when the conversation became personal—although they left the bedroom door ajar. Morgan seated herself on a wooden chest at the foot of the bed.

"He doesn't deserve you either, if he doesn't marry you."

"You know? He told you?" she asked in a surprised but angry voice that quietly dropped in shame. She was looking in Peter's direction, but her eyes could not meet his compassionate ones. "Why?"

"Because he wanted to lessen my pain, my distress at finding out what kind of woman Catherine is. Nick thought he'd share some of his distress. I'd say you're in quite a predicament. He does not know what to do."

"I know. Neither do I."

"Yet he cares for you, Morgan. And, strange as it may sound, he wants to do what is right."

"He'd better hurry, Peter. Before . . . well, before everyone finds out."

"No one will, I assure you. But Morgan," he leaned forward, "Nick is a good, decent man. He would never have planned it this way. You must believe that."

"Oh, I realize that, Peter. It is more my fault. Did he tell you that too?"

"No. Here," he slapped the bed. "Nick is more a gentleman

than I gave him credit for."

"Or me," she sadly smiled.

"Well, my girl, I seem to have a lot of time and I am not the least bit sleepy. Are you?"

"Where should I begin?"

"Neither of you ever told me how you actually met. I can't believe that rubbish about running into you." His dark eyes twinkled with mischief as well as the effects of the brandy fumes.

"Oh, but it is true, Peter," she laughed, a light pleasant sound to his ears.

The story emerged hesitantly at first. But with Peter's friendly smile and encouraging words, Morgan decided to tell him everything.

"You must already think the worst of me for being his mistress. This will only confirm your thoughts," she decided aloud.

If he were suitably shocked, he did not appear so. Rather, Peter had a much better understanding of the complicated relationship between Morgan and Nicholas. They were bound together by sympathetic promises as much as by some physical attraction. No, the little girl was becoming a woman, and Nicholas was teaching her as much about pleasure as she was teaching him about trust.

Well before she had ended her tragic story, Peter was convinced that Nicholas and Morgan were perfect for one another.

"And if that pirate does not help you find Andrews, by God, I promise I will be on the next ship bound for the Colonies."

Chapter 14

With each passing week, Morgan had convinced herself that returning to her former life, to her family, would be impossible. Charlotte had forgiven Morgan for rashly running away, although judging from the tone of her recent letter, she still was expecting a better explanation than the one Lizzie had provided. However, she had drawn her own conclusions about her daughter's living arrangements in Halifax. Nicholas Rhodes was most certainly not in the same house, let alone the same bedroom as Morgan. From what Morgan had deliberately left out in the letter, one could easily assume that she was staying at the home of a darling, elderly, childless couple named the Gleasons, who had immediately assumed guardianship of the young woman just as soon as the *Anastasia* had docked.

But Morgan had become accustomed to her deceitful ways. Nevertheless, there was one thing she had not planned on as she enjoyed the fictitious life as Mrs. Nicholas Rhodes.

The captain's "wife" was going to have a baby! By late summer.

Morgan had overlooked so much the last few weeks following her arrival in this British province. Naive and finding herself caught up in the excitement of being with Nicholas in a new land, as his wife, she had not worried about missing her first monthly. But one learns quickly. Catherine Stevens had planted the notion in Morgan's mind weeks ago. Thereafter, Morgan began counting the days in earnest, again discounting the real possibility of being with child.

It could not happen to her. Too much had already happened. How much worse could her life get?

She was to find out in the weeks ahead.

As soon as Nicholas had recovered from the beating, he set about looking to find the person behind the attack.

"This was no accident," he had explained to Morgan, Peter, and the Gleasons the day after the assault. His ribs had been tightly bound, making movement difficult. His handsome face was slightly swollen, but to Morgan he only looked more rakishly handsome than ever before.

Thereafter, there was never an appropriate moment to talk to him about her "problem"—or their future. Nicholas and Peter had completed a new set of business negotiations, agreeing to take on a new cargo. Some of the manufactured merchandise would come from up North. Nicholas had proudly announced that this smuggled cargo would be taken to New York, not Boston. He would sail into New York Harbor, under his father's upturned nose.

But there was still more—Catherine Stevens for one.

While Nicholas had been looking for the person behind their beating, Peter had gone about disassociating himself from Catherine. He had sent a note to Catherine's father; then, after his bruises faded, he met with both Stevens and his daughter.

Taking full responsibility for his change in attitude about the marriage, Peter graciously offered to pay the promised dowry. When rumors began to spread about the reasons for the "disengagement" of the couple, Peter merely smiled even after hearing some of the exaggerated claims that were being circulated. One had him labeled a fop! No doubt, Morgan decided, Miss Stevens had promulgated those slanderous tales. It was learned that Catherine would be leaving on an extended visit to England. In the meantime, her steady escort was none other than Bennett Williams.

With Catherine out of her immediate sight, the social evenings had become pleasant. One such evening, Nicholas had taken Morgan to the theater, insisting that they have a late supper in their home immediately after the performance.

It was the perfect opportunity to tell him of her

condition. Although she did not appear to have any symptoms, other than missing her monthly, Morgan felt that she needed someone to talk to—someone to reassure her, to tell her she was mistaken. She wanted to talk to Nicholas.

When they had arrived home, Nicholas ushered her up the steps, removing her sable-lined cloak, then leading her toward the dining room.

"Oh, Morgan," he had stopped before the panelled door, his arm wrapped around her shoulders, "I cannot find my good cigars." He fumbled in his waistcoat pocket. "I think I left them in the library."

"But Nick, I saw . . ."

"Come with me. Perhaps we'll share a brandy first. Who knows," he smiled, his eyes darkening in promise, "perhaps we should forget supper and go directly upstairs." He kissed her ripe lips, removing any reasonable objection she might have had over his odd behavior.

She followed him across the foyer, smiling when he held the library doors open for her to enter.

"Happy birthday, Morgan!" Voices called from the darkened room.

"Oh Lord." She felt faint. "Nick," she turned to face him, her face revealing her total surprise, "I forgot all about my birthday."

"Well, I did not, neither did Agatha. Today's the day. You're still very beautiful, my love, despite your advanced age."

The ten people in the room had crowded around to congratulate her—Peter leading the way. Morgan was happy to see them all, including Mr. McNeil.

It had been such a wonderful evening that Morgan could not bring up her concern. The next day, Nicholas had been called away. He had to take the *Anastasia* further up the Atlantic Coast to Québec for a special cargo of silks, Belgian lace, and French brandy. The trip would take at least eight days.

Now, one week later alone in the library, Morgan clutched the beautiful pin in her hands. It was a most unusual birthday present that Nicholas had gone to great lengths to have made. The pin was the exact duplicate of his jeweled anchor ring.

151

Even the diamonds and sapphires in the center were matched to his. Morgan had been so touched by this gift that whenever she was not wearing it, which was rare, she held it in the palm of her hand.

Soon, he would be back. Soon, she would tell him.

Comfortably settled in the window seat, she dreamily gazed outside. The barren rows of trees, the gray skies, reminded her that it was the time between autumn and winter; a time when nature is arrested. It was a gloomy sight outside. Inside, despite the logs burning in the fireplace, the hot chocolate beside her, the fur skin around her legs, Morgan felt ill at ease.

The Gleasons were occupied in different parts of the house, not within earshot. Suddenly, she heard the unmistakable sound of a carriage rolling up the drive. Knowing it was not Nicholas, she decided to wait before greeting the caller.

Bennett Williams arrogantly emerged from the coach, taking his time as he straightened his cuffs and cravat, then smoothed the long black cloak behind his shoulders. He must have liked the results, for he briskly strode upstairs to the wide entrance door, firmly announcing his arrival.

Morgan had no idea what she should do next. It was not proper to entertain a gentleman when Nicholas was not at home, especially since he had voiced his suspicions about Bennett Williams. Perhaps, Morgan could gather information from him. Besides, she thought, what harm could come of a short conversation at the door? She did not have to let him in. If her "husband" were home, there would not be a problem, she decided, not aware of her circuitous logic. Now that the blame was squarely placed on Nicholas, she took a deep breath, wrapped her paisley woolen shawl around her, and opened the door.

"Mr. Williams, I am sorry but my husband is not here."

"I know that Mrs. Rhodes. That is why I am here. Now," he doffed his dark hat, "may I come inside?"

Flustered, she allowed him entrance. "Perhaps you can warm up a bit before you go out again."

Ignoring her message, Bennett strode into the library as if he, not Nicholas, were the owner of the house.

"Excuse me, Mr. Williams, but I think the parlor would be

152

more appropriate for your short visit."

"I think not, not for what I have to say. Why don't you take my cloak and hat? Then tell Mrs. Gleason to serve tea."

"Pardon me, but I think you must be suffering from a lapse of memory. I am not visiting you in your home. This is not Bedford Basin." She resolutely stood by the library door, unwilling to enter the room with him. The insufferable clod was finally succeeding in his effort to infuriate her.

What Morgan could not realize was that the sight of her standing a few feet away from him, her beautiful face glowing from suppressed anger, entranced Bennett. He craved her body, and he did not know how much longer he could be patient. The long black hair through which he so desired to run his hands was softly pulled back, secured by a red velvet ribbon. Her pale skin looked more wan when contrasted against the high-necked dark purple wool dress. Her voluptuous body was hidden beneath that dress, but Bennett's mind visualized it all the same. Especially what he would do when he got her into his bed.

"Sir, my husband will be home shortly. You can come back then," Morgan said acidly. It was stupid of her to think this man could behave as a gentleman. She wanted him out of the house, now.

"Mrs. Rhodes, I am well aware of the captain's whereabouts. If he is home by tomorrow, it will be a day early."

"Excuse me. I'll go fetch Arthur." She turned to walk away, but Bennett's hand grasped her wrist.

"I think not, my dove. What I have come here to say will not take long." His dark, fathomless eyes carefully concealed his burning hunger for his enemy's wife. "I presume you would like to keep your husband alive."

Now it was her turn to stare, her topaz eyes widening in shock. Snatching her wrist away from his cool hand, she failed to notice his nails streak across her delicate skin, leaving two thin red lines.

Bennett stepped closer. Not giving a damn about leaving this horrid man alone in the room, she wanted to bolt away, needing to find Arthur. Yet Morgan knew she had to hear his threat.

153

"Go on." Her voice sounded cool, but inside she was steaming.

"May I help myself?" He slowly walked over to Nicholas's liquor cabinet. Removing the port decanter and a crystal glass, he generously poured the ruby liquid, took a small sip, lowered the glass onto the table, then smoothed the wrinkles on his well-tailored bottle-green jacket and breeches.

"It will all be mine soon," he casually informed her. Including you, he silently amended. "Do you recall your husband's 'accident' a few weeks ago? Your husband and his partner fought surprisingly well, considering the quantity of whiskey they had consumed."

"You arranged that? Well, my husband already assumed as much." She walked over to Nicholas's desk, idly running one hand over its top while the other hand appeared to remain in front of her.

"I am quite sure that he did. But I made one mistake. The next time I will not fail."

"There won't be a next time, Mr. Williams. My husband is too clever for that."

"Do you think so?" His ruthless smile chilled her. "There are many ways to arrange accidents. His ship could catch fire, or his office, or his horse could go wild. But those are simple. I'd prefer something a little less obvious," he paused to gauge the beauty's reaction. Stiffly moving to the window, her hand playing with some ridiculous charm, she tried to exude a calm he knew was not there.

"The patrols might catch him. A fight could ensue. And your husband would surely be hung for the pirate he is. Now that is only one scenario. I can think of at least half a dozen more."

"What do you want Mr. Williams?"

"You," he bluntly stated. "I see you are not surprised."

"Rodents like you can be quite predictable."

"Touché, my dear. But you have not heard me out."

Williams walked over to Nicholas's desk, seating himself in the dark Moroccan leather armchair. Then he helped himself to one of the imported cigars that were stocked in the humidor on top of the desk.

"You see, I would like you to become my mistress. Oh, I will not tell anyone. You have my word as a gentleman." He smelled the aromatic cigar. "Your husband seems to have good taste," his dark eyes suggestively roamed over her body, "in everything. Now, if you'd care to meet me at my home, perhaps once or twice a week, I can arrange for your husband to live a trifle longer."

"You are insane! I shall not hear of this any longer. Get out of my house—this instant. For if you don't, I swear I will not wait for Arthur to shoot you. I shall do it myself!"

Without warning, Bennett Williams found himself looking into the barrel of a loaded pistol, the hammer efficiently cocked.

"Now," she stepped forward, "you have two minutes to leave my home."

"I would comply with my wife's request, Williams. I instructed her well in the use of firearms. She has never missed yet."

Nicholas's firm voice was a surprisingly soothing sound to her ears. His presence filled the doorway, lightening Morgan's spirit for the first time in days.

"Welcome home, darling," she walked over to him, offering him her cheek and the pistol. "Will you be needing this?"

Nicholas's murderous glare had pinned Williams to the seat. "No, I'd prefer to strangle the bastard." In two long strides, Nicholas was upon him.

"Williams," he grabbed Bennett's lapels. With a strength born of fury, he easily lifted Bennett out of the chair.

The rending of cloth was music to Morgan. "Nick, you are ruining his beautiful jacket."

"I am, aren't I?"

"See here, Rhodes," Bennett finally found his voice, but Nicholas effectively silenced the protest by tightly grabbing his cravat, cutting off his outraged breath.

"You will stay away from my wife. She will not be your mistress. But she thanks you for your generous offer to spare my life. You know, I always wanted to throttle you. Killing you in an act of self-defense would please me to no end."

His powerful grip tightened around Bennett's throat.

Without mercy, Nicholas's fist flashed forward into his enemy's stomach. Not once, but in three rapid movements.

When Williams was doubled over, Nicholas hauled him up again. "This one is for Peter," he connected with Bennett's jaw. "And this is for my wife." His fist smashed into Williams's nose, the bone crunching beneath his strong punch.

"You broke it," Bennett moaned, trying to stem the flow of blood with his coat sleeve.

Morgan had seen enough. Nick's fury would soon be out of control. She knew he meant to beat Williams to death. When she saw Nick's arm pull back once more, she cried, "Enough! Stop it Nick! He'll not dare to threaten either of us again."

The red haze finally lifted. Williams was a bloody mess. Yet, the sight of that man comfortably seated in his house, propositioning Morgan was indelibly etched in his mind. Someday, he would have to kill Bennett Williams. Nicholas knew that Williams had no intention of staying out of their lives. Certainly not after this humiliation. But despite Morgan's brave facade, Nicholas could see that it was a matter of minutes before she lost hold of her emotions.

"Thank you for visiting us, Williams. I hope you enjoyed your stay. Here, you can keep the cigar." Nicholas hauled Bennett out of the house, ignoring his curse. Morgan followed with the cloak and hat.

Bennett was nursing his broken nose, but his venomous look could not be overlooked, or underestimated.

"It is not over yet, Rhodes. You'll see." Finding his way into the coach, Bennett still looked at the couple as his carriage hurriedly pulled away from the house.

Morgan's hand was no longer squeezing his. In fact, her face had become deathly white as she stared at the departing carriage. Her hands dropped to her sides. Her legs refused to support her. And for the first time since he had known her, Morgan fainted in his waiting arms, her pin clattering to the ground.

"Morgan, sweetheart, it is over now. You are going to be fine," he crooned in her ear.

156

Holding her left hand in his, Nicholas was bent over her prone body. For the first time in a long while, Nicholas had felt something alien creep into his bones: fear. When he had hurried along the road, urging the horse to a faster gallop, the cold wind biting his cheeks, he had felt an overwhelming desire to be home with Morgan, hoping that she'd be standing near the door waiting for him.

Nicholas had envisioned what she would wear, how her hair would be coiffed, what she might have been doing while she waited. He also decided what they would do as soon as he had a short, hot bath.

The trip to Québec had been completed with dispatch. Selecting the new cargo and negotiating with the merchants took much less time than previous trips. The crew of the *Anastasia* knew why their captain was in such a hurry. They had forgiven him for the few times he pushed them hard in order to get extra wind into the sails. The missus was waiting, they said. Who wouldn't rush home to her?

The captain had politely refused an invitation by a wealthy merchant to be the guest of honor at a dinner. That would have postponed his departure by two more days. Uppermost on his mind was Morgan, waiting at home—their home, he had conceded. The need to hold her, to talk to her, and of course to make love to her was clouding all else.

While the *Anastasia* was smoothly cutting through the choppy waters, Nicholas remained above deck, thinking about this strange woman. She was expecting a marriage proposal. Living and enjoying an immoral relationship—according to her—would definitely reserve her a special place in purgatory. Before he met her, she had been so young, so innocent, so naive about life. Now, a scant three months later, she'd experienced more with him than most women would ever dream of.

Perhaps, he decided, he owed her that much. If giving her his name restored her peace of mind, then maybe he should make the magnanimous gesture. If their marriage did not prove to be a happy or rather tolerant one, then he would figure out a way to dissolve their union.

Nicholas warred within himself. The noble, gentlemanly side of him could do no less. After all, he was far more experienced than she; therefore, he was ultimately responsible for compromising her. But the roguish side said that this made no difference. There had been many women who schemed to have his name: Margaret Lawson, for one. He did not succumb to them. If, he told himself, you want to remain a free man with no whining, clutching female begging you to stay home, to do something respectable, then do not, under any circumstances, marry.

Now that Peter Mackenzie knew the entire truth, he had consistently railed at Nicholas each day up to the time the *Anastasia* had set sail for Québec.

"Are you daft, man? You cannot be so inconsiderate. Besides, I would give both of my arms to have Morgan as my wife. You must marry her. Before you take her back to New York," he'd scolded.

"Peter, even if I agreed to marry her in Halifax, who is to say that our marriage would be a legal one under British or American law?"

"What difference does that make, Nick? At least Morgan would be at peace. Then as soon as you dock in New York, you can marry her again."

Nicholas had mulled over Peter's words, putting off the decision to marry Morgan until he saw her once more.

As soon as he had arrived home, he leaped off the horse in front of the stable, swiftly striding toward the front of the house. No one seemed to be about. It might be better that no one was here, for he could surprise Morgan. Since she'd probably be at the window seat in the library, Nicholas had decided to sneak up on her and surprise her with his early arrival.

That was before he had seen the carriage in front of his house. It was not a coach he immediately recognized.

When he had heard Bennett Williams's odious voice, Nicholas thought he'd go beserk. As Morgan answered one of his questions, her voice was strained but in control. Stealthily approaching the library door, Nicholas heard Williams threaten Morgan, bargaining with her for her husband's life, then offering what he considered to be a wonderful opportunity—the chance to be Bennett Williams's mistress.

Nicholas had been prepared to attack, his fists clenched in leashed fury. Hearing Morgan reply to Williams's demand with a cocked pistol, he decided to act.

The pleasure he'd felt in beating Bennett nearly senseless was better than any triumph he had encountered in the open sea. Nicholas wanted to kill the bastard, but Morgan's voice finally reached him.

At the sight of Williams's departure, Nicholas wanted to laugh off the entire episode, but Morgan's sudden swoon had changed his plans.

Now, in the library with the Gleasons nervously hovering over them, Nicholas willed Morgan to come out of her faint.

"I think she is finally coming round, Captain," Arthur said, still staring at the lovely woman.

"Yes, see," Agatha added, "her hand just moved. Seems like she's reaching for something."

Intuitively, Nicholas knew what she was searching for. Lifting her palm up, he placed the tiny anchor pin in her hand, then closed her fist over it. Lowering his head, he tenderly kissed each finger.

The unmistakable mixture of voices penetrated her trance-like state. With a sudden, unrelenting speed, the events of the last hour overwhelmed her. Wide topaz eyes snapped open in fright.

Nicholas was seated beside her. He was there, so full of robust life, so reassuring, so handsome. And he was smiling down at her.

"Well, have you decided to join us?"

"Oh, Nick. It was awful. That man . . ." she looked about the room wanting to reassure herself that Bennett was indeed gone. "Did I really faint?"

"Dead away, sweetheart. It was a good thing my reflexes were in such good form," he gently teased.

"I have never swooned in my life."

The full truth of that statement hit her hard, like a clenched fist in her stomach. How much longer could she deny the truth? From herself and from Nicholas? But she wanted to postpone it—just a little longer—at least until her fear subsided.

"Oh God," she let out a small sob. With a burst of strength, Morgan clutched Nick's arm, throwing herself into his comforting embrace.

"I think I'll put you to bed now, my love. We'll talk when you are ready."

Allowing him to lift her up, Morgan rested her weary head against his shoulder, closing her eyes, shutting out what lay ahead.

Chapter 15

"Nick, I still can't believe the audacity of that man. He acted as if this were his home, as if everything in it—including me—was his."

They were in the master bedroom, Morgan settled on the sofa beside the fireplace. It was early evening. After a brief but refreshing nap, Morgan awakened in their bed to find Nicholas seated at his secretary, brooding over something. Seeing her awake, he brightly smiled, then carried her close to the fire. He solicitously attended to her every need, insisting upon undressing her, placing tiny kisses on her neck as he helped her into a flannel nightdress.

"Very attractive," he wryly said. He fastened the tiny buttons on the neck, still smiling as he placed a heavy shawl around her slender shoulders. "You are so lovely, even in flannel."

He must have bathed while she was napping, for he smelled of the spicy lotion she loved so much. His hair, still slightly damp, curled at the nape of his neck. Wearing a cambric shirt open at the neck and dark blue breeches, he looked as if he'd not been to sea at all, but had been resting at home, playing cards, going to the pub. Aside from his still suntanned skin, Nicholas looked like a country gentleman.

"Now, my love, if I give you a sherry, will you quietly contemplate the fire while I finish my journal entries?"

"For whom?"

"Peter and I keep records of everything—each sale and

purchase—including a description of each of the manufactured items. We have never lost, mishandled, or undersold any item."

"From what I have seen of these merchants, you and Peter could easily become the wealthiest of the lot," she smiled at him, enjoying the light conversation.

"That kind of life is not for me. Never will be. I'd rather be at sea, taking my chances with nature and the patrols. Now, may I finish? And if you are good," he winked at her, "I'll let you come downstairs for dinner."

Allowing him to complete his task, Morgan became mesmerized by the burning fire, occasionally sipping the sherry. It was wonderful to be here in this room, with him so close. Of late, she mused more about making a life with him. Perhaps they would fall in love with one another. Even if she never found love, what she felt now—the peace and contentment of being with him—could be enough. If . . . he wanted her and a baby.

"Sweetheart, what is so fascinating about that fire that you have not answered me."

"Oh," she looked into his handsome face, feeling a twinge of desire. "I am sorry. What did you say, Nick?"

"I asked if you are feeling better?"

"Yes, yes, of course," she smiled back.

"Now do you think you can tell me everything? And please," his smile faded, "don't spare me any of the details. Morgan, he didn't try to, um, to take any liberties, did he?"

"No, of course not. I would have shot him, you see. By the way, I really am a good shot. My father taught me. However, I appreciate your telling Bennett that I knew how to shoot— even though you claimed to have taught me."

"I suspected as much from the way you held the gun. Now, start from the beginning."

Reviewing the entire episode with Williams, Morgan doubted she had left out any detail.

"He hired those men to attack you and Peter."

"I knew that right away. It was something one of those thugs said before he knocked me out."

"What will you do?"

"There is nothing I can do now, not if we want to leave Halifax next month. But I'll have him watched, you can be sure of that. And I have no intention of letting him within fifty feet of you."

"He's too smug about his position here. It is as if he knows something you don't. Something that is important to you."

"Well, I cannot worry about that. Morgan," he turned to face her, one hand leaning over the top of the chair, "I think this weather has affected your health. I never thought you the fragile type."

"You mean my fainting? Well, you have to admit I had a difficult day." She lowered her dark lashes, steeling herself for what she knew had to be said.

"Besides, you weren't home to defend us, and I . . ."

"Us?" he laughed. "Since when does old Arthur need to be protected?"

"Not Arthur, not Agatha," she began finding the fringe of the shawl incredibly interesting. "Nick, this is going to alter your plans, and mine. I cannot very well hide it from you."

An icy chill ran along his spine. He stood to approach her, knowing something was very wrong. And she was having difficulty expressing it.

Seeing his towering form over her, Morgan felt intimidated. But in a gentle voice he said, "Morgan look at me. What are you trying to tell me?"

"Sit here Nick." She patted the space next to her on the sofa.

When he did, she took a deep breath. "Nicholas, it may be all my fault. But I, that is we, oh . . . Nick, I am going to have a baby!" she blurted it out at last.

Frozen to the seat, he dumbly stared at her, sure yet unsure of what she said.

"Pardon me? Let me repeat what you said to determine if I heard you correctly. You said that you are expecting a baby?"

"Your baby."

"Of course, whose child could it be?" he stupidly asked. Still staring at her, Nicholas noted how forlorn she looked. "Well, this certainly changes a few things, my beauty."

"Yes it does."

"I'll have to alter our plans. But I do not think it will take too long to arrange things," he continued, carefully watching her expression. "We'll be married by the end of the week."

With a suspicious gleam in her eyes, she finally met his amused look. "Really Nick? You don't have to, not really. I could manage."

"Could you? Would you want to be alone? Is there something wrong with me? No," he firmly stated, "it is all settled. We will marry as soon as I can make the appropriate arrangements. Peter will help me. We will visit the doctor again tomorrow. I want to make sure you're all right."

"Nick," her brow lifted, "I feel fine. It was the excitement that caused me to faint today."

"No. I insist." Taking her cold hand in his, he added, "Imagine that. I am about to become a father and a husband."

"Do you think it has ever happened to you before?" At his confused look, she clarified her statement. "I mean, I know you have not led a celibate life. Do you know if you have any other children?"

"None that I know of." He dismissed her question. "Now Morgan, everything will be fine. I promise to take care of you and the baby."

"But what about my search for Andrews?"

"We will continue to do whatever we can when we reach New York. Afterwards, I'll do what I can on my own or, if necessary, I will hire someone."

"You will?"

"Why, of course. Morgan," he took her into his arms, "I am not going to desert you. What do you think I am?"

"A smuggler and a rogue," she readily replied, inhaling his spicy scent. "You know, I should hold out a little longer, make you beg me to marry you. But then you might change your mind."

"Impossible. You and our child deserve my name."

A log in the fireplace suddenly popped, startling her. Nicholas merely laughed, a deep throaty sound that reminded her of how lonely she had been without him.

"Well, Mrs. Rhodes. I guess it's time to learn to trust me. Can you?"

Morgan found the courage to gaze into his face. "Nick, I will try not to be too much of a nuisance. But would you promise me one thing?"

"Anything." He rested his cheek on the top of her black hair.

"Don't let me find out about the other women in your life. I mean, can we try—for the baby's sake, of course—to make a good marriage? To really try?"

"Morgan, if you are prematurely accusing me of philandering, you owe me an apology. I will not take our marriage vows lightly. Nor, I assume, will you."

"Oh no, Nick, never." She burrowed deeper into his arms, hiding her wide smile from him.

"Good. Then we will settle things tomorrow. Now, I no longer think I have an appetite for food. However," his arm traveled along her neck to her chin, pulling her face up to his, "I am very hungry for your sweet lips."

The long, sensual kiss left both of them breathless. Without wanting to alter their positions on the couch, Nicholas slowly undressed her then himself before he made love to Morgan. The sound of the crackling fire mingled with her soft moans of pleasure.

Three days after Thanksgiving, Nicholas and Morgan were secretly married. Peter attended, along with the Gleasons. Upon hearing of the captain's duplicity, both Arthur and Agatha had let forth a tirade unfit for the most experienced ears. After two days of not speaking to the captain—they spoke to Morgan, deciding that the entire charade was Nicholas's idea and not hers—they finally relented. After all, he was really going to marry her, and who else should witness the ceremony but the people who lovingly cared for them.

Peter had found an Anglican priest who, after a sizable donation, managed to assist Captain Rhodes in securing a special bishop's license. Therefore, the posting of the banns—which would have meant another three weeks before they could wed—was unnecessary.

The priest was willing to marry them in the privacy of his

church. Morgan was dressed in a pale blue satin dress with tiny white embroidered flowers trimming the bodice, the wrist of the long billowing sleeves, and the hem. Around her head she wore a coronet of yellow and blue flowers that Nicholas had miraculously managed to produce. Agatha created a loose, flowing hairstyle by braiding the sides of her thick black hair then twisting them behind her head.

When he first saw her slowly descend the stairs from their bedroom, Nicholas thought he had never seen Morgan look this beautiful or angelic. She proudly held her tall frame erect, her face pale except for the two tiny spots of color on her high cheekbones. The black hair fell in waves behind her, nearly touching the small of her back. Her topaz eyes held his silver gaze and Nicholas knew he had made the right decision.

"Madam, you humble me with your beauty," he'd whispered, bowing low before her. Her soft giggle was a balm to his almost-nervous state.

Nicholas had no idea how equally marvelous he looked to his soon-to-be wife: resplendent in blue-black satin breeches, a matching coat, a crisp white silk shirt, underneath an embroidered waistcoat of muted colors. It was the first time that she had seen him wearing dark silk hose and black buckled shoes instead of his leather boots.

"You only marry once," he'd teased when she asked him about his shoes. "I shall happily make the sacrifice, although this is probably the last time you will see me wear this ugly dress shoes."

They rode to the Church on Prince Street with Peter, who also looked quite the gentleman.

"Remember to name the bairn after me," he smiled when he presented Morgan with his mother's bible.

"You are such a wonderful friend, Peter Mackenzie."

The ceremony was quick and surprisingly, thought Nicholas, quite painless. The priest asked them to sign two documents: He gave one to Morgan to keep and the other was to be placed in the rectory. At Nicholas's request, the marriage would not be recorded in the usual registry but in another one where it would be privately kept. Morgan understood immediately why he was making this unusual request. He was doing it for her, so that the town could not learn of their true marriage date. The elderly priest, intrigued by the little mystery, readily agreed. The bride's look of gratitude when he did so made it all worthwhile.

Assuming her distaste for the golden wedding band she had been wearing, Nicholas had another more elaborate one designed. It was in the shape of a V. He told her it was similar to an African symbol of love.

Even though Nicholas was unwilling to part with his anchor ring, Morgan presented him with a silver and gold wedding ring and a beautiful pocket watch. Inside was a tiny painted miniature of herself.

"I was wearing the gold ballgown, but you would never know. I know you won't wear the ring, but I hope you will keep it with your favorite momentos."

"Absolutely, my lovely wife." He was deeply touched by her thoughtful, loving gesture, wishing that he could always keep her happy.

Later they enjoyed a delicious, yet simple meal—one of Agatha's best. Since Thanksgiving was not observed in British Halifax, Agatha had decided to serve the traditional meal for the wedding dinner. The thick soup, roasted turkey, sweet potatoes, cranberries, and apple pie were a rare American treat.

"Agatha, are you certain you won't want to take Cook's place on the *Anastasia?* I shall miss your meals," Morgan playfully informed her, waving the fork in the air.

"Just see to it that the captain brings you back with him after the birth of the bairn."

"Have no fear of that Agatha. Nick is not going to sail around the world without us."

It snowed the next day. The Rhodeses took it as a sign from the gods to remain indoors, inside their bedroom for two days. When they eventually emerged, it was to enjoy the cold, wintry day. Nicholas promised to take Morgan on a sleigh ride, something she'd only had the pleasure of once before. Securely wrapped in her fur cloak with blankets around her lap, they toured the countryside, laughing at the playful antics of the children, feeling wonderment over their unalloyed bliss.

Only once in the days that followed their wedding did

167

Morgan consider the one flaw in their marriage. It had come upon her as she penned a long, loving letter to her mother and Lizzie. She told of her marriage, giving them the early date, describing every detail of the private ceremony. Of course she happily informed them that their baby would be born in the summer. Pledging not to give up her search for her father's murderer, she reiterated Nicholas's promise to help her— alone if she were unable to assist.

But in rereading the letter, Morgan realized the glaring omission: There was no mention of love.

That they enjoyed each other's company was obvious to her. She could also recall that weeks ago they talked about love, had even joked about it. Nicholas had proven to be more considerate and compassionate than she would have thought possible. Yet, even when she told him about the baby, he carefully considered his words, speaking in the same business-like manner he often used aboard the *Anastasia*.

And she was no different. Morgan savored his embraces, reveled in his kind words and his almost loving gestures. He taught her everything. Did she marry Nicholas for the sake of her tarnished reputation? For the baby? Or did she truly desire, above all else, to live with him, to live for him, to enjoy growing old with him and their healthy brood of children?

The omission hit her hard. For Morgan could not answer her own question: Do I love Nicholas Rhodes?

Their first heated argument was caused by Nicholas's concern for her.

"Morgan, love, I've been thinking about our departure. I must go to New York. The *Anastasia* must sail before Christmas. The seas will be very choppy and cold. It may not be safe for you and the baby."

"Don't be absurd, Nick. I will be fine. You were with me at the doctor's office. You heard what he said about traveling again."

"Yes, yes, I know. Keep in mind that we could run into another incident with the patrols. It could be very dangerous."

It had snowed again. But the air was so cold that Nicholas chose to stay home, knowing it was the only way to keep Morgan indoors. Of late, Morgan's moods had become erratic.

She would find fault with him and everyone else, then for no apparent reason would burst into tears. It was, of course, related to her pregnancy, so he shrugged it off, realizing that this would pass.

The more he considered their voyage to New York, however, the more concerned he became for her welfare. The trip could be hazardous. Rather than take the risk, Nicholas began to consider the alternatives. She could remain in Halifax with the Gleasons and Peter to protect her. He could—with any luck— be back in Halifax within eight to ten weeks.

"Nick, that is unreasonable," she declared after he slowly and rather calmly, explained his plan. "I don't want to be here without you. I would rather take my chances at sea."

They were in the dining room, enjoying a light lunch. Morgan had taken to wearing her wire-rimmed spectacles when there were no visitors. She had complained of looking like a spinsterish school teacher when wearing them, which, according to Nicholas, was one of the most absurd things he'd ever heard her say.

"No one can look the way you do—with or without your spectacles—and be considered an ugly spinster, I assure you, my love. Now, about the other matter . . ."

"No! I will not hear of it, Nicholas. I am not staying in Halifax without you." The fork clattered to the plate before her.

"It is for your best . . ."

"Nonsense," she spat. "You don't care about me. You care about the baby—your precious heir. You care about getting your equally precious cargo into New York," her voice steadily rose with each accusation she hurled at him. "You care not one whit!"

"Enough!" he commanded. He knew he had tried to keep his temper in check, but she was saying things that were ridiculous. "You don't know what you are saying. All I ask," his voice became conciliatory, "is that you think about this when you are calm."

"Calm? I am calm!" she shouted. "I simply will not hear of it." She angrily stormed out of the room, leaving a bewildered Nicholas to dine alone.

"She'll be fine, Captain," Agatha tried to soothe him. "It is new to her too."

"Agatha, I hope I have the strength."

Half an hour later Morgan returned, feeling contrite. She slowly approached him, putting her arms around his neck. "I guess I behaved foolishly, Nick. I apologize. But I did think about it and I do not want you to leave without me. I am afraid to be here without you." She kissed the nape of his stiff neck, then moved her head around to see his expression. He did not appear angry. "Nick?"

"Oh, all right Morgan," he moved his chair, cradling her. "But be warned, madam. I will lock you in the cabin if you disobey my orders. Not even your tears will dissuade me."

Although they did not formally announce Morgan's condition, people seemed to know. They were congratulated wherever they went. Morgan doubted if there was anyone left who did not know. Even Catherine Stevens was aware of her condition.

Morgan considered herself quite lucky for not seeing Catherine since Peter broke the betrothal. But when Catherine appeared at a late afternoon tea Morgan cursed aloud, having decided to attend primarily because Nick thought it a good idea that she be present at social events. Rachel Tucker, who had appointed herself Morgan's best friend, had insisted she attend this small gathering.

Morgan knew most of the ladies, many of whom were the wives of government officials. Wearing a heavy, but fashionable rose velvet dress, Morgan did not feel uncomfortable with these women. They sincerely wanted to welcome her into their society. Their easy, often innocuous chatter reminded Morgan of how much she knew about social amenities. Moreover, having listened to Peter and Nicholas so often, Morgan firmly believed that she knew more about politics and business than all of these ladies combined.

No one thought to tell her that Catherine would be a late arrival. Gossip had it that Catherine blamed Morgan for her broken betrothal, claiming that Peter was influenced by

Morgan Rhodes and her pirate husband. Catherine preferred a more refined gentleman like her newest beau, Bennett Williams, whose discreet business ventures were less significant than his quest for knighthood.

Catherine grandly stepped into the room, wearing a magnificent fur cape. Immediately, her dark brown eyes surveyed the room, turning to slits when she spotted the demure Morgan Rhodes. Finding her way toward her, Catherine pretended to warmly greet the women around Morgan.

"Nice to see you again, dear Morgan. I apologize for not visiting you, but I've been so busy with the plans for my departure. How is Nicky? Still buried in his paperwork?" she purred.

"My husband is fine, thank you Catherine."

"He looked so tired when I saw him last. Ah, but he is such a charmer, you know."

"Yes, I do know. He makes friends easily." Morgan wanted to move to a different corner of the room, but how could she do so without appearing obvious? Nor did she want to give Catherine the satisfaction of seeing her uncomfortable.

"Please send your husband my warmest wishes. Tell him I hope we can all visit with each other before my departure." Catherine took a seat across from Morgan, closing off her last avenue of escape.

"We both so admire art. Why Nicky's told me on a number of occasions that he intends to start his own collection. He asked me to assist."

"Why thank you, but that, I am sure, will no longer be necessary. I seriously doubt that he is interested, if he ever was, Catherine. He hates Gainsborough. It seems to have something to do with the evening you showed him that painting." She chose her words carefully, hoping that Catherine would finally get the message that Nicholas was well beyond her grasp.

"One can't be too sure Morgan. Did I hear that you were enceinte? How delightful for you. I hope Nicky is tolerant of your whims. He doesn't strike me as the patient type of man. Why I recall a former friend of mine whose husband simply

171

left her because he could not take her clumsy size or her silly demands."

"Catherine," Rachel Tucker appeared, "I believe you have not seen the way Captain Rhodes protects his wife. Why we were telling Morgan—before you arrived—how lucky she is to have such a handsome, loving husband. That man adores her. Weren't you aware of that?"

"Men can be capricious," she stated in a peculiar voice. "Anything can happen," she added, looking directly at Morgan.

For the rest of the afternoon, Morgan could not stop the shivers that trailed along her arms.

Chapter 16

If Morgan knew why Catherine was late to the tea, she would have been astounded and infuriated.

Catherine had decided to visit Nicholas in his office. Since she was aware of Morgan's whereabouts and acquainted with the business activities of Nick and Peter, Catherine had timed her visit perfectly. She had even contrived to find some emergency errand for the lone clerk in the office. Captain Rhodes would be alone, for she knew that Peter was out of town.

Peter had been long forgotten—almost immediately after she got over the embarrassment of the broken engagement. With a few well-placed rumors about Mr. Mackenzie's less than honorable intentions toward her, Catherine had convinced herself that this was all for the best. Her blossoming association with Bennett Williams was also a great salve to her ego. He was so handsome. He came from a wealthy, titled family, and was such a marvelous companion. Best of all, Bennett was a good lover! Afraid that Peter would tell Nicholas she was not a virtuous woman, she had never given him the opportunity to bed her. But it did not matter to Bennett; he had told her so on the few occasions they had managed to be together. Those glorious encounters in Bennett's home would never be forgotten.

Yet, above all else, there was only one name, one face, that haunted Catherine's days and nights. And now that Bennett had mysteriously disappeared for a few weeks—some family emergency his butler had said—Catherine once again became obsessed with Nicholas Rhodes.

He was before her, bent over the desk, dark blond hair spilling across his forehead that was propped up by one hand. Contemplating the figures on the sheaves of paper, Nicholas was oblivious to her silent entry. Catherine continued studying him, allowing hatred to consume her—hatred for Morgan Rhodes.

She patiently stood in the doorway, drinking in his masculine perfection, smiling to herself.

"Hello Nicky," she purred. "I have missed you." She glided toward him, placing a gloved hand on his shoulder. "I was hoping for a more intimate setting, but I suppose this will have to do."

"Catherine," he pushed back the chair, resting his hands against the edge of the desk, "I don't have time for this. Now, if you will excuse me."

"No, I will not. I went to a great deal of trouble to see you alone," she said, ignoring his look of annoyance. "I thought we needed some time alone." Removing her gloves, she slowly— seductively, she thought—opened her fur cloak. Wanting his eyes to remain riveted on her body, Catherine began undoing the tiny pearl buttons at the neckline of her velvet dress.

Nicholas, however, had no intention of letting her go further. "Catherine, we do not need any time alone. I thought I made that abundantly clear," his tone was impersonal. Intending to help her out of the office, Nicholas moved around the desk to offer his hand.

Taking his hand into her still-gloved one, Catherine looked up into molten eyes, mistaking his anger for desire.

"I am yours, Nicky. I'd like to prove it to you. After one night with me, you would never think of that skinny country bumpkin. She is not for you, Nicky." Catherine's smug manner was as offnesive as the arrogant airs of tilted aristocrats. "I am the one for you. I've waited for you. With Peter no longer in our way, why I simply . . ."

"Shut up! I do not know who you think you are talking to. I am not an innocent, nor am I disloyal to my friends and family."

174

"Oh Nicky," she placed her arms on his lean waist. "You don't have to pretend with me. There is no one here. I promise not to tell a soul. As soon as you rid yourself of your wife, we can be together."

Clearly, Catherine could not understand him. But he was not in the mood to cajole her. Too much rested on his mind. He wanted to be rid of her.

"Catherine, I am happily married. Morgan is going to have my child. We will . . ."

"That cannot be true! She can't be!"

"Look, none of this is your concern. Morgan was correct in her assessment of you. Get out, Catherine. Now. Or I will forget you were ever engaged to my best friend." His gray eyes darkened as they bore into her. His mouth was grimly set. If he could strangle the little bitch he'd do it, without remorse. "Now," he firmly took her elbow. "Good day and good-bye."

The door slammed and locked behind her. Never, never would she offer herself to him again. Why he was as arrogant and boorish as Bennett had argued. She straightened her back, placing her gloved hand on the outer doorknob. There was still Mrs. Morgan Rhodes to deal with. And Catherine was on her way to see the lady. A baby! Hah!

"Just wait, Nicky. Someday, you will beg me for my favors. I will spit in your arrogant face," she said aloud to no one.

It did not matter. As Catherine was assisted into her carriage, a twisted smile marred her pretty face and a high-pitched cackle filled the coach.

After that fateful afternoon, Morgan had dismissed Catherine Stevens. She had seen her two more times that week, but fortunately, Catherine never got close to Morgan.

It was now the beginning of the Christmas holiday. Excitement, gaiety, above all cheerful times, were prevalent among the Haligonians. There were parties, teas, charity balls, so many, that on more than one occasion the Rhodeses had to decline.

There was one theater performance that Morgan was especially looking forward to seeing. A traveling theater company—direct from the London stage—was in Halifax for only one week performing Shakespeare's *Romeo and Juliet* at the Old Grand Theater on Argyle Street. Dressed and ready to go, she waited in the library for Nicholas to return home. He had been gone since dawn. By six o'clock Morgan was anxious. It was not his safety that worried her, but whether he would be home too late for the theater.

"Agatha, when is he coming back?" She sought the housekeeper in the kitchen, deciding it was better to talk to someone than pace across the room. Wearing a peacock-blue velvet dress with a lovely embroidered short bolero jacket, Morgan felt quite good about her appearance.

Agatha knew that despite Morgan's flat stomach, there was the delightful sparkle in her eyes, the tiny smile that appeared for no reason, which gave the impression that Morgan Rhinehart knew something wonderful was going to happen.

But that sparkle turned to fire when her husband still had not returned.

"Why don't you have Arthur drive you into town. That way you can meet the captain in his office and go to the play from there. If the captain has left, you are bound to meet him on the road."

"What an excellent idea, Agatha! I shall do it. You are such a dear." She kissed Agatha's plump cheek.

Twenty minutes later, Arthur pulled the carriage in front of Nicholas's office on Buckingham Street.

The lanterns brightly glowed within the office. Peter, Nicholas, and another man she had previously met were deeply engrossed in conversation.

"I tell you, Captain, you could have a good deal of trouble if you sail into New York," the third man said. "The war between France and England has escalated according to your newspapers."

"I am well aware of that, Mr. Davidson. I'm also aware that President Jefferson continues to ignore the pleas from the New England merchants, and has no intention of rescinding this blasted Embargo Act."

"Just think, Captain, if the President did rescind the Embargo, you would be out of business."

"On the contrary," Peter cut in, "we would be in a much better financial position. Think of how many ships we could buy or build, how many cargoes we could acquire, if we were free to trade."

"I did not think . . ."

"I know, Davidson. Now, we must settle our business this evening. My wife . . ."

"Is here to escort you to the play, Nick," her melodic voice startled the men.

The room smelled of stale tobacco, leftover lunch, and wine. One could barely detect Morgan's faint scent of jasmine. Nicholas noticed it immediately. Standing in the doorway wrapped in her white cloak, she had the look of an angel cascading down an enchanting waterfall.

Quickly excusing himself from his associates—who stood at attention as soon as she entered the room—Nicholas gently ushered her into another room.

"I apologize, beauty, but this is going to take much more time. I don't think you'd care to wait for me here, so . . ."

"Nick, how could you!" she flared. "You knew how much I was looking forward to this evening."

He tried to mollify her, but Morgan would hear none of it. "Morgan, I am sorry. I lost track of the time."

"You never lose track of the time when it comes to doing something you want. Only when it comes to me."

His patience was rapidly diminishing. "I told you I did not plan to disappoint you. But on occasion, when I am interested in earning money, unforeseen things can happen. You'll have to get used to it. This won't be the first or last time."

Morgan was more than half a foot shorter than he, but her fury rose to new heights. Arms akimbo, foot stomping, topaz eyes flashing, she snarled, "That is just fine, Nicholas. I will go alone. I should have done it in the first place, but I thought you'd be concerned if I wasn't home when you finally decided to go there."

"I don't want you to . . ." His hand touched her shoulder, but Morgan recoiled.

"I don't care what you want. The Tuckers are meeting us in our theater box. I shall not disappoint them or myself. I

177

am going."

"I said no! You will go home." He wanted to grab her shoulders and shake some sense into her.

"No! I will not wait at home like some empty-headed concubine for the great master to pay attention to me." Morgan's anger began to take over. She was panting. Once her fury finally erupted, there was no controlling it.

Their voices were clearly heard in the other room. Peter, thinking he could make a difference, quietly emerged.

"Excuse me, Nick. Why don't you go with Morgan. I'll take care of things." Seeing those two angrily facing one another made Peter want to laugh. On closer inspection, though, Nick looked furious enough to throttle her.

As soon as Peter spoke Nicholas turned, ready to throttle him as well.

"Peter, thank you, but stay out of this. Our business—in case you and my wife forget that I have a say in things—must be finished tonight with me here. I am staying here and my lovely, determined bride is going to the theater without me."

"Good. I'd rather be alone than with you. Take care of your important business, Captain Rhodes."

"If I finish before the end of the play, I'll meet you at the theater." He tried to sound conciliatory, but the tone was more caustic than kind.

"Don't bother," she snapped. Replacing the hood over her head, Morgan marched out of the room, leaving an open-mouthed Peter and a furious Nicholas behind.

She was late. Arthur reluctantly drove Morgan to the theater, knowing that otherwise she would walk through the streets unescorted.

"I'll wait out here for you, Mrs."

"Fine," she sounded angry with him too.

Morgan quickly walked up the theater's marble steps. A footman held the door. Once inside, she marched across the foyer and up the carpeted stairs to their box, removing the white cloak as she walked.

The play had just begun. Rachel Tucker anxiously looked at Morgan.

"Where is . . ."

"He is not coming. Business," she muttered, still angry with Nick and everyone else who dared to ask about him.

By the intermission, Morgan's temper had slightly abated. Determined not to think about that man, she nevertheless sought his tall form among the crowd. All she had to do was look up, for Nick was taller than most. Of course, the collective sighs of the women around the room usually indicated that he was near.

"Why Morgan dear, he left you alone already?" The unmistakable voice of Catherine Stevens assaulted Morgan's ears.

"No, he's detained. He'll be here shortly," she lied smoothly.

"I don't believe that dear. Neither do you. It's just as I said. Nicky would run away as soon as he grew tired of you and the brat you're carrying."

Morgan was dying to scratch out her dark eyes.

"Catherine," she began in a honeyed voice, a false smile pasted on her face, "don't you ever give up? I am not the least bit interested in anything you have to say. Particularly about my husband. So why don't you find another victim for your vituperation." She quickly turned away without waiting for a response.

Morgan did not realize—not until this moment—that when angered she was perfectly capable of holding her own against the formidable Catherine Stevens. Being around Nicholas must have something to do with it. After her confrontation with Nick and now Catherine's assault, Morgan felt as if she could deal with a snake. Straightening her spine, feeling quite proud, knowing now that things could be accomplished on her own, Morgan kept walking. That independent streak she'd always possessed—albeit somewhat hidden of late—was emerging and was redefined. Morgan Rhodes could take care of herself. Although, she reluctantly admitted, it was more fun being with Nicholas.

She could indeed take care of herself . . . if she were dealing with normal people.

*   *   *

179

Nicholas was angry, yet still able to concentrate on what was being said. At any other time he might have laughed at her ridiculous temper tantrum. But two hours later, looking at the wall clock for the tenth time, he realized that if the meeting were ended now he could meet Morgan at the theater and take her home. Then he stopped himself. Why the hell was he thinking about her? She was probably still angry anyhow. Why not postpone the confrontation, instead of meeting it head-on?

That's what he meant to do. But inexplicably, Nicholas looked at Peter.

"Well, I think we solved the pressing issues this evening, gentlemen. The rest we can straighten out as soon as you provide a complete inventory, Mr. Davidson."

Surprised by his partner's sudden change, Peter looked at Nicholas who again was staring at the clock. Then Peter understood.

"You are right, Nick. It's a trifling matter."

"So," Nicholas rose, reaching for his cloak, "I think I'll leave. You'll excuse me, Mr. Davidson?"

As soon as he left, Peter smiled. "The man does not know that he's smitten."

What Nicholas could not know was that the night was far from over. Years later, he would still curse himself for being so intransigent.

The performance ended shortly after half past eight. As the crowd slowly made its way out of the theater, Morgan continued to look for Nicholas. Her anger had cooled considerably and she was now anxious to see him, to settle their differences. Rachel's husband assisted her into the white woolen cloak. The three followed the crowd, first down the staircase, then outside to the marble steps. The front of the theater was alight with torches and lanterns. But Nicholas was not there.

"It was such a lovely performance, don't you agree Morgan?" Rachel asked.

"Oh yes, I am so glad I saw it. I've never seen this performance. Although," she laughed, "I must have read it and cried over it at least a dozen times."

They had reached the stone ledge. Morgan, still pressed by the crowd, did not see the two street urchins standing behind a large pillar. At a gloved signal, the two boys ran into the crowd, jostling the people in their way. No one could have realized that they were heading in a carefully planned direction—for the black-haired lady in the white cloak.

One ran behind her; the other got in between her and Rachel Tucker. Just as Morgan was about to step down, the boy in the back pushed her—hard. The other extended his foot.

Morgan did not have a chance. She felt the shove. She felt herself tripping over someone's foot. She knew she was going to fall. Voices screamed—hers mingled with those of the people around—as she crashed into the white marble. Like a leaf caught in a heavy wind, she relentlessly, helplessly, tumbled down the five stone steps. Protectively clutching her stomach, Morgan bruised her face and back in the process. Her thoughts passed quickly; yet she knew she was losing consciousness. When she hit the bottom, Morgan was no longer aware of the people rushing toward her. She had no idea that one tall blond-haired man had desperately run to assist her, shouting her name as if she would awaken to the deep, demanding voice, as if time would miraculously turn back a few minutes. He would have been standing next to her, at the top of the stairs, securely holding her about the waist. If he were there, she would not have fallen.

Lanterns were brought closer to them. Nicholas did not care about the friendly, concerned faces asking him if they could assist. Nor did he notice that Arthur had run for the doctor. Careful not to move her body, he gently lifted and placed her head on the side of his lap.

"Someone get a doctor!" he ordered, his eyes riveted on Morgan's still form. "Now!"

With tears in her eyes, Rachel Tucker knelt beside him. "Arthur already has left for the doctor."

Oblivious to the crowd surrounding them and the approaching soldiers, he stroked her hair, whispering, "Morgan, my love. I want you to open your eyes. Please, Morgan, I want to help you."

As powerless as a sea urchin in a rising tide, Nicholas was thoroughly helpless to do anything for Morgan. And he was afraid for her. A fall like that could do irreparable damage. Already bluish stains grew on her forehead and cheek. He wanted to examine her body for more bruises or possible breaks, but the dark winter air and the surging crowd prevented that. Tearing off his own cloak to blanket her body, he waited for what he knew was the worst.

"Nick, what about the baby?" Rachel Tucker voiced his morbid fear.

"I don't know," he brokenly whispered, "I just don't know."

Suddenly he heard a soft, muffled whimper. Morgan's head moved. It appeared as if she were trying to open her eyes.

"Morgan, love. I've sent for the doctor. Just hold my hand."

"Nick?" she painfully sighed. "I don't think . . . the baby . . . Oh!" she groaned, squeezing her eyes shut, her hand still clutching her stomach.

Nicholas watched in agonizing sympathy as the golden eyes filled with tears of pain.

"Nick. Please . . . take . . . me . . . home." In a stronger voice, she repeated, "I want to go home."

"Yes, yes, of course. We'll wait for the doctor."

"No! Nick," she squeezed his hand. "I don't want to . . . lose the baby here. Please," the tears rolled into her tangled hair. "Please."

"Anything you say, my love."

Rachel Tucker heard the exchange. Luckily, Arthur was half running up the street with the doctor alongside.

"Captain. Arthur is coming with the doctor."

"Thank God. Rachel, tell Arthur to bring the carriage around."

"But, Nick . . ."

"Please, Rachel. I don't want her to suffer a miscarriage on a cold slab of marble. Do it Rachel."

She ran to do his bidding.

The doctor pushed his way through the crowd. A fall of this kind could be fatal to the young woman. It would surely kill the babe. Seeing the crumpled woman in the captain's lap confirmed the doctor's worst suspicions.

"Doctor Craig. She wants me to take her home. I want to do as she asks. She thinks she is losing the baby." His voice cracked, "Is it true?"

"Take that lantern," the doctor instructed Nicholas, lowering to the fallen pair. "Let me see if anything is broken. The ride will be a difficult one if she can be moved. I'd prefer to bring her to my office but . . ." Dr. Craig saw the captain's determined look. "Let me see. Hold the lantern close to her face."

The examination was cursory. "I don't think anything is broken," he smiled. "Let's see what we can do for her. It is going to be a difficult, painful time."

"I know, more than you can imagine. You see, this is all my fault."

The doctor thought the captain was making no sense. "I'll follow you in my coach."

Nicholas gave the lantern to someone. Shifting his body, he gently lifted Morgan into his strong, steady embrace. For one brief moment, her eyes opened, focusing on him. He placed her arms around his neck, then rose to his feet, finally noticing the blood stains on her white cloak.

"We're going home, Morgan. I'll hold you in my arms. I promise not to let you go. I will stay with you throughout . . ." There was no need to finish the words.

Despite her haze of pain, Morgan knew with a woman's intuition that she was going to lose the baby.

"I am sorry Nick. I did not mean . . ."

"Hush. I am responsible. Not you Morgan." He walked to the waiting coach. Morgan's head rested against his coatless chest. "Close your eyes Morgan, I'll get you home safely."

The hushed crowd parted, allowing the man to carry his wife toward the waiting coach. Someone managed to bring blankets, which Nicholas used to pad the leather carriage seat. Cushioning her body he stepped within, then gave Arthur the signal to head home.

"Slowly, Arthur. Her life depends on it."

As soon as the coach departed, the crowd began chattering in earnest. Rachel Tucker turned to her husband, sobbing, "It is too terrible for words. They do not deserve this. No one does."

Peter Mackenzie saw the soldiers trying to disperse the crowd in front of the theater. Wondering what was going on, he hurried toward the theater, thinking he would find Nick and Morgan to explain the late night activity. Deciding to walk up a side street where the crowd was thin, he saw a most curious sight.

Catherine Stevens was leaning against a marble pillar, laughing, her gloved hand covering her mouth in an effort to stifle the uncontrollable laughter.

"Catherine!" he sharply called to her. "What is going on here?"

"What a wonderful evening, Peter. You should have seen it," she said. "But I am in a terrible hurry, Peter dear. My Bennett will be home today. Ta, dear." She scurried away, leaving a baffled Peter Mackenzie to stare openmouthed at her odd behavior.

When he finally found the Tuckers he fully understood what had happened. In a nearly hysterical voice, Rachel explained that two beggars had pushed their way into the crowd, tripping Morgan in the process.

"I could swear they saw her. But they would not stop. You know," she added, "the more I think about this, I could swear their action was intentional. What do you think?" She turned to her husband and Peter.

"I have a very good theory. But I will speak with the soldiers first." Peter hastily bade good-bye.

Alone in the carriage with his semiconscious wife, Nicholas's torturous thoughts became overwhelming. How could he ever block out the vision of Morgan lying on the cold ground, alone with her pain? Thinking about the events made him feel far worse.

He had briskly walked to the theater, thinking it would take less time than riding through the busy streets. The whole time his primary goal was finding Morgan, hoping to greet her in front of the theater. He could not help but anticipate the sight of her exquisite face, remembering the scent of her skin, her

184

elegantly styled black hair, her body beneath the white cloak. Eagerly wanting to make her forget their stupid argument, he walked faster. It was odd, he had thought, how Morgan could simultaneously bring out the best and worst in him. Unused to living with a woman, he had not realized that his freedom would be curtailed.

His memory of Morgan standing in the doorway of the office, angrily demanding that he leave with her, jolted him. He could not do as he pleased; he could not stay away from his home all night if it suited him. No, he had someone who would demand explanations. This did not sit well with him. Living an unfettered life before ever setting eyes on Morgan had not prepared him for marriage.

Much later, though, when his temper had cooled, Nicholas conceded that Morgan might have a right to expect some explanations; that perhaps he did need to take her feelings into consideration—some of the time.

It simply was not going to be easy.

When he had made his way around the corner to Argyle Street, Nicholas's somber mood had lifted. He was only one street away, yet he saw the patrons leaving the well-lit theater. Locating Morgan at the top of the stairs saying something to the Tuckers, he smiled. Even in the semidarkness, he could locate Morgan.

At that distance, Nicholas could see the entire top landing, including the two boys who dashed out from behind a pillar. As they approached Morgan, Nicholas became alarmed. He began to run, but it felt like his feet were stuck in mud. It took only two seconds to trip Morgan.

"No!" he had shouted.

But like a man seeing his worst nightmare unfold before startled eyes, Nicholas watched Morgan tumble down the stairs. Five hard marble steps. Enough to . . .

"Morgan! Oh God. No!"

Too late, he had made his way to her side. What he saw would forever remain indelibly etched in his mind.

She was curled on the ground, people surrounding her. Arthur was running toward her too. But for Morgan, it did not matter whose concerned face was above hers. She was in a private hell. Whoever had caused the fall would suffer twentyfold.

It took another twenty minutes to reach the home on Oakland Drive. Nicholas could not bear her mournful cries, her pain. He would have done anything to make her pain his.

"Just be well, my love. You've gone through so much." He smoothed her perspiring forehead.

"Nick?" It was hardly a whisper.

"Yes, my love."

"Will you stay with me?"

"I'll never leave your side, I won't let go of your hand."

"Nick, the cramps. They are getting worse."

"We will be home soon, darling." He closed his eyes against their loss. "I wish I could do more for you."

Once the carriage stopped at the front of the house, Arthur scurried down to hold the coach door or Nicholas. All the while Arthur shouted for Agatha to assist.

"My Lord! Captain. Is it very serious?" she sobbed into her apron.

"Yes, Agatha. I'm afraid so. Get the bed ready, then get plenty of clean white linen and whatever else Dr. Craig requires."

The doctor was behind them. After Nicholas settled her in their large four-poster bed, the doctor cleared his throat.

"Captain, I think you ought to leave. Mrs. Gleason and I will take over."

"No! I will not let her go through this all alone. I will be here."

"Stay Nick. Please?" Morgan pleaded in a childlike voice. And he did.

For two hours, he let her puncture his hand with sharpened nails while trying to wipe her brow, saying nonsensical things, anything so that in her semiconscious state Morgan would at least hear his reassuring, familiar voice.

"I love you." The words were uttered in such a low voice that he doubted she heard. But the words continued to flow: all of his promises for her happiness, pledging that they would make many more babies—if she wanted—anything she wanted.

"Just smile for me again, Morgan."

In all the years at sea, Nicholas had seen every conceivable injury, but none compared to the agony Morgan was experiencing. He would never forget.

Finally, Dr. Craig announced that it was over.

"She will need plenty of rest. Captain, she is going to be very dispirited. It could take quite a while to get over this loss."

"Can we, I mean has there been any permanent damage?"

"None, I assure you. Mrs. Rhodes will be able to have many children—if she desires."

"I was planning to leave Halifax with her in two weeks."

"I think not, Captain. Although the change in environment would greatly help. Let's see how she feels in one week."

Positive that Morgan was peacefully oblivious in her laudanum-induced sleep, he pried his hand loose from her strong grip and escorted the doctor downstairs.

"I am so sorry, Captain. Miscarriages are unpleasant. Particularly those caused by a fall. I will be back tomorrow."

The heavy oak door closed. Nicholas leaned his forehead against the door, fighting the urge to cry.

Two snifters of brandy fortified him, but it also brought back the murderous rage now directed at those two boys and the person who must have paid them to do it.

He would find them. And God help them.

Chapter 17

She awoke late the following afternoon. The gray, overcast skies perfectly fit her state of mind. Despite her half-conscious state, Morgan knew everything that had happened. She also knew that Nicholas had remained by her side throughout the entire ordeal. Slowly looking around the room, she could see that the fire was still brightly glowing; someone must have been tending it all night. Then she saw who it was. Nicholas was sitting on the edge of the sofa, leaning forward, elbows balancing on his knees, the palms of his hands supporting his face.

Unable to tell if he were sleeping, she decided to leave him in peace. Morgan tried to shift her body, ignoring the soreness in her limbs. A small groan escaped her lips. Nicholas's head instantly picked up and within two seconds he was by her side, holding her hand.

"You know?"

"Yes. I can feel it. I am sorry to have caused so much trouble." Morgan looked into his eyes, which were ringed with black smudges. His unruly hair fell onto his forehead. It looked as if Nick must have run his fingers through it many times last night. Still wearing the same clothes as yesterday, he had the appearance of a man who had been to hell and back.

"Morgan. I don't want to hear you talk that way any more. What happened was a deliberate act. I do not know who is responsible, but you can be damn sure I will find out."

"Am I going to be all right?" she hesitantly asked.

Nicholas thought he knew what she was trying to say. Lost among the large white pillows, Morgan looked so fragile and so defeated.

"Morgan, Dr. Craig said you are going to be fine—perfectly normal. We can have more babies, a whole passel of them if you want." He tried to smile, but it was a poor attempt. Seeing her like this saddened and hurt him. She was missing the spark of life. After what she had gone through it was certainly a natural reaction; he knew this, but still was concerned and wondered if he'd ever see her carefree smile again.

"I don't know what I want. Not anymore."

"Sweetheart, do you think you could tell me what happened? What you saw?"

In a monotone voice, she explained as much as she could recall, from the moment she'd stormed out of his office to the conversation with the people during the intermission.

"Then Catherine showed up." Morgan said more but Nicholas's mind began to wander. Some strange notion took hold in his head, but he needed to confirm it before he made any accusations.

". . . and Nick, she said that you'd grow tired of a fat, useless wife," she faltered, but he was alert to the catch in her voice.

"You know better than to believe that tripe."

"Do I?"

"Morgan, my God, what do you think I am?"

"Oh," one tear slid down her cheek, then another. "I don't know anymore. It just hurts. I feel so empty. I didn't know if I wanted this baby when I first discovered I was pregnant. But then I felt the small changes begin and I kept thinking about this new life we created and Nick," she caught her breath on a sob, "I wanted it. I wanted it so badly."

They reached for each other at the same moment. The emotions of the last twenty-four hours were finally released in a flood of tears.

"Hush Morgan. I'd do anything—anything to make you smile once more." He moved her to arm's length, studying the tear-stained, sunken eyes. "Morgan, I wanted that baby too. The more I thought about it, the happier I became. This may not be the appropriate time to tell you this. But I swore last

190

night that I'd not let another moment pass without telling you how much you have come to mean to me." Damn, he swore to himself, knowing he was saying it badly.

"You mean a lot to me too," she replied, her voice back to monotone.

"No, that's not what I mean. Morgan, all through the night, I kept thinking about our last few months together. I did not want to love you. But you see," he paused, "I don't think I can live without you."

"Nicholas," her eyes were suspiciously bright again. He even detected the beginning of a smile. "What are you trying to tell me?"

"You know for a man who is usually so glib, who is so experienced in, ah, certain matters, I seem to be botching this one up. I suppose it's because I never told a woman that I love her."

"You are just feeling sorry for me."

"Morgan, I don't say things I don't mean. I love you. All right? Is that clear enough for you?"

Unsure of whether she should laugh or cry, she did neither. She just stared at him—her mouth open, her eyes saucer wide. It was what she had wanted to hear him say for so long. But too much had happened. In her numbed state, Morgan could not say the words Nicholas wanted to hear.

"I don't know what to say," she muttered, looking down at the quilt cover.

"Woman! I just told you that I love you. While I did not expect you to leap across the room with joy, the very least I expected was 'I love you too, Nick'. Is that asking too much?"

Baffled by her behavior, Nicholas simply leaned against the bedpost, studying her expression—or lack of one.

"I'm sorry," she placed her hand on his lap. "Yes, I suppose I love you. But Nick, I can't think about that now. Can't you understand? All I can think of is the baby I lost. Give me time, please Nicholas. I need time."

"You are right. I apologize. I just wanted to let you know how I feel about you. I did not mean to shock you. Don't worry, I won't change my mind and I won't bring it up again. Not until you're more receptive. But I swear, I'll get an enthusiastic response from you yet!" he grinned.

If he were shaken by her omission, he did not let it show. They would have plenty of time together. Time for him to convince her that he did love her.

"Nick, one more thing. When can we leave Halifax? I really," she choked, feeling the tears well up, "want to go home. Back to America, I mean."

"As soon as Dr. Craig says you are fit to travel. I postponed our departure until I am positive you can sail with me. I won't leave you here."

"Nicholas?"

"Hmmm?"

"Thank you," she earnestly said, ignoring the tears that spilled over her pale cheeks.

He left her alone with her thoughts. Morgan slept intermittently for the rest of the day and the next one. She dreamed many things, but even in the dreams, her husband was there to comfort, to console her.

Peter appeared at their home the next day. He patiently remained in the library, waiting for Nicholas who had been upstairs with his wife.

Nicholas's haggard, unshaved face told Peter everything he wanted to know.

"I am worried about her, Peter." He sunk into his leather armchair, pouring himself a liberal glass of whiskey. "I need to take her out of here, back to America, to New York. As much as I hate to admit it, she needs to become involved again in her search for her father's murderer."

"Nick, you told me that whole story. What happens if she finds out about your pledge to your father?"

"She won't," his voice hardened. "I will see to it. Christ! What a mess!"

"Nick, there is more." Peter waited for Nicholas to finish his drink, then explained his theory about Catherine Stevens's involvement in Morgan's accident.

"It had to be either Catherine or Bennett Williams. I just didn't want to think Catherine would be that vicious. She's unbalanced, Peter."

"I know that now. I am sorry I did not see it sooner. I could

192

have prevented this."

"You are no more responsible than Morgan is. Yes," he noticed Peter's surprised look, "Morgan blames herself too. Damn!" he violently swore, throwing his glass into the fireplace, unmindful of the scattered glass. "I will have to attend to Catherine."

"You can't Nick. She is gone."

"What? Gone where? I'll find her, Peter."

"I've tried. When I became sure of my suspicions, I went to her home. Mr. Stevens said she left early that morning to visit relatives in Montreal. From there, she is off to England."

"I am sending someone after her. That bitch will not get away with murdering my child and hurting my wife. Never, Peter!" his voice rose alarmingly.

"We'll send Gordon to track her. Nick, I know less about the law than you do. If Gordon finds her, he will have to bring her back here to Halifax to face charges. You and Morgan will have to press formal charges with the magistrate. Are you willing to stay here until then?"

Sadly shaking his head, Nicholas said, "I want to take Morgan away. Within the next two weeks." He stood up and walked over to the walnut bookcase. "I am going to press charges. I am going to hound the authorities until something is done. I'll come back alone if I have to. I am also going to her father's home to let him know everything that has happened."

"I'll go with you."

"Thanks, Peter. I have to go alone. Don't worry," he grimly smiled, "I will not kill him. But I do want revenge."

True to his word, Nicholas had done everything he said. The next day he asked Peter to stay with Morgan and the Gleasons, while he rode over to the Stevens' home in Bedford Basin.

Their exchange was blunt and heated. After assimilating the captain's accusations, Catherine's father threatened to kill him.

Nicholas did not care, except when Mr. Stevens began to sob, admitting that he had suspected his daughter was not well.

"Too spoiled. I gave her everything. She did not understand what it meant to be denied. Captain," he begged, "if I swear that I will see to it that she never comes back to Halifax and remains in England—I have a home in a small village near Cornwall—I will hire someone to watch her day and night. Will that satisfy you? Please?"

The old man's tears did affect him. Would he have done any less for his child? Wouldn't his parents have done the same for him? Could he put Morgan through any more heartache?

Feeling drained, he sympathized with the broken man before him.

"All right, Stevens. I have your word. If, however, she ever sets foot on this Continent, I will find her and deal with her myself!"

Before he returned home, Nicholas stopped to meet with his crew aboard the *Anastasia*.

They seemed to know everything. A few words of sympathy from Mr. McNeil on behalf of the entire crew pleased him. In addition, the crew had collected funds for a special get-well gift for the captain's wife. He was deeply moved by their thoughts, promising to tell Morgan their kind words. He then advised McNeil to be prepared to sail immediately after the New Year.

By the end of the week, Morgan was feeling physically well enough to go down for dinner. Her spirits, however, had not yet improved. If she wasn't sitting on the window seat in the library, staring out the frosted panes, then she was sitting on the sofa in their bedroom, studying the roaring fire that was constantly blazing in the marble fireplace.

When he was not busy in town, Nicholas tried to spend as much time as possible with Morgan. He'd bring her pretty trinkets, tell her amusing anecdotes, then he would massage her neck or brush her long raven hair. Rarely did she smile. Despite Dr. Craig's words, Nicholas was very concerned.

They had a quiet Christmas celebration. As was their annual custom, Agatha and Arthur put a tree with handmade decorations and stockings in the house. Morgan did not take any interest in the festivities, preferring to remain in their bedroom.

Her despondency was taking its toll on Nicholas. Morgan ignored the many kindnesses of others—especially the Gleasons and Peter. Each day since the accident, Nicholas or one of the others would plan some activity, some small project with her. Or they would simply try to entertain her, ensuring that Morgan spent as little time as possible alone. Peter insisted she learn how to play chess, but after two futile attempts—she did not want to concentrate on the board—he gave up.

Two weeks had passed and still Morgan remained unresponsive. Nicholas felt that if he did not bring her back to life—now—she would never recover. Moreover, he was afraid that she would harm herself. He dared not think that she would even consider taking her own life, but the tiny fear lodged somewhere in his brain, especially if she were aboard the *Anastasia* where there would be time alone. He had to do something.

Nicholas took action on the eve of the New Year.

Again Morgan refused to leave the confines of her bedroom. Dr. Craig had been to see her earlier in the day. Physically, he said, she was recovered, although he did not think they should resume their marital relationship for another week.

"She could go out, if she's bundled up properly. And she can leave Halifax with you as early as next week." Dr. Craig added, though, that he too was becoming concerned about her emotional state.

"I am going to do something about it," Nicholas had said in a determined voice.

It should have been an evening of celebration, of being with close friends, of sharing more than one glass of champagne. He bounded up the stairs, taking two at a time, charging into their bedroom without knocking. She was sitting in bed, hair braided behind her, the wire-rimmed spectacles high on her nose, an open book on her lap.

"Come on, Morgan. Get dressed."

Her head rose less than an inch. "Why?"

"I am taking you for a midnight sleigh ride. What better way to bring in the New Year."

His enthusiasm did not affect her. "I'd rather not," she stated.

"I am not taking no for an answer. Now," he approached the bed, "either you get out of that bed, into your warmest clothes, or I will drag you out and dress you myself!"

"Nick . . ."

"I can do it, you know." Although he was grinning, there was that familiar authoritative edge to his voice. He disappeared through the dressing room and went into her bedroom to fling open the doors of the armoire.

Morgan heard the banging, which ultimately piqued her curiosity. What could he possibly be doing? The banging continued, punctuated by objects being thrown against the wall.

"Nick? What are you doing?" she called.

"I can't hear you Morgan."

"I said . . . Oh wait a minute," she tossed aside the bedcovers, walking barefoot into the next room.

"Nicholas! What is going on in here?" In less than five minutes he had made a mess of her room. Dresses were strewn about, shoes and boots were scattered on opposite ends of the room. When his hands found her jewelry case, she walked over to him.

"Why are you doing this?"

"Because madam, I am looking for your warmest clothes. I cannot find them. And you will not help me."

"Well they are not in my jewelry case," she replied.

"Ah hah," he turned his attention to the rear of the armoire, finding the old pair of breeches she had used aboard the ship. "These will do."

"Nick, you are not paying attention to me. I am not going out with you. Why, it's cold and dark out there! And it's late."

"I don't care Morgan. I am having bricks heated for your delicate feet. I've got scores of blankets and furs. I have mittens for your hands. And another surprise or two," he flashed a wicked grin.

"I am not leaving this room."

"You are. Do you know why, sweetheart?" He took a menacing step toward her. "Because I demand it."

"You what?" she stood rooted to the floor, feeling the sparks of anger ignite.

Because he was warmly dressed in breeches, dark boots, and a dark blue wool sweater that reached his neck, Nicholas did not feel the chill in the room.

"Nick, I'm cold. I'm going back to bed," she turned away

heading for the other room.

Something snapped inside him.

"Don't you dare turn your back on me, Morgan Rhodes. Just who in the hell do you think you are!" he shouted, his voice carrying to the floor below. "I am sick and tired of your 'poor little me attitude.' I know you've experienced a terrible loss. But dammit, so have I! I wanted that baby too," he grabbed her arms, still shouting. "In the last few weeks, I find that I am also losing my wife. Should I mourn for you too? Should I Morgan?"

"No!" she shouted back. "Stop shaking me Nicholas. What do you want?"

"I want you back. I want to start our lives again—together. I want to take you to New York to meet my family. I want to help you find Andrews and those missing currency plates. But I'll be damned if I'll do it alone. I won't Morgan. I'd just as soon leave you buried here."

"You would leave me?"

"Yes! I don't want to be married to a mummy. I've got a life to lead. I'll gladly share everything with you. But you have to help me. You have to meet me part of the way. I am not asking for much. I know you are still mourning." Nicholas pulled her stiff body into his loving embrace. Placing her head against his chest, he murmured, "I am too. Help me Morgan. Please."

Her silence disturbed him. Feeling a small tremor, he looked down to see her shoulders shaking.

Tenderly, he placed two fingers under her chin, lifting her face. Tears streamed down, spilling onto his hand.

"Oh God, Nick," she wailed. "It's been so hard."

"I know, sweetheart. Believe me." He continued holding her, allowing the pent-up emotions of the last few weeks to finally emerge. Her sobs shook her body and broke his heart.

"My love," he said minutes later, in an odd but gentle tone, "let's try to make this a better year."

Gradually the sobs diminished. When she was able to breathe normally once more, Morgan looked up into his handsome face.

"If you'd still like to take the sleigh ride, I can be ready in a few minutes."

"Absolutely!" his face brightened. "Come on, I'll even help you clean up this mess."

Bundled in layers of clothing, it was difficult for Morgan to climb into the waiting sleigh. Arthur held the team of mares while Nicholas gallantly assisted her into the sleigh then neatly arranged the blankets around her.

They rode at a brisk pace, the cold night wind coloring Morgan's pale cheeks. Her spirits did lift, and when Nicholas offered brandy from a flask hidden in his coat pocket, she actually laughed.

At midnight, the distant sounds of church bells, guns, and horns blended into a cheerful welcome of the New Year. Nicholas stopped the sleigh, took Morgan into his arms, and sweetly kissed her cold lips.

He tasted of winter, brandy, and warmth. Morgan lifted her arms from beneath the myriad of blankets to capture his neck. It was a prolonged kiss that fired her emotions into a state of bliss.

"Morgan, I want you to have this," he murmured. "It's another Christmas present that I wanted to give you."

It was a small box with red wrapping and a bright green bow on top. She clumsily tried to undo the wrapping, but her mittens made it nearly impossible. Tearing one end off with her mouth, she finally succeeded. Her jaw sagged with awe at the beautiful, delicate heart-shaped locket surrounded by black velvet. Lifting it up by the gold chain to the moonlight, she nearly cried at its exquisite beauty.

"When we get home, you'll read what is on the back."

"Tell me."

"It has your initials and mine, plus three dates: the date of our accident in Boston, the date we said we were married, and our real wedding date. I hope you like it."

"I love it Nick," she whispered, still staring at the locket.

"I hope you'll put something inside."

"I will."

"I wanted to have a miniature painted of both of us, but I was not sure you would want my ugly face."

"Oh, you know I want your handsome face in my constant

embrace. Tomorrow we will take care of it. Can we Nicholas?" she smiled.

"Indeed, madam, even if I have to go to the artist's home."

They raced some more along the snowy paths, generously partaking of the brandy. In her heart, Morgan felt warm and secure—and very happy for the first time in weeks.

Chapter 18

JANUARY, 1809

The *Anastasia* set sail from Halifax, bound for New York, on the tenth day of the New Year. In her hold once more was an extremely valuable and, when sold, highly profitable cargo. There were articles of leather, silk, hemp, glass, silver, paper, tools, woolen hosiery, ready-made clothing, malt liquors, pictures, millinery, prints, even playing cards. Nicholas also managed to load some large wooden and marble pieces of furniture—armchairs, tables, and highboys.

The captain was confident about the sale of the goods, and believed that their extremely late departure in the heart of the winter almost guaranteed that there would be no patrol ships scouring the coast for smugglers. Only fools and a handful of fearless men would consider a winter voyage with expensive cargo and a woman on board. Perhaps, Nicholas mused, he was a little of both.

Their departure had been a sad one for Morgan. Eager to leave the town that caused such heartache, she found it difficult to say good-bye to the Gleasons and Peter. They had fussed over her, cried over her, and Arthur even considered going with her. Few people would ever experience the kind of friendship and loyalty that she was given. They were three very special people in her life.

Nicholas had promised that he would come back with his wife in the late spring. Morgan promised to send letters;

hopefully, she would be able to tell of their successful quest for her father's murderer.

The admonition in Peter's eye when he had strongly slapped Nicholas on the back was a reminder. Again Peter cautioned Nicholas to tell Morgan the truth—before someone else did. He also urged Nicholas to marry her in New York.

"Just to be safe and cautious. If nothing else, my friend, do it for me," he had advised the day before they sailed.

Nicholas would probably do everything Peter had suggested. But not until they were settled in New York, for he suspected that Morgan was terrified of meeting his family—especially his father.

Whenever they talked about New York, they invariably ended up discussing the same subjects, such as meeting his family and their involvement in New York society. Despite her training in Halifax, Morgan knew it would be a different experience in New York. It was larger, the population so diverse, and New York was becoming known for its sophistication. The wealthy families were intent on establishing their own dynasties. And Warren Rhodes was among them.

"Nick," she asked one evening while they were enjoying an early supper, "where is your house?"

"It's a small town house, farther uptown from my parents' home. It's on a lovely street called Greenwich. You'll love it, Morgan. It is very different from the house in Halifax. The rooms are smaller, but just think, the house is in the middle of New York, in the prettiest part of the town."

"Who keeps this home?"

"No one. I closed the house before I left the city. You, my love," he raised his wineglass, "can hire whomever you want."

"I hope I can keep up with all of your homes. In Philadelphia, I lived in the same house for eighteen years—until we had to leave, of course."

"You will manage beautifully. I am confident of that."

"I can just imagine what your parents will think of me," she stared into her plate.

"I already told you. My mother will be thrilled."

"It's what you didn't tell me. Your father and brother, for example."

"My brother will think exactly what my father tells him to think. As for my father," he sighed, leaning back into the chair, a faraway look in his eyes, "I cannot say. But don't worry. I will not leave you to his mercy. He'll probably come to love you."

"You don't sound very positive."

It was difficult to imagine Warren Rhodes ever approving their marriage, unless he and Morgan could quickly solve the mystery of the stolen currency plates. Nicholas would have to prove to Warren how very wrong he had been about Samuel Rhinehart and his beautiful daughter. If necessary, he'd make his father apologize to Morgan.

"Nick? What are you staring at? I've been talking to you and you haven't heard a word I've said," she mildly scolded.

"How can I possibly ignore your mellifluous voice Morgan?" he sobered. "I promise you that we will not stay in New York very long. I will take care of the cargo transfer. If necessary, the New York agent can purchase the new cargo to bring back to Halifax. That way we can leave on a moment's notice in case we find out where Andrews has gone."

"That's fine with me." Morgan was trying not to be overwhelmed by the new developments in her life. If Nicholas said she would like New York, then hopefully, she would. It was too late to turn back. She would have to trust Nicholas.

Lately, she found herself placing a good deal of trust in her husband. It was hard to believe that this godlike creature could love her. But he had said it—only once, that day after the accident. Perhaps he did not think it necessary to tell her again. He had shown her so much, had done so much for her. Then again, she thought, perhaps Nicholas had not meant those words. Maybe they were said in the heat of the moment—not out of passion, but compassion. Thinking about it made her head ache. Nicholas was her husband. He said he'd care for her, help her, and had done far more than that.

Did it matter if he didn't love her?

Yes, to Morgan it mattered a great deal. For she was hopelessly, irrevocably in love with Nicholas Rhodes. When the realization had hit her, Morgan could not say. During those dreadful days after the accident and convalescence, she had spent so much time alone with her thoughts, dreams, and nightmares. But no matter what her state of mind, Nicholas was omnipresent. She could no more get him out of her heart and mind than she could remove the past from her distant memory. His towering presence warmed her, comforted her. He freely offered himself to her. Yet Morgan could not accept it was done out of love.

Nicholas was as solicitous of her needs as a lioness protecting her cubs. Was that love or sympathy? Perhaps he could not abandon her—not after everything that had happened. Nicholas was an honorable man. He felt responsible for her, nothing more.

Or was it that simple?

Damn, she silently cursed, she did not know what to think.

"Sweetheart," his deep voice intruded on her thoughts, "look who is not paying attention."

The heat in her face surely betrayed her—as it always did. "Sorry. I guess the wine is more potent than I thought."

"It has been too cold to take you above deck. It must be hard being cooped up in here all night."

"And most of the day too, Captain. I wouldn't mind the feel of the cold wind against my cheeks. Weren't you the one who introduced me to late night outings?" she gently teased him, recalling their wonderful midnight ride. How could she forget. It was the night they referred to as the "night Morgan woke up." The small gold locket nestled between her breasts was a constant reminder.

The voyage was rough. The seas were choppy, the winds cold and fierce. Nicholas did not appear to mind these conditions. He was above deck at dawn, giving the day's orders. Often, he was at the wheel wearing a heavy sweater, a blue wool jacket with brass buttons and a high collar, wool breeches, black knee-high boots, and a woolen cap. Occasionally, he wore gloves. He would stroll across the deck, his silver eyes scanning the sea for signs of trouble.

Fortunately, there were none. New York Harbor was only a few days away.

Each day, just after noon, Morgan could hear the unmistakable sound of Nicholas's firm footsteps as he approached their cabin. Without knocking, he would enter the cabin, kiss Morgan on the lips, then march over to the heated stove to warm his cold hands.

She never tired of watching his movements. Nicholas was a tall, well-proportioned man. The bulky clothes made him appear so much larger. One by one, he would carelessly remove the winter garments. She'd seen him do it many times now, yet whenever he tugged the woolen cap off his head onto the bed, exposing his dark gold wavy hair, she'd suddenly lose her breath. To Morgan, it seemed as if Nicholas took his masculinity for granted and was unaware of the effect he had on women—particularly her.

Knowing that he would be joining her for lunch, Morgan always straightened up the cabin before ten o'clock. It was an activity she had insisted on doing alone, despite Nicholas's offer to have one of the men do it. She wanted this warm cabin with the wide gallery window, dark wood furniture, and brightly colored rug to remain as their private sanctuary. Morgan had brought along a few feminine touches. There was a rose-colored satin coverlet for the bed, a new multi-colored porcelain basin and pitcher, dried flowers in pretty vases, white Venetian lace curtains for the gallery window, and a new set of dishes.

Morgan felt like she belonged in this cabin, aboard the large ship. Once a day, she would venture into the galley, offering her meager culinary skills to Cook. He didn't mind; none of the crew minded her serene presence aboard the *Anastasia,* despite the old wives' tale that a woman on a ship is bad luck. Sometimes Morgan would remain in the galley until the crew filed in for dinner. Their coarse words would immediately soften as they removed their woolen caps and smiled in greeting to the beauty before them. She'd pour them coffee and say a kind word or two. She was the captain's wife now and they would protect her with their lives, if necessary, as they would their highly respected captain.

Even the captain, they noted, would soften his voice around her. Known for his mercurial moods, the captain displayed a pleasant, even disposition during the entire voyage. If his wife could soften him that way, then they were glad to have her aboard.

The peaceful interlude lasted throughout the voyage. Nicholas joined her for lunch and dinner each day. Twice, he invited Mr. McNeil and the surgeon to join them. But Nicholas also preferred the quiet solitude in their cabin, savoring the moments alone with Morgan. Their conversations covered a range of topics: from politics—she was extremely interested in his stories about President Jefferson, his cabinet, and the struggles of the new nation; to travel—she especially loved his tales about his sea voyages, making him promise to take her to the Continent, if there were no war; to books—she loved Shakespeare, he loved the Greek philosophers. They shared their thoughts and sometimes argued about them. But always, their discussions ended on a light, playful note.

If Nicholas was concerned about any problem in his life, he chose not to show it. It was also true that despite their amicable times together, they had not resumed their physical relationship.

Each night after supper, Nicholas would go back above deck for an hour or more. Usually, Morgan waited for his return. By that time, however, she was undressed, wearing a warm nightgown and robe. Sometimes she'd already be in bed beneath the covers reading a book, or seated at his desk writing a letter to her family. The spectacles she had come to need but still loathed were perched on her nose.

They shared small intimacies. Morgan always had a hot bath ready for him and a snifter of brandy beside the tub. She was not shy about his bathing before her. Occasionally, she offered to scrub his neck, which nearly drove him insane with desire. He'd walk about the cabin wearing a towel around his trim waist and nothing else!

Morgan freely offered her kisses too. Each night, she'd snuggle against his well-muscled body, seeking his warmth and protection, falling asleep in his arms.

It was Nicholas, however, who remained wide awake, watching her, feeling the slow rise of her chest, seeing her dark sooty lashes, closed in trouble-free sleep, touch her face. Then he'd watch the darkness fill the cabin and he'd wait hours, wondering if he should broach the subject with her. In their daily conversations, they began to share so much with one another. Perhaps, he wondered, she was waiting for him to approach her. Maybe she was afraid of him. Or maybe she was no longer interested in him.

Where this black-haired, golden-eyed minx was concerned, Nicholas could no longer be certain of himself. She tied him in knots. She was fire and innocence, beauty and simplicity, tenderness and passion. She was unique. She was his wife. And he loved her.

He knew that with an unambiguous certainty. He would always love and want her beside him. The problem as he now saw it was how to convince her of his love. How could he awaken Morgan to her own emotions, so she could admit that she loved him? He knew she cared for him, that she was attracted to him. But did she love him? When he told her his true feelings that night after the accident and did not get a response, he was disappointed. Although he promised to give her time, he no longer wanted to mention it again. Nick, he told himself, you are a coward. You are afraid to hear her answer.

Nicholas did not think he could tell her again how much he cared, not until he was sure of her love. Yet, he felt that time was his ally. For he would court her, charm her, show her how much he cared. Knowing he was capable of doing all these things and more, he sought a plan of action.

Throughout the long nights, he would think, rejecting some ideas, accepting others. But first, before he did anything else, Morgan must willingly come to him. He would have to help her come to that realization.

Early the next morning, Nicholas decided to make enough noise to wake her. Standing naked before the washstand, he hummed a little sea ditty to himself. A quick glance in the shaving mirror told him that she was stirring. When he started to shave, his tune became louder. Morgan turned her face to the source of the noise.

One eye partially opened, but she saw what he intended for her to see. In the early morning light, she had an unobstructed view of his tall, lithe, bronzed muscular body. As he shaved, she clearly saw the bunching of his back muscles as his arm moved. As if that were not enough, Nicholas felt the need to stretch his body. His taut rounded buttocks and powerful thighs were so inviting to touch. With the razor in one hand, he stood on his toes, lifting his arms to touch the beamed ceiling. The dim rays of sunlight creeped through the lace curtains, creating little patterns on his torso.

When he turned around for his towel, Morgan felt a stirring of desire for him. Stealing another look, she started with the top of his wavy head, then slowly savored each downward glance, from his corded neck to his wide furry chest and narrow waist. Looking lower still, she could see his manhood resting against his thighs. Did he not know that he was sending her a message with his body? When he took two pantherlike strides across the room to rummage through his sea chest, Morgan was resentful that he slowly pulled on his skintight leather breeches instead of reaching for her.

She was afraid to move, afraid to let him know how much he was affecting her. The simple act of shaving and dressing had become erotic torture for her. As he approached the bed, she tried to keep her eyes closed. He was smiling. Lowering his tall body, he lightly kissed the top of her head.

"See you later, my love," he whispered, his husky voice giving her the chills. When his fingertips slowly roamed along the fine contours of her face, Morgan thought she'd moan aloud. It was such a soft, featherlike touch that when it suddenly stopped, Morgan opened her eyes to find that he had gone.

Now she was wide awake, alone with nothing but her aroused state. Morgan decided that Nicholas respected her too much. It dawned on her that they had not resumed their physical relationship because he must be waiting for some signal that she wanted him again.

Morgan was not afraid to have him make love to her. In fact, Dr. Craig had told her that as soon as she felt able, there was no harm in trying for another baby. At the moment, that was not what she wanted—not yet.

Morgan had hoped that before she became pregnant again, she and Nicholas would have firmly declared their love for one another. She also wanted all the other loose ends to be neatly tied, among them, finding Andrews and settling the differences that were sure to arise with Nick's family. When she was sure of Nick's love for her, she would think about the rest of their lives together.

This afternoon, Morgan would give her husband the signal that she was ready to be his loving wife again.

He did not appear in the cabin for their lunch. Morgan was wearing what she considered to be one of her more flattering day dresses—a deep crimson velvet dress with white lace trimming. The gold locket peeked out beneath the lace and her anchor pin was settled above the bodice. Deciding to add a little sophistication to her look, she spent two hours styling and restyling her long raven hair. Satisfied at last, she studied the finished product: The hair was piled high atop her head, black curls were artfully twisted to fall down the back of her head, while tiny wisps framed her forehead and temple. Given more time and practice, Morgan thought she could create more curls and could dress her hair with ribbons or jewels.

As it turned out, she had a lot of time to admire herself. The entire afternoon. Where was he? she wondered for the hundredth time. If she went above deck to look, he'd surely be furious with her for disobeying his order. As patiently as possible, Morgan waited, then alternated between pacing across the cabin and staring out the gallery window.

At sunset, Nicholas returned. She heard his descent and quickly smoothed the dress and her hair. Scooting over to the desk chair, she pretended to be engrossed in writing a letter.

Casually striding into the room, he pulled the dark cap off his head.

"Hello, sweetheart. Did you have a nice afternoon?"

"Hmm? What? Oh yes, Nick. I've been writing letters to Agatha and Peter."

"Indeed. You look very lovely, Morgan. Your hair is different, very becoming."

Removing his heavy jacket, Nicholas hid his knowing smile. She had been expecting him. Dressed like that, she must have been disappointed when he did not arrive for lunch. His plan was working better than expected.

"I apologize about lunch. The winds were stronger than usual today, and I had to stay on the quarterdeck."

"That's all right. I was busy."

"Are you ready for dinner, love? I asked Cook to prepare chicken. I hope you don't mind."

"No, not at all," she replied, still not looking at him.

There was a soft knock at the door. Morgan looked at Nicholas questioningly. "Isn't it too soon for dinner?"

"Yes, but I decided to bathe first. It was so cold out there today. I thought it might be comforting to take a hot bath."

Two sailors brought hot water buckets into the cabin, greeting the captain's wife before departing. Morgan tried to feign indifference, but it was difficult when Nicholas removed every layer of clothing.

"Morgan, I can't seem to get this damn boot off. Can you assist me?"

Seated on the edge of the bed, bare to the waist, Nicholas appeared to be struggling with his boots. How could he possibly remove those boots when his leather breeches were so damn tight? No wonder he could barely cross his legs. A rosy hue filled her face. Ducking her head to avoid the rest of his anatomy, she concentrated on the boots. It was more difficult than she thought.

"It's best if you turn around," he instructed.

Giving him a perfect view of her derrière, Nicholas stifled his groan by pretending to yawn.

"Hard day. We'll be in New York soon. The boys deserve something special for all their hard work." He continued the one-sided conversation. Morgan was clearly frustrated with his boots. "You have to pull at the heel, Morgan. Otherwise, they will never come off. Pull harder."

Morgan had to step over one outstretched leg, her red velvet dress covering him. He wanted to laugh, but doubted she'd see the humor in it.

"Dammit, Nick. You have to help me!"

"Here," he leaned forward, his hands spanning her waist. "There, it's loosening."

"I've got it Nick!" she enthusiastically announced, unaware that his hands moved to rub her velvet-clad backside. "Give me the other foot."

He did. It came off a little easier than the first. When it fell free, Morgan was caught unaware and almost fell forward.

Snaking an arm about her waist, he easily caught her. She fell on top of him, her laughter filling the cabin. It sounded like sparrows in the early morning. He was delighted to see her this way. Black curls loosened about her face. Wanting to keep her in his arms while his hands roamed all over her velvet body, Nick resisted. Not yet, not until she showed him how much she wanted him.

"Thank you, my love," he kissed her lightly on the cheek. "I couldn't have done it without you. Now," he lifted her off his body, "I think I better take this bath before Cook sends in our food."

Realizing that she was in his arms, Morgan became annoyed when he pushed her aside with nothing more than a chaste kiss. What was wrong with him?

He stood up, stripping off the rest of his clothes. "I won't be long, love." He stepped into the copper tub without first feeling the water temperature.

As with the morning, Nicholas began humming a little tune. His bass voice was quite good, Morgan thought, but she tried not to look at him. He was difficult to ignore. His body was too large for the tub. His long muscular legs, shadowed with golden hair, spilled over the sides. His upper torso was hardly wet. Hearing him splash about, she still refused to look at his body.

"Oh, Morgan. I dropped the sponge. Can you get it for me? It's near the desk."

Now what could she do? Pretend she didn't hear? She tried to move quickly and toss the sponge at him, but thought it would look too obvious. Handing it to him, she averted her head.

"Morgan," he caught her wrist with his wet fingers. "Can I ask another favor of you?"

"What is it, Nick?"

"I cannot move too much. Lord, it will be great to be in a real tub again. Would you mind helping me with my back?" he innocently asked, enjoying her flustered look.

"I'd rather not get wet."

"Oh come on. I've got salt through my skin. I could use your help."

Placing a towel in front of the tub, Morgan lifted her velvet dress, then lowered to her knees.

"Give me the sponge."

Since he kept talking to her, asking questions, Morgan could not keep her head turned away. The sponge glided up and down his back.

"Harder, Morgan. Here, use the soap," he handed the unscented bar to her. "Wait, let me get more comfortable." He moved his legs into the tub, exposing his waist and back.

There was so little water by now that Morgan could see all of him beneath the surface.

"Morgan, take the soap."

Why, she asked herself, was she allowing him to do this? Lathering the soap onto the sponge, she vigorously scrubbed his back.

Thinking he was making her mission easy, Nicholas bent farther forward.

"Morgan, what did you say?"

She didn't recall saying anything—unless the low groan she only thought about had really been uttered aloud.

"I did not say a word, Nick," she replied in an irritated voice. "You are getting my dress wet." She straightened, tossing the sponge in the water, hoping the soap would blind him. "Do it yourself."

Nicholas leaned back in the tub, hoping she could not see his sly grin. She found it hard to maintain her composure; she did want him. Not much longer, he thought, before her true desire surfaced.

Deliberately extending his stay in the tub, Nicholas felt the water turn cool before he decided to get out. He stood tall in all his male magnificence, then said, "Morgan, I hate to disturb you again, but I'd like my towel before I step out of this thing."

"Here," she tossed it in his face, fighting the impulse to look at the drops of moisture glistening all over his naked body. Stay composed, Morgan, she repeated. Giving him her back, she returned to the desk.

"Well, I feel much better now. I could eat three meals."

212

Vigorously rubbing the white towel through his wet hair, he approached her. Blesssedly, he was wearing a black silk robe.

After the meal was served, they ate in silence until Nicholas began a light conversation about the weather.

It seemed to Morgan, though, that each move he made, each word he said, had another sensual meaning. Well, she did want him. Why not admit it now?

She could not.

He was in a quandry. Would she readily offer herself to him tonight? How much further should he push her?

"Shall we have a brandy?"

"I'd love one Nick," she readily replied.

She enjoyed two snifters. He knew what that would do to her defenses, and so did she.

"Have I told you how beautiful you look this evening? Red suits you so well."

"You look quite handsome too. I suppose you are aware of that. You have such a . . . such a . . . a casual grace. Even in your robe, you don't seem to realize it. You are so han . . ." she stopped herself, realizing she was going too far.

"I like your hair this way too," he ignored her blunder. "It is very becoming. But you know there is something about your long, black wavy hair, cascading down your back, that I find so appealing." His voice deepened. "Undo it for me, Morgan. Now. Stand over here so I can see." He pointed to a spot directly in front of him.

His hypnotic voice directed her movements. Morgan slowly left the chair, moving to stand a few feet before him. One by one, the pins were eased out of her hair. Long black ringlets tantalizingly fell down her red velvet back.

"Put your hair in front of you." His silver eyes compelled her to look at him.

Everything in the room blurred, except the soft glow of the candles still on the table. It matched the glow in Nicholas's eyes. She could deny him nothing. Her hand moved to her neck. Fingers spread through the heavy raven hair, pulling it around to slide down the front of the crimson gown. Delicate strands rested on her breast.

She was an enchantress.

"Take off your dress," he ordered, but his voice held more passion than authority. Nicholas could not move. His body ached for the beautiful vision before him.

Beginning with her neck, Morgan leisurely released the buttons down the front of the dress. Only when they were all undone did she spread the material, exposing a white satin chemise underneath.

Not until the dress fell in a crimson pool around her slim ankles did Nicholas realize he was holding his breath.

Standing proudly before him, she was a golden statue. Her chest rose with each quick breath, her full mouth slightly parted in expectation.

"Take off the rest, Morgan."

The tiny ribbons were pulled; the thin straps of the white chemise were gently pushed off the slim shoulders.

Oh how he wanted to jump out of his seat and claim her body with his mouth and hands!

But Morgan seemed to be enjoying the game. Their roles suddenly reversed. Seeing he was about to rise, she spoke in a low whisper, "Not yet, Nick. Let me finish. Then I want to watch you."

Like a curtain being pulled open, the white satin chemise slithered off her, exposing her ripe breasts, the coral nipples jutting out at him. The garment was lowered past her narrow waist, her flat tummy. Morgan was not wearing any other undergarment. All that remained were the silk stockings. Once the chemise fell, Nicholas's eyes were riveted to the black curly hair that hid the centermost part of her being. One shapely leg lifted to his lap as she lowered her head to slowly roll off the silk stocking. Repeating the same motion with the other leg, Nicholas felt his hands gripping the arms of the chair. He would not touch her yet. But the gossamer black curtain of hair obscured her body, and he felt denied.

Again standing before him Morgan brazenly said, "Now it is your turn, my love."

"Ah, but I've had an advantage. I do not have those many layers to undo."

"A pity."

Reaching for the sash of the robe, he said in a throaty voice,

"You are a vixen, Morgan. You instinctively know exactly how to tease and please me."

"You taught me."

"Not this, my beauty. Not this. But surprise me with your resourcefulness."

She took one step closer to him, the candlelight outlining only one side of her naked body.

"Your robe, Nick." She held her hand out for the garment.

"Of course, madam." His eyes still could not tear away from her exquisite face. The topaz eyes glittered like the finest jewels. More than anything, Nicholas wanted to make this night last a lifetime. He stood, kicking the chair away, but did not move any closer to Morgan.

They were separated by a few feet, but the heat that passed between them melted the distance.

"Undo my sash, love."

"With pleasure."

Taking the extra step, her hands reached for the silk sash that was knotted about his waist.

"It's stuck, Nick," she pursed her lips in concentration.

"Here, let me."

His hands touched hers, their first contact since dinner. Each one felt an electric shock.

Let me wait, he groaned to himself. Please give me the strength to wait.

"Nicholas," his name was a tortured moan on her lips.

The sash undone, he waited as Morgan spread the garment, pushing it off his lean body.

They stood facing one another, completely naked. The sound of his heavy breathing fused with hers. Morgan had to touch him. Tentatively, her hand reached out to trace a path, which began with his high forehead, down his nose, rounding his parted lips. His tongue flicked her fingers, but she continued the descent to his firm chin, down to the thick column of his neck, finally becoming lost in the soft curly mat of chest hairs, locating his nipples and rounding each one, not once, but three times.

"Mmmm, this is fun Nick."

"Remind me never to suggest this again. You are driving me

215

mad with your sultry looks, your hot touch, your luscious body."

"No more than I, sweet husband."

"I will not hurt you, Morgan. You must believe me."

"I do, Nick."

Pulling her into his hard embrace, Nicholas sought her mouth while his hands leisurely roamed along the curves he knew so well, resting on her derrière, then gently pressing her closer to his pulsing manhood.

"Ah Morgan, my beauty, you do have a way with your body," he whispered in her ear, burying his face in her hair. In one quick movement, Nicholas held Morgan at arm's length.

Feeling bereft without his body pressed against hers, slender arms moved to grab him. But he stayed away.

"Open your eyes Morgan. I want you to see how I intend to love you."

When she complied, Nicholas partially lowered to one knee, placing one hand firmly against the small of her back. First nuzzling her breasts, he continued exploring her ivory flesh with his mouth. Making small circular patterns with his tongue, Nicholas heard her whimper, but he was just beginning this adventure.

Hands firmly holding her rounded buttocks, pulling her body toward his waiting mouth, his tongue sought her moist center.

Morgan could only see the top of his head moving to and fro, playing with her body. The sensations, as always, were exquisite, but Morgan almost exploded when his hand gently urged her thighs apart and inserted one finger into her center, joining it with his tongue.

Looking up, Nicholas saw her eyes closed in ecstasy, her tongue gliding over parched lips. He smiled. She was ready for him, and he would make her remember this and every night they were joined together.

When his hand left her weak with passion, Morgan did not think she could stand it any longer. Apparently, Nicholas knew that too, for in one quick movement she was lifted into his arms as his mouth again claimed the ripe lips.

"Taste yourself, Morgan," he ordered, easing his tongue

deep into her waiting mouth. "You are sweet everywhere."

Arms enclosed her neck. Morgan wanted to remain locked in his embrace forever.

Refusing to let go of her mouth, Nicholas stood a few moments longer with the voluptuous body in his embrace. Slowly, he walked over to their bed lowering their bodies onto the soft mattress.

She was staring up at him, her eyes feverishly glazed with passion. Knowing exactly what was going to happen, her desire was fueled to greater heights. She could never have enough of this man with the quicksilver eyes.

"I want to feel you too," she moaned, repeating the phrase until the request was granted.

Moving out of his arms, Morgan leaned on her knees, facing him. Tossing the hair out of her eyes, she throatily laughed when Nicholas's eyes widened in anticipation.

One delicate hand settled on his stomach, seeking then feeling the length of his hardness. Her mouth closed over him, enjoying the thrills she was creating. This night would be memorable for him too.

"Ah Morgan. You don't need any more lessons."

"I wasn't asking for any."

In one smooth movement, Nicholas pulled Morgan underneath him. Looking down at her sultry eyes, he knew she was ready for more rapture.

Silver eyes riveted on her, Nicholas inserted his thigh between her legs, nudging them apart. Force was not necessary, for Morgan easily complied with his body's commands.

"You are so beautiful," he whispered, seconds before his mouth sought hers.

Lost in his deep kiss, Morgan barely felt him settling above her, lightly touching her with the tip of his manhood. There was no resistance. Morgan's liquid body beckoned him to enter, to fill her with his maleness.

"Am I hurting you?" he paused upon hearing a loud groan.

"Never, darling." Her arms pulled his head back down on her mouth. They moved as one, as smoothly as a bird gliding on a spring breeze. Turning onto their sides, Nicholas's hands stroked her back, pushing their bodies closer until they were one. Their heartbeats mingled while their sighs of sublime pleasure harmonized.

Unable to part from one another, Morgan rested her head against his shoulder. The golden eyes were still closed, but a tiny smile tugged at the corners of her mouth.

Seeing her so content, Nicholas kissed her forehead. Together they fell asleep, locked in a lover's powerful embrace.

Chapter 19

NEW YORK—FEBRUARY, 1809

The *Anastasia* proudly sailed into New York Harbor on a late winter night. The starless sky was near black and the cold air was filled with the threat of snow. The city had already been blanketed with six inches.

Nicholas could not have planned a better moment to arrive. The docks were almost deserted. Only the cargo agent, Ben Camden, and his crew were there to greet the ship and its captain, before swiftly unloading the cargo. The lucrative cargo would be brought farther up South Street to a warehouse.

"If the cargo is half as good as your letter indicated, I'd wager that the whole lot will be sold off before noon tomorrow," Ben commented, his eyes aglow with dollar signs.

"You should have commitments for more than half of the cargo by now," the captain stated.

"Absolutely right, Captain Rhodes. Sailing that ship into New York was a daring move on your part. The patrols were here only two nights ago. I was sure you would be caught. But you have the luck with you, my boy." He affectionately slapped the captain's back. "And I'm glad to be a part of it."

Morgan nervously paced across the cabin floor. When Nick returned, they would go to his town house on Greenwich Street. What would happen after that, she could only guess. Nicholas already informed her that he would not notify the elder Rhodeses of their arrival, not for another day. The time, he hoped, would give Morgan a chance to become acclimated to the new environment.

"Believe me, Morgan, once I introduce you to my family, I'll be thankful if we ever have five minutes alone."

Of course Nicholas neglected to mention the real reason for postponing the meeting: He was going to tell his father Morgan's true identity. Then he would tell his parents that he married her. Knowing now how much Morgan meant to him, Nicholas would not stand for his father rejecting her. If it meant cutting off his ties with his father, he was willing to do that. Hopefully, his mother would prove to be far more understanding. In time, Warren Rhodes would relent, or else lose the affection of his younger son.

"Morgan, are you ready?" he called down the stairway. "The coach is waiting for us."

Opening the cabin door, Nicholas saw Morgan standing in front of their bed. "I shall have fond memories of that bed," he announced. "I hope you will too. But let's not dawdle. Come on. It's time to go to your new home."

Her portmanteau was carefully packed and sitting on the floor. Morgan was dressed in dark blue, with the sable cloak already around her shoulders.

"You'll blend into the night, my beauty. No one could find you in those colors."

"I have no intention of being the woman who turns in the infamous smuggler Nicholas Rhodes. I've grown accustomed to sharing a room with you." She took one look at him and exclaimed, "You can't go like that! Why Nick, you're dirty and I'll wager that underneath that sweater you are perspiring from all the work you've been doing."

"Please don't worry about me." He reached for his sailor's jacket. "Will this make me more presentable, madam?" She nodded. "Good," he took her arm, "I'll have our trunks delivered tomorrow."

The ride to Greenwich Street took longer than anticipated. The snowy paths made driving hazardous.

"The settled area in New York is not that large. Actually, our home is almost considered the boundary of the fashionably habitable area. But that won't last long. Each year, new people arrive, more space is required, and the boundaries keep pushing further north."

"You like New York, don't you?"

"I even attended college here. Except for my years at sea or the time in Halifax, New York has been my home. I was born in the same grand house my parents still live in. I think you will find it interesting."

"But I hope we will not stay too long. Not this time," she turned to face him. Nicholas could not see her face in the darkened coach, but assumed that her expectant eyes were focused on him.

"Yes, of course, my love. I give you my word as a gentleman. In fact, tomorrow, I shall see if we have any messages from your friend George Taggart. In any case, I shall begin my own investigation."

"Good," she breathed easier, believing his promise.

The coach pulled in front of a red brick three-storied town house. There were kerosene lanterns on the sides of the red doorway. Five other homes were on the same street.

Lighting the lanterns, Nicholas turned to collect his wife. "I hope you will like it."

"Oh, I will Nick. It looks very much like the homes in Boston, not the red door though."

"I wanted to add a nice touch."

Finding the keys, Nicholas opened the front door. "Wait here a moment."

She stood in front of the door while Nicholas went inside, apparently to ascertain that nothing was amiss. Returning a few minutes later, he said, "Everything appears to be in order."

Inside, Morgan immediately noticed the curved, carpeted staircase ahead of her that led to the second floor. On the left side of the foyer was his library, the dining room on the right, and a smaller room behind the stairwell.

"The kitchen is behind the dining room. It's connected; I added that last year. If I hated going outside in the cold for a meal, how could I ask the servants to do it?"

Holding a lit candelabrum to guide them, he proudly showed

her about the lower floor.

Morgan was impressed with the wealthy surroundings.

"Nick, where did you get all this beautiful furniture? I didn't know you collected paintings," she exclaimed, immediately recognizing the lovely oils along the panelled library walls.

"Tomorrow, you shall have the complete tour. We'll need to hire a cook and housekeeper. I'll have some people sent over for you to interview. If you think we'll need more help, I'll take care of that too," his voice held the unmistakable air of authority.

Maintaining a steady stream of conversation, Nicholas led her up the narrow staircase. "The parlor is over there," he pointed to the left. "Our bedroom suite is behind you. In front is another bedroom. Over there," he pointed to a dark corner, "is the stairwell to the third floor."

In the dim light, it was difficult to see the colors of the papered walls. "I cannot wait to explore this house."

"You'll have most of tomorrow alone, I'm afraid. I'll have business to attend to. And you'll have to be here to interview the servants."

Circling the landing, Nicholas again asked her to wait outside the bedroom while he examined the general appearance.

"No problem. It's just that all the furniture is covered with those damn white sheets. I have no idea about the condition of the bedding."

After one look, she did.

"Where are the clean linens kept?"

"Over here," he pointed to a cedar chest. "That bad, huh?"

"I wish the light were even more dim," she wryly said. "When was the last time you slept in this bed?"

"I, uh," he scratched his head, "I can't recall."

"I thought so. Well," she removed her cloak, carefully placing it over a chair, "let's have some more light and then you can help me."

"Sweetheart, it's after two A.M."

"Nick, you don't think I'd sleep in a filthy bed, do you?"

"My, my. I did not know I married royalty," he said, but he

was smiling. "I suppose my bachelor ways need some mending."

"Overhauling is more likely."

An hour later, Morgan felt the room was habitable for at least this night.

Nicholas woke her early the next monring to announce his departure.

"I made your breakfast. Not quite up to Agatha's standard, but it will do. I left the tray on the table over there. I'll be back around three o'clock. Morgan? Do you hear me?"

"Hmmm?" she turned her head to the sound of his voice, but could not open her eyes.

"Morgan, I said I'm leaving now," he gently shook her shoulder.

"All right. I hear you," she half moaned. "I'm getting up. Later."

By ten o'clock she was up, exploring the house. It was obvious that it had not been lived in for months. The dust was everywhere, under and over the white sheets. Sneezing a few times, Morgan decided that she had to begin somewhere and the bedroom was the most logical choice.

It really was quite a lovely room. Tall windows faced the front of the tree-lined street. If the windows were clean, the room would be bathed in bright afternoon sunlight. The dark mahogany furniture was definitely a late eighteenth-century design. Included were two large armchairs covered with the same blue and white damask material as the curtains, and a deep burgundy velvet chaise lounge that was the exact duplicate of the lounge in their Halifax bedroom.

"He probably made a good bargain for the two," she said aloud.

Alongside the chaise was a small, round wooden table with a brass lantern for easy reading. Two large mahogany highboy dressers, one of which she would immediately appropriate for her clothing, were against a long wall. A large gilt-edged cheval mirror stood off to the side, near the fireplace. There were what appeared to be two dressing rooms, but upon closer inspection one served a completely different purpose; it was a washroom. A large porcelain tub with a small stove nearby took

223

up most of the space. The rest of the small area contained a washstand and a shelf for towels.

All in all, Morgan realized that the bedsuite had almost everything. Yet the room needed a little more color. She intended to add a dressing table and mirror for herself, and some lace . . . something she would tend to quickly.

After reviewing the downstairs rooms, Morgan decided she was pleased with this town house. Suddenly, an insistent knocking on the red door attracted her attention.

Rushing to the entrance, Morgan peered out of the tiny window panel alongside the door to see who was calling. A middle-aged woman and a much younger one patiently stood outside.

Upon greeting them, Morgan learned that the women— mother and daughter—were sent by Nicholas.

"I've known your husband a long time, madam. I used to work for Jonathan Rhodes. My name is Mary Carlton and this is my daughter, Betty. We'll work hard for you, Mrs. Rhodes," the elder woman said. Both had the same shade of dark red hair and were of identical height—taller than Morgan.

"Seems to me your husband hasn't spent much time here. But Betty and I can clean it in no time. I'm the cook, she's the housekeeper. You won't be needing anyone else as long as you have us."

"Mrs. Carlton, if you can help straighten up the first floor before my husband comes home, the job is yours." Morgan smiled at the woman. She did not feel the same friendly warmth she had felt at her first meeting with Agatha Gleason, but Mary and Betty Carlton appeared to be efficient.

Feeling completely idle, Morgan returned to the upstairs bedroom, doing the best she could with it. Finally satisfied, she returned to the first floor to discover that the Carltons were almost finished.

"You work well together, and so fast. I'd be delighted to have you work for us."

"I knew you would, Mrs. Rhodes," Mary attempted to smile. "Now if it's all right with you, my daughter and I would prefer to come in each day, early. Our little house is not too far away, on Morton Street. I promise we'll stay late in the

224

evening, if you need us."

"That's fine with me," Morgan said, deciding this would be a very satisfactory arrangement. She and Nick could have their evenings alone. "I am sure my husband will agree."

"The captain is a fine man," Betty spoke for the first time. The girl seemed painfully shy.

"I think we should investigate the kitchen," Morgan suggested.

"No need. Betty and I did while you were upstairs. It's in excellent condition and the captain told me that the food is on its way."

Minutes later, a wagonload of supplies and food were hauled around the back of the house. The three women unloaded the foodstuff. Their conversation was sparse but informative.

Mary Carlton was a widow. Betty was the youngest daughter still living with her. Although both women were quiet-spoken and not prone to gossip, Morgan was able to find out a little about the mysterious Rhodes family.

They were known to be quite wealthy, something she already suspected. Some of the money was inherited, but Warren Rhodes made the rest of his fortune through his lucrative law practice and various business interests. They were a highly respected family, considered to be among the most socially prominent. Christine Rhodes was supposed to be a beautiful woman who appeared unaffected by her wealth and social status. Her husband was concerned with money and respectability, and he too was still considered a handsome man.

As for Jonathan and his wife, Mary said very little . . . except that Jonathan tried very hard to win his father's respect.

"They're very nice people—all of them. I am sure you will be warmly received," Mary tried to smile again.

Thankfully, Morgan remained unaware of her husband's activities. After going to the South Street Wharf, Nicholas visited the warehouse. Since most of the cargo had potential buyers, Nicholas penned brief notes to these merchants, informing them of the *Anastasia*'s arrival and the date the cargo was to be sold. Hopefully, the warehouse would be emptied of the cargo within a few weeks. As for the rest of the cargo, a discreet word here and there would take care of that. His cargo was too desirable to remain unsold for very long. No, Nicholas was not concerned about his smuggled goods.

What did concern him was the late afternoon unannounced visit to his parents' house on Broadway, near Bowling Green. The house, as well as the area surrounding it, was considered the most elegant and expensive in all of New York.

It was a large mansion of yellow brick and brownstone, with yellow shutters on each of the many windows. The house was three stories plus an attic, above which was a tiled and slightly sloping roof, encircled by two rows of balustrades. The main entrance boasted a massive portico with fluted columns.

Nicholas was born here, and loved this old house with the same sense of attachment a child has to his first toy. Yet as soon as he strode up to the white picket fence, he knew that something was wrong.

The massive front door was ajar. This was most unusual. Either word had reached Warren that his son was home, or something odd was happening. Nicholas always trusted his instincts; the hair bristled on his neck.

Charging into the house, Nicholas was further surprised to see no one in the hallway, the spacious drawing rooms on each side of the wide mahogany staircase, or the library, the doors to which were wide open. The library looked unusually neat. Ordinarily Warren spread his files and other paperwork across the oak desk and onto the floor, but the room was immaculate.

Concerned, he wandered to the back of the house, toward the kitchen. At this time of day, his mother usually spent time consulting the cook about dinner. The cook was alone in the big kitchen.

"Oh it is sure good to see you, Captain Rhodes," she began to sob, which intensified his concern.

"What is going on here Hattie? Where are my mother and father? Aren't they home?"

The old woman cried into her apron. "So much has happened since you left."

"Tell me, woman." Impatience made his voice seem harsh.

"It's Mr. Rhodes sir, your father. He's had a seizure."

"A what?"

"Hattie, who is here? I thought I heard Nick's . . . Thank God it is you." Christine Rhodes hurried into the room, heading for her son. Only this time her arms were not outstretched in welcome and support. His were. "Oh Nicholas, it is so good to see you home again. We were so worried that you would not make it home in time."

"In time for what, Mother? Tell me exactly what is going on here."

Leading his mother to a chair near the hearth, Nicholas waited for her to be settled before repeating his questions.

Her silver eyes, so much like his, were filled with tears. Her pale blond hair was tightly coiled at the nape of her neck. But her head was bowed, slumped in despair.

"Mother, please. What is wrong? What happened to Father?"

"He had a seizure. It happened one month after you sailed. He had been anxious about something. Then your father received a message from Secretary Albert Gallatin about some stolen currency plates. Your father was angry . . . very angry, Nick. A few days later, he received another message. That evening he had the seizure. I was not sure he'd survive, but," she smiled, her features softening, "you know your father. He wouldn't let go. He fought for weeks. Until," she smiled despite the tear that slid down her cheek, "one day he woke up complaining that there wasn't enough light in the room for him to see his files. After that, the doctor announced he was on the road to recovery."

"How is he now?" he asked, trying to mask his concern.

"He has good days and bad ones. Sometimes I think your father is ready to jump out of bed, dress himself, and leave for his office. But then," she paused, studying her son's face, "there are those times when he's very tired, occasionally forgetful, and not interested in many things. Ah," she brightened, her silver eyes twinkling, "with you home, Nicholas, I think it will make a difference for your father. He'll be so thrilled to see you."

Nicholas let go of her hand, rising out of the wooden chair. His head was a few inches lower than the wood-beamed ceiling.

Christine proudly smiled at her handsome son, but quickly noted that he was not smiling. In fact, he seemed preoccupied as he paced across the floor.

"Hattie dear, would you excuse us?"

The cook graciously complied with the request, leaving Christine and Nicholas alone in the kitchen. The sounds of meat slowly roasting over a metal spit, the simmering soup, the ticking of the wall clock, all seemed loud to Nicholas.

"Nick, what is wrong?"

He turned to face her, unsure of what he could or should say about the major change in his life.

"Mother, so much has happened since I left New York—to you, Father, and to me."

"Were you arrested?" she suspiciously inquired.

"No," he smiled, "but I suppose you could say I am serving a sentence. That's not true," he quickly amended, "my sense of humor is not what it used to be."

"Will you please tell me what is wrong?" She began to rise, but Nicholas motioned to remain seated.

"I will. In a minute. Tell me something first, Mother. How are Jonathan and Sally?"

"They're fine. They've been very kind and of great assistance to me throughout this ordeal."

Still the same, he told himself. "And Uncle Eric, has he arrived?"

"No, but I did send him letters, as I did to you. I have no idea if Eric ever received them."

"I didn't receive any letters. Perhaps you should send another letter."

"I did. Two weeks ago. I'd like him to be here, although it's not as critical as it was last month. Nick," she stiffened her spine, smoothing the dark green brocade dress, "stop avoiding my question. What is wrong?"

"Everything and nothing."

"Nicholas. Please."

"Do you have any sherry in here?"

"Yes, in that cupboard to your left. On the top shelf."

"Hattie is still keeping it for medicinal purposes?" he smiled, an expression so like his mother's.

228

"Yes. She says it's better than any other medicine for her rheumatism."

Helping himself to a large glass, Nicholas drank all of it in one large gulp. After pouring another, he returned to the oak kitchen table to sit next to his mother.

"Mother, did you know congratulations are in order?"

"They are?" she was perplexed. "For what, dear?"

"I was married in Nova Scotia."

The words were softly spoken but to Christine they sounded like cannon fire. "Nick, this is not the time for your pranks."

"It's not. I assure you I was married in Halifax. Morgan has the paper to prove it."

"Morgan?"

"Yes," he took another swallow, "this gets much more difficult. You see, Mother, I came to New York to bring my wife to my home, to introduce her to my family, and to help her find her father's murderer."

"No, it cannot be that family."

Nicholas swirled the red liquid in the glass. "Father told you everything?"

She nodded.

"Even my promise to him?"

Again she nodded, adding, "He was so pleased that you agreed to help him find those currency plates and the girl. He thought it was the beginning of a closer relationship with you. You married her?" Christine wished she had heard him incorrectly.

"She's an incredible young woman. I married her for many reasons. Most important, though, is that I love her." He looked into Christine's troubled gaze. "I've hurt her very much. I cannot hurt her again."

"Tell me everything, Nicholas. I need to understand. Please, give me a sherry too, dear. I know I will need it."

"You will."

When he finished the long story, Christine Rhodes did not know that crystal tears were sliding down her cheeks.

"How dreadful for her—and for you. I am so sorry about the baby."

"Morgan is finally free of the nightmares, Mother. She is

229

looking forward, albeit with some trepidation, to meeting all of you. She is also anxious to begin the search for the real murderer. And together, we will find those currency plates."

"There is no doubt in your mind . . ."

"None, Mother," he cut in, anticipating her words. "I tell you—and you will know once you meet her—Morgan and, more importantly, Samuel Rhinehart are innocent. I was hoping to explain all of this to Father. I didn't want Morgan to know anything about my promise to him. Mother," he looked more troubled than Christine had seen in a long time, "it would break her heart. I can't do this to her. Not now." Nicholas's hands framed his face.

"What about your father's heart?"

He lifted one questioning eyebrow, unsure of what she was going to say next.

"Nick, dear. I don't think it is wise to tell your father the truth. I don't know what the shock would do to him. It could . . . it could kill him. Do you want to bear that burden?"

"Of course not! But what do you expect me to tell my wife? That I cannot introduce her as my wife because of my father's health? And," he impatiently rummaged fingers through his hair, "how do you expect me to explain her presence in my home. Our home?"

"I hadn't thought of that," her voice lowered. "But I am sure we can come up with something."

"Mother, I will not hurt her. I told you that. I will explain the situation to Morgan. If she is willing to go along with whatever plans you hatch, I will too. But I am leaving it up to her. However," he looked directly into her concerned face, "if Morgan wants to leave New York, I am going with her."

"Nick, let me meet her. I am confident that she is everything you say and more. I'm sure she will do what's right."

"Why don't you come to our house tomorrow for tea?"

"Fine. Now, would you like to make your father a happy man by visiting his room?"

Together they walked up the long, curved staircase to the second floor. His father's suite of rooms was on the north side of the house.

Whenever Nicholas was about to see his father, it became

230

slightly difficult to swallow, and his hands felt clammy. This time was no different. Taking a deep breath, he smoothed his unruly hair, then waited for his mother's signal to join them.

"Warren," he heard her say, "I have a wonderful surprise for you."

"I doubt it, Christine." The voice was still deep and tinged with paternal authority. "Not unless you're going to tell me that the young rascal has finally come home."

"I am and he is. Nicholas," she called, "make a believer out of your father."

Boldly walking into the well-lit room, Nicholas tried to hide his shock. Warren looked ten years older than his fifty-four years, much thinner than the last time Nicholas had seen him, and his hair was completely white. Spectacles were perched on his straight nose, a newspaper lay open on his lap. He was wearing a heavy cotton nightshirt with an elegant blue silk robe over it. Warren looked old. The seizure had sapped his usual boundless strength.

"My son," he stretched out his hand, "how good it is to see you home." He was smiling broadly, genuinely pleased to see his errant offspring. Nicholas noticed the slight tremor in his hand.

Grasping the hand, Nicholas said, "I'm glad to be back. In a couple of days, I expect you to be up, in your office, screaming at me for some indiscretion."

"Come closer," Warren softly ordered, pulling Nicholas into his arms. "I've missed you, boy. We've got a lot to discuss."

"We will." For one brief minute, Nicholas allowed Warren to hold him. How could he deny the feelings of love and sympathy from this prideful man? His once robust father was only a shell of his former self. Looking up at his mother, Nicholas understood her sorrowful expression. She too wanted to bring back the whole man, the one who was healthy and so excitable.

"Sit over there, Nick. I want to hear about your trip. Not about your smuggling—you know very well what I think about that—but about the other matter. Did you learn anything about the missing currency plates and Rhinehart's daughter?"

Slumping into the cushioned armchair near the window,

Nicholas allowed the despair to wash over him. He could tell Warren the whole truth—and watch his father sicken again—or he could indulge the wishes of his mother and not tell the truth. Biding time might be valuable to Warren, but detrimental to Morgan and himself.

Well before the words came out, Nicholas had chosen the path of deception.

"I've learned some things, Father. I met Miss Rhinehart. She is not what you think. She is rather young, very beautiful, and quite nice. In fact . . ."

"Rubbish! It was just an act, boy. You must know that."

"No, I don't think so. I met her family. Her uncle is a wealthy Bostonian businessman, you know. They have a very different story to tell. But one thing I do know is that Miss Rhinehart is as anxious to find the stolen plates as we are."

"I am sure she is," Warren snorted, tossing the paper aside. "She wants to sell them to the French! Or the British!"

"Father," he tried to sound patient, but this interview was more difficult than anticipated, "perhaps I can arrange for you to meet her."

"No! Absolutely not! It's bad enough my son is involved in illegal activity. But no, never will I make the acquaintance of a traitor!"

"Warren, darling." Christine decided it was time to cut in. "I think you are getting too excited over this ridiculous matter."

"Ridiculous, huh? Did you know, Christine, that another set of currency plates were stolen? You didn't either, Nick? How could you, gallivanting on the high seas? Well, it's true. Remember the messages I received from Albert Gallatin? The currency plates from the U.S. Bank in Boston were stolen. Less than six weeks ago. Did you not say the lady was in Boston, with her—ahem—family?"

"But that cannot be Morgan. I know."

"How the hell do you know? Was she with you wherever you sailed?"

"Well, if you must know . . ." he began, forgetting everything but the need to vindicate his wife.

"Nicholas!" Christine scolded. "I think this conversation

has gone far enough. You can discuss this again with your father when he is much calmer. And not now!"

"I tell you, I have a feeling about this one, Nick. I know. Find Miss Morgan Rhinehart and you've found the plates and the leader of this group of traitors."

Christine shot her son a warning look. Settling back into the chair and crossing his booted legs in an effort to appear nonchalant, Nicholas concentrated on the scene outside the curtained windows, hoping it would calm his jumbled nerves. "All right. We'll resume this delightful conversation another time. I must leave soon. I have my own business to attend to."

"Join us for dinner, son." Warren appeared calm once more. "I feel strong enough to join you all at the dinner table. Jon will be here too."

"Not tonight, Father. Perhaps tomorrow. I'll let Mother know. Now," he rose, "I think I should take my leave. I've caused enough excitement for one day."

Chapter 20

The short ride to the Greenwich Street town house did not clear Nicholas's mind. He had no idea what to tell Morgan. The all-too-familiar feeling of being torn between his loyalty to family and the woman he loved created inner turmoil.

Could he dare risk being the cause of his father's fatal seizure? Could he live with himself if that happened? Who was being selfish? Nicholas, for wanting to live a peaceful life with Morgan? Or his family, for wanting to remain together?

"God, this is awful," he muttered aloud.

It was late in the afternoon. Certainly Morgan would be waiting, thinking that she would be meeting the Rhodes family at dinner. The horse slowed in front of the brick town house.

Dreading what must be done, yet knowing there was no alternative, Nicholas jumped off the animal, secured the reins, then deliberately strode up the steps. The door was unlocked. Unbuttoning his sea jacket, he neatly hung it on the brass rack.

"Morgan? Where are you?" he called, checking the two rooms closest to him. The sheets were off the furniture, the rooms were spotless. She must have worked most of the day getting the house in order, he realized. "Morgan?" he called again, running up the stairs. hoping to find her alone.

He found her soaking in the large porcelain tub, lavender-scented bubbles covering all but her shoulders and neck. The long black hair was piled haphazardly on top of her head. She was humming one of his sea ditties.

"What a delicious picture you make."

His deep voice startled her, causing some of the bubbles to spill over the sides of the tub. It also gave Nicholas a clear view of her round, upturned breasts.

"Can't you ever enter a room after you've knocked?"

"I did. But you were so busy humming the verse about the sailor and the tavern wench." He was leaning against the doorjamb, silver eyes devouring every exposed inch of her.

"Nick," she warned, "there isn't time. Not if you want me to be dressed and ready for your parents this evening."

The amused expression immediately disappeared. Nick unfolded his arms, cleared his throat more than once, then clamped his mouth shut.

"Captain Rhodes. I know you are trying to tell me something and you are not doing a very effective job. What is it?"

"Would you like me to scrub your back?"

Never one to turn down an opportunity, Morgan smiled, "I'd love it. But it won't make me forget that you are hiding something."

Pushing the sweater sleeves high above his elbows, Nicholas bent beside the tub, taking the sponge from her hand.

"Some day you will do this for me," he gently stroked her slender back.

"I have, as you well know. But I will gladly do it again and again. Always with pleasure," she smiled into his eyes.

"Tell me about your day, dear wife. Did you like the Carlton ladies?"

"They are perfect for us," she replied before happily chatting about her day in their house. "It's such a lovely house, Nick. I only need to make a few changes."

"Hmmm," his hand lowered to her waist. "Do you want to remain in New York?"

The question surprised her. "Yes, if you do. Besides, you thought we would find much more information about Andrews here than in any other city."

"I did say that, didn't I?"

"Nicholas!" she moved away, leaving him sponging the air. "You are acting so strangely. Now either you tell me what is wrong, or so help me, I will splash you."

Throwing his head back, Nicholas laughed loudly. "What a

236

terrible threat, my love. I think you better get out of the tub before I lose track of everything I want to say."

She did, and he sucked in his breath at the glistening body before him. Morgan was a vision of perfection. Now, if only she could be happy with him.

"You tempt me, woman."

"I know," she seductively lowered her lashes, parting her ripe lips for a kiss.

"I will only give you one kiss, then I want you to dry yourself and join me inside. Wear my bathrobe; it hides more of that luscious body. I'll stoke the fire."

Morgan's wet, lavender-scented body rubbed against his scratchy wool sweater.

"You smell good, Captain. Like the sea air."

"And you, my tempting sea nymph, smell like a spring garden in full bloom." His lips found hers, taking what was so generously offered.

"Would you like to tell me now?"

"Is that why you kissed me like a wanton?" he looked into her laughing gold eyes. In one quick motion, she was lifted out of the tub into his woolen embrace.

"Nick, it itches."

"You should have thought of that before you teased me with your delectable body," he nuzzled her neck, enjoying the spontaneous reaction to him. Morgan was a rare treasure that enraptured him.

"Here," he grabbed a white fluffy towel. "I'll dry you."

"If you do, you will never get to tell me what is plaguing you. Put me down by the fireplace and I'll dry myself."

"What a bossy woman you've become, Mrs. Rhodes." Yet he did as she bid, realizing that the ensuing conversation could no longer be put off. Better to tell her now and get it over with. Hopefully, she would not remain angry and would reach a decision with him.

When Morgan was sufficiently wrapped in his robe and seated by the fireplace, Nicholas stood in front of her. Leaning against the white marble, one arm propped on the mantle, he hesitantly began. "My father is very ill, Morgan. He had a seizure."

"That's terrible!" she gasped. "Is there anything we can do?"

"Don't get up Morgan. I have a lot more to tell you."

"Shouldn't we go there?"

"No. Not yet. You see I had a very long conversation with my mother. I told her everything about us. She is quite delighted and is looking forward to meeting you. However . . ."

"What?"

"She asked us to consider my father's fragile health. You know how politically involved he was—I mean is. Before his seizure he had received a letter from Secretary of the Treasury, Albert Gallatin. Another set of currency plates were stolen, Morgan. From the U.S. Bank in, of all places, Boston."

"I don't believe it! Boston? We could have been there. Oh this is dreadful." Suddenly, she brightened, "But surely you see it proves my father was innocent. Don't you see Nick?" A mixture of emotions chased across her lovely, expectant face.

"I do, love. But my father knows nothing about the Morgan Rhinehart I married. What he knew was what most people considered to be the truth: that your father was guilty. Remember Morgan, we have to prove his innocence now. People who knew or read about your father's arrest and trial discounted your father's testimony regarding Andrews."

"Particularly your father? Is that what you are trying to tell me? Why, Nick," she implored, "why did you wait until I gave up everything to come to New York with you to tell me this?"

"I don't know. It wasn't important to me at the time. I suppose I forgot." It was a blatant lie that sickened him.

"You forgot? That's preposterous! You are not one to forget details, Nicholas. Particularly about your father's willingness to accept me or our marriage."

He could not face her penetrating glare. Instead, Nicholas presented his back as he suddenly found it necessary to stoke the still-blazing fire. "Morgan, I did not think this would happen. I had every intention of explaining the issues to both of my parents, not just my mother. He is ill. Am I supposed to barge in on him, tell him I don't give a damn about his

238

misguided notion or his health? How much should I be responsible for, Morgan? His death?"

"No, but . . ."

"But what? What would you do? What would you say to your mother if she begged you to wait a little longer?"

Morgan stared into the orange fire, searching for the right answer. "I don't know. I suppose the same thing," her voice dropped. "I don't know."

"I am torn, sweetheart," he kneeled in front of her, a troubled expression marring his handsome face. "I cannot be responsible for that kind of grief. I have caused enough trouble over the years." Nicholas took her left hand. "I also know, Morgan, that you are my wife, that I will do anything for you. If you want to leave New York, we will go together. I shall not abandon you."

"I believe you. You have to stay here in New York." At his sharp glance, she amended, "We will stay in New York."

"Are you certain?"

"No. But I will not change my mind. It has to be. Just as we both know what our nondeclaration of marriage will mean." Morgan leaned into the blue and white sofa.

"I can't do that to you or to me, love."

"What? As an 'unmarried' woman I cannot be living in the same house as you. Can I? Or," she tried to lift her lips in a smile, "are you trying to tell me that you cannot live without me?"

"Both. But I really mean the latter."

"And what do you propose?"

"Dammit!" He rose, slamming one hand against the marble mantle. "I've run out of ideas and schemes. I want to live with you openly—as your legally wedded husband." Those last words suddenly reminded Nicholas of Peter's warning to marry again in New York. This was definitely not the time to tell Morgan about that. What a mess he was in! And he saw no way out of it without hurting some or all of the people he most deeply cared about.

"Nick. I cannot live here with you."

"I know." His head fell against his forearms. "But you will not leave this house. I will go. I'll stay with my family. That, or

239

rent rooms at the City Hotel."

"Not tonight, Nick." She stood behind him now, arms folded around the front of his lean waist. "We have this last night together."

Spinning her around, Nicholas tenderly gazed into the trusting golden eyes. With one hand fondling the back of her neck, he slowly lowered his mouth to hers. The long, sensuous kiss inflamed their bodies and minds. In a moment, Morgan was abruptly swept into his arms. Nicholas reached for her hairpins, glorying in the sensation of the long raven curls swirling over them.

Lowering her onto the large bed, Nicholas undid the robe's sash. Hands reached inside the thick material, sensuously roaming up then down the tantalizing body that was waiting for more.

They loved one another many times through that dark, cold night, knowing that their days ahead would be similarly dark and cold.

Late the following afternoon, Christine Rhodes called upon her son and daughter-in-law.

She was the most beautiful woman Morgan had ever seen. And why not? Nicholas obviously favored his mother. All morning worry had been gnawing at Morgan. What would this woman think of her? Would she think that Morgan was not suitable for her son? Would she want Morgan to leave New York—alone?

The petite blond-haired woman removed her gloves while climbing the steps to the town house. Anticipating the soft knock, Morgan opened the door. The knots in her stomach were making it difficult to stand straight.

"Hello Mrs. Rhodes. I am . . ."

"I know." Her voice was pleasant. "It is I who should say hello Mrs. Rhodes," she smiled.

"Please come in. I have been looking forward to meeting you."

"As I you. Now, may I congratulate you?" she kissed Morgan's flushed cheek. "I want to welcome you into the

240

family. Nick has wonderful taste. I am only sorry you could not have some family at your wedding."

Christine removed her hat, placing it on the marble table beside the red door.

"Mother." Nicholas cheerfully called, running down the stairs. "Aren't you early?"

"Well," she laughed self-consciously, "I could not wait to meet my daughter-in-law."

They walked into the library, the two women strolling arm in arm behind Nicholas.

"Mary will be in shortly with tea and cakes." Morgan sat on the leather sofa beside her husband.

"Thank you, dear." Christine was perfectly dressed in a turquoise brocade dress and matching jacket. Silver eyes shining with friendship, she said, "Tell me about yourself, Morgan. I heard you have an adorable sister."

They amiably chatted for an hour. Christine could not help but notice that Nicholas did not let go of Morgan's hand. Finally, she brought up the subject they had all been dreading.

"I've agonized over this situation last night, Morgan. I would not make such a difficult request if I did not believe my husband's life depended upon it. I am terribly sorry, my dear."

"Morgan and I have discussed this, Mother. We are willing to pretend—for Father's sake only—that we are not married. But," he leaned forward, "not for long, Mother. We will go along with this for a few weeks. I want to give Father time to meet Morgan, to get to know her. However, as I've told you both, I will not see Morgan hurt." Two matching pairs of silver eyes stared at one another.

"I understand. And I deeply appreciate what you are going to do. I have a plan, if you'd both like to hear it:

"You see, I think Morgan should stay with us." Christine hurried on, amused by their surprised expressions. "We can tell people part of the truth; that Morgan sailed with you from Halifax at the request of her brother—your partner, Peter Mackenzie. She's in New York to visit relatives and seek some minor medical treatment. After all, if the political conditions among France, England, and our country are as difficult as you and your father have said, this might be Morgan's last chance to visit her family in the United States."

Morgan looked at Nick. "Well, it might work."

"Sounds plausible," he added. "But Morgan will have to use another name. Maryann Richards . . . uh no," he chuckled, "Mackenzie. Peter will be honored, my love."

"I promise that this situation will not last long. Warren needs a little more time. And with a beautiful young woman under his roof, his recovery may be more rapid than we anticipated. I've already informed him that I will not tolerate any more political conversations, particularly about missing currency plates."

"I intend to court Miss Mackenzie."

"I may not permit it," Morgan laughed. It was going to be a difficult, strenuous few weeks, but at least Christine Rhodes would certainly make her feel welcome in their home.

"I have the perfect room for you, my dear. It's on the same floor as Nick's old room."

Caught in a situation in which she was giving up voluntary control, Morgan felt as if her life were sliding down into a whirlpool where free will was submerged by the force of sheer momentum. Nicholas must have felt the same way too, but it was harder for Morgan who was a stranger in an unfamiliar city. Since her marriage in November, she had yet to find a place to call home.

It was decided that Morgan would join the Rhodes family early the next day. There was no point in prolonging their inevitable separation. Their last evening alone was filled with little conversation and bittersweet thoughts. Like the final golden sunset of an autumn day, Nicholas studied Morgan's moves as she prepared for bed. He counted the number of brush strokes, admiring the way she quickly and efficiently plaited her hair. Although Morgan sat in front of the cheval glass, Nicholas was positive that she did not really see herself. Her movements were mechanical, but he would miss this nightly ritual.

When she came to bed, Nicholas opened his arms. They did not make love this night. They just slept wrapped in each other's arms.

"I am staying there tonight," he announced the next

242

morning at the last breakfast they would share in this house.

Morgan openly admired her husband. His unknowing charm and casual grace continuously amazed her and never failed to make her fall a little more in love with him. Wearing black leather breeches and boots, an open-necked red and black checkered wool shirt with full sleeves, Nicholas reminded her again of a country gentleman. He was standing by the sideboard, loading his plate with food, unaware that Morgan was staring at his backside.

He suddenly turned, "What did you say love?"

"I didn't say anything. I only sighed. Very loudly, I suppose."

He sat beside her, settling long legs underneath the table. "I am going to be very lonely without you. I mean that Morgan," he earnestly said. "And as I already told you, I plan on staying in my parents' home more often than I'd like, but I'll do anything to be near you."

"Ha! If I am going to fit the image of the perfect little houseguest, I don't think you should visit my room too often."

"Your assumption is totally incorrect. I'll be in your room. And you had better be there waiting for me," he half seriously threatened.

"We will see," she sweetly smiled, making his heart beat erratically.

"Come on, woman. It's time for you to make me an eligible bachelor again. I'll have your trunk delivered tomorrow. Have you packed your portmanteau?"

"Yes, of course. I put some clothes in last night. And my more treasured momentos," she smiled demurely, "like our marriage license, letters from my mother, and your—no my—blue silk shirt. Nick? Do I have to remove my ring?" her face lost all traces of humor.

"Not if you don't want to."

"Good. I don't. Let people think what they want."

"I'm glad," he reached over to touch her left hand.

It seemed as if the entire Rhodes household—servants and family—were waiting for their arrival. A kindly looking elderly butler opened the wide double doors for the handsome couple. Nick protectively held Morgan by the elbow as they were led inside the spacious house.

Morgan was immediately struck by the elegant grandeur of the home. Marble tops covered light wood tables designed and made by the well-known New York cabinetmaker, Duncan Phyfe. Large double doors led to a series of rooms on either side of the long hallway.

"Nick, it is all so lovely and so very intimidating."

"I know. My parents believe in collecting valuable pieces of furniture. The rooms reflect different styles. You'll see for yourself. Personally, I think it overdone," he whispered.

They were escorted into the parlor where Nick's family waited.

"Hello Jon, Sally," Nick's voice was less than friendly as he slightly bowed.

Jonathan quickly rose to greet them. He didn't look anything like Nicholas. Although he was almost as tall, his hair was much darker, his eyes a nondescript blue.

"Nick, good to see you home again," he warmly said, extending one hand. "And this is the lovely Maryann Mackenzie Mother has been raving over." Jonathan turned to her, his eyes crinkling in the corners in amusement and friendship. "Welcome to New York, to the United States. In fact, I am sure you will enjoy your visit. My mother is a marvelous hostess."

This enthusiastically friendly man could not be the same Jonathan Rhodes about whom Nick had spoken of. Why doesn't Nick get along with him? she wondered.

"Jon, it is nice to be back. However, my home is on Greenwich Street, not here." Nick was annoyed.

"You know what I mean brother. You have no sense of humor."

"You think so?" Nick remained standing next to Morgan.

"It is a pleasure to meet you sir," Morgan quickly interjected. "Your brother has told me so much about you."

"Has he really?" Jonathan seemed to brighten. "Please, Miss Mackenzie, may I introduce my wife, Sally? And you must call me Jonathan."

"Call me Mor—Maryann," she dared not look at her husband. Instead her gaze settled on Sally Rhodes, who was now standing beside Jonathan. Sally was petite. Her light brown hair, though neatly combed, would not remain in the tight coil. Long, thin strands escaped down her back. Sally nervously fussed with these hairs, but to no avail. Light brown eyes darted from Jonathan to Christine then settled uncertainly on Morgan.

"It is so nice to meet you," she said, her voice lacking expression. "It will be nice to have a friend."

Sally appeared friendly, but there was something else Morgan had trouble defining. She smiled at the proper time, said the correct words, was perfectly dressed. Then Morgan realized what was missing. There was so little animation in Sally.

"Maryann has relatives in Boston and New York. Her parents insisted she come to this country to meet them in case, well, in case there is any trouble between our countries," Christine pleasantly said.

"Mother, Maryann has marvelous taste in clothing. I . . . that is Peter gave me money to purchase a new wardrobe for her."

"Oh that's not necessary," she turned to Nicholas.

"Not necessary, dear lady. Well you are wrong," he looked into her topaz eyes. "It will be my pleasure."

The look that passed between them was not unnoticed by the occupants of the room.

"We must have a dinner party for Maryann," Christine quickly announced. "We will invite your friends Nick and some of ours."

A bell insistently tinkled near the settee, attracting everyone's attention.

"That's Warren," Christine laughed. "This bell was installed at his insistence. It keeps all of us busy. Actually, it was a good idea."

"It jingles so much these days that you know he's getting well," Jonathan lightly added.

"I know what he wants. He is waiting to meet you, Maryann."

"Oh really? Now?"

"When Father commands . . . Come on, I'll volunteer to take you upstairs," Nick told her.

The walk up the many stairs felt like a long, arduous climb up a steep mountain. Her heart pounding in her ears, Morgan had no idea if her knees could provide adequate support.

"Courage, beauty. I won't let him browbeat you."

Just before they reached the bedroom door Nicholas pulled her into a dark corner, stealing a passionate kiss.

"You're not fair Nick. Not at all fair," she whispered against his mouth.

"Whoever said I was?" he nuzzled her neck. "Ready?"

In the middle of the overly bright room was a massive carved oak-framed bed. The occupant, propped up by three huge pillows, had a tray over his lap. It was not covered with food, but with papers. He had a pair of spectacles on his face—like Morgan's—and wore a pale yellow sweater over his wide chest. Waving a quill pen in one hand, the other held a mug of hot tea.

"I hate tea. Tea is for the sick. I am not sick," he grumbled. Blue eyes looked up at the couple standing in front of the bed. "You are the young woman my wife has been chattering about for the last day? Well, you are as pretty as she says. Do you have a clipped accent like the rest of those damned, oh excuse me, British?"

"Uh, no. I don't have any accent." But I do have a stammer around you, she wanted to add. Instead she said, "Neither does my brother Peter."

"Did you enjoy sailing with this young sea captain? Was he a gentleman?"

"Why yes, yes of course. I was treated very well by the entire crew." She was positive that the words gave a different meaning to her phrase.

"She had my cabin."

"Did she now? Where were you?" Warren did not blink.

Neither did Nicholas as he glared at Warren curtly replying, "With McNeil. Any more questions? Are we still in court? Would you like to know how old Maryann is? Nineteen. If she has had any diseases? If she steals?"

"Well, have you?" Warren switched to Morgan.

She watched Nicholas clench his jaw in suppressed fury. But then Warren smiled, "I am not that nosy, Nick. But I am sure you don't steal, Miss Mackenzie."

Only currency plates. Nicholas wanted to throw the words at Warren, but stifled the urge.

"Sit down Miss Mackenzie," Warren gestured to a cherrywood rocker. "Did you know that you squint? Do you have trouble seeing clearly?"

Morgan nervously tittered, "Why yes, yes I do Mr. Rhodes. In fact, if you would be willing to keep my secret, I will show you something."

Warren leaned forward in curiosity. When she dug into her tiny reticule and withdrew the wire-rimmed spectacles, Warren chuckled.

"Ah hah! I knew I could recognize a fellow sufferer. Things are blurry for you. Don't be ashamed to wear them, my dear. You could ruin your eyesight if you don't wear those things. In fact, if you are more comfortable wearing them when you read to me, then don't be a coward."

"I don't recall your asking Maryann to read to you. Do you Maryann?" Nick tried to hide his irritation.

"Oh, I didn't. I apologize. You have such a lovely voice, and it would be a rare treat if you would read to me." The pale blue eyes looked over the spectacles to whisper conspiratorially, "I don't like Sally's voice. Too plain. She whines, too."

The man might have a gruff exterior, but Morgan was willing to wager that Warren Rhodes had a very kind heart . . . something his son could not see, although Nicholas shared the same trait.

"I would be delighted to read to you, Mr. Rhodes. I do not need the spectacles for reading. My problem is distance."

"She is a very sweet girl, Nick."

"Yes, I know. In a few weeks you will tell me you love her like a daughter. Perhaps I should marry her."

Warren may have been physically ill, even occasionally forgetful, but he could still judge people. His son was very protective of the young woman, and appeared to care for her. A great deal too, he decided.

"You'd better explain that to Margaret Lawson, son. She's

247

been a bit anxious for your arrival. She reads to me too."

Morgan glanced sharply at Nicholas who had the good sense to appear indignant.

"I am not and never have been seriously involved with Miss Lawson. You are quite aware of that. If I told you that Maryann's family is wealthier than Miss Lawson's, would you change your affiliation?"

"Nick, I think we should not discuss this in front of Miss Mackenzie." Warren's voice grew firm. "Perhaps if you will do us the honor of remaining for dinner this evening, you and I might have a chance to chat privately."

"I shall be happy to oblige. Now, can I show Maryann to her room? You will excuse us Father?"

Once in the hallway, Morgan let out a deep breath.

"A bit of a curmudgeon, isn't he?" Nick asked.

"He is not that bad Nick. Used to having his way though. Like his son," she patted his cheek.

"I am not that hardheaded."

"Really darling?"

"Morgan, I don't know if I can go along with this mad scheme of my mother's. It will not work. Sooner or later he will find out who you really are. You are as likely as I am to mistakenly use your real name. Besides, why wouldn't a Haligonian have a clipped accent?" Nicholas spun her about to face his stern expression. "I will not have you hurt."

"How will I be hurt? Nick, that makes no sense to me. I believe it is too late to turn back. We'll see what happens. I don't want to upset your parents. Apparently, you do that for the both of us."

It was not going to work. He believed that now. If only Morgan could leave the house before the whole mess blew up in her beautiful face.

248

Chapter 21

That evening Warren Rhodes joined the family for dinner. It wasn't an unpleasant experience, but Morgan could certainly recall other dinners that were filled with less tension. It was obvious that Nicholas was uncomfortable with his father and brother.

Jonathan was well dressed in a dark gray jacket, white shirt with neatly tied cravat, black breeches, silk hose, and shoes. Warren dressed up as well.

Not Nicholas. He defiantly chose to wear a black silk shirt with billowing sleeves and black leather breeches with his usual high black Hessian boots.

"I am happy to see you dressed for the occasion, Nicholas," Warren dryly commented.

Seated next to Morgan, Nicholas seductively rubbed his thigh against hers. It took tremendous willpower to ignore such a gesture. Then, halfway through the meal, Morgan gave up resisting his advances. Not only did she respond, but Morgan made a few advances too. Once she pretended to drop the linen napkin. Allowing Nicholas to retrieve it, she playfully ran her fingers through his wavy hair and almost burst out laughing when his head bumped against the mahogany table.

After dinner the ladies retired to Christine's parlor, while the brothers helped Warren to the library.

"Excuse me Mrs. Rhodes," the kindly butler intoned, "but Mr. Nicholas has a visitor."

Morgan was sure it was Margaret Lawson.

"Show our guest in."

Expecting to see a beautiful blond-haired woman, Morgan was surprised to see the tall, dark-haired gentleman approach.

"Why Ian Kendall! When did your ship arrive?" Christine was delighted to see her son's friend.

"My ship docked this morning. I've been trying to find Nick all day."

"How was the weather in New Orleans?"

"Warm and sunny, as usual. A far cry from this chilly town. My blood is too old and thin for this," his hazel eyes glowed in merriment.

"Not you, Ian Kendall. You are too warm-blooded," Sally added with surprising wit.

Ian paused before the entrancing creature. When golden eyes demurely raised to greet his, he felt a sudden shock. She was magnificent!

"Oh, I apologize for my lack of manners, Ian. May I introduce Miss Maryann Mackenzie—our houseguest. She arrived from Halifax with Nicholas."

"Peter's sister. I did not know he had one. Certainly not one as beautiful as you," he lifted her hand to his warm lips, "or I might have gone to Halifax with Nick when he invited me."

"Hello Mr. Kendall."

"No one in this formal house calls me that. Ian, please. Did that pirate take good care of you?" At the moment he didn't care what she said as long as he could hear her throaty voice.

"Indeed. I have no complaints," she smiled, lowering her lashes. This man was very charming and very handsome, she told herself, noticing the firelight play with his mahogany hair. "May I have my hand back, Mr. . . . Ian."

Reluctantly, he let go of her hand. Seated between the two fair-haired women, Miss Mackenzie's dark beauty enthralled him. Except for the golden eyes, she could have been mistaken for a Creole woman. How did Nick keep his hands off this one during the voyage? Ian wondered. Or did he?

Noticing the unusual V-shaped ring, he commented. "What a lovely ring you have, Maryann. It's a shame you wear it on your left hand. Confuses us single men."

"Yes," she hesitated, ignoring the latter part of his statement, "it was a present from my brother."

"So, where is the pirate? I have not seen him in months. Is he in the library with the elders?" He drawled in a lightly accented voice that Morgan found unusual and pleasant to the ears.

Christine hastily explained Warren's health, then sent Ian to the library.

"He is such a charmer," Sally said. "He is from New Orleans, but Ian's family has so many business interests that he ends up spending quite a bit of time in New York."

"Are he and Nick very friendly?" Morgan had never heard his name mentioned before.

"Whenever they're both in New York. They share the wanderlust, I think," Christine informed her. "Personally, I think Nick smuggles some of Ian's goods. But I am not certain."

The ladies chatted about New York and the upcoming social activities. Although Christine had declined many invitations, she now felt it necessary to accept some, if for no other reason than to keep Morgan and Nick occupied.

"You will love the theater. It is the best in this country. You will find, my dear, that New York can be as sophisticated as Paris."

"I've never been to Paris."

"That should be remedied, and soon." Christine winked at her daughter-in-law. She was a lovely young woman, who was endowed with a strength of character few women could recognize, much less be lucky enough to possess. Morgan was right for her son. Now, Christine sighed, if only Warren could be made to see the truth.

When the men rejoined them, Morgan immediately noticed how irritated Nick looked. As he stalked into the room, his lips were pursed and his eyes turned a shade of deep steel-gray. Clearly something was displeasing him.

"Father sends his regrets, but he was fatigued," Jonathan said. "Did you meet Ian Kendall, Maryann?"

"Yes, I did."

"By the way, you did say you were not married or affianced?" Ian asked her.

"No," she began, but Nicholas quickly interjected.

"She has a steady beau in Halifax. As soon as she returns, her father was planning on announcing their betrothal."

"Oh," Ian's voice dramatically dropped. "I am terribly disappointed. But there still may be some time for me to win your heart. It is far more exciting in New Orleans than Halifax or any other part of this country for that matter." He sat beside Morgan on the dark blue damask settee. "I could just smell the fish, the coffee, the exotic foods that are sold in the French Market. Oh and the nights, the restaurants—so gay, so . . ."

"Ian, she is not going to New Orleans, so forget the Southern flowery speech of yours."

"My, my," his laughing eyes looked at Nick's glowering ones, "you sound as if you are the lady's keeper or brother."

"Peter entrusted me with her safety, and I will protect Maryann from anything, especially lechers like you."

"Hah! Look who is calling the kettle black. Why I can recall the dozen or more times in the last year that you and I cornered many 'protected' ladies. Why . . ."

"Enough Ian," Nicholas's sharp voice cut in. "I think you've said enough. Now, when did you say you were leaving New York?"

"I didn't." Ian did not bother to look at his friend. He was captivated by Miss Mackenzie.

"I'm over here, Kendall." Nicholas stood before them.

At first, Morgan wanted to hide from Mr. Kendall's overtures. But he was so charming and Nick was so furious that she found the situation to her liking. Could her husband be jealous?

"I have plans to leave in one month. But things can happen, you know."

Nicholas wanted to murder his former friend. Ian's hands would be all over Morgan if no one was in the room.

"Kendall, it is late. Why don't you go home now? I'll catch up with you tomorrow."

"Nick, I thought we would go to a tavern or two this evening."

Christine, who had been avidly watching this exchange, decided to help her son. Never had she seen him act so rudely.

But a man in love with his wife can often behave rashly and foolishly.

"Ian, I have asked Nicholas to remain with us this evening. We haven't spent much time with him since his return from Halifax," her silver eyes beseeched Ian.

"Another time, Captain," Ian winked at his friend. "I will take my leave now but, Miss Mackenzie," he took her hand again, "I hope to be calling on you soon. Very soon."

"Good night, Ian. I'll walk you to the door." Nicholas couldn't wait to be rid of him.

Morgan watched Nick lead Ian out of the room. They were almost of the same height; perhaps Nick was an inch or two taller. Ian, however, was slightly leaner than Nick, but judging from the superb fit of his clothing he seemed just as muscular.

Sauntering into the room, Nicholas sat next to her. "Well, did you enjoy yourself this evening?"

"Your family is very nice," she glanced at the people in the room. Sally and Jonathan were involved in a game of backgammon. "I am sure I will feel welcome."

Alone in her room, Morgan stared at the brass headboard of the small bed. Room enough for one. This night would be the first of many lonely nights without Nick by her side.

Tying the sash of the red satin wrapper around her waist, Morgan walked over to the curtained window. It was after nine o'clock but there was still some activity on Broadway. A hand-holding couple bravely walked along the snow-covered street. A driver gamely struggled with his horse and cart. A sleigh—similar to the vehicle she had ridden in with Nick— easily passed the slow-moving cart. Remembering that midnight ride with her husband, Morgan smiled.

"What are you thinking of, beauty?"

Did she conjure up his husky voice? Was she so desperately wishing to see his tall form fill the room, his distinctively male scent fill her nostrils? Morgan was afraid to turn around.

"Well, aren't you going to greet me?"

It was Nick. Standing inside the room, his black shirt opened to the waist exposed his mat of curly blond hairs.

"Nick, this is not proper."

"Don't be ridiculous, my love. I am willing to go through this charade during the day, but not," he emphasized, "never the nights. I intend to spend them with you, in that god-awful bed. Now," he closed the distance between them, "are you asking me to leave?"

"Never, my husband." She let him pull her into a hard embrace. "I could use some company."

An hour before dawn, Nicholas left his sleeping wife, vowing two things to himself: one, that he would not remain parted from her much longer; and the other, that he must get a larger bed for the room.

Time dragged by. It seemed that the strain of maintaining this charade was taking its toll on Nicholas. One week passed, yet he swore it was more like one year.

For Morgan, being in the warm, gracious company of Christine—and even Sally—made her feel welcome and comfortable. Charlotte Rhinehart would like Nick's mother. And Morgan hoped that in the near future the women would have the chance to meet.

Morgan sorely missed her family. Writing them once or twice a week did little to ease the sense of loneliness. So much had happened. It was difficult to explain everything on paper, but she tried. When Sally was not around, Morgan would spend many hours telling Christine about her family, including her father.

"I have not visited his grave since our hasty departure from Philadelphia. I wonder if someone is taking care of it," she said in a melancholy voice. "Nick said he would take me. Soon, I hope."

"Have you received any word from Mr. Taggart?" Christine knew of her recent efforts to contact Mr. Taggart and that Nick had begun the search for Andrews.

"Yes," Morgan's eyes suddenly brightened. "We received a letter two days ago. Mr. Taggart gave us the names of some possible associates of Andrews here in New York! Perhaps one of the accomplices we have been looking for is right here. Nick thinks these people may not have participated in the theft of the plates, but might have been contacted by Andrews. As far

254

as Mr. Taggart knows, the plates have not been sold to any person. Not yet. Nick still thinks there is a pattern to the thefts and believes it will happen a third time. It bothers him not to know where."

"I hope, dear, that this ugly situation is over very soon. I too would like to see your father's name cleared. I'd also like for you and Nick to begin living your lives—together."

Morgan was making a terrible attempt at embroidering a handkerchief for her husband. "So do we. I don't know how many more of these ugly things I can ruin," she laughed, a trifle self-consciously. "It has been harder on him, you know."

"I can see that. Morgan, I am aware of where you go in the afternoons—when I am not dragging you about the city—and I want you to know I have no objection to you and Nick meeting privately. I know you can both use some time alone. Why, I have never seen my son so smitten or so irritable. Also, I cannot recall a time when he spent so much time in this house. Not since the day he moved out, more than seven years ago."

Controlling the flush that threatened to surface in her cheeks, Morgan said, "It is unfortunate that Nick does not have more patience with his father and Jonathan."

"It's been that way for quite some time. They are so different. Nick is as headstrong as his father. Jonathan does not have that stubborn streak. He is easygoing. Nick thinks it is a sign of weakness."

"It doesn't have to be."

"Jon is not weak. I am well aware of that. I seem to be in the minority, however."

Their conversation continued a while longer. They both heard the loud knock at the front door, yet remained in the sunny parlor.

"Mrs. Rhodes, Mr. Kendall and Miss Lawson are here."

Morgan paled. Hoping that she would not have to make the acquaintance of Nick's former lady friend, Morgan thought her good fortune would continue. Now the New York society beauty was seeking Morgan. No doubt she had heard the rumors of the Rhodeses' mysterious houseguest who happened to have been on Nick's ship. No doubt, Miss Lawson was interested in studying her rival. Sally had already innocently

255

informed Morgan of how anxiously Margaret Lawson awaited Nick's return and the hopeful announcement of their betrothal.

Amused, but also tired of these silly games, Morgan patiently pretended to sew tiny embroidery stitches.

In his usual energetic state, Ian burst into the room. Behind him sashayed Margaret Lawson. She was very pretty; approximately the same height as Morgan, Miss Lawson was the epitome of sophistication. Her dark red hair was elegantly twisted and curled with a yellow satin ribbon. Margaret was wearing a white fur cloak over a pale green dress that perfectly matched her eyes. Even her thin lips seemed to be set in a permanent pout. Morgan hoped that when Margaret spoke her voice would be high-pitched and shrill. But that was not the case. It was deep, yet well-modulated. Every characteristic of Margaret Lawson made Morgan feel clumsy and unattractive. Afraid her composure would crumble, she stilled her hands and waited for Margaret to speak.

"How do you do, Miss Mackenzie. I've been so anxious to meet you. Ian can speak of nothing else but you." Margaret's lips formed a perfect smile, showing flawless white teeth.

Morgan had trouble lifting her eyes to this new rival, but it was important to be polite. Ian was seated beside her; his buoyant presence gave Morgan courage.

"I have heard many kind things about you too, Miss Lawson."

"Margaret, please."

"Yes, of course. Please sit down."

Christine ordered tea while managing to maintain a polite conversation.

"Mrs. Rhodes," Margaret began, curious now that both women simultaneously looked up, "I have not seen Nick. Has he been so busy that he has failed to call on me? I must admit I am offended."

"My son has been occupied, Margaret dear. I am sure he will visit all of his friends soon."

"She was hoping they were more than friends," Ian said, not at all perturbed by Miss Lawson's murderous look.

"Ian," she warned.

256

"Oh, don't worry, angel. You're talking to Nick's family. I'm sure they understand. But we all know how difficult he is to pin down. The man never stays in one place very long. Say," he brightened, unaware of the tension he was creating, "why don't we all go for a ride. It's warm today, Maryann. And I would be delighted to give you a Southerner's tour of New York."

"I don't think . . ."

"No. I will not take another refusal. Your big brother is not here to answer for you, and I would cherish the opportunity to have two beautiful ladies, one on each arm. Three, Mrs. Rhodes, if you'd care to join us."

"Thank you, no," Christine softly laughed. "You are some charmer, Ian Kendall."

"I know. I only wish some people would fall as helplessly in love with me as I did with her—I mean them." His eyes locked on Morgan's face.

"I think I will stay here, Ian. I have not warmed up yet," Margaret pleasantly said. "Why don't you two go without me? Have you seen much of our beautiful city, Maryann?"

"Yes I have. Nicholas did show me about."

"I'll wager he's only shown you the harbor sights and the taverns. Has he shown you the lovely homes along Broadway? The historical sights from the Revolutionary War? The theater, the races?"

"Well . . ."

"No, of course not. Come, I will not take no for an answer. Mrs. Rhodes, do I have your permission to escort Maryann?" His laughing eyes beseeched her.

"You don't need my approval."

Christine's nonchalance and Ian's sorrowful hazel eyes made her decision easy. "Well, I suppose I could use a little fresh air."

Helping her secure the sable-lined cloak about her shoulders, Ian declared, "I promise to take marvelous care of her, Mrs. Rhodes. We will be back within two hours."

They leisurely drove south toward the tip of Manhattan Island. Ian pointed out the major streets and historical landmarks.

257

"Did you know, Maryann, that Bowling Green became the city's first park in 1733? There used to be a statue of King George III dressed as a Roman emperor in this park, but after the Declaration of Independence was read in front of City Hall, an angry mob marched to Bowling Green and tore the statue down."

"For a Southerner, sir, you are very knowledgeable about New York."

"It is my second home. I grew up in New Orleans; my family and our business are still there. But I went to college in New York—Columbia College. It used to be called King's College before the war," he added with a smirk. "That, by the way, was where I met Nick."

"I wasn't aware of that," she mused aloud, curious now that Nick had told her very little about Ian Kendall.

Despite the closed carriage, Morgan felt the afternoon's cold air and shivered.

Noticing her discomfort, Ian gallantly offered his lap blanket. "I may be a Southerner, but I've grown accustomed to cold weather."

"I never will. It is so cold in Halifax. I don't go very far unless I have plenty of pelts to cover me."

"It must be beautiful in Halifax in the spring and summer, though."

"Yes, it is," she replied without enthusiasm. Morgan hadn't been in Halifax long enough to know what the warm seasons were like. Nick had begun to explain the weather to her, but had been interrupted and never resumed the conversation.

Ian studied her bland face. "I am sure it is similar to New York and Boston. They must have lovely theaters, outdoor restaurants, dance halls, and markets. Like here."

"Yes, they do," she looked out the window studying the scenery.

"We will be passing our most famous concert hall—Delacroix Vauxhall. What is the name of yours?"

"Ummm," she laughed, "I uh, suddenly forgot. You must think me a ninny. But I thought you were giving me a tour of your adopted city?"

"I am. I'm also curious about you. Who are you really,

Maryann Mackenzie? You don't sound British. You know very little about your hometown. But I've heard your enthusiasm and knowledge displayed whenever you speak of Boston—even Philadelphia." He peered into her troubled golden gaze. "As a Southerner, I have no trouble recognizing other accents. Yours is northern, but not Nova Scotian. Perhaps you are really an American spy sent to the British Provinces. Or perhaps . . ."

"Don't be foolish, Ian. I have no idea what you are talking about," she nervously toyed with the fur blanket.

"I do." He took her left hand, touching the gold ring. "You are an enigma, Miss Mackenzie. And I would love to know who you truly are. Perhaps, if you learn to trust me, to know me as well as I hope to know you . . ." His sincere smile touched her. "I hope you will realize that I would do anything for you. Anything."

For no reason, Morgan's eyes suddenly misted. "Thank you Ian. I am not really that mysterious. But I will remember your kind words."

"I am positive that my friend the pirate is involved in this matter. But I will find out everything. And I give you my word that I will not desert you if you are ever in need of another shoulder. Will you remember that?"

She quickly nodded her hooded head, unable to say any more.

"Well, let me show you some more old New York sights. We are heading toward another park—Battery Park. It was named after the battery of guns that were kept by the British in the late seventeenth century. Along the water's edge is the newly built fort—West Battery. You know with all the tension between our country and yours, there is talk of war. This fort is our attempt at protection."

"Ian, do you think there will be a war?"

"I'm afraid so. Unless tempers cool. Our government has to change some of its policies too. We cannot forever remain neutral in the war between England and France."

"Nick says the same thing. He says that the Embargo Act of President Jefferson's is foolish."

"I'll wager he does," Ian wryly said.

"Oh Ian. You are not going to accuse Nicholas of being unpatriotic, are you? He has heard that accusation too many times."

"No," he looked at her animated expression. Whenever she spoke of Nick her face displayed a myriad of expressions, not the least of which was love. Was she in love with Nick? Ian wondered. Judging from his fierce protectiveness toward the beauty, Ian believed that Nick must feel something for his friend's "sister." He had not visited his usual night haunts; nor, Ian recalled now, had he accepted any one of the dozen invitations from willing females . . . something that was highly unusual for the lusty Captain Rhodes.

Even Margaret Lawson had commented to Ian that Nick was staying away from her. That was certainly unusual. Nick had deftly managed to escape becoming engaged to Margaret; yet most people thought it was merely a matter of time before she ensnared him.

Ian now thought differently. Miss Mackenzie had much to do with it. Margaret Lawson must have thought so too, otherwise she never would have insisted that they drive over to the Rhodeses' home, knowing perfectly well that Nick was not there.

Ian had no intention of giving up his pursuit of Miss Mackenzie—or whoever she was. Not yet. He had only known this woman for a short while, but he did not need any more time to know that he was falling in love with this exotic creature.

Their drive was punctuated by comments of historical information, personal questions, and general good humor. Feeling carefree and young again, Morgan did not realize how much time elapsed. The dying rays of the late afternoon sun suddenly reminded her that they should have returned an hour before.

"Oh, Ian," she was anxious, "I think we should return now. I don't want the Rhodeses to worry about me."

"Which one?" he muttered before turning the carriage onto Broadway.

Chapter 22

When they reached the side of the house, Morgan waited for Ian to assist her from the coach. She was barely up the stairs to the front door, when it was jerked open.

"Nice to see you remembered to join us for dinner," Nicholas drawled.

Morgan knew he was livid. His rigid stance and clenched jaw indicated as much . . . not half as much, though, as the metallic gleam sparking from his half-closed eyes. Who, she wildly wondered, was the anger directed toward?

"Let me help you with your fur cloak, Maryann," he ground out the name, his hands painfully biting into her shoulders.

At least now she knew with whom he was angry. "Thank you, Nicholas, but I can help myself."

"Can you?"

"What is wrong Rhodes? Why are you so piqued? She is not officially your ward. I acted as always with great propriety . . . the perfect gentleman," he calmly said, but his accent seemed more pronounced. Seeing Nick's furious glare, Ian refrained from making further comments.

"Keep out of this Kendall. I know too much about your 'southern ways.' Remember? I've prowled the streets with you."

"Nicholas. What on earth are you carrying on about?" Margaret intruded on the scene. Her pale green dress and demeanor did not look the least bit ruffled. "We heard you in the parlor. Oh," she casually glanced at Morgan and Ian, "you're finally back. Mrs. Rhodes invited us to stay for dinner, Ian."

"She did?" Nicholas asked, including his mother into the circle of anger.

"How kind." Ian's enthusiasm irritated Nicholas.

"Mr. Rhodes will be joining us too."

"Great," Nick muttered.

Morgan was too upset with Nicholas to see the humor in this ridiculous situation.

Throughout dinner, Warren and Ian carried most of the conversation. Nick sulked in his wineglass. Morgan anxiously looked his way, then at Christine. The evening was not going to be pleasant. Margaret attempted to draw Nick into conversation, but failed miserably.

When dessert arrived, Nicholas finally appeared to come out of his irritable mood.

"Nick, tell me about your voyage to Halifax. Was it dangerous? Did you run into border patrols?" Margaret asked in a concerned voice.

Nicholas mechanically replied to her question, but when she "oohed" and "ahhed" and fretted over his well-being, he suddenly warmed to the story.

"It is so dangerous," Margaret said for the third time.

"And illegal," Warren reminded the dinner guests.

"Not now, dear," Christine soothed him, relaxing when Ian drew Warren into a different conversation.

But Morgan was observing all of it. All too soon, her anger bubbled to the surface. Nick was flirting with Margaret Lawson, seemingly unaware that she hung onto his words. His story of outmaneuvering the patrol boats sickened Morgan. Margaret loved it, commenting on his bravery and brilliant thinking.

By the time Ian turned her way, a more receptive Morgan listened to his light conversation about his travels abroad.

"You have met Napoleon?"

"Well, only briefly. I was presented to him at a fabulous ball the empress was hosting. I have many relatives in France. My family tries to travel aboard every two years."

With a dreadful feeling, Christine Rhodes anxiously

watched the odd dynamics among the four young people seated around her dinner table. Because she had begged her son to accept this deception, his relationship with Morgan could be damaged—permanently. Each person was playing a dangerous game with the emotions of the others. She had to stop this charade.

"Excuse me; I think we need to clarify something."

"Wait a minute, Chrissie. Did I tell you about the letter I received today?" Warren interrupted her. "It's about those stolen currency plates."

"Warren!" Christine admonished. Having made him promise not to discuss the subject in front of anyone, Christine wished he had kept his word. "You gave your word, dear."

"I know, I know. But this is good news. It is good enough to share with these people."

Nicholas was stunned. How could his father speak so carelessly in front of strangers? What had happened to his discretion? Was this another example of his memory lapses? Darting a look at Morgan, Nicholas saw the way she nervously clutched the stem of the wineglass. How much worse could this get?

"Excuse me, Father. I do not think the ladies are particularly interested in this topic."

"Not now, Warren. Please." Christine's voice softened.

As if to orient himself, Warren blinked a few times then noticed all the stares of the dinner guests.

"I, uh, I am deeply sorry. I forgot." Realizing the breach in conduct, Warren was acutely embarrassed.

"Well, did I tell you, Nick, that I met your Uncle Eric in New Orleans?" Ian felt the need to say something.

He had told him before, but Nicholas thought this conversation was safer than the other. "How is he?"

"Ian, did my brother-in-law receive my letters?"

"Well, I am not really sure. I was entering the restaurant as he was leaving—always in a tremendous rush. Just like you, eh Nick?"

"So how did my brother look?" Warren asked.

"Very well. He was heading to a ship. Does he still own one?"

"Three, as far as I know. If he didn't lose them in a card game." Warren mumbled the last sentence.

"Well, I hope he received my messages. I dearly hope he will visit soon. I'd love to see him again. It has been over two years."

"Mother, I am sure that if Uncle Eric received your letters he will be here. We are his only family."

"Your uncle sounds so mysterious. Don't you think so, Maryann?" Margaret politely asked.

"Hmmm? Oh yes, Margaret," she responded in a distracted voice.

"I would love to hear the story about your travels with your uncle, Nicholas. It must have been so exciting. You are so adventurous." Margaret openly flirted with Nicholas, who once more seemed to be enjoying it.

When did Margaret Lawson become the hostess? Morgan asked herself. Wishing that the night would miraculously end, she silently watched as Margaret continued a private conversation with Nick. As soon as the dessert was served, Morgan politely excused herself, pleading a headache.

She knew that Nick would not be spending the night. It was beginning to look strange that he was staying at his parents' home when his house was so close by. Besides, Nick was running out of excuses. How many more times could his town house be in disrepair? How many more windows could be broken? How often could the fireplaces need cleaning?

Alone in the tiny room, Morgan wondered how much longer she could bear being in this house, separated from the man she loved, separated from her family.

She could not know that Nicholas had the very same thoughts. Riding to his own home, the keen sense of loneliness would not go away.

He needed Morgan. And he needed to get her away from Ian, who obviously was smitten with her. To make matters worse, Nicholas had received a long letter from Peter Mackenzie that morning.

When he was comfortably settled in his library, a snifter of brandy by his side, Nicholas pulled the letter out of his coat pocket. He had almost committed to memory the first part of the letter:

"Nick, I hope you followed my advice and married Morgan as soon as you arrived in New York. If so, the information I am about to relate is irrelevant. I hope to God that is so.

"Yesterday a devastating fire destroyed St. Peter's Church. The whole building, Nick. Including the rectory and the priest's office. EVERYTHING. Do you understand that, man? Everything was destroyed. All of the records! The records of births, deaths, and marriages. All of the marriages, Nick. The priest has been asking his parishioners for their duplicate certificates. He is going to write to London. Most of the certificates will be reissued. But Nick, you will have to bring your document to Halifax. Yourself. The priest will not accept the certificate from me.

"I hope you see the gravity of the situation, yet I pray to God that a trip here is unnecessary. If you were foolish enough not to marry her, then DO IT NOW. You know what can happen with outside interferences, particularly your father. Just do it my friend . . ."

The letter went on explaining other business matters, none of which Nicholas cared about at the moment. He had to do something. To tell Morgan the truth now was not a good idea. He had to get her away from here. How the hell was he going to accomplish that?

Morgan had promised to meet him tomorrow at the town house. They had managed this secret rendezvous at least twice a week. The Carlton women were out of the house at that time. How ridiculous, he snorted; husband and wife forced to steal precious moments alone. Some day, Morgan once said, they would laugh about this absurdity. But not yet. How would she react upon learning that once again their legal marriage might be a farce?

But Morgan did not arrive at the usual two o'clock. By three o'clock Nicholas alternated between worry and anger. Did something happen to her? His father? Or did she forget? Was

Ian Kendall hovering over her today? Was she enjoying it?

By four o'clock Nicholas was on his horse heading south on Broadway. In the stables he saw an extra horse; from the looks of the old mare, it was a rented hack. Entering the house from the kitchen, Nicholas heard voices in one of the downstairs parlors. Morgan's clear, bell-like laugh was heard above the others.

"Damn," he cursed aloud, wanting to kill Ian. "Not again."

Just as he entered the room, Nicholas recognized another voice. Deep and sure, he knew of no other such baritone.

"Uncle Eric!" Nicholas charged into the room, all anger having quickly evaporated. "How good it is to see you." Nicholas affectionately embraced his uncle.

"I was just as surprised to learn that you were in New York. But I should have known that if your mother could find me, she'd easily locate you."

Eric looked much younger than his forty-three years. There was no trace of gray in his light brown hair. His deep blue eyes sparkled with vitality—like Warren's used to look.

"Come here boy," he placed an arm around his nephew's shoulders. "Let's see how you look."

"The same, Uncle. I assure you." Only Eric could call him "boy" and not be beaten. Standing next to his uncle, Nicholas was only a few inches taller. Yet their resemblance was evident. They had the same broad build, the same easy smile.

"I can see from the company you are keeping that you are still doing very well." Eric smiled at Morgan who was quietly sitting on the Sheraton armchair nearest the window. She was trying to hide a smile.

"I see Maryann has captured your heart too."

"Mine went to her the moment I walked into this room. And she's British!"

"Enough Eric. You see I am not dead, I am not going to die. So now what are you doing in New York?" Warren exhorted.

"My brother is direct as always," Eric laughed, then faced Warren. "Fool, I came here to see if I am in your will. Then I am taking your wife across the sea—to China perhaps."

"You know she hates sailing, Eric."

Morgan had never heard this repartee between family

266

members. Shocked at first, she became amused by the laughter and clever rejoinders.

When Eric Rhodes had charged through the front door at exactly one P.M., Morgan thought those booted steps belonged to Nicholas. Running down the long staircase, she darted to the front door just in time to see this other man drop two bags on the marble floor.

"Why hello. Who are you, pretty lady?" his voice seemed so familiar and friendly.

"I am a guest. Who are you?" she quickly replied, not feeling the least bit afraid.

"Eric Rhodes."

"You're Nick's uncle Eric?" her smile lighting up the golden eyes.

"The same." He approached the dark-haired beauty. "Now can I have the pleasure of knowing your name?"

"Oh. I apologize. My name is Mor—Maryann Mackenzie. I am a friend of Nick's. And Peter Mackenzie's sister."

"I never knew Peter had such a beautiful sister. Well, how is my brother? Is he . . . uh . . . he is . . ."

"He's fine, Mr. Rhodes. I think he's just as feisty and hardheaded as ever. So I've been told by everyone else."

Eric's presence had a miraculous effect on each person present in the room. Warren felt better physically. Christine felt the release of pressure. When Jon and Sally appeared, they too were pleased.

Morgan was greatly impressed by this man who was a cross between Nicholas and his father. She was looking forward to knowing him better, believing that Eric would become her friend.

Nicholas believed that Eric would help him with this mess. As soon as possible he would find time alone with him. Perhaps his uncle could shed some light on the situation and could even suggest an alternative plan.

"Uncle Eric, why don't you stay with me tonight? I seem to be alone in my town house."

"Never bothered you before lad."

"No. Not until recently," he looked at his wife—who might not be his wife.

267

Hating to be out of Morgan's presence but eager to talk to his uncle, Nicholas forced himself to remain seated, listening to the clever chatter around him. At dinner, Nicholas sought the seat next to his wife. More than once, his hand located hers under the table, reassuringly squeezing it. When it strayed up her arm, Morgan must have blushed as she jerked it away.

It was not unnoticed by Eric, who though engaged in conversation with Jonathan missed nothing at the table. What, he wondered, was going on between those two? The veiled looks, the funny hand motions beneath the table were adorable—if one enjoyed adolescent playfulness. But this, after all, was Eric's wild, fun-loving, womanizing nephew. Oh no, something was not quite right here.

After dinner, Morgan excused herself. Seconds later, Nicholas found an excuse to leave the room. He caught her on the wide mahogany staircase.

"Why are you running away from me?" he kissed her exposed neck.

"Nick, please. I am unwell. Remember? This is the time of the month."

"I'm sorry, I forgot." Then he noticed her pale cheeks. "You really are unwell. Here, let me escort you upstairs."

"Nicholas! How can you?"

"I don't give a damn. I missed you today. I want to at least hold you in my arms and kiss you good night."

His husky voice affected her. "This is silly."

"I know. Now, can I walk you to your room?"

They could not know that as they walked up the stairs, arms wrapped about each other's waist, a pair of dark blue eyes looked on in mild surprise.

"What is my nephew up to now?" Eric wondered aloud before turning back.

Once inside the bedroom, Nicholas could not wait to hold Morgan. "My love, I think it time we moved on. I won't go on without you sharing my bed."

"Didn't you say you were waiting for some letters from contacts of yours? Wasn't it going to give us some information about the currency plates? What about the metting you arranged with a so-called British agent? What about the cargo

268

you were waiting to purchase?"

"Wait a minute, will you my love? All you ask is important, but . . ."

"Then let's wait. I want to, Nick. We have to. I feel that we are close to something. I believe we will find the information we need. Then we can leave."

"Why must you be so damn sensible?" His hands idly roamed under her bodice.

"Nick," she warned.

"Morgan, meet me tomorrow at our usual time. I must talk to you. Alone. I received a letter from Peter today, and . . ."

"Oh, how is he? I miss him and the Gleasons so much."

"Everyone is fine. He . . . Oh hell, Morgan, kiss me."

It was not as long and passionate as he would have liked, but it would do for now.

Warren was feeling well enough to walk unaided to the drawing room. No one but Eric seemed to notice that Nicholas had been gone for a long time. Once Eric thought he saw Christine look at the door, but that meant nothing. Or did it?

After Nick returned, Eric could see that his nephew's mind was elsewhere . . . perhaps upstairs with the black-haired beauty. Putting the matter aside for a moment, Eric again studied the people in the room. For a man who had suffered a near-fatal seizure, Warren Rhodes looked great. Somewhat more subdued than usual, but it was only a matter of time before Warren began barking at everyone who dared to disagree with him.

It took six weeks for Christine's alarming letter to reach him. For two months he had been deep in the Spanish Territory as a guest of a local Spanish don. His stay was prolonged because of a certain niece of the don. But the letter had reached Eric and he departed at dawn the following day—never saying good-bye to the black-eyed señorita.

While Warren and Eric had not been very close, Eric could never think of abandoning his only family. Warren, being much older, had always treated Eric as his son. Their father died when Eric was barely three years old. Warren immediately filled the void, always offering advice—even if not asked—and generally telling Eric what was considered proper behavior. Eric had no love of the law profession; it was the sea that had always called to him. Given the earliest opportunity, Eric fled. Warren was left a brief note and empty promises of someday returning to the law practice.

In some respects, Nicholas was more Eric's son than Warren's. They were kindred spirits. Eric recalled the first time he'd taken Nicholas to his ship, the *Falcon*. The boy refused to leave his perch in the crow's nest for hours. When Nick was thirteen, Eric finally convinced Warren and Christine to let the lad sail across the Atlantic on the *Falcon*. It was a trip neither of them could ever forget. With Eric's assistance, Nick saw the world open before his eager gray eyes. He had become the most important person in Eric's life.

Now that his nephew was troubled by something, Eric knew he had to help. First, they needed to talk.

It was a quiet ride back to Nicholas's town house. The men headed for the library and the imported French wine.

"Now lad, tell me what all this mystery is about." Eric settled onto the leather sofa.

Nicholas seated by his desk leaned back, lifting booted feet to the inlaid cherrywood top. "It is an extremely long story. One I have repeated a few times."

"Who is that black-haired siren who calls herself Maryann Mackenzie? Did you forget that I met Peter? He does not have a sister."

"She is my wife."

To his credit, Eric did not choke on the wine.

"Congratulations. When?"

"Less than four months ago—or six, depending upon who you ask."

"Do you think you could try to make the story simple? Or do you want to see your old uncle become a drunken sod?"

Nicholas frowned. "Believe me Eric, I would rather be the drunken sod. Because I don't see how things could get much worse."

"Tell me lad." Eric's blue eyes studied his nephew's scowl.

"She is my wife. But she may not be my wife. She is the daughter of a man falsely convicted of treason, subsequently murdered by the real traitor. She is the woman my father

270

believes is a traitor. She is a remarkable woman."

"So, you love her?"

"Without a doubt."

"Why are you living apart? Is it because she is the daughter of a traitor?"

"Falsely convicted, Eric. Have you ever heard of Samuel Rhinehart?" Nicholas crossed and uncrossed his long legs.

Eric thought a few moments, then looked up. "Not the missing currency plates your father has been talking about?"

"The same."

"His daughter?"

"Morgan Ann Rhinehart Rhodes. Age nineteen. Beautiful, defiant, childlike, charming. We were married in Halifax. In an Anglican Church. Peter just sent me a letter. The church has been destroyed by fire, along with every record in it."

"Does that include the record of your marriage?" Eric's legal mind considered the problem. Nicholas was in serious trouble.

"Destroyed. According to Peter, our marriage may not have been a legal one. American citizens married in British Territory have a peculiar status. I don't know if the marriage was legal. Nor did I have this checked out when we arrived here. I suppose I wanted the problem to disappear. Anyway, Peter warned me to marry Morgan again in New York. But how can I even see her for a kiss, let alone a marriage ceremony!" Nicholas morosely looked out the window, seeing nothing but darkness and white snow.

"Nick, if you don't make this tale of woe easier for me to understand, I shall fall asleep."

Restless now, Nicholas uncurled his legs and walked over to the marble fireplace. Sitting on his haunches, he took an extraordinary amount of time to light the fire. Once done, Nicholas remained unmoving in front of the logs.

"Now lad. Suppose you tell me the whole story. I seem to have the rest of the night free."

Chapter 23

"I have an ugly suspicion, Uncle Eric, that I may never see my wife alone again." Nicholas crumpled the letter that had been delivered. Morgan was unable to meet him today. Christine and Sally were taking her shopping and then to lunch.

"You will need some patience, boy. After all, you are as much responsible for this as anyone else."

"It is all my fault. Do you think I didn't realize that last night?" Nicholas's bloodshot eyes barely focused on his uncle, who looked no better than he.

"Haven't drunk or smoked that much since that card game in New Orleans," he muttered. "I hope you feel cleansed today, lad."

"Far from it, Eric. I talked too much last night. You heard every sordid detail. But you know," Nicholas pushed his breakfast plate away, the sight of all that food suddenly nauseating him, "I heard myelf trying to logically explain what is anything but logical. I am the fool. I'm in love with a woman."

"That in itself is highly unusual for you, Nick. It takes time to adjust to it." Eric tried consoling him, but knew as early as last night that Nick blamed himself for all the problems.

"Don't patronize me, Eric. Not you. I made two promises that could not be kept. One cancels the other out. If I help Father, I hurt Morgan, and vice versa. I am weak-willed."

Eric could not stand the self-pity. Never had he seen Nick

273

like this before.

"Enough lad. Stop this nonsense. You have a dual responsibility, that's true. One does not negate the other. You are a brave man, and a clever one too. All you have to do is find the real traitor-murderer."

"Thanks, Uncle Eric, for shedding new light on this matter," he sarcastically said. Lifting the hot coffee cup to his mouth, he grumbled, "I don't know if I want coffee or more wine."

"Lad," Eric plopped his linen napkin onto the dining table, "I am going to help you. I will stay in New York as long as it takes."

"I was waiting for your offer," he smiled.

"I thought so. Now, I think we should visit the New York Bank today. Didn't you say that there are nine Federal Banks?"

"Yes."

"Name them."

"Well, the Second U.S. Bank has eight branches, or state banks. The bank itself, as you know, is in Philadelphia. The others are in: New York, Boston, Baltimore, Washington, Norfolk, Charleston, Savannah, and New Orleans."

"Each bank has plates?"

"Yes. Each state, much to Albert Gallatin's dismay, still prints its own currency. Very messy and very complicated," he chuckled, finding this turn in the conversation stimulating.

"Would this Andrews chap need to steal all of the currency plates?"

"I don't know," he wrinkled his brow.

"Think lad. Let's assume the plates are going to be sold or destroyed. Why? This Andrews and his accomplices want to destroy our economy. Or hold it hostage for a reason. Or help the British and French. Their motives?"

"Money—or a foolish act of patriotism."

"Which country? England, France, or America?"

"I don't know. Certainly not our country."

"Well, don't you think we should find out? If we can discover the motive, perhaps we can outfox the murderer."

Nicholas became enthusiastic. "We will know Andrews's next move before he does—and be there, waiting."

"Correct."

Nicholas pulled the plate before him. "I think I've just rediscovered my appetite. If we can solve this riddle, I'll have my wife and my life back."

"You still need to marry the girl again."

"As soon as I can find a moment alone with her, I will tell her the distasteful truth."

Not on that day. Nicholas did not hear from Morgan at all. Eric had gone out on some business of his own and theirs, confident that he would have some information to start with by the end of the week.

There was nothing else for Nicholas to do but keep his appointment with a prospective buyer at the South Street warehouse. It was cold outside, but he chose to ride on horseback rather than take the coach.

Setting a leisurely pace, Nicholas rode down Broadway before heading further east. Passing Whitehall Street, he turned onto Pearl Street and could not believe what he saw.

Fraunces Tavern, on the corner of Pearl and Broad Streets, was one of the more popular meeting houses in New York. A familiar black coach pulled in front of the tavern. Sure that it was his friend Ian Kendall, Nicholas kneed the horse to a fast pace. A hatless Ian emerged, extending his arm to another person in the carriage.

He did not need to see the black sable-lined cloak to know who it was. As Morgan gracefully stepped down, the hood of the cloak fell back, exposing raven curls that were artfully arranged. It was her charming, light laughter that tore at Nicholas's heart.

What was she doing with Ian? Didn't her note say that she was lunching with his mother and Sally? It appeared to Nicholas as if Ian held Morgan's waist too tightly and intimately.

Jealousy and anger consumed him. Why would Morgan lie to him? Determined to investigate this unusual turn of events,

Nicholas waited for the couple to enter the tavern before approaching. Quickly tying the horse to the hitching post, he removed his woolen cap and walked toward the entrance door.

Suddenly he froze. He could not go inside. Why, he asked himself; are you afraid to confront the truth?

Questioning himself numerous times without receiving a satisfactory response, Nicholas opened the tavern door.

"Nick? What a wonderful surprise!" Margaret's voice stopped him from going further.

Seated in her carriage, she frantically waved and called until he saw her. But Nicholas seemed rooted to a spot and Margaret decided to be bold. Opening the coach door she half leaned outside, calling, almost shouting, his name. Eager to see him alone—away from Miss Mackenzie and the whole Rhodes family—Margaret would gladly forfeit her ladylike rectitude for this opportunity.

Since his return to New York, Margaret had not seen Nick alone. The days and, more importantly, those long loving nights without him were torturous.

Their affair had been ongoing for less than three months before he left New York last August. He had never mentioned marriage. In fact, before their first passionate night together, Nick warned her that he would not be forced into marriage—no matter what the circumstances. However, he was determined to safeguard against "accidents." Knowing little about men, she was first unaware of what he meant. But he quickly showed her that there were ways a man could prevent spreading his seed within a woman. Dismayed, Margaret saw the only chance of snatching Nicholas Rhodes slip away.

In time, however, she had realized it was not the only way of catching the infamous smuggler. He was afraid of marriage, afraid of long-standing relationships with women. His reputation among the New York ladies and their doting mamas was legendary. Nick never got seriously involved. Yet the Lawsons were as wealthy as the Rhodes family and, Margaret smugly thought, none of those women were as pretty as she. Nor had any of them enjoyed an intimate relationship with Nick.

276

Margaret devised a rather simple plan. She would let it be known among family and friends that she and Captain Rhodes were very fond of one another. She'd let Nick know that even if marriage was not in his plans, they could continue to enjoy an intimate and friendly relationship. Then perhaps he would marry her if he became accustomed to this comfortable arrangement. Margaret would not pressure him. Instead, she'd patiently wait for him to accept the inevitable.

Until last August, the plan had been working beautifully. Nicholas escorted her everywhere. Friends and family naturally assumed that a betrothal announcement was imminent. But Margaret never said a word to her nosy friends. When pressed, she smiled sweetly, saying that she and Nick were only good friends.

The last night they had spent together, Nicholas told her he was leaving and when he was planning to return. It was more than any woman had gotten out of him and Margaret was satisfied. Time would be on her side. During the long months he was away, Margaret made a point of visiting Mr. and Mrs. Rhodes. When Warren suffered the seizure, Margaret was there every day, offering sympathy and a solid, dependable presence. Warren loved her. According to Sally, she was the hand-picked choice to be Nick Rhodes's bride.

He was gone longer than expected. Worse, he showed up in New York with his partner's gorgeous sister. Margaret knew Nick well enough to realize that there was something going on between those two. And she was determined to find out.

But for now, Nick was alone in front of Fraunces Tavern.

"Nick, I was meeting my father and his partner for lunch. Would you care to join us?" she inquired when he approached her coach.

"I don't think so. Thanks."

"Well," she persisted, "were you meeting someone in there for lunch?"

"Well, no. No I wasn't. Oh hell, Margaret. Let's go to lunch somewhere else. It's too crowded in there. I'll take you to a nice seafood house near the wharf."

She had no time to demur, for he quickly tied his horse

behind the coach, grabbed her arm, and hopped into the carriage.

Well, she smugly thought, this was going to be a wonderful day.

Inside the tavern, Morgan tried to concentrate on Ian's words over the noise.

"I am so glad you agreed to let me escort you, Maryann. Mrs. Rhodes and Sally should be joining us any minute. May I," he cleared his throat, "speak boldly?"

"I don't know what you mean, Ian," she smiled kindly. Never before had Ian Kendall appeared at a loss for words. But today he appeared nervous, almost unsure of himself.

"What is wrong, Ian?"

"Maryann," he took her right hand, "I feel I must tell you how deeply I care for you."

"Ian, please." She tried to remove her hand.

"No. I must say it while I still have the courage. I love you; I want to marry you. I would like to write your family in Halifax and ask permission to court you."

"But you can't," she blurted.

"Maryann, I can wait if I must. It's just that I did not think I could let another day pass without telling you how deeply I care."

"But Nicholas . . ." she began, not knowing what she had meant to say.

"He is very protective. I am aware of that. I'm sure you can remain with his parents during our betrothal. I was hoping you might come to New Orleans with me. We could marry at my parents' home."

"No Ian. You do not understand. It's far more complicated than that. Why, you don't even know very much about me."

"I've seen all I need to know," his hazel eyes earnestly stared into her troubled face. "I know you have captivated my heart with your smile, beauty, and intelligence. What more need I know?"

It was time to confide in yet another person. "Ian, there is something you must know. I am not what you think. I am mar . . ."

278

"Finally!" Sally almost sounded excited. "We thought we'd never find you in this crowd. Mother went to the Long Room to see if you were standing there. But Ian, I did not think that you would stand near that bar with a lady."

Ian rose to help Sally remove her cloak.

"Oh, there she is. Mother," she called above the din, "I've found them."

Christine's arrival ruled out Morgan's confession.

"Where is Nicholas?" Sally asked Ian. "I was sure he was joining us."

"He has no idea that I was fortunate enough to meet you charming ladies as you were leaving the house. Otherwise, I would not have had the honor of taking three lovely young ladies to lunch."

"You exaggerate Ian, as always. But I love it," Christine smiled. However, she was not completely unaware of what was happening. Ian had cleverly manipulated them, inviting himself to lunch. When Nick found out he would be furious with everyone, but especially his wife.

Poor Morgan was being tested to the limit of her mental endurance. It was so difficult to be separated from her husband, pretending she was another person . . . all for Warren's sake. Was it fair? Christine asked herself this question over and over. Did she have any right to make such a difficult request of her son and his wife?

Of course Morgan was perfect for her wayward son. They loved one another. But was this test of their love necessary? No, it was all taking a terrible toll on the girl. Of late, Morgan refused to participate in the many social activities. Afraid that she might forget her charade or suggest something about her past, Morgan preferred the quiet solitude of the Rhodes home, except when she visited Nick.

Today Christine and Sally had prevented that meeting. It was not intentional, but after Christine realized what she had done, it was awkward to rescind the invitation. Morgan realized that as well and politely excused herself to send a message to Nicholas.

Christine was also aware of something else. Ian Kendall was obviously in love with Morgan. How would they deal with this new problem? If only Ian could fall in love with **Margaret**

Lawson, then two of their problems could be solved at once. But Margaret was not letting go of her imaginary hold on Nick.

Warren, she said to herself, I hope this is all worth it. You must get well and you must accept this woman into our home. Otherwise . . .

Nick did not appear for dinner that evening. Wondering why he hadn't returned to the town house, Eric decided to leave for Warren's house. Nick was probably tied up with business and would join them later.

Throughout dinner, each person present wondered where Nicholas was. It was Warren who finally said it.

"I think Nick slipped into his old ways again. Shows up when and if he feels like it. The lad will never change."

Morgan felt ill. There had to be a reason for his delay. Hating the sympathetic look Christine offered, she wanted to escape from the dining room.

"I think I will take a walk," she unexpectedly announced after dessert.

"It is still cold out there Maryann. Stay inside. I'll let you read another legal brief to me," Warren generously offered. She was such a fine young woman and he had begun to look forward to her daily visits. She read whatever he requested. Warren insisted that she wear her spectacles around the house.

"I really would like some fresh air, Mr. Rhodes."

"May I join you, Maryann?" Eric offered to accompany her after noticing that she was perilously close to tears.

The late night chill did not affect her. Morgan was too hurt and angry to worry about the weather. Determined not to cry, Morgan left the house with Eric, heading for Bowling Green. Her quickened pace despite the icy path gave Eric some indication of the lady's inner turmoil.

"I never knew a woman to walk that fast unless she was furious with something or someone."

"Both, I guess." She slowed, but would not look at him.

"I knew a young woman once—long ago. She was the prettiest little thing I had seen, so sweet and young. But for one so young she had to grow up fast. You see, her parents were killed in a tragic accident and Nellie had to support two sisters and a brother. It wasn't easy, I recall. Overnight, the sweet, even-tempered girl, became a hard, embittered woman. She worked in a tavern, took in sewing. She was determined not to split up the family."

"And what happened?"

"I saw her three years ago. She looked much older than her years, but the gleam was back in her eyes. She met a man—a good man. He was much older and not a very handsome man. But he loved her and her family and would do anything to make them happy. Nellie believed in herself. She was stronger than she thought. She found the right man and she held onto him."

Morgan suddenly stopped. Looking up at his merry blue eyes, she inquired, "Are you trying to tell me something?"

"Indeed I am." He smiled, taking her arm to resume their walk. "I am trying to tell you that if you strongly believe in something you must stick with your belief. If you strongly believe or love someone, that is also true. Everything will unfold properly in time."

"Don't tell me you know," she whispered, her soft voice creating white puffs against the night air. "Before long, it will be printed in the newspaper."

"It probably should be," he chuckled. "My God, *Morgan*," he emphasized her real name, "you have nothing to hide and everything to be proud of."

"Did you tell your brother?"

"No, of course not. But he is as bullheaded and cynical as you appear to be. I do not think you've been dealt a fair hand. Neither has Nick. But I know you will see things through— together. And do you know what, dear niece?" Eric put an arm around her shoulders. "I think you are a fine addition to our family. You are just what my nephew needs."

"Then where the devil is he?" she blurted. "I will wager he is with Margaret or some other beauty."

"He is not like that and you know it, Morgan."

"Do I?" She stood tall. "What do I really know about my husband?"

"He cares a great deal for you. He would never hurt you. I'll tell you what," Eric paused, wanting to change the subject. "I give you my solemn vow that no matter what happens, I will assist you in this search for the murderer. In fact, Nick and I began today."

"You did?"

"Yes. We have an idea, Morgan." Quickly, Eric reiterated the theory that Andrews would strike yet again. "Nor do we think he has sold the stolen plates. We think he is still waiting for the highest bidder—England, France, maybe the U.S. What we need to do is provide them with the contacts. Have you heard my French?"

"Could we speak it?" she giggled.

"How is your French?"

"Quite good. Have you heard my British accent?" she perfectly imitated the clipped nasal aristocratic sound. "I've had better practice with that accent, although I have difficulty maintaining it for a long time."

"It may mean leaving New York."

"When?" she eagerly asked.

"As soon as Nick says so. He'll know."

"Oh." Her face fell.

"Still won't trust him?"

"Well, perhaps a little."

"Just remember, my niece. I will be there too. I have not had an adventure like this in two years. It's good for the heart. Come on, I think your pretty nose is turning blue. Can we go back now?"

Well after midnight, Morgan woke from a deep, dreamless sleep, thinking she had heard a scraping sound against the window. Or was it the door? Then she heard the door creak open. Sitting against the headboard, Morgan waited. It had to be him—sneaking into her bed in the middle of the night.

Leaning headfirst into the room, he loudly whispered, "Morgan? Wake up. It's me."

The whiskey fumes reached her before he did.

"I am not surprised, Nicholas. Where have you been all evening?" she accused.

"Where have *you* been all afternoon?" he countered.

Managing to find his way to the bedside in the darkened room, he waited for her to say something.

"Well, aren't you going to answer me dear *wife?*" he sneered.

A small white candle was lit. The tiny glow did not hide the dangerous gleam in his eyes.

"Nick, I don't know what you are talking about."

"Really? Has your deception become a regular habit? How often did you neglect to tell me when you were meeting your lover?"

The quilt cover dropped, exposing the lacy trim of her blue nightdress. "My lover? Nicholas, what is wrong with you?"

"Why nothing. I receive a note this morning from my wife, telling me she is unable to keep our appointment. Something about lunch with my mother. I am, needless to say, somewhat disappointed. I go to the warehouse. But en route I pass Fraunces Tavern. I see my wife going inside with my friend. Now," he grabbed her bare arm, "tell me if that is not unusual."

"Let go of my arm. You're hurting me."

"Am I?" He did not release her. Instead, Nicholas roughly hauled her out of the bed to stand before him.

"Now, tell me about you and Ian Kendall."

"There is nothing to tell. Ian joined us for lunch. Nick, I was with your mother and Sally too. Ian happened to join us." She defiantly faced him.

"Why don't I believe you? I want to, but all I can see is Ian with his arms around you, his mouth on yours, his hands . . ."

"Stop this!" her voice rose. "You will wake everyone in this house."

"I don't care anymore. I have had enough. You are my woman." The long black braid swung in the opposite direction of her when he shook her.

Frightened but angered by his behavior, Morgan did not think she could reason with him. "Nicholas."

"Don't talk. There is nothing you can say. Did he kiss you Morgan? Like this?" He grabbed the back of her head, making any escape impossible while his mouth brutally attacked hers. It was a passionless kiss.

Twisting free, Morgan slapped Nick's face with all the strength she could muster.

"Get out of here, Nicholas, this minute. I have nothing to say to a brute."

Stunned, he blinked a few times before focusing on her

heaving body. Then he shoved her onto the bed, falling on top of her, pinning her hands above her head. His liquored breath assailed her nostrils. "Listen to me. You will do as I say. I do not want to wait for you to come to me. I do not want to watch you flirt with every man you meet. Even Margaret says that Ian loves you. He wants to marry you!" The absurdity of their ridiculous situation made him laugh. "You cannot marry twice. But then," he briefly sobered, "you can marry once."

"You are making no sense. Let me go Nicholas. You are hurting me." He seemed not to hear her words. "I will scream."

"You are my woman. Do you hear me? You will marry me again to prove it. I'll marry you in front of the whole damn town if I have to."

"Please Nick. Please," she begged.

Wanting to claim her sweet lips, Nicholas lowered his mouth. The feel of tears against his lips communicated more than words. Startled, Nicholas moved a thumb to wipe the salty wetness from her cheeks.

"Morgan . . . I'm sorry. I don't . . ."

"Get out!" she hissed.

"There is something I have to tell you."

Morgan scrambled away from his touch. Taking the quilt cover, she defiantly stood at the other end of the bed.

"I want you to get out of here. I am not interested in anything you have to say to me. Now—or ever!"

Chapter 24

"She won't speak to me, Eric. It's been one week and I can't get close to her."

Eric quirked one eyebrow. "What did you expect? You only stopped drinking three days ago."

"I saw her with Ian Kendall. All right, so I jumped to the wrong conclusion. But tell me, Uncle, whose company has Morgan been keeping this week? Who escorted her to the theater, one charity ball, and one damn sleigh ride?"

"Stop pacing like that. You're wearing a hole in your beautiful carpet and you are making me dizzy."

Nicholas dropped into his desk chair. Reaching for a cheroot, he continued to complain. "How can I possibly tell her about our marriage now? Why she'd marry Kendall just to spite me!"

"I doubt that lad."

"Don't. You haven't seen her when she's blind with fury. She's some wildcat." His eyes followed the path of the smoke. "Yes, angry. Her eyes spit fire, her cheeks become red, small fists clench and unclench by her side—or at me."

His nephew's bemused smile told Eric enough. Yet Nick had no idea how far he had pushed his wife that night. She was making him pay now, and would probably continue if someone didn't intervene—soon. They were two of a kind, Eric thought: headstrong, stubborn, impulsive, and passionate.

"Listen to me, you fool. You cannot let this go much further. Kendall is over that house all the damn time. He is enthralled with Morgan."

"Who can blame him?" Nicholas put out one cheroot to light another. A stark white linen shirt contrasted with the black buckskin breeches and boots. Although he was clean, there was an unkempt look to him. Perhaps it was the long hair, which curled below his ears, or the heavy stubble on his face. Nicholas hadn't shaved in three days.

Women must be falling all over him, Eric thought. And the young besotted fool had not noticed. His eyes were only for one vixen. "As I was about to say, lad, I don't think you can wait much longer. She has to know the truth. One of us must leave for New Orleans in a few weeks. If our assumptions and contacts are correct, the 'Andrews Gang'—for lack of a better identification—will be visiting the U.S. Bank in New Orleans very soon. We should be there before them."

"I am perfectly aware of that." Nicholas left the chair to wander toward the tall curtained window. The glare of the sun against the window hurt his eyes, but he remained immobile. The weather was warming. Soon the snow would melt. There would be no more sleigh rides. Sleigh rides! Why am I thinking about those, he asked, then quickly answered his own question. They reminded him of the happier days with Morgan, he miserably thought.

"Perhaps I should speak to her."

Turning to face his uncle, Nicholas threatened, "Don't you dare. This is my problem, my business. I must take care of this."

Eric tried to hide a smile by strolling over to the teakwood card table. They had had some long nights at this table recently. Despite the liquor-induced haze, Nick was quite a sharp cardplayer. I wonder how sharp he will be when he confronts his wife and Ian Kendall? Clearing his throat, Eric said, "I heard there is another charity ball tomorrow night. At the Winthrop's mansion in Lipsenard's Meadows. I know your family is planning to attend—including my brother. Yes," he acknowledged Nick's surprised look, "Warren's been bellowing so much lately that the doctor said it was time to let him out. They are all going—including your wife."

"With Ian Kendall, I assume."

"Of course. You are not around to interfere."

"Well," Nicholas slapped his thigh, "I will be tomorrow. And I am not going alone. I think," he impishly grinned, "I will be escorting Miss Lawson."

"Nick," Eric warned, "you may be stirring up a hornet's nest."

"No. Now that I think of it, I believe it is what Morgan needs. Some healthy competition for my affections."

"Perhaps I should come too."

Morgan was bored. It was the fourth consecutive night that she'd been out. The people were the same—wealthy, snobbish, and very pretentious. Morgan was easily accepted into this social group by virtue of being the Rhodeses' houseguest. But she was tired of answering questions about her life in Halifax. How much more could she improvise? However, she was more alluring because they believed she was British. The Americans still loved to hear about British social life and royalty, and it was rumored that she was the same beauty who captured Ian Kendall's heart, not to mention the eye of Captain Nicholas Rhodes.

Then there was Ian; dear, sweet Ian, who was the perfect friend and escort. He said he loved her. Moreover, he proposed again two nights ago. Morgan managed to postpone any further talk about marriage by telling Ian that she could not think of marriage at this time. Not until she settled some family matters. Being the wonderful man that he was, Ian agreed to wait for an answer . . . no matter, he said, how long it took.

She liked Ian too much to go on deceiving him. Either she would tell him the truth, or in a more cowardly fashion let Nick handle the situation. It was, she reasoned, all Nick's fault anyway.

Reluctantly, Morgan admitted that she sorely missed Nick. But anger still dominated her actions and seeing Nick, especially after that awful night, would mean listening to his explanation and excuses. He might even apologize. Of course, Morgan would be lost in his metallic gaze and no doubt would forgive him.

"Maryann, cherie, you seem lost in some trance. This is our first of many, I hope, dances of the evening." Ian formally bowed, but winked at the same time.

"Ian, must you be so formal?" she giggled. "I daresay I am most flattered."

"That is my intent," he murmured before leading her into the center of the crowded ballroom floor, gracefully twirling Morgan about the room in a lively waltz.

"You are the most beautiful woman here," he said aloud.

"Thank you kind sir. But you shouldn't fill my head with such lies."

"Lies! Maryann, you could not think you are anything less than stunning. That gold dress perfectly matches the sparkle and color of your eyes. Your hair is so fashionably styled and curled—so many curls, Maryann. Your smile is the most genuine I have seen. You radiate beauty." Ian's hazel eyes held no trace of laughter. "I truly mean it, Maryann."

"Well, thank you. You make a very handsome picture too." She couldn't help but notice the well-tailored dark burgundy velvet jacket and embroidered waistcoat of blue, pink, and yellow. Quite fashionable, yet very appropriate on Ian's tall frame. The only understated thing about Ian was his white breeches and silk shirt and cravat.

"We make a lovely couple. Even Warren Rhodes told me as much."

The musical set ended and Ian led her to the Rhodes family.

"It is so good to see him outside of that house," she fondly looked at Warren. She had learned much about Warren Rhodes from their daily conversations and reading. Despite his gruff exterior, he was a kind man who dearly loved his youngest son—perhaps in excess. If it weren't for this terrible, deceitful life, Morgan could love this man as a parent.

"I wish I could dance, my dear. You look lovely this evening. I have never seen such a becoming gown," Warren complimented.

Remembering the gown had been a surprise gift from Nick, Morgan hoped her blush was not as obvious as it felt.

"That is a beautiful locket," Sally added.

"Why thank you," she stammered. Morgan had reluctantly

hid most of her jewelry. When she was sure no one was about she'd take out the anchor pin, reminiscing about the halcyon days with Nick. The locket, likewise the ring, she could not take off. They were a part of her. Without them, Morgan felt that a portion of her past would disappear.

"Was it a gift from an admirer?" Sally innocently persisted.

"A relative." She felt the heart and tried to recall the touch of long, lean fingers on her neck as he whispered delicious words in her ear.

Recognizing the look of longing and sadness, Christine loathed herself for making this difficult request of her children.

"Doesn't my bride look beautiful?" Warren proudly asked.

Wearing a turquoise watered silk gown, Christine looked far prettier than most of the young girls in attendance. Pearls were woven through her pale blond tresses. A single strand diamond and pearl necklace adorned her slim neck.

"It's a shame that Nick couldn't join us," Warren said. "He hasn't been around much lately. Nothing new I suppose. Either it's business or someone that keeps him away. By the way, where is my brother, the one Nick truly takes after?"

"Oh, he will join us later. He promised me so this afternoon. I think Eric was trying to bribe a tailor into finishing his formal clothes. He did not think he'd need to pack those clothes, Warren."

"Thought he'd be attending my funeral, huh? Well, I showed that rogue a thing or two. By God," Warren chuckled, "I feel well enough for a turn around the dance floor." Extending his arm to Christine, he asked, "Would you do me the honor, my lovely wife?"

"I don't think you should . . ."

"Nonsense. I'm fine."

They were such a handsome couple slowly turning around the marble floor. Christine's diamonds sparkled under the brilliant glow of the enormous crystal chandeliers. When they returned, she was more breathless than her husband.

After a few glasses of champagne punch, Morgan found that she was having a better time. Forgetting her most immediate problems, she allowed the glitter, good food, and music to lift her spirits. Before long, she was in the center of a charming group of men, all vying for a place on her dance card or the opportunity to do her bidding. Punch, food, anything the beautiful Miss Mackenzie wanted. Ian was having a difficult time keeping those potential suitors away. Without any qualms, he would have cheerfully announced their engagement. If only that would keep all the men away.

Comfortably seated in the middle of the pleasant group, Morgan was unaware of the envious stares the single and married ladies directed at her. Nor did she hear them collectively sigh when another couple entered the ballroom.

"What's he doing here? I thought he hated these affairs?" one of the gentlemen said loud enough to catch Morgan's attention.

"He's probably bored or looking for a new conquest," said another.

"I thought he was through with her."

"Well perhaps she finally won him over."

"I don't think so," the young man closest to Morgan said. "He's not that eager to settle down, despite his father's wishes."

Morgan briefly wondered why these men sounded more like jealous young ladies than the refined gentlemen they were supposed to be.

When the crowd hushed, her curiosity won out over propriety. Standing beside Ian, she tried to peek through the parting suitors.

"Ian, what is going on?"

"You don't want to know."

"Don't be absurd." She moved toward the front of the group and stopped short upon seeing the object of everyone's attention.

Nicholas was resplendent in a dove-gray broadcloth coat, black satin breeches, and the shoes he hated. He wore a stark white silk shirt and cravat, which was ornamented with a diamond stickpin. His hair was slightly longer than usual. Silver eyes disdainfully wandered across the crowded room, looking for and finding her. For one brief moment, their silver and gold gazes locked. But Nick's shuttered expression revealed nothing. He looked away.

Morgan was mortified. He acted as if he had never seen her before. Margaret Lawson proudly stood beside him, one hand delicately perched on his arm. Morgan wished the floor would open up and claim her.

"Maryann, I believe this is our dance again," Ian's mellow voice reminded her of where she was.

It wasn't their dance, but Ian immediately noticed how uncomfortable she had become. There was much more going on between his friend and this woman. Ian had every intention of finding out about it. Already, he knew quite a few things about the black-haired beauty, but it was not appropriate to discuss them with her. Until she opened up to him, Ian vowed to wait patiently to gain her trust. He was convinced it was simply a matter of time.

Thank heaven it was a lively quadrille. As Morgan moved from partner to partner, she lost track of where Nicholas was.

Feigning gaiety, Morgan laughed when she thought it was expected, fanned herself to keep her hands occupied, drank when the glass was handed to her, and finally allowed Ian to lead her to the giant buffet in another room.

Hot and cold dishes of meats, fresh fish, tureens of soup, and assorted vegetables adorned the long tables. Ian found a small table toward the back of the room—somewhat removed, he hoped, from the ardent suitors. The food smelled delicious, but as soon as Morgan lifted the silver fork, she could not summon the appetite. Her stomach was tied in knots. Her head pounded from champagne and tension.

Squinting hard while looking about the room, Morgan thought she saw Christine and Warren Rhodes. She knew that even if Nick could not be spotted at a distance, she'd still see him—or feel his presence. His picture was permanently stamped before her imperfect eyesight.

"Maryann, you're wrinkling your forehead. Why don't you wear those spectacles?"

"They are too ugly," she focused on Ian's pleasant face. He would have been the most handsome man in the room—if Nick hadn't shown up.

"Nothing on you could ever be ugly. Who was it you were

looking for? Perhaps I can be of service."

"I was looking for Mr. and Mrs. Rhodes. I should let them know where I am."

"I am sure they know you are with me and that, much to my dismay, I shall not whisk you away tonight." Taking a cursory look around, he said, "They are across the room. With Jonathan and Nick."

"Oh." For some reason Morgan did not think Nick would spend any time with his family. "I wonder if Eric Rhodes is joining us this evening."

"He has and did. Maryann, you must possess some strange powers. Eric just walked in."

All of a sudden the room, the aromatic food, and dozens of people began to close in on Morgan. Wishing she could escape into the cold night air, Morgan decided that a private moment might revive her sagging spirits.

"Ian," she touched his arm, "would you excuse me? I want to freshen up."

Morgan tried to exit swiftly, but along the way she was stopped by new acquaintances. She was almost at the door when Eric found her.

"My dear. How good it is to see you. I've been looking for you. I intend to claim at least two waltzes with you," his dark blue eyes twinkled with merriment.

Admiring the perfectly tailored dark blue jacket and breeches, Morgan said, "You look quite handsome tonight, Eric."

"Only tonight? Why I thought you considered me the most handsome man in all of New York," he laughed.

"And Boston too," she demurely smiled.

"What's wrong, Morgan?" his voice lowered. "Is my nephew still being as difficult as you?"

"Worse. Have you seen him?"

"Only for a moment. He's not in the best of moods this evening."

"You could fool me and every other woman in this house. Why, they're swarming and swooning all over him," her eyes flashed.

"He's your husband. And I . . ."

292

"I'm afraid being my husband is meaningless to him, Uncle Eric. It probably always was. Would you excuse me? I have a slight headache."

Gathering her composure once again, Morgan proudly walked out of the room, the golden skirts rustling behind her. The upstairs salon was empty. All she needed was a few moments alone. Then she could go back and probably face Nick. Seated behind a screen, Morgan could not see the two young women enter the room but heard their hushed voices.

"He's the most handsome man I've ever seen. Did you notice the way he held my hand? Oh Lord, and such a winsome smile. I thought I'd die of ecstasy!" one exclaimed.

"I think Ian Kendall is more handsome. Ooh, but Nick is such a rake. I heard he was chasing his parents' houseguest, then tired of her and went right back to Margaret."

"Margaret will not snare him. Nick Rhodes is not meant for one woman. But I don't mind. I would accept him on any terms." Both girls giggled.

Morgan's head shot up. "Tired of her" they had said. How could these busybodies know such things?

"I don't believe he'll be in town much longer. It's either another woman or business or both, but in another city. Well, there is still Ian. Do you suppose he'll stay in New York for awhile?"

"I hope so. Come, let's leave. Perhaps Nick or Ian will dance with us."

So Nicholas Rhodes was leaving, was he? Did he plan on leaving without me? she wondered. What about his promise to find Andrews?

Morgan placed a cold cloth on her burning brow. If Nick meant to leave her, then there was nothing she could do about it. If he wouldn't help her, others would. Uncle Eric had already offered. And so would Ian—if she ever told him the truth. Determined not to allow Nick to hurt her or undermine her quest, Morgan listed the things she must do. She would give Nicholas one more chance to approach her. If he didn't, she would worry about it then. For now, Morgan would enjoy the rest of the evening. Tomorrow morning she would think about how she would deal with her difficult husband.

Feeling better yet still longing for the feel of the cold night air, Morgan quietly descended the wide staircase, looking for the unoccupied morning room. Surely she could open a window and remain undetected for a few more minutes.

The door softly closed behind her. Morgan stood in the semi-darkened room, heading for the tall French window. But she could not undo the lock.

"Oh damn!" she muttered while toying with the stubborn latch.

"May I be of assistance?" a deep, familiar voice drawled.

Turning sharply, Morgan felt her throat tighten at the sight of her husband. Sitting in a large armchair off to the side of the room, smoking a cheroot, he seemed perfectly at ease.

"Well, may I?"

It took a minute to comprehend his question. "Yes, please. I'd like some air."

Snuffing the cheroot in a glass tray, Nicholas smoothly rose to assist her. The fresh scent of bayberry rum lotion drifted by her nose. In one easy movement, Nicholas opened the window.

The cold air filled her lungs and head. It also hardened her resolve to remain as unaffected as he appeared to be upon seeing her.

"Aren't you concerned that your escort may be looking for you?" he quietly asked.

"No. Aren't you? I'm sure Margaret must be frantic by now."

"I suppose so. But I don't care."

"About Margaret?"

"About everything." He was within touching distance, yet did not move close to her.

The room was too dim for Morgan to see the hard set of his features or the cold expression in his eyes. Yet his impersonal tone gave some indication of his state of mind.

"I hear you are leaving New York soon."

"I am? Who told you that? Ian? Is he so anxious to be rid of me?"

"No. Believe it or not, Ian thinks very highly of you. No," she partially turned away, "I heard it from two giddy, lovesick girls who seem to be aware of everything you do and say."

294

"I seem to have almost as many admirers as you do, my love."

"Don't call me that!" she spat.

"Why?" he touched her arm. "Are you surprised to know that I still consider myself a married man?"

"I certainly am!" she sardonically laughed. "From what I've heard and seen, you certainly haven't acted like my husband."

"Oh? And how should your husband act?" he mocked her. "Should he allow you to collect as many beaus as your fickle heart desires? Should he watch you laugh, flirt, and dance with almost every eligible bachelor who drools over your nearly bare cleavage?"

"How dare you!" Without thinking, Morgan's arm shot out, placing a stinging slap on his cheek.

Nicholas did not move. "That was most unwise, Morgan. Tell me," he crossed his arms over his chest, "when are you planning to tell Ian Kendall the truth about us? Before or after he proposes?"

"He already has," she blurted.

"Another poor lovesick fool who has fallen under your magic spell. Morgan, if you don't tell him tonight, I will. Better yet," he seemed to smile, "why don't we tell him together?"

Intending to lead them out of the room, Nicholas took her arm, but Morgan tried to pull away. Nicholas responded by tightening his grip.

"Let go of me! You have no right . . ."

Hurling her about, Nicholas grabbed the bare forearms, shaking her. "I, madam, have every right. Lest you forget, you are my wife. That makes you my responsibility. It also," he pulled her resistant body closer, "makes you my property. You will do as I say."

"Like hell I will," she snarled.

"Why, then, are you wearing my locket?" he curiously asked. "Shouldn't you be sporting one of Ian's presents? Then you can tell the world who you now belong to," he jeered. "Since when did you become such a hypocrite, my dear?"

Tearing the offensive piece of jewelry off, Nicholas did not wait for a response.

"Nick, you broke it," she cried, staring at the lovely

necklace clutched in his hand.

"Here," he shoved it at her. "Take it back. You can show it to your fiancé. Or should I do that too?" Then completely reversing himself, he angrily announced, "You will never accept anything from anyone but me."

"But you just said . . ."

"Silence!" He still had a viselike grip on her arm. "In case you are hard of hearing, I shall repeat what I've said. You are my woman until I say otherwise." His voice lowered, "And I shall prove it to you now."

Without giving her a chance to protest, Nicholas roughly claimed her mouth. It was a hard, bruising kiss that cut off her breath. His hand snaked up one bare arm to clutch the back of her head, preventing any release.

Shocked at first, then angry, Morgan lifted a slippered foot to step on his toe. Aware of the movement, Nicholas twisted her body, throwing her off balance. Still he did not stop possessing her mouth. Morgan was unaware of the subtle change in the kiss. It softened, beckoning her to respond to the deep longing he felt. Slowly, his tongue insinuated itself between her teeth. She allowed it, welcomed it. The cold night air suddenly became a hot summer gust that gradually touched each part of her aroused body.

There was little resistance. Morgan's hands rose to circle his neck, playing with the curling hairs at the nape. Her tongue dueled with his. There was no more distance between the two. Their bodies fused as one. Morgan felt the desire building, burning, and dearly wished she could feel his naked skin.

A low groan escaped her throat, but was swallowed by his passionate possession of her mouth. She would let him have his way with her, here and now. As long as he never let her go.

Nicholas broke the kiss to whisper in her ear, "I've missed you, my love. I long for you." Nibbling her neck, strong hands glided under then over the golden bodice, exploring her upturned breasts. "We have to talk. But not here, not now. I want to take you home."

Once again, he took her expectant mouth. Lost in the reawakened sensation of intense longing for him, Morgan tried to speak. "We can't Nick. I must not let you do this to me.

296

I . . . I mean we'll . . ." The protest was silenced by another searing kiss.

"Am I intruding?" another voice asked, then repeated the question in a louder voice.

"Ian," Morgan breathed into Nick's shoulder.

"Pardon me. I seem to have made a dreadful mistake." He turned to leave, but Nicholas's calm voice stopped him.

"Don't leave Ian. Come in. There is much you don't know."

"I doubt it Rhodes." He moved again to the door.

"No, please. Ian, wait!" Morgan called, moving out of Nick's embrace. "My name is not Maryann Mackenzie. It is Morgan . . ."

"I know that," Ian snapped. "It's Morgan Rhinehart. I know all about your father and the terrible tragedy. I was waiting for the most propitious moment to tell you. Then I realized that what I really wanted was for you to love and trust me enough to tell me yourself. I wanted you to know how deeply I care for you—whoever you are. I wanted to believe you felt the same way."

Ian's heart-wrenching words and dignified manner sliced through Morgan's cool demeanor. "I am so sorry Ian. But . . ."

"But you don't know everything." Nicholas finished the sentence. "I don't know who your source of information is, but whoever he is, some vital news was omitted."

"Really?" Ian stepped farther into the room. "I thought I was very thorough."

"You did not get Morgan's whole name. Morgan Ann Rhinehart *Rhodes*. Does the last name ring a bell?" Nicholas sat on the arm of the couch, crossing one leg over the other, arms again casually folded across his chest.

Morgan was annoyed with Nick's abrupt manner. He seemed to be enjoying himself. Standing between the two men, she gave Nicholas a sharp glance then turned to Ian.

"I never meant for this to happen, Ian. There are reasons for this charade."

"It's true, Kendall. Morgan has been completely selfless about this. It was all for my family's sake. I never should have allowed her to become involved," he added for Morgan's ears.

"How long have you been married?"

"Since November. We were married in Halifax." Morgan tried to smile, but her eyes felt too watery. "I could never find the proper time to tell you. You are so charming, so enthusiastic about life, that I lost my nerve. It was a cowardly act on my part, Ian. I have acted selfishly." The only sound was the rustling dress as she moved closer to Ian, offering one hand. "I hope you find it in your heart to forgive me some day."

Ian was speechless, his mind confused by previous bits of conversation, Morgan's reluctance to speak of marriage, Nick's fierce and unusual protectiveness. The signs were always there. He simply chose to ignore them. Everything about Morgan was beautiful. She was intelligent, witty, and completely oblivious to her physical beauty and charm. Ian wanted Morgan more than he wanted anything in his life.

From the first minute he'd met her, Ian suspected that the story about Halifax and being Peter's sister were false. Sailing with Nick, Ian went so far as to assume that Morgan might have shared his cabin. But it did not matter. Ian had decided to find out exactly who Maryann Mackenzie was. One letter to Halifax answered that question. An old family friend of the Kendalls was a longtime resident of Halifax. There was no Maryann Mackenzie.

Another well-placed inquiry in Boston gave Ian her true identity. Upon learning her real name, he would gladly help her—if she wanted it. If she wanted to keep this other identity, that was fine with him too.

But never, never did he consider that Nick actually married her.

"This is none of my business. Then again," he smiled, "perhaps it is. Since I seem to have made a perfect fool out of myself in front of my good friend and the woman I am in love with, I would like to know why you two are married yet living apart."

"It was out of respect for my father's health, Kendall. My mother wanted us to wait."

"She knows?"

"Yes, and so does Eric. No one else does, Ian, not yet." Morgan's implied request to remain silent affected him.

"You have nothing to fear from me. I shall fade away and remain mute. If you will excuse me, I need a drink and a moment alone."

"So do I," Nicholas rose to join him. "Mind if I accompany you?"

"Yes." Ian turned and quietly strode out of the room.

"That was very nice, Nick. Anything else you'd care to ruin? Why don't we find your father? Better yet, let's make a public announcement," she said waspishly.

"That would be fine with me." Offering his arm, Nick asked, "Shall we?"

Confused by his apparent lack of concern, Morgan stammered, "I don't understand you, Nicholas. I thought you were worried about your father."

"I am. But as you can see, he has made a swift recovery. He'll be fine. I see no reason why we cannot go on with our lives, Morgan. I've waited long enough; so have you. I want my wife back," he said heatedly.

If he would have spoken with a little more feeling, Morgan might have relented. He seemed so uncaring; he was not the person to whom she was accustomed.

"Perhaps we should discuss this another time," she turned to go.

"Wait, I have something else to say."

Morgan closed her eyes in anticipation of the words she so longed to hear, words that would make all the difference. She'd go home with him this very second if he told her that he loved her. Swiveling her head toward his commanding voice, Morgan held her breath as she waited for his words.

"I'll have this necklace repaired tomorow." In one long stride, he was before her. "Did you know how ravishing you look tonight? You smell like summer lilacs and roses," he huskily said, watching for a reaction. When there was none, Nicholas took her hand in both of his, raising the palm to his mouth. "Would you do me the honor of dancing with me, Morgan?"

It was the last thing she would have expected to hear him say. But his voice, his mouth, sent heat and chills along her arms. Too late, she must have swayed toward him, for once again Morgan was in his powerful embrace.

Nicholas placed tiny kisses along the slender column of her neck, eventually seeking her moist lips. Passion, tenderness, and pain combined to melt her resolve. Lost in his kiss, Morgan would have cheerfully stayed in the darkened room all evening.

It was Nicholas who broke the trance. "We must meet Morgan, tomorrow at the town house at four P.M. Morgan," he breathed into her ear, "promise you will meet me."

"I will."

"May I claim that dance now?" he rakishly grinned.

Chapter 25

True to her word, Morgan met Nicholas in their Greenwich Street house. She barely reached the red door when he swung it wide open, pulling her into his arms. A booted foot kicked the door closed. Wordlessly, he undid the white cloak, letting it drop. Then he lifted her into his arms and carried her up the carpeted stairs to their bedroom.

Still fully clothed, they lay on the bed; Nicholas was above her, cushioning his weight with his elbows. Looking deep into the topaz depths, his eyes told her what words could not as his hands roamed her body roughly.

The desperate need to feel was communicated to Morgan. Now she too clutched his linen shirt, feverishly unbuttoning it, sliding her hands over his skin.

As her tongue surged into his mouth, Nicholas sensed her surrender to the desire that pulsed through her blood and his. One moment his hands were loosening her bound hair, while the next his hands massaged her uplifted breasts and then roamed over her skirt. Her arousal was as great as his. Moving against him, Morgan felt his swollen manhood straining against the confinse of his breeches.

"Do you want more, my love?" he passionately whispered at last while sliding one hand beneath the skirt, the petticoat, stroking her, feeling the moisture against her satin chemise. "You do, sweetheart; you need more."

The ribbons undone, Nicholas chuckled upon hearing Morgan's groan. Writhing against his hand, she nearly lost control when one finger then another dipped into her moist center, moving in and out in a rhythm that foretold of much more pleasure—if she wanted it.

"Now Nick," she groped for the buttons on his breeches. "I cannot wait. I want to feel you deep inside me—now."

Skirts were lifted, satin underthings and breeches pulled out of the way. Nicholas forcefully thrust deep inside her. It was bliss. They needed to be consumed by one another. He didn't care how he took her, clothed or unclothed; it mattered not, as long as he did not leave her. Fueling her fire with kisses and his stroking hands, saying words of passion and phrases she never heard before, Morgan was like a comet riding on the flames of desire.

"Take all of me, Morgan. Let go with me. Do you feel the tremors, Morgan? I do. Now," he groaned into her mouth, "please, now!"

Together they soared to a new dimension beyond the heavens; a blending of souls from the elements of attraction to the compound of love.

"I must be a harlot," she finally said much later.

They were still entwined in each other's arms, their clothes crumpled.

"Nick, you still have your boots on. I have no idea what happened to my shoes," she self-conciously laughed.

"Ah," he sighed with satisfaction. "I've never felt so good. Morgan, you can't do this to me again," he kissed her temple. "Here, let me help you."

He tried to straighten her clothes, but was not successful, which only made them both laugh. Then Morgan remembered the clothes she had left the armoire and sought a pale blue day dress.

"Morgan, love, there is something we must discuss. I've postponed talking to you about this matter, but it can no longer wait." He leaned against the headboard, one arm casually supporting his head.

"I don't think I'll get into that bed—now that I'm dressed again." Morgan, half reclining in the chaise lounge, stared seriously and said, "Nick, before you tell me anything, I want to ask you a few questions." She tried to comb the tangles out

302

of her hair with her fingers, but quickly gave up. Spotting her silver-backed hair brush, Morgan retrieved it then took her seat. "Sorry. I was about to ask if you are going to help me with Andrews."

"Of course, Morgan. You've always known that."

"Well, not in the last two weeks."

"That is part of what I need to talk to you about. Let me begin. I think it will answer your questions. All right sweetheart?"

His brilliant smile caught her unawares. He was so handsome, so masculine. It was a good thing there was some distance between them. Nicholas had not dressed. Instead, he removed his shirt, tossing it across the room. He was half clad in open breeches and boots and Morgan felt flushed from staring at him.

"Morgan, don't give me those sultry looks or we will be lovemaking on that chaise. Stop," he lifted one hand seeing her about to speak, "I still have the floor.

"First, I intend to settle the matter with my father tonight. We will not live apart."

"But Nick . . ."

"I don't care Morgan. We've waited too long. He is strong enough to learn the truth. Second, I think we owe Ian some explanation. We can speak to him together, or I'll handle it."

"No you won't," she sharply said. "It's my responsibility and my problem. I will talk to Ian. Stay out of this one Nicholas," she warned.

Repressing his grin, he relented. "Fine, you take care of Ian. Now, the last and most important issue," he moved across the bed to sit on the edge, facing her. "I want us to marry again. Here, in New York." Ignoring her shocked look, he blithely continued speaking. "The arrangements have been made. We will go tomorrow afternoon to Trinity Church. We will inform the family tonight and invite them to attend. In either case, Eric will be there."

Paralyzed at first, Morgan absorbed his surprising words then sprang out of the lounge. "What are you talking about, Nicholas?"

"Morgan, you only call me 'Nicholas' when you are angry

or upset."

"Answer my question. Why are we marrying again?"

Casually unfolding his legs, Nicholas eased off the bed to sit in front of her. "Do you remember when, or rather where we married?"

"Of course I do!"

"I mean, sweetheart, we were married on British soil. Do you remember my telling you that I believed it wise for us to marry again on American soil? Just to be sure. Well," he paused, still smiling, "we must do it now."

There was something too casual about his manner that alerted Morgan. He wasn't telling her everything. She was positive that he was avoiding something. Sitting beside him, she inquired, "What aren't you telling me, Nicholas? You are hiding something and I know it."

Nicholas reached for her hand, but Morgan angrily pulled away. "Well, it really is not very important. I received a letter from Peter a few weeks ago. Do you remember that lovely church we were married in?"

"Nick," she warned impatiently.

"All right. There was a fire. Unfortunately the church was destroyed—along with everything inside."

"Our marriage documents," she breathed.

"I'm afraid so, beauty. You have in your possession—you do have it, I hope—the only original documentation. However, I think this is as good a time as any to marry—again." He grinned.

"Are we still legally married?"

"Of course we are," he said too quickly. "Just don't lose the paper. You do have it, don't you Morgan?"

"Yes, yes. I know exactly where it is. In my jewel box."

Seeing her troubled look, Nicholas took her left hand. "Some day, beauty, we will have a marvelous laugh about the early months of our marriage. It will be a great story to tell our grandchildren."

Leaning her head on his broad shoulder, Morgan wondered how much more she could endure and if she would ever fondly remember this time.

*   *   *

Two hours later, Morgan and Nicholas left for the Rhodes home to attend a family dinner. Nicholas's mind was firmly made up. Everyone would be told of their marriage. Damn the consequences.

They were late. The others had already set down to dinner. Holding hands, they leisurely walked into the formal dining room and were shocked to see both Ian and Margaret at the table.

"Damn," he muttered in a low voice.

"How nice of you to join us, Nick." Warren sounded very healthy. "Maryann, I am sorry you did not have time to change into dinner clothes."

She was definitely underdressed. Margaret looked as if she were at another charity ball, while Sally and Christine appeared to have spent the entire afternoon preparing for the evening meal.

"I apologize. If you'll excuse me, I will find something more appropriate."

"No." Nicholas stayed her hand. "I am confident that my father will forgive us this major transgression this once. Won't you Father?" he coolly inquired.

"Oh sit down, Nick. I'm not dressed either." Eric tried to inject some humor, "If my brother doesn't like it, we will all go to your house."

"The world is not the same anymore," Warren grumbled to himself.

The situation could not have been any more uncomfortable, but the evening was still far from over. Morgan, seated between Nick and Ian, felt her husband's icy stare whenever Ian spoke a word to her. And Ian was so subdued that Morgan dearly wished she could have spoken privately with him before this dinner. Apparently, Ian and Margaret had been invited the week before . . . something Morgan obviously forgot.

Perhaps it was the stilted environment that made the wine flow too freely. Not one of the nine adults declined the offer for more wine. Once, Christine admonished her husband.

"Warren, I don't think you should have any more wine. You are not used to this much . . ."

"Nonsense, Chrissie. I feel wonderful. Do you know what?" he brandished the crystal wineglass. "I intend to visit my office

305

tomorrow. There are too many things left undone," his rising voice matched each arm movement. "Ah, yes, I feel great. And I am pleased my family and friends are here to share my good fortune."

When Nicholas was momentarily distracted by Margaret and Eric, Ian took that moment to whisper, "Morgan, I would like you to know that I still care very deeply for you." His hazel eyes studied her exquisite face. "I will always be your devoted friend. If you ever need me . . ."

"Thank you," she softly replied. "I—it means so much to me."

Noting his wife patting Ian's hand, Nicholas cleared his throat. "Excuse me, I'd like to say something."

Christine looked at her son, knowing what was going to be said. Nor could she blame him. At last night's ball she had vowed to say something, but once more she became a coward. Then before midnight she had observed a beautiful sight—one that would forever remain in her mind: Nicholas whirling Morgan around the dance floor. They had moved as one, leaning and swaying into the other, mesmerized by one another. For them, there was no charity ball, no crowded dance floor, no flickering candlelight. Nicholas had all he needed in his arms. He was consumed by the loving eyes of his wife.

Yes, she decided, it was definitely time. Without a doubt, Christine knew she would protect her son and his wife.

Studying each curious face, Nicholas's silver gaze settled on his father. "I want to introduce someone to you." Taking Morgan's right hand, Nicholas continued, "Father, this is my wife."

"Your what!" he sputtered. "When did you marry? Today? Yesterday? Christine, did you know about this?"

"Father, I am not finished. There is much more you need to know. Morgan and I have been married for four months."

"Morgan?" Jonathan and Warren questioned in unison.

"Yes, Morgan. Meet my wife, Morgan Rhinehart Rhodes."

"For God's sake, son! You didn't have to marry her to get the information I wanted!"

Morgan's hand tightened on Nick's. Color fled from her face. "What are you saying?" she asked her father-in-law.

"It wasn't necessary to sacrifice yourself for the plates. Nick," Warren continued to blunder, ignoring the stricken look on the young woman's face. "I asked for your help in locating Miss Rhinehart and the stolen plates, but son . . ."

"Father, you don't understand. This has nothing . . ."

"Well, did you find the plates, son? Where are they? Wasn't I correct about the traitor?" Warren continued speaking, unaware of the words that spilled forth. The wine was speaking, but that did not matter to Morgan who was painfully shocked. Married her for the plates? The daughter of a traitor? Could Morgan be hearing correctly?

"Mr. Rhodes," she found her voice, snatching her hand away from Nick. "What are you saying? Do you mean that Nicholas was requested to find me?"

"Of course. I was asked to do whatever is necessary to find those currency plates. It means a lot, young woman. You know that! So did your father. Back in June I asked Nick to help me locate the plates and the traitor's daughter. He's done an admirable but overzealous job. Why, I never . . ."

"Stop it. Stop!" she shouted. There was a wild, haunted look in her eyes now. Swinging her head toward the man she had loved with all her heart, she asked, "Is this true? Is it, Nick?"

"Morgan, my love, it is not exactly the way it sounds," he answered, still sitting beside her, a goblet of wine in his hand. It was supposed to be for the toast he would propose.

The armchair Morgan pushed back slid across the fine Persian rug. Facing him, fired with rage and pain, she persisted, "Answer me, Nick—now. Did you agree to help find me and the plates last June?"

"Morgan, let's discuss this in private." Nicholas stood, seeking her arm.

"What difference should it make? Of course he did. So?" Warren had no idea of the havoc he was causing with his careless words. He had no idea of how deeply he was wounding Morgan. As Maryann Mackenzie, he had genuinely liked the girl. His mind was too befuddled by wine and at the moment he could only recall that Nicholas had married the daughter of a traitor! All his plans for joining the Rhodes and Lawson families were lost. Unless . . .

"Don't concern yourself, Nick. I can have this marriag annulled. Margaret, I pray you will have patience."

The young woman was as speechless as the others. Nick— married? The daughter of a traitor? Feeling like an intrude Margaret looked at Ian. "I think we should leave. This is private family matter."

She quickly rose, giving Ian no other choice but to follow "Yes, yes of course. I'll be available, Morgan, if you need m You know where to find me."

"No! No one has to leave but me. I am the one who does n belong. I believe I made a dreadful mistake. Ian," Morga looked beseechingly at him, "would you please wait for me? will only take a moment to gather a few things."

"You are not going anywhere, Morgan, but with me. We ar going home." Nicholas's voice was deceptively cool.

With the last shred of her dignity, Morgan looked at eac person at the table. "Mrs. Rhodes, thank you for you hospitality. Jon and Sally, you've been most kind. And Eri thank you for being a friend." She did not look at Nick c Warren. Her heart was too heavy. But not for one minut would she remain in the same house with any member of th Rhodes family. With her head high, Morgan turned to exit

Nicholas was right behind her. "Morgan, don't be a fool. M father does not know what he is saying."

Turning on him, she asked, her voice raw with pain, "Di you agree to help your father look for me last June? Did you?

"Well yes, but Morgan . . ."

"Were you in Boston looking for me or a cargo?"

"Well, both I suppose."

"Wait here Nick. I will be right down."

Having no idea what she meant to do, Nicholas stood at th base of the wide staircase. She was gone for five minutes.

When Morgan returned wearing the sable cloak, she brief placed the small portmanteau on the bottom step. A piece c parchment paper was clutched in her left hand.

It took a moment for Nicholas to recognize the documen

"Morgan, what are you doing with our marriage ce tificate?"

"I said I had something for you, didn't I?" She appeare

devoid of emotion. Holding the paper between her hands, Morgan stared into Nicholas's surprised eyes while methodically tearing the document into shreds that settled around her feet.

"I loved you Nick. So much that it became a terrible ache when I could not see or touch you. You meant everything to me. At times I thought I could not live without you." She paused but held his startled gaze. "I really loved you."

"Morgan, please. Listen to me," his hand reached for her shoulder.

"No! Never again. As I said, Nicholas, I *loved* you. That is all in the past. I have learned so much in the last hour. You betrayed me. You mocked my love. You never loved me. All you ever cared about was locating the daughter of a traitor and returning the damn plates to your father. But I was naive and actually quite stupid to believe that a few whispered words of passion and some baubles meant anything more than what, Nick? Lust? A way to keep the traitor's daughter in your bed while you searched for the bronze plates? How you must have laughed behind my back.

"Perhaps it was for the best that I lost our child. There is nothing that binds me to you any longer Nicholas. Nothing. I never want to see you again." She took a step, but Nicholas blocked the path.

"Do you honestly believe that by tearing up that ridiculous piece of paper it is over between us?"

"As far as I am concerned, I have no husband. My name is Miss Morgan Rhinehart. Daughter of Samuel Rhinehart of Philadelphia."

Retrieving the bag, Morgan walked to the front door just as Ian and Eric entered the hallway.

"Do you need any help?" Ian kindly asked.

"Absolutely."

"Where will you go Morgan?" Nicholas could not believe she was actually walking away from him. Her words had sliced through his heart. Shoulders slumped in defeat, he helplessly watched as the only woman he had ever loved calmly walked out of his life.

Morgan did not bother to turn around to answer the

question. "Where I go, Captain Rhodes, is none of your concern. You are free to marry Margaret or sail around the world."

In one last desperate attempt to stop her, Nicholas headed for the departing couple. But Eric's strong arm clutched his shoulder.

"Leave it alone Nick. She's hurting. She's been humiliated. Allow her some dignity, with time to think things over. She will come around."

"Uncle Eric," Nicholas's full gray eyes were as bleak as a winter storm, "she's not coming back."

Silently, they watched the black carriage pull away. The sounds of horses' hooves echoed through Nicholas's mind.

"She said she loved me." His anguished whisper hurt Eric, who had never seen his nephew this way. "I never heard her say those words before tonight. Isn't that ironic, Eric? She loved me and now she is walking out of my life. Our marriage was not real. Nothing is real—except that she is gone."

Without reaching for his jacket, Nicholas walked into the dark, cold shadows of the night.

Chapter 26

NEW ORLEANS—MARCH, 1809

"Ian, I am positive that Andrews is here in New Orleans," Morgan waved a letter at him. "It's all here in Eric's letter to me. Listen:

"'It was a stupid error on my part to overlook the obvious. Andrews and his two accomplices are systematically stealing the currency plates from the U.S. Banks. Perhaps all. We traced their thefts. They are making a small circle around the states. There is little doubt that New Orleans is next.

"'I have a plan, Morgan dear. I want you to wait. Do not do anything until you hear from me again . . . certainly within the next three weeks.

"'So much has happened since your hasty departure . . .'"

Morgan looked up, hesitant to reveal the contents in the balance of the letter. "I think that is the important part of his letter, Ian." She neatly folded the paper, placing it in the pocket of her riding skirt.

"Then we must wait until we hear from Eric, Morgan. He made that perfectly clear. No more inquiries at the Governor's office. No more visits to the bank," Ian's tone was too light for chastising.

"Well, I suppose I can wait a few more weeks."

"Good. Now, how about that ride you promised me?" He reached for her hand. "I had no idea you were such an accomplished horsewoman."

"There are many things about me you do not know, Mr. Kendall," she smiled fetchingly.

"I intend to learn them all. By the time we marry, I shall know so much about you that you will never have to ask me for anything. It will all be there for you," his hazel eyes lit up in amusement.

"Give me a moment. I must get my hat and jacket. Although I cannot understand such propriety in this heat." She hurriedly walked out of the music room.

It gave Ian such pleasure to see Morgan laugh again. Leaning into the brocade settee, Ian thought about the recent changes in their lives.

After that disastrous night in New York, Ian had taken Morgan to the City Hotel. She did not cry; she did not speak. Morgan was like a cold statue. But Ian knew she needed someone to depend on and there was no doubt that he would do anything for Morgan Rhinehart.

The next day he had appeared at the hotel with two one-way tickets on the next passenger ship bound for New Orleans. She politely refused at first. Ian, however, was adamant. There was no place else for her to go. If she went to her mother in Boston, it would be a matter of days before Nick trailed her. And surely, he contended, if she wanted to continue her search for Andrews, Boston was not the place to begin and New Orleans was.

"Besides, Morgan, my family is there. I have a lovely house in the Garden District and a magnificent plantation less than two hours outside of New Orleans," he'd explained. "It's perfect for you. My family will adore you. You need some time for yourself. I am not asking for any promises or anything in return—except your friendship and trust. Perhaps the rest will follow."

"I am not sure. Ian, how can I travel with you alone? What would your family think?"

He had wanted to tell her that he cared nothing for people's thoughts. He only wanted to protect her and help her get over this terrible trauma. He'd do whatever he could to make her laugh again; to see the flash of delight in her golden eyes, not the hollow look in the wraith before him.

"You will go with me as my fiancée. I will hire a woman as your chaperone. Trust me, Morgan. I know it is difficult at the moment to believe anyone. But I think this is for the best."

"But your fiancée? Ian, less than forty-eight hours ago I discovered that I am not legally married, that the man I loved was using me for personal gain. Please," her hands had cradled her throbbing temples, "it's too much."

"Morgan, we will say you are my fiancée. There will be no official announcements, posting of the banns, no date of marriage. I hope to God you come to love me as much as I do you, but I will wait, cherie, for as long as you want. I promise to wait."

It was not necessary for Morgan to ask for proof of his devotion; it was there in his expression.

"All right. But please, Ian, give me time to get over my disappointment and pain," her voice had cracked a fraction.

It was a fragile beginning for Morgan Rhinehart. Ian Kendall knew he would be there when her spirits were restored.

Less than one month had passed since their arrival in New Orleans. Ian's family fawned all over Morgan.

Not wanting to deceive his family about her identity, Morgan had insisted Ian tell them who she was and who her father was. If she were not welcome in their home, so be it. But Morgan would not lie to Ian's family.

They had silently listened to Ian's story about the Rhinehart trial and murder. Ian's father was the first to react.

"Mon Dieu!" Paul exclaimed. "How terrible for you and your family. Is there something we can do?" he had asked, his eyes so much like Ian's.

They were wonderful. Ian's mother, Marie, and sister, Celeste, took Morgan out for a new wardrobe the very next day. Celeste was delighted to have a companion who was not so much older than she.

In the days that followed, Ian knew that Morgan was coming back to life. His family had made the difference, as he had known they would.

Now all he had to do was convince Morgan that her happiness lay with Ian Kendall and not with the pirate who broke her heart. As far as he was concerned, Nicholas Rhodes was no longer his friend. Not after the cruelty he had inflicted on this beautiful creature. He prayed he'd never have to see Nick's face again, for he did not know what he would do—challenge him to a duel or have him killed.

"I am ready, Ian," her sweet voice made Ian scoff at his absurd thoughts.

Yet, Ian wondered for the thousandth time, was she over the heartbreak? Sometimes he'd see that faraway look in her golden eyes and knew she was thinking of Nick. It tore him apart, but he had pledged to be patient. She will love me, he vowed. I know she will.

Morgan slowly adapted to the social life in New Orleans, even though the city was so different from any other place she had visited. There was laughter and gaiety everywhere. People were so warm and friendly that she felt as if she had been a longtime resident of the city. Her new summer wardrobe added a sophistication she had not previously displayed. She was drawn to the simple yet elegant Empire style. But she had no idea how deeply she insulted Ian when she promised to reimburse him for the costly wardrobe.

Because she was a houseguest of the prominent Kendall family, Morgan's relationship with the handsome, eligible Ian Kendall was uppermost on many minds. Yet the talk was not scandalous or vicious. Of course, the young women simply wanted to know who this lovely woman was and whether they still had a chance of snaring Mr. Kendall. Most people had no recognition of the Rhinehart name. To those that recalled it, the scandal was out of their ken. This was the South . . . New Orleans. Life was grand and so different from the stuffy North. Since there was no betrothal announcement, the ladies relaxed. Perhaps Miss Rhinehart was only visiting.

Uppermost on Morgan's mind was Andrews and his accomplices. They were in New Orleans. She felt it in the marrow of her bones. With a single-mindedness that occasionally worried Ian, Morgan's every move, every thought, was on finding the murderers. Only at that moment did she feel her life could start anew.

314

She would start again. Nicholas's treachery was buried deep in her heart. Only at night did he haunt her dreams. But Morgan would try to resist it. She'd never see him again, although she did receive letters from Eric who kept her well-informed about the Rhodes family—all except Nicholas.

Only in the first letter did he briefly explain that Nick had decided to make another cargo run. One week after Morgan's departure, Nicholas had left New York. The other family members were fine, albeit quite upset over the unfolding of events. Warren's health continued to improve despite the fact that he shouldered the responsibility for the shattering episode. Blaming himself for too much wine and too much pride, Warren finally listened to Christine's explanations. But it was too late. Nick was gone, and so was Morgan.

It did not matter, Morgan continued to tell herself each morning. She'd never see them again. Looking into the large gilt-edged cheval glass, Morgan saw the determined face of a young woman who had a mission. Until she heard from Eric, she would make the best of her time with the Kendall family. Tonight was an elegant theater party and dinner. She would look her best and say the right words. The amber-gold eyes would focus on the hundreds of people in the room, searching for new faces, one of whom had a birthmark on his cheek.

A soft knock on the door finally caught Morgan's attention.

"Are you almost ready Morgan?" Celeste called. "Ian swears we will be the last to arrive at the theater. And you know how he feels about late entrances."

"Yes I do," she laughed, remembering how upset Ian became whenever she was tardy. Grabbing her Chinese silk print shawl and fan, Morgan met Celeste's smiling face and Ian's adoring gaze.

He was a very handsome man. Morgan was well aware of the looks the young women gave Ian. He did not seem to mind the attention. In fact, he often stopped to chat with a group of fluttering females, enjoying their flattery while doling out some of his own compliments. Standing at the base of the steps, wearing cream-colored breeches and a dark blue jacket with embroidered waistcoat, Ian looked every inch the gentleman. She was fortunate to have such an attractive man as her escort and friend. Ian was reliable, good-natured, and even-tempered. Not like . . . Morgan shook her head, forcing that unwanted thought away.

"Morgan, you are beautiful. I knew that you would look enchanting in lavender silk." Ian's eyes did not leave the low-cut bodice of the dress. Although Morgan no longer had her marriage band, she did wear the gold locket. Was it simply a fondness for the piece of jewelry or the donor, he jealously wondered. She had refused to accept his gifts of jewelry, saying it was not appropriate or warranted considering the extravagant wardrobe he had purchased. The few pieces she had would do nicely. Occasionally, Marie insisted on loaning a necklace or bracelet, which Morgan graciously accepted.

"Well, Ian, I thought you were the one who hated to be late. Are you ready?" She tossed her head, but the black curls that were intricately woven into a fashionable style did not move, except for the wisps of hair on her forehead and the curls on the side of her face.

"My parents have already left. Celeste, you and Morgan are never on time. Come," he led the woman outside the waiting coach. "I have been looking forward to this opera, *The Barber of Seville*. I saw it in Paris last year."

"I would love to go to France, Italy, and Spain," Morgan wistfully said.

"You shall. There are many adventures that we could have."

Morgan did not need to see Ian's downcast eyes to know what he meant. Yet she deliberately chose to ignore it. This evening was not meant for serious discussion. Tonight she would let Ian entertain her with witticisms and delightful stories.

"Ian," she locked an arm through his, "do you think we will see the Governor tonight?"

"Oh, I doubt it. Governor Claiborne is not very social. Nor is he well liked by most. Yet I think he tries very hard and is quite devoted to this city."

"I wonder what people think of you. You are such an enigma. You come from a very prominent, highly respected family. Yet your work and travel are all related to your import-export company. Most of the men I have met have very little interest in work. They would rather hunt, fish, ride horses, and of course gamble. I also know that most men of your ilk have a . . . ahem . . . a mistress—a quadroon in the French Quarter."

Celeste's giggles did not stop Morgan from continuing.

"Well Ian, do you?"

Ian must have blushed to the roots of his dark brown hair. Celeste laughed harder, and Morgan merely smiled. After hearing Celeste's countless stories about the eligible bachelors and their quadroon mistresses, she was extremely curious about Ian.

"Morgan," he coughed, "who has been feeding you such information? Ah," he glanced at his cringing sister, "I should have known, imp, that it was you. Do you ever stop gossiping?"

"Oh no, never Ian. It's too much fun."

Mercifully, the coach pulled in front of the St. Peter Street Theater.

"I am not finished with you," he scolded as the coach door opened.

"Don't be a brute, Ian. I simply asked a question and Celeste happily answered. But, my dear, you have not answered my questions," Morgan teased.

"That's right, and I shall not."

"Coward," she muttered.

The opera was magnificent. Morgan had never enjoyed an evening as much as this. Sitting in the Kendall box, she could see the many beautifully coiffed ladies and elegant gentlemen. Theater in New Orleans was unlike anything Morgan had experienced before. People here loved theater, music, the opera, the balls, and all forms of amusement. Life was slower than in the North. Southerners knew how to enjoy life. Perhaps, she briefly considered, she could be very happy settling in New Orleans . . . with Ian alongside, protecting and loving her.

During intermission, Morgan continued to study the impressive crowd.

"Oh look," Marie called over her shoulder, "there are my dear friends, Etienne and Jeanette Lysle. I haven't seen them since they returned from France. But there are others in their box I do not recognize."

Morgan's head snapped up. A slight chill ran along her spine. Lifting the opera glass, Morgan studied the people in the box across from theirs.

The Lysles were a short, elderly couple, but the other two who quietly stood behind the chairs held Morgan's attention.

"Perhaps they are relatives from France," Marie pondered aloud.

"Maman, you know everyone and everything. How could the Lysles bring people you do not know. It is unthinkable," Ian dryly said. "And unforgivable."

"Mon fils, you take too many liberties with your poor maman," she smiled. "But I still love you, you rogue."

Morgan laughed when Marie pinched her son's cheek. However, her eyes did not stray from the foursome across the theater. If only she could see their faces.

"Come, let us visit their box. Morgan, would you care to accompany us?"

"Of course, Madame Kendall. I would be delighted. Besides, I would love to stretch my legs."

With Ian as escort, Morgan and Marie walked along the carpeted hallway to the opposite side of the brilliantly lit theater. There was not much room in the box for all of the visitors, so Morgan and Ian waited just outside the curtained box. She could only hear voices, two of which were heavily accented in French; the others—well they were difficult to identify. A southern drawl? No, not really, she decided. Definitely not New England. Continental then?

"Mes infants," Marie called. "Let me introduce you to my dear friends." Marie grabbed Ian's arm. "You certainly remember Ian. Come, come dear," Marie gestured to Morgan who stood behind Ian's broad back, "don't be shy."

Moving in front of Ian, she half curtsied to Marie's friends.

"May I introduce our houseguests, Charles and Jane Gray? They recently joined us. The Grays are from Ohio."

318

Morgan quickly studied the couple. They were of medium height, Charles only an inch or two taller than Jane. Both had the same dull coloring: pale brown hair and eyes. They had to be related.

"My sister and I are grateful to the generosity of the Lysles," Charles Gray said in a plain voice.

At least Morgan had correctly assessed their parentage. Still, they appeared so plain and so frumpy. Jane's hair was severely coiled at the base of her neck and tightly pulled back at the sides, accentuating her long nose. The dress was a dull green velvet, which was not at all fashionable and dramatized her hips and full bust. But Morgan thought she detected an alertness in those pale brown, almost colorless eyes.

"May I introduce my son and our delightful houseguest, Miss Morgan Rhinehart."

Morgan's gaze remained riveted on Jane Gray. Upon hearing the name, the woman sharply inhaled, then stiffened her already rigid spine while reaching for her brother's hand. He seemed momentarily at a loss for words, but quickly recovered offering his hand to Morgan and then to Ian.

"A pleasure," he intoned.

"I hope you enjoy your stay in New Orleans. Are you planning to remain awhile?" Ian tried to sound polite, but he did not care for these people at all. What the devil were the Lysles doing with them? he wondered.

"We will stay for perhaps one month. My sister and I must be back in Ohio before the summer. Family business, you understand."

"What sort of family business?" Morgan brazenly inquired.

Ian cast an odd look in her direction, but waited to hear the response.

"Lumber." Charles quickly replied.

"Not too much lumber in New Orleans." Marie laughed, "unless you go into the Louisiana Territory."

"No, no," Jane laughed—a trifle nervously, Morgan thought. "We are on an extended tour. Charles is taking me to relatives in the Spanish Territory. I have never met them and I so need a trip. I've had some health problems, you see."

On closer inspection, the woman could not be much older

than twenty-five, yet her matronly appearance gave the impression that Jane Gray was much older. Odd, Morgan thought, it was almost as if Jane were concealing much about herself.

Continuing her appraisal of Jane Gray, Morgan was unaware of Charles's assessment of her. Ian, however, was not. Charles stared through Morgan. It was not a lustful look; rather, it was the look of a cat gauging its prey. Thankfully, the orchestra reappeared, signaling the end of the intermission.

"Ian," Morgan whispered as they walked away from the Lysles' box, "I have a very strange feeling about the Grays."

"So do I, cherie. They did not seem to be all that they say. Lumber, indeed," he snorted.

"Exactly. Ian," she turned to him, "I had this feeling all day. I think, no I am positive that the Grays are the people I have been looking for." Her chin lifted in a stubborn tilt that always brought a tender smile to Ian's lips.

"Morgan, you just met them. How can you be so sure?"

"I can feel it, that's all," she pressed her gloved hands together. "Did you see the way they reacted to my name?"

"Yes I did. It was somewhat odd," Ian conceded.

Escorting Morgan to her seat, Ian inhaled the sweet fragrance of her hair. Restraint was often difficult, he painfully decided.

"Ian, I have a request," her tawny eyes hypnotized him. "I am well aware of your, shall we say, 'contacts.' I would like you to find out something, anything about those two strangers. Would you?"

"I will try, cherie. I promise to try."

Her rewarding smile warmed his already fevered soul.

The following day, Ian began his investigation. While he was gone, Morgan decided to make an inquiry of her own. The waterfront was the best place to begin. However, a well-dressed young woman could not roam unescorted. There was only one thing to do. It was a stroke of genius that Morgan secretly purchased the clothing on one of the many shopping spreads.

Rummaging into the back of the armoire, Morgan pulled out

320

a pair of fawn nankeen breeches and an oversized beige linen shirt. It was the woolen cap that completed the outfit. Pulled down low over her head, it effectively hid the mass of black curls.

"Well?" she asked herself. "Do I look like a lad?"

Despite the warm, summerlike day, Morgan put on an oversized woolen jacket. Taking the servants' staircase to the rear entrance, she stealthily left the house. She would have to remain partially hidden. Therefore, hiring a coach was out of the question. Morgan decided to walk the few miles to the waterfront. By the time she reached her destination, she was perspiring and very uncomfortable in the scratchy wool jacket and cap.

The entire area was crowded with ships. Which one should she approach? Who could assist her? Perhaps, she thought, this was silly. After all, Ian was acting on her behalf. Why couldn't she have patiently waited for him? An approaching sailor cut short further ruminations.

"Excuse me, mate," she hoped her voice sounded low and husky. "Can you tell me which ship recently arrived from France?"

"There's two new arrivals over there," the sailor pointed to an area not too far away.

Morgan could barely make out the shape of two ships bobbing together in the water. Squinting in the direction to which the man pointed, she asked, "Which one? The left or the right?"

"That one," he still pointed.

"Thank you, mate," she gave up questioning the old man. Following the path ahead, Morgan sauntered along the docks.

There appeared to be more activity on the small schooner. Perhaps she should begin her inquiry on that one. The plank was down, so Morgan walked onto the ship.

"Ahoy! Is the captain aboard?"

"We don't need no cabin boy. We just docked. Christ!" a sailor cursed aloud.

"No. No, I am looking for your captain. I have some information."

"He's busy," another answered, although he did not look up

from the sail he was mending.

"Well, it's important," she persisted. "I must see him now! Don't you lads know Ian Kendall? Well, he sent me to see the captain."

"Yeah, I heard of him. But I said the captain's busy. So go away, runt!"

Knowing a bit about ships, Morgan immediately located the stairs leading below deck. The captain must be in his cabin. Pretending to leave the ship, Morgan darted around the two men, down the stairs to the captain's quarters.

Rapping twice on the door, she waited for the man to bid her entry.

"Come in," a muffled voice called.

Refusing to remove the cap, Morgan entered the well-lit cabin. The captain was leaning over the washbasin.

"I, um, apologize for barging in, captain. I am trying to obtain some information. I can pay."

Shocked by the words and strangely familiar voice, the man glanced up.

"My God, Morgan! What the blazes are you doing here? How did you know that I would be arriving today?"

The friendly, albeit shocked voice sang through her ears. His light brown hair and dark blue eyes were a joyous sight.

"Oh Eric!" she cried, running into his outstretched arms. "What are you doing here?"

"I should ask the same of you, Miss. What are you doing about this area, dressed like that?" He held Morgan at arm's length. "Did you honestly think those breeches could disguise your shape? Lord, you are a handful."

"Eric, you sound too much like someone I was once married to. Why didn't you tell me you were arriving?" she scolded. "Your letter said nothing."

"I know. I did not want you to do something rash without me. And, of course, you do exactly that," he replied in a milder tone. "Now tell me why you are here?" He led her to the desk chair.

"This ship is very similar to the *Anastasia*."

"Yes. Same builder, same year. But the *Christine* doesn't carry guns. Will you please answer my questions?"

322

"Eric, I think I found Andrews. Well," she amended, "I found his two accomplices."

Morgan eagerly explained her unusual introduction to the Grays, giving a complete description of them and their reaction to her name. "It may be trivial, but it's a feeling I have, Eric. Those two are not who they claim to be. I thought that by coming to the docks, I could locate the ship that supposedly brought them from the Spanish Territory."

"If you mean the ship docked alongside, it sailed out of London—a British registry vessel. That cannot be the one you are looking for. All right," Eric slapped his thigh, "I suppose it's time to tell you what I have found out."

Morgan gripped the sides of the chair in anticipation.

"You are correct about the Grays. The description fits the one I received from Boston and Philadelphia. Damned if I know where Andrews is though. The Grays—I think that is their real name—are originally from Pittsburgh."

"Then it must be. It must!" she excitedly exclaimed. "What are we going to do?"

"Not very much. Not yet. They must be here for one reason: to steal the currency plates from the New Orleans Bank. My sources reveal that the plates that were stolen have not been sold or exchanged."

"Well, they cannot hold onto the plates indefinitely. They must make a move."

"That's right. We finally figured out the pattern to their thievery. I told you as much in my last letter. They are stealing from most—if not all—of the major U.S. Banks. It stands to reason that New Orleans is next. Now I do have a plan, and that is one of the reasons I am here."

"And the other?" she suspiciously asked.

"Take your hat off, Morgan. Here, have a drink with me."

The long black curls fell onto her shoulders. With a few deft movements, Morgan twisted the heavy mass of them into a knot.

While Eric sought the drinks, Morgan studied the cabin. It was a painful reminder of her life aboard the *Anastasia.*

The wood-framed bed was not as wide as the *Anastasia*'s; the Persian rug was smaller and in different shades. Eric's cabin did have a gallery window—without lace curtains, a beamed ceiling, and a sea chest in the same place that Nick kept his. Even the desks were identical. She could not bear it.

"Eric, it is so warm in here. Could we have our drink in one of the outdoor cafes. I must confess I am a little hungry."

"Of course. Although I have no idea what sort of commotion you will create in your breeches," his smile was achingly familiar.

"I care not one whit. Haven't you always said it does not matter what people say about you since they will talk no matter what you do?"

"Something like that. Though not in as many genteel words." Also, Eric wanted to add that the Morgan Rhodes he remembered from New York would never have thought of—let alone voiced—such words.

They walked to a nearby cafe. Morgan ignored the curious looks of the sailors and other passersby. Eric merely smiled to himself. This woman had changed; she was more independent and, unfortunately, hardened. There was a determined look in her eyes, and her smile did not readily appear.

"Tell me what you think about New Orleans," he said once they were seated.

"Eric, it is such a beautiful, magical city, unlike any other place I have seen. Ian says New Orleans is very European. Where, by the way, is your home?"

"My house is in the Vieux Carré."

"But that is not possible. I thought Americans were not allowed to live near the Creoles." She saw his mysterious smile, "Except of course rogues like yourself. I don't know how you remained unmarried for so long, Eric. Surely there are one or two women who meet your standard."

"There are. But I am demanding. Now . . . well, I suppose it might be interesting to have a woman to share one's advancing years."

"Posh! 'Advancing years.' You sound like my mother. She is only forty-one, yet she thinks life ended with my father," her eyes briefly clouded. "Actually I cannot blame her. I did too, until I met . . ." She paused, then falsely brightened. "You would like my mother, Eric. And my sister Lizzie. She can be

324

quite a handful. She must have grown since last October."

"You miss them?"

"Terribly. After Andrews is arrested, I will go to Boston."

"With Ian or alone?"

"I don't know, Eric. Ian is such a wonderful friend."

"I'm sure. But is he the man you want to marry?"

Morgan studied her coffee cup. "Perhaps. He would never hurt me. Not like Nicholas. I could not go through that again."

"Morgan, can we talk about him now?" Eric's dark blue eyes would not let go of hers. "You have avoided all references to Nick. Aren't you curious about him? Don't you ever wonder where he is?"

"No," she snapped. "I don't care. I don't want to care. It's over, Eric. It was a terrible, bitter lesson, but I will go on living. Without him," her voice was steady and firm.

"You did not ask me the other reason why I am here. Nor did you ask—although I am quite positive you knew—who the 'we' was in my statement about the Grays."

"No. I said I don't care." She looked away from Eric's sympathetic face, noticing the stares from the other patrons. "It's in the past. I do not want to hear about it."

"Well, I think before you permanently close off your mind, you should at least know that Nick has not forgotten his promise to help you find Andrews."

"I can't tell you how pleased I am to hear that he kept his word," she sarcastically said.

"You have misjudged my nephew. Morgan, please," he saw she was about to rise, "don't run away from it. At least listen to me. Just this once."

"Well," she relented, "I suppose it won't hurt to listen."

"Morgan dear, Nick has changed—as have you. Not necessarily for the better, either. Some days after you left, Nick did too. A wealthy merchant begged him to take a special cargo to France, promising a better cargo once he docked in Marseilles. The young fool agreed. He'd been drunk for three days. I cannot believe that he would have accepted such a dangerous trip—unless he were despondent or inconsolable.

"He was devastated when you left. He wanted to talk to you, to explain why things happened the way they did."

325

"That's absurd, Eric. There are no excuses for that kind of behavior. I loved him! I thought he was my husband. I truly thought he cared about me."

"He did. He still does. Morgan, he loves you."

"Rubbish!" She angrily swiped at a tear that inadvertently fell from the corner of her eye.

"He is hurt and confused. And very bitter. Moreover, I have never known my nephew to be reckless. He is taking too many chances. It is as if he's daring the patrols to find him."

"Nick can take care of himself."

"I am not so sure. He left his parents' home the same night you did, Morgan. He never said a word to his family. He wouldn't have seen me if I didn't track him down in a tavern. He talked about you; how he would never get over your leaving him. Then he became angry because you refused to listen to his explanations.

"Nonetheless he wanted to keep his promise about Andrews. It was Nick who found out about the Grays. He encouraged me to come to you." Fumbling through his coat pocket, Eric said, "Morgan, he asked me to give this to you." Eric handed her a pale blue silk handkerchief.

The silk smelled of Nick. It was a combination of tobacco and bay rum lotion. Raising it to her cheek, Morgan smiled involuntarily.

Eric noticed. He also noted her wistful expression. The woman was still in love with Nick . . . just too hurt to know it, he decided. Eric was now more determined than ever to remedy this bloody mess, before she married Ian and before Nick got himself killed.

Unfolding the silk, Morgan's throat tightened. She thought she had lost the anchor pin. Apparently, it was left at Nick's town house. The sapphires and diamonds twinkled in the afternoon sun. She was blinded by memories of the rogue she had married: his laughter, his handsome face, his lovemaking.

"Oh God. I forgot," she moaned.

"Well, he has not. Morgan, please. All I ask is that you don't marry Ian until you are positive you no longer love Nick. Will you promise me?"

"I . . . I don't know, Eric. It is too painful to think about."

"Just remember that I am here for you. As far as I am concerned, you are and always will be my niece. I have a home here, as you know. But I came back for you."

Morgan took his hand, squeezing it affectionately, ignoring the tears that slid down her sunburned cheeks. "I love you too, Uncle Eric. And I do thank you."

Chapter 27

Ian was patiently waiting for Morgan's return. If he were alarmed at seeing Eric Rhodes, he did not show it.

"I should have known you would join us," he said in a friendly voice. "Come in Eric, I want to hear about Morgan's reckless behavior. Although," he noticed her breeches, "I can guess."

"Now Ian," Morgan started.

"I will not be silent. I think you should know what I feel. What you did could have been dangerous. I thought you trusted me, cherie. I assumed you would wait for my return."

"I cannot wait. This is my problem, my family's name that needs to be cleared. Tell me, Ian, if it were you would you idly wait for someone to bring you information? Or would you do something on your own?"

It wasn't fair to upbraid Ian. But Morgan's temper compensated for her confusion. "I am sorry Ian. I should not be taking my frustrations out on you. Forgive me," she kissed his cheek. "I think I will go to my room and change. Would that please you Ian?"

Alone with Eric in the study, Ian listened to the information that he had obtained.

"What can be done now?"

"Two things. We must go to the bank. Devereaux is still in charge, isn't he? We must tell him what we know. We cannot wait for these currency plates to be stolen before we act. We have to set a trap for the Grays.

"The second thing I plan to do—with your assistance, Ian—is let it be known to the Grays that I am a potential buyer of the plates . . . a representative of the French Government. Ian, I will need your cooperation. We must see the Grays at some social function. I want you to introduce me. We will think of what to say after that. We have to convince them that I am here exclusively for those plates."

"That shouldn't be difficult. But I will tell you what is difficult. What are we going to do about Morgan?"

"That, my good man, is your problem," Eric affectionately slapped Ian's back.

"Eric, haven't you left something out?"

"Not that I know of."

"Eric," Ian sighed, "where is he?"

"In France, of all places. My nephew wants to tempt the fates."

"How—um—how did he take her hasty departure?" Ian nervously pulled on his cravat.

"What would you do, Ian, if you lost Morgan?"

"I think about it all the time," he morosely replied.

"Then you know, don't you?"

Fortunately, Eric Rhodes found the opportunity to meet Charles Gray. It was late on a Thursday night. Ian had learned that Mr. Gray enjoyed midnight card games at a club not far from the Vieux Carré. Securing an invitation for Eric and himself was not a problem.

The warm, humid night air could sap the strength of the heartiest man. But gambling was a passionate pastime among the Creoles, and nothing could stand in the way of a chance in a smoke-filled, brightly lit room. For the gentleman who needed diversion, there was always an attractive lady for entertainment. There were fancy roulette tables and carved card tables from the Louis XV period, and a long bar replete with the finest foreign brandy, whiskey, and wines.

Although Eric had a home here, he rarely mixed with the Creole society. New Orleans was usually where he returned after his travels. To his advantage, few of these Creoles knew

Eric Rhodes. Certainly no one knew of his relationship with Miss Morgan Rhinehart.

It was a stroke of luck that placed Eric and Ian at the same card table as Charles Gray. One look at Charles's sallow face, beady eyes, and dour expression convinced Eric there was something suspicious about the man. It was obvious that Charles had been at the table for quite some time. And he was not winning.

"Good to see you again, Charles," Ian cheerfully intoned. "Gentlemen, I don't believe you have met Captain Eric Rhodes. He is recently back from France. Eric travels a great deal. What he does, eludes me," Ian chuckled, all the while judging Charles's face. Was he mistaken or did he see a flicker of interest?

"Oh, you must realize by now, Ian, that my export business takes me all over the world. But for now, I call France my home. It is more expedient. The emperor would not have it any other way."

"Etes-vous Americain, non?" asked one of the cardplayers.

"Well, yes I am. For now," he laughed loudly.

By three A.M. Charles Gray owed Eric Rhodes three thousand dollars! Sweating profusely, Charles tried to appear unaffected by his losses. "I do not have the money with me at the moment, sir. But if you will consider accepting my mark, I shall settle with you tomorrow."

"That's fine, Charles. I am in no hurry. Perhaps we can play again. In a day or two?"

Charles actually smiled. "My pleasure, Eric."

It was a glorious day. The customary morning rain did not appear. The sun so bright in the cloudless southern sky hinted that summer was coming early this year.

Morgan was buoyant; she seemed to blossom in this weather. Her lightweight day clothes were of the finest materials and the prettiest designs. The humidity, which most women abhorred, created tiny black curls that delicately framed her face, while her skin looked as creamy as finely polished marble.

331

Ian was simultaneously pleased and pained. Seeing the way she adapted to the climate and southern way of life convinced him that Morgan could indeed adjust to life in his city. Yet he dared not touch her, although he yearned to do so. He no longer visited any of the elegant bordellos, no matter how fine they were. Morgan was all he wanted. Nothing and no one could sate his desire for her.

With Eric Rhodes in New Orleans, Ian believed that Morgan must be constantly reminded of Nicholas. How could she think of marrying again? Although he wanted to keep his promise of not pressuring her, Ian did not know if waiting would help or hurt his cause. He decided to take the chance and propose to Morgan once more.

She was in the walled garden. The scents of hibiscus, magnolias, and jasmine blended into one sweet fragrance that filled the pregnant summer air. Seated by the fountain, one hand idly running through the water while the other playfully turned a white magnolia, she was nothing less than enchanting.

"Hello cherie, you look so serene." He sat beside her. "Here, allow me."

Taking the flower, Ian tenderly placed it in her hair. "Give me a pin." After securing it, he moved back a bit to study the effect. "Ah, so beautiful. I do not know which is lovelier or brighter, the magnolia or your golden eyes," his voice became husky.

Recognizing yet ignoring the tone, Morgan gaily said, "I like it here Ian. For a Northerner who loves seasons, crowds, and roaring fires, I am surprised by my reaction."

"Have you heard from your mother yet?" Ian idly crossed his legs.

As always, he dressed like a perfect gentleman. Despite the heat, his dark brown hair remained well groomed, not a lock of it being out of place. It seemed as if the only concession to the heat was his open white linen shirt, worn under a lightweight jacket. He was truly a handsome man. Morgan had never kissed his full lips, and she quickly wondered if they would be soft or firm. Be careful, she admonished herself.

"I received a letter yesterday," she replied, quickly

recovering her senses. "Mother and Lizzie are very well. Lizzie has grown another inch. Mother swears that she will be wearing my clothes soon. Oh, and Ian," she suddenly exclaimed, remembering the best news of all, "guess what? Oh, never mind," she cut off any possible response. "You can never guess."

"Thank you for your confidence. Pray continue, my dear. I am simply dying of curiosity."

He smiled and Morgan finally noticed that Ian had a dimple in his right cheek. Why haven't I seen these things before? she wondered.

"I apologize, Ian, but wait. This is such delightful news. Mother and Lizzie have their own home now! Isn't that wonderful! Just to be away from my cousin Alice I think they would have gone back to Philadelphia. She did not say how they were able to pay for the house, but I assume my uncle must have finally understood how unpleasant it is living with that—that viper." She quickly covered her mouth having astonished herself. "Excuse me, but there is no other word to accurately describe Alice. My mother and Lizzie are now living on Chestnut Street, not far from Uncle Benjamin. Mother wrote that it is a small but lovely house, within walking distance of Copley Square. There are three small bedrooms, a parlor, and dining room. She thinks it is a beautiful house. I am so pleased for them," she gushed.

"What did she say about us? Did you inform her that I have proposed marriage? Can I write her asking for permission?" his hazel eyes implored.

"That will not be necessary, Ian. Mother believes that the choices are mine to make. Whatever I decide to do will satisfy her." Morgan flashed a deceptively brilliant smile. Because she neglected to mention that Charlotte also though it might be wise to wait a little longer before marrying Ian. She had even suggested that Morgan return to Boston for a brief visit and that Ian travel there too—but not together.

Deciding not to press his luck, Ian softly implored, "Would you allow me to escort you tonight to a wonderful new restaurant I have discovered? It is small and very French. The cuisine and wines, I hear, are superb. Just the two of us?"

"I would love it," she whispered, enjoying the feel of his hand on her bare arm.

It was well past eleven P.M. when they returned to the Kendall home. Morgan allowed Ian to hold her about the waist as they made their way into the house. She needed his support, for they must have consumed two bottles of the finest French cabernet and more than two glasses of sherry. The splendid dinner was served over three and one-half hours. Morgan could not remember which course she liked best: the cold lobster and shrimp, the veal in brown sauce, or the dessert tart.

Ian's pleasant banter kept her smiling. He was such a delightful companion. In between the sips of wine, Morgan again noticed how very urbane and handsome he was. When he had placed the silk shawl over her bared shoulders, she actually wished he would kiss her, right there in the restaurant in front of all of the admiring faces.

"Mmmm. Ian, I had a wonderful evening. I wish it did not have to end."

"Let's not end it. Come," he pulled her toward the drawing room, "would you care to join me for a brandy?"

She knew it wasn't proper, but she did so anyway.

Morgan kicked off her white satin slippers before sitting on the settee, comfortably curling her legs underneath the white chiffon dress.

She could not know how ethereal she appeared. The contrast between the curled raven locks swirling around the crown of her head and the white dress unsettled Ian. Instead of wearing the gold locket, Morgan wore the double strand of pearls with a diamond clasp around her slender neck. She had no need for artificial coloring. Her skin, slightly tanned by the New Orleans sun, hinted of robust health. Even the tawny eyes that he wished would lovingly gaze at him were clear and bright.

Ian knew she had consumed more than a reasonable allotment of wine. He was hoping that something special would happen tonight, something the wine might unfurl. If Morgan could let go of the tight rein that held her heart, perhaps she would realize how happy he could make her.

"Morgan, I am so very happy to see you this way. I have

longed to see you look at me and smile the way you are this very moment. I hope you will consider staying in New Orleans," his smile deepened, "with me, as my wife."

She looked up, but did not seem surprised. Not wanting to give her time to think about his words, Ian pulled his chair in front of the settee.

"I would make you happy, you know that, cherie. Please, Morgan. Say yes."

"Ian, I am not being fair to you. I am not sure that I love you." The words were hard to say, but necessary. Morgan's head leaned against the high back of the settee, languidly focusing on his face. "I must be honest with you. I think you are so handsome, Ian. And you have made me happier than I have been in months. And . . ."

"Please, don't say anymore, and for heaven's sake don't list my virtues," he whispered. "I love you Morgan. You have known that. What you do not know is that I believe you care a great deal for me. Oh, maybe not the same passion or love you felt for Nick, but ours will be a more enduring love, one that does not ripen then quickly dissipate. No, my dearest, not like that. Our love will last, will flourish over the years. Because you can depend on me, and I shall always cherish you."

A tear slowly rolled down one cheek, followed by others. "You say such beautiful things."

"Morgan, I know you will love me—if you don't already. Listen to me," he sat beside her now, wiping the tears with a silk handkerchief. "Don't cry, please." Ian softly kissed one damp cheek, cupping her chin in his large hand. Her ripe lips were barely inches away. The temptation was too great. Slowly, Ian found her mouth, his lips firmly fusing with hers.

Morgan did not want to protest. A thousand thoughts filled her mind. The kiss was lovely, yet not as passionate as the ones with Nicholas. However, wasn't Ian correct about the heights and depth of her marriage to Nick? Wouldn't it be wonderful to have a stable, solid relationship with a reliable man who swore to cherish her? He would protect her; Ian was not like Nick. Couldn't she learn to forget Nick with this man by her side?

Ian's kiss deepened, his hand leisurely stroking one soft, still wet cheek while his tongue softly insinuated itself into her mouth. Morgan could not resist placing one arm about his neck. She did feel something for him. It was a warm glow, something she had not expected to experience with any man again. It was so pleasant that Morgan did not discourage his other hand as it traveled down her neck and arms, then gently pulled her pliant body into his hard embrace.

"Ah Morgan. You taste so sweet," he murmured in her ear, outlining the shell with his tongue. Her soft moan gave him the courage to continue. Once more, Ian's mouth claimed hers. "Morgan, will you marry me?" It was a low, husky request, filled with all the yearning and desire that had been held inside for so long. "I love you. Say you will marry me."

Was it the heady wine, the soft touch of his hands and lips, or the compelling tone in his voice that made Morgan whisper, "Yes, Ian. I would be honored to accept your proposal."

Hugging her while raining kisses on her forehead and cheeks, Ian laughed. "You have made me the happiest man alive, cherie. Truly. Ah, but I have something for you, my wife to be. I have carried it with me for so long, wondering if ever I would be given the opportunity to present it to you."

Disengaging herself, Morgan stared into Ian's radiant face. "What are you talking about, Ian?"

Reaching into his coat pocket, Ian withdrew a velvet box. "This, my dearest love, is my betrothal gift to you."

Morgan gasped upon seeing the exquisitely designed diamond and topaz necklace nestled in the black velvet box. Carefully removing it, she stared in awe at the sparkling gems and the lone heart-shaped topaz in the middle.

"The first time I saw your golden eyes, I knew I had to have the jewel that matched your color. May I?" he asked, removing the pearl choker and replacing it with the diamond one about her neck. "Go to the mirror. Tell me if you like it."

Scurrying off the settee, Morgan stood transfixed before the tiny mirror. It was magnificent! Her eyes were as bright as the topaz stone. "It is the most beautiful piece of jewelry I have ever seen," she whispered.

Ian's reflection appeared in the mirror. "I was hoping you would say that. So I realized that if I purchased the necklace, I would need something else too."

"Oh no Ian. You can't!"

336

"Cherie, you are my fiancée. I would give you the stars if you asked for them. But until you do," his hazel eyes darkened and the dimple in his cheek deepened with his broad smile, "you must possess these."

Again he withdrew a box. Morgan was afraid to look inside, but of course could not resist. "Ian, my goodness, you shouldn't have!"

The topaz and diamond ear bobs were perfect mates to the necklace. "I have never possessed such beautiful jewelry," she honestly said, stunned by his gesture.

"I could not conceive of anything less for you. You do not have to wear them now."

"Oh no, Ian, I must." She easily managed to remove the small pearl studs.

The radiance of the earrings and necklace along with Morgan's exhilaration took Ian's breath away.

"It will give me great pleasure always, cherie, to see you wear my presents." His arm snaked about her slender waist.

Morgan eagerly turned to him. "Thank you so much Ian. I shall try, with all my heart, to make you happy too."

Her face was so serious, so beautiful. "You always will. Never think otherwise. I am so honored to have you as my wife."

Their promises were sealed in a long, deep kiss.

It was pleasant, Morgan told herself, as she struggled to keep her weary eyes open. It would be a good marriage, she tried to convince herself. Ian loved her and she felt the stirring of love for him.

In time, the memory of quicksilver eyes would be replaced by laughing hazel ones; the sun-bleached, dark blond hair would be replaced by dark brown hair. It would not be Nick's rakish grin that twisted her insides, but Ian's dimpled, smiling face.

For the first time in weeks, Morgan fell into a deep, dreamless sleep. Not once did Nick's face haunt her. Soon he would be completely out of her system. It would simply take a little more time; Ian would see to that.

Morgan was up early the next morning, but was still the last one to arrive for breakfast. The Kendalls were seated, chattering and enjoying the morning meal.

Donning a lilac muslin day dress with tiny embroidered flowers along the hem, Morgan lightly stepped into the room. She was enthusiastically greeted by all.

"Oh Morgan, at last. I am so very happy that you will be joining our family," Marie Kendall joyously announced.

"And I shall really have a sister," Celeste added.

"We are, as you can hear and see, very happy for both of you," Paul said. "Just look at my son. He has never looked better."

Ian rose to take Morgan's arm. "Sleep well, cherie?" he asked.

His loving touch and warm smile reinforced her decision to marry. "The best night I have had in weeks," she answered honestly.

"You look splendid. But I fear Maman has much to say and plan. You may be quite fatigued before the morning is over."

How right he was! Marie had decided that a ball must be given in their honor. The formal announcement would be made that evening. The ball would be held in two weeks. Lists must be made, dresses ordered, the ballroom cleaned, plans for the evening's entertainment arranged, the decorations ordered, the menu planned.

"There is so much to do. My head will swim, but I shall love every moment," Marie enthusiastically exclaimed.

"Have you set a date for the marriage?" Paul asked the only sensible question thus far.

"Yes, Papa, we have. We would like to be married by the end of April—before it gets too hot. But," Ian looked at the expectant faces of his family, "Morgan and I wish to have a small, private wedding. I hope you will not be disappointed if we do not invite all of New Orleans."

The Kendalls looked at one another. Finally, Paul spoke. "If that is your desire we shall, of course, abide by your wishes."

"That is why this betrothal ball must be perfectly planned and executed. Morgan dear, you will send for your mother and sister. If it is a matter of money . . ."

"Maman, please. Of course we will send for Morgan's

amily. Money is unimportant."

"I hope you will not be upset. You have been so wonderful
to me. I do not want to distress you. It's just that, under the
circumstances, Ian and I thought a small wedding would be
best."

Above all, Morgan did not want to alienate the Kendalls.
They had welcomed her into their home like a daughter. But
the thought of a large wedding was somehow overwhelming
and absurd—given the circumstances of her previous mar-
iage.

"No, no. But promise me, Morgan, that you will allow me to
accompany you to the dressmaker for your ball gown. I would
love to see you in white, you know," Marie cautiously said,
unwilling to sound domineering. "Will you consider it?"

"Of course, Mrs. Kendall."

"I want you to start calling me 'Maman.' Will you Morgan?"

"Yes, Maman," she laughed. The word—despite the French
pronunciation—was difficult to say; but given time, it would
be easy.

The grand party was planned for a Saturday evening.
Everyone who mattered would be invited . . . even Governor
William Claiborne. Morgan offered to help write the invita-
tions, thinking of nothing else she could do.

After breakfast, Ian escorted her to the music room. "Are
you happy, cherie?"

"Oh yes," she breathed. "Your family is wonderful. I am
pleased they so graciously welcomed me into their hearts."

"They love you as I do," he kissed her hand but could not
resist a bolder move. Twirling her about, Ian enfolded Morgan
in a tender embrace. Lowering his head, he took possession of
her soft lips.

The kiss felt much the same as last night. Morgan was
pleased, for she briefly worried that only the wine's effect had
made the kiss satisfying. Ian's tongue enticed hers into his
mouth, while one arm leisurely roamed along her slender
spine, pulling Morgan's body close. She could not ignore the
growing presence against her stomach. Pushing him away, she
nervously laughed, "Ian dear. I think we should wait."

"Yes, of course," he looked contrite. "I do apologize."

"Ian, may I make another request?" Morgan faced him allowing his hand to remain on her waist.

"Perfect timing, cherie," he dryly said.

It took a minute for her to grasp the meaning. Then she laughed. "I did not mean to entice and embarrass you into granting a request."

"I believe you, I think."

"Ian, I must see Eric. I think it only proper that he be informed about our engagement by me—not anyone else. Besides, I would like to know what is going on with the Grays."

"You can certainly see Eric Rhodes. If you like, I will escort you. As far as the Grays are concerned, we have discovered that Charles likes to gamble."

"Really?" she was surprised.

"Two nights ago, Eric and I met Charles in a card game. Charles owes Eric three thousand dollars."

"My goodness, so much money!"

"It will be interesting to see how or if he can pay."

"Ian, was there any mention of Andrews? Hasn't anyone seen him?"

"No. I think it odd too."

"I wonder where he is. Perhaps his disguise is better than any of us imagined. He may be here in New Orleans and we do not know who he is yet."

"That's very possible, but I simply do not know. Neither does Eric. If you recall, Eric could not get any information about Andrews. We will have to see."

"Perhaps it will not matter if we trap the Grays now. Once caught, they will have to lead us to Andrews."

She said it with such conviction that Ian could not gainsay her words. It was so odd . . .

"Well Ian, will you take me to Eric's this afternoon?"

"Yes. But I will have to leave you there. I have some business matters to attend to. I'll come back for you—if you'll wait. Otherwise, I'm sure Eric will escort you home."

"Thank you Ian." She kissed his lips.

"For what?" He was nonplussed.

"For letting me see Eric. I intend to remain his friend, you know. You have made it easy for me. You also trust me."

"Morgan, you silly goose, of course I trust you. And Eric still loves you as his niece. I won't take that away from either of you."

"Ian, I am not sure I deserve you."

She looked so serious he could not help but laugh. "Don't you dare cry on me, Morgan Rhinehart. I will run right out and buy you another present. I cannot stand it when you cry."

"I won't," she recovered her composure. "But you should never have admitted to that secret."

In the early afternoon, Ian drove Morgan to the old section of New Orleans. She loved the houses with the Spanish colonial wrought iron grillwork decorating the fronts of them. Magnolia trees and other flowers grew in profusion. What Morgan truly adored were the private courtyards—little parks, she called them—behind the homes, where more trees, flowers, and fountains shaded part of the house from the hot Louisiana sun. Many homes still had the Spanish carriageway leading to their rear entrances, where long stairwells showed the direction of the upper quarters.

Eric's house on the Rue Bienville was the perfect image of these homes.

"I wondered how long you would be able to stay away," Eric teased as they entered the house. "Come in, please." He led them into the drawing room.

Morgan stared at the tastefully decorated, brightly lit room. It was light and airy—perfectly suitable to this climate. Eric, too, was well dressed in nankeen breeches and a cream-colored linen shirt, which outlined his strong physique. Blue eyes darkened, however, upon noting the possessive way Ian held Morgan's waist.

"Most of the rooms on this floor are connected. The library adjoins this one through that door," he pointed to the small white wood panel. "Let me show you."

They quickly toured the lower portion of the house and went back to the drawing room.

"Eric, I could not wait any longer. What happened with Charles Gray?" Morgan settled herself in the white cushioned armchair.

"It is as we have suspected." Eric explained about the card

game with Charles and the money now owed.

"Eric, Ian and I think it odd that Andrews has not been seen—or discovered."

"I don't know. Perhaps Charles will lead us to him."

Drinks were served. Ian quickly noted the time, then excused himself. "Eric, I must leave. Would you see Morgan home for me?"

"With pleasure," he grinned at the beautiful woman demurely seated across from him. She was a rare jewel and he knew now that he loved her as a daughter—and would protect her any way he could.

"Ah Ian, before you leave I think we should tell Eric . . ."

"Of course. Eric old chap, I hope you will be pleased. You are the first to know that Morgan has accepted my marriage proposal. With one little 'yes' she has made me the happiest and most fortunate man alive!"

"Why that is good news," he lied, hoping the words and tone sounded cheery. Ian Kendall was a terrific young man, and he would make most women gloriously happy. But he was not the man for Morgan. Only one man could make her happy. And that fool was somewhere sailing across the Atlantic Ocean. "When are you planning to marry?"

"The end of April. However, the Kendalls are planning a betrothal ball in three weeks. You will stay for the party, won't you Eric?" she pleaded.

"Why certainly. And I hope you ask me to give the bride away."

Morgan jumped into his outstretched arms. "Oh, I do love you Eric. I am so happy you approve."

"I want to see you happy, my dear. That's what counts." His troubled blue eyes looked away from the couple.

After Ian left, Eric regaled Morgan with stories about his wandering ways.

"I tell you, lass, I have had some wild times. But now I suppose a person needs to settle down. I love New Orleans almost as much as New York. I guess I will have to find a woman who does not mind spending six months in each place."

"I wouldn't mind. After I had been to Europe, of course."

"But you are taken."

"Eric," her expression became serious. "You do think I have made the correct decision?"

"I cannot answer that for you Morgan. Ian is a wonderful lad. I see how much he loves you. I hope you will eventually feel the same way about him."

"You can tell?" she whispered. Morgan nervously played with the lilac ribbon on the dress.

"If you think you can erase Nick from your mind and heart—well . . . I . . ."

"I must and I will," she countered. "He is out of my life—permanently, Eric." The tawny eyes revealed sadness.

"As you wish," he sounded resigned. "Will you have a drink with me, angel?"

A soft knocking on the door startled them. "It couldn't be Ian. I wonder . . . Wait here Morgan. I will be a moment."

Morgan stood by the door waiting for his return. Checking her appearance in the window, she smoothed her dress and hair, wondering who else would drop by unannounced.

"Morgan," Eric urgently whispered. "It's Charles Gray! He must not see you here. Please stay in this room and," he winked, "do not stand too close to the door lest your presence be discovered."

She had closed the adjoining door when Charles Gray's voice filled the library.

"I apologize for calling on you unannounced, Captain Rhodes. But we have an important issue to discuss . . . my marker."

Morgan thought he sounded nervous; there was a hesitancy in his voice. Placing her ear against the door, she eagerly waited to hear Eric's response.

"That is very kind of you, sir. I could have waited another week or two. Here, sit down. Would you care to join me in an early afternoon libation?"

"I am not supposed to drink this early. Jane thinks it is bad for my stomach," he replied, wiping his perspiring brow with a linen handkerchief. "Uh, Captain, the problem is that I do not have three thousand dollars."

"Well, that's all right," Eric smoothly said. "You have

343

something far more important to me."

"I do? I have no idea what you mean."

"Yes you do, Charles. May I call you Charles?" Not waiting for a response, he continued to talk. "I thought you understood my hints the other evening."

Morgan placed a hand over her mouth to muffle any gasp. Eric was so bold! Wasn't he taking a chance by accusing Gray of having the plates?

"Charles, I came to New Orleans at this particular time for a reason. You could say I was sent here."

"Sent? By whom?" Charles tried to sound nonchalant.

"The Emperor Napoleon received your message about the possible sale of some bronze plates. He is interested in, shall we say, purchasing the goods—if they are what I think they are. You see Charles," Eric leaned forward, "it is all up to me. If they are authentic, I might be interested in purchasing them. I would need to see them first, of course."

"You will excuse my lack of enthusiasm, Captain. I, too, would like to see some proof."

Morgan shoved a fist in her mouth to prevent the loud sigh. Eric was right! He took a chance and Charles Gray fell for it. But where, she wondered, would Eric get the proof Gray wanted?

"It's right here, Charles."

Morgan heard the muffled scraping sounds against wood. A drawer opened and closed. Footsteps. Eric must be walking to a different side of the room. Again a creaking sound. What could that be? Ah—she recalled the painting. Perhaps there was a wall safe behind the painting.

"Is this what you are looking for?"

Silence.

When Charles spoke, his voice was slight. "My God. I have waited a long time for this moment. It is authentic, all right. Here," the paper or whatever it was must have been handed back to Eric.

"When are you going to 'visit' the Bank of New Orleans?" Eric questioned in a nonchalant manner.

"That is my problem, Captain Rhodes, not yours. Soon enough."

"Mr. Gray, I am prepared to offer you a large sum. Larger than the English, I hope. But I still need to see some proof."

"You shall have it. I am not so stupid as to have all of the plates with me in New Orleans. They are safely hidden and easy to retrieve—if we come to terms."

Suddenly Morgan hated his overly confident voice.

"I am prepared to show you one plate, from the U.S. Bank in Philadelphia. Perhaps in a day or two."

"Mr. Gray, I am in no rush. I have homes in many cities in the United States and in France. I can wait as long as you would like. Can you afford to wait?" Eric's question was direct. "How many plates are for sale?"

"Twelve—after New Orleans."

"And your opening price?"

"Four hundred thousand francs."

Eric whistled. "Quite a large sum."

"I will sell you two plates immediately. I want two hundred fifty thousand francs at that time. The rest you can have in five weeks. And, Captain, there is no negotiation. If you and I can agree on this matter, I will bring one plate this evening."

"I shall have an answer for you then. Oh and, Charles, if we can negotiate a deal, you can forget the three thousand dollars. If not," he smiled, "we'll have to discuss it another time."

"How generous of you," he snapped, grabbed his hat and, without waiting to be shown the way, left the house.

Morgan dared not move from her spot—not even when the voices faded away. When Eric finally opened the door, she practically fell into his arms.

"Oh my God, Eric. I cannot believe it. I cannot believe what I have heard!" she exclaimed. "It is here. They are here, so close," she clutched his shirt. "I am so excited, Eric. It is almost over. Do you think Gray is meeting with Andrews? And, Eric, what did you show him as 'proof' of your intent?"

"Ah Morgan, that was simplest of all. Here, I will show you."

"And Eric," she caught his arm, "how could you have been so bold to say the emperor received a message? Was it a guess?"

"No, it wasn't. I told you that we have many contacts on

345

both sides of the Atlantic. One was lucky enough to intercept the message before Napoleon received it."

Morgan fell into the nearest chair. "I still cannot believe it. After all this time. Wait! Show me the document."

Eric presented a beautiful piece of parchment decorated in red and blue ribbons with a raised seal at the bottom. "It is almost the real thing. We forged it from an official French document Nick had. The seal was a bit difficult, but Nick managed quite perfectly I think."

Morgan was too excited to care about the many references to Nicholas. Soon, she told herself, soon this part of the nightmare would be over.

"Eric, I love you. I cannot tell you what this means to me," her eyes looked suspiciously bright.

"I would be dishonest if I did not tell you that I am not doing this only for you. I am also a loyal citizen to this country. I too want to catch the traitors and see them hung for their crimes."

"I still love you. And I will never ever forget your friendship."

"Wait until it is all over before you thank me. Besides, I have to watch over my girl. You will never be rid of Uncle Eric Rhodes."

Their light laughter blended and filled the white room. Morgan could almost forget the struggles and heartache experienced on the long, lonely road of the last year.

She took this as an omen. Life with Ian would be grand.

However, Eric held Morgan and stared at the family portrait on the wall. Where the devil are you, Nick? he silently asked.

Chapter 28

LATE MARCH, 1809

Swept up in the excitement and plans for the engagement ball, Morgan could not believe the day had arrived. It was a glorious springlike afternoon; unusual for New Orleans, where it rained at least once a day.

Reclining in a cool tub filled with scented verbena perfume, Morgan thought about a future with Ian Kendall. After their honeymoon abroad, they would return to New Orleans and proceed to Ian's plantation. Only last week they had taken the ride to the house. It was on the same property as his parents' large farmhouse, which was built along the banks of the Mississippi.

She had been surprised to see such a lovely home. The house was not very large, although the graceful hipped roof with three small vertical dormers in the front gave a different impression. A long gallery ran along the front of the house, so that each of the front bedrooms on the second floor had access. It was supported by eight long white columns. Ian explained that an eighteenth-century technique of "bousillage-entre-poteaux" or mud between the posts was used for the basic construction of the house. The kitchen was connected to the main house.

On the ground floor was a music room, a formal dining room, a library, and another small room which, he laughingly said, could be used as their ballroom. Upstairs was a sitting room, two large, connected master bedroom suites, and two more bedrooms. Having learned of her fondness for a separate room for washing, Ian had already begun to renovate an adjoining room to Morgan's specification. The large French window opened onto the beautifully manicured garden, surrounded by dozens of live oak trees clad in Spanish moss.

Yes, she sighed, dipping lower into the tub, I will be happy with Ian in that darling home.

The dress for the evening lay across most of her bed. Morgan could not get used to the idea that most southern young ladies wore dresses of white or pastels. Yet with her dark features, the pale colors enhanced her appearance. The ivory china silk and lace dress was an exquisite fit. Unlike most dresses in the Empire style, this one did not flare so much beneath the high waistline, which meant that as she walked one could almost see the outline of the long, lean legs beneath the silken material. It was the most daring dress Morgan had ever owned. But Marie Kendall swore it was perfectly decorous to wear such a dress. The entire upper portion of it was made of white Venetian lace: the bodice, the high neck, and the long, tight sleeves that angled at the wrists. A single layer of silk at the bodice outlined her full creamy breasts. The back, with dozens of tiny seed pearl buttons, was also half lace, half silk. Even her white satin slippers had lace trimming.

It was decadent, Morgan thought. But then, why not?

One of the maids artfully arranged pearl strands into her long raven curls. When the toilette was finished, Morgan stepped into the gown, then stood before the cheval glass staring at her gorgeous visage.

"I cannot believe this is me," she breathed. "I look pretty." The sparkling diamond and topaz necklace and ear bobs twinkled in the candlelight.

"You look ravishing," Ian told her when she descended the stairs. "I shall not be able to greet our guests, for my eyes will be glued to you. Ah Morgan, I am such a lucky man," he tenderly kissed her temple and hands.

"I am honored since you are the most nattily dressed man in all of New Orleans."

He was, without doubt, very handsome in a stark white linen

jacket and matching breeches. The whiteness accentuated his dark brown hair and sparkling hazel eyes.

"Only in New Orleans?" he teased. If it were possible, his wide smile made her spirits soar higher than before.

"I am so excited, Ian. I hope I don't disgrace you by tripping over my feet when we dance alone on that huge dance floor."

"Impossible. I have never known anyone as graceful as you. Here," Ian took her arm, "stand next to me."

"And me," added Paul, who was also quite taken by Morgan's sophisticated beauty.

The Kendall women happily gave the spotlight to Morgan. This was her night. Whoever entered the gracious Kendall home could not help but admire the attractive couple at the head of the receiving line. Morgan Rhinehart, they whispered, has thoroughly captured Ian's heart. Several mamas looked around the room for other suitable bachelors for their daughters.

Eric Rhodes was one of the last to arrive.

"It's about time you arrived," her dazzling smile mystified him. "I would like to have a cold drink and then a dance with my betrothed. I believe, however, there is space on my dance card for my Uncle Eric."

"Ah, you wound me by calling me 'uncle' on this night. I feel like an old man."

"You are one of the most handsome men here. I am sure the anxious mothers and daughters will be at your side in an instant."

The flickering candlelight reflected against the cut crystal pieces of the huge chandelier in the ballroom. It caught and held Morgan's glittering jewelry and golden eyes. Whenever she glided past, heads turned in admiration and jealousy.

"Ian, it is all a beautiful dream. I wish Mother and Lizzie could be with us tonight. But at least they will be here for our wedding."

Afraid to leave her side, Ian protectively hovered near Morgan, casting angry glares at the men vying for her attention. But her carefree laughter and flushed face made him forget some of his jealousy. Loving Morgan with such unselfish devotion, Ian was prepared for a life full of lusty remarks, bold

349

advances, envious glares, and perhaps a duel or two. It would, however, all be worthwhile. For at night it would be Morgan who lovingly slept at his side, who bestowed loving glances, whose gay laughter would fill his days for a lifetime.

Whirling about the dance floor, they ignored the knowing glances and murmurs from the others, managing to escape onto the veranda for a few moments.

As she held a cold glass of champagne to her lips, Ian wished it could have been his lips that moistened hers.

"Having a good time?" he queried.

"Wonderful. Simply wonderful," she leaned against the white pillar, dreamily staring at the moon and stars. "I shall remember this night forever, Ian. You have made me so happy."

Suddenly, she shivered.

"What is it, Morgan? Certainly you're not cold."

"I—I really don't know, Ian. It was such a strange feeling. Like someone was watching me from the shadows out there. I cannot explain. Ah," she laughed, "I must sound very foolish. Champagne does strange things to me."

She smiled, but Ian recognized a problem. "Come, let's go inside. I know my father wants to make the announcement soon."

No sooner had they returned when Paul anxiously strode toward them. "There you are! We were wondering if you decided to elope this evening. Now," he took Morgan's arm, "follow me to the front of the room."

Within moments, the chattering voices hushed, closing around the Kendall family and the beaming, handsome young couple. Morgan's golden eyes scanned the room, settling on Eric's smiling countenance. She squinted and saw him wink, which made her smile broaden.

"My dear friends," Paul began, "we welcome you to our home this evening. Marie and I have shared so many things with you dear people. And this evening is the happiest of all."

The crowd moved closer.

"You have all had the pleasure, I hope, of meeting Miss Morgan Rhinehart. Well, she has graciously consented to accept my wayward son and turn him into a respectable, solid citizen. Dear friends," he beamed, "may I present the future Morgan Kendall."

People applauded, exclaimed, whispered, stared, and sighed. Morgan heard none of it. She saw Ian lovingly gaze into her eyes, and she returned the look. Seconds before people descended upon them, Morgan whispered, "Ian, I hope I never wake up from this dream."

"It is no dream, cherie. You will soon be mine."

Toasts were offered. A few young men were bold enough to approach the couple, offering congratulations while begging Ian for one kiss or dance with the future bride.

As the evening sped by, everything in the room—lights, crystal, people—blurred into one fuzzy image. Four times Morgan was obliged to switch dance partners, returning their smiles and thanking them for the lovely compliments.

It was the way the fifth dance partner held Morgan familiarly that jogged her out of this stupor. But it was too late, for this man made her heart stop, her legs turn to lead, and her eyes widen in shock and dismay. All color drained from her face.

"Keep dancing, beauty, or your fiancé may become suspicious. We wouldn't want to cause a scene. Your present husband meeting your future one under the dueling oaks in the morning would cause quite a scandal. This city would never forget . . . neither would you."

The oh so familiar deep voice that used to whisper such passionate love words in her ear heated her blood. He was here. She was in his arms. But she was not his.

"Nicholas! What are you doing here?" she recovered her voice.

"Why I have come to wish my wife well," he drawled. "But Morgan, I am afraid you have made a serious mistake. Kendall is not for you. Why I'll wager that you already have him eating out of your hand. No my love," his arm tightened about her slender waist, "you need a stronger man."

"Well it is not you!" she snapped. "Now, if you will excuse me," she tried to stop but Nicholas deftly swirled her about the room, practically lifting Morgan off her feet.

"I shall not. After all, I have come across the Atlantic to see you. I will not be cheated."

With great trepidation, Morgan finally looked up at his face. Later, she would only remember the fathomless molten silver eyes that consumed her with hatred and, was it possible, desire?

"You are truly the southern beauty, Morgan. More beautiful than I can ever recall," the words were seductive but the tone harsh.

"Get out of my life, Nicholas!" She summoned the courage to stare back at him, but he merely laughed. It was an unpleasant sound. She experienced a chilly tremor—the same one as before on the veranda with Ian. "It was you! You were here all evening! How long have you been spying on me!" she asked accusingly.

Nicholas whirled her past an approaching young man whose intention of cutting in was obvious.

"If you mean did I see the touching scene on the veranda before, I did. You have no trouble freely bestowing your favors, do you?"

Before she could respond, Nicholas had managed to sweep her clear across the ballroom to the veranda, to the same spot she had shared before with Ian.

"How dare you!" she pulled back an arm to slap his arrogant face, but Nicholas was prepared.

"Oh no you don't." He grabbed her wrist, twisting it behind her back. "Is this a way to greet your long, lost husband? Come now, Morgan, you can do better than that," he coldly mocked her.

Never had she heard such a hateful comment. Why then, she wondered, was he here? To torment her more than he already had? To ruin the only decent chance left in her life?

"Stay away from me, Nick. I mean it. You are *not*—contrary to what you say or think—my husband. You never were," she spat, her fear turning to anger. "Who invited you to my party?"

"So the kitten has claws. You have changed, Morgan." He eased the pressure on her wrist while his other hand captured her stubborn chin. "I think it becomes you."

Opening her mouth to speak, Nicholas's tawny head

swooped down to take what he believed to be his. His tone and glare were cold, but his lips were warm and inviting. Morgan refused to respond. But her trembling hands betrayed how much she sorely missed this man's touch.

She was roughly pulled against his length, confined in his hard, unrelenting embrace. When did she kiss him back? She could not recall anything but the softening of his mouth on hers, his tongue searching for and insisting on entry. Did she allow that? She submitted to a calling beyond her senses.

All of Morgan's emotions focused on the man who held her. His spicy scent combined with the smell of the sea, his calloused hands plucking at the lace bodice, his quicksilver eyes matching her gaze.

"You can never, never forget me, Morgan. You're a fool if you think you can," he smugly whispered against her mouth.

It was enough for her to return to sobriety. With surprising strength, Morgan's hand snaked across his cheek in a resounding smack.

"You selfish bastard! What is the matter, Nick? Your immodesty cannot accept rejection? I don't want you here. I do not love you."

The moonlight caught the jeweled glow of his anchor ring as he touched his cheek. "Who said anything about love, sweetheart? I am only here to collect what is due me . . . you."

His humorless chuckle nauseated her. Taking a small step back, then another, Morgan sounded surprisingly calm as she said, "Do you remember how good I am with a pistol? Why you even gave me a few lessons to perfect my skill. If you come near me again, Nicholas, I swear I will find that little pearl-handled pistol you gave me and shoot you between those hateful eyes!"

His loud laughter chilled her blood. "Never, Morgan. You see, I taught you many things. And I remember many more. You are still mine. Perhaps another lesson," he grabbed her arm.

"No!" She moved back, desperate to run but frozen in place. Was it fear or something else that kept her only inches away from him? When he took her mouth once more, did she want him or was she too numb to respond?

How could she explain her arms winding around his neck, holding him close as she allowed his tongue easy entry into her mouth? Would she have allowed him to go further? As far as he wanted?

She would never know, for another voice brought this flight of fantasy to an embarrassing end.

"What the devil are you doing here, Nick?"

It was Eric. Thank God it was Eric and not Ian. Yet Nick refused to release her arm.

"Hello, Uncle Eric. Good to see you again. I did not know that you were chummy with the Kendall family," he forced a smile.

"You damn young fool. You cannot walk in here uninvited. Do you want to call undo attention to yourself and ruin everything we have worked for?" Eric was surprised by Nick's cavalier behavior.

Meanwhile, Morgan was confused. What did Eric mean? "Everything they worked for?" Pulling away from Nick, she said, "Please excuse me, Eric. My behavior was unforgivable. That happens whenever your nephew is around."

"You are not leaving, Morgan. I am not finished with you," Nick warned.

Morgan was not fooled by the dim light that obscured Nick's face. He was scowling and so furious that she knew he would throttle her if given the opportunity.

"Thank you for reminding me of what your odious presence can do to a respectable woman," she turned her back.

"Respectable! Hah! I suppose you will tell me that you haven't bedded Kendall—or anyone else who would promise to find your father's damned murderer. Or are you waiting for the highest bidder? Perhaps," he sneered, "I can join the bidding."

Only her head turned, but the topaz eyes greeted his callous remarks with unalloyed fury. "You could never pay my price. Besides, I have already bedded you. I am ready for a far more experienced and tender lover. Good evening, Eric," she regally strolled away.

Her head was held high, her shoulders straight, and Morgan could not help but smile. She amazed herself by summoning the courage and the right words to wound him, hopefully as much as he had wounded her.

Without looking back, Morgan blinked a few times to adjust to the bright light in the ballroom. Ian was there, somewhere. He would comfort her this night and each night thereafter.

"I will kill the black-haired bitch!" Nicholas snarled, starting out after her.

"You've already made a fool out of yourself. What do you intend to do now? Waltz into the room and announce to the crowd that Morgan is your wife?" Eric wanted to reason with him, but Nick's behavior was far from reasonable. "Nick, you were supposed to arrive two weeks ago. What happened?"

Leaning against the balustrade, Nicholas lit a cheroot. "We came up against not one, but two patrols. It was one hell of a run, Eric. There was slight damage to the *Anastasia*. But she is fine now."

"And you?" Eric knew Nicholas understood his meaning.

"Don't worry, Uncle. I will not cause an embarrassing scene this evening. I am calm now," he blew the smoke into the air.

"You said this evening. What about tomorrow or the day after?" Eric leaned against the balustrade.

"I don't know. Damn," he flung the lit cheroot into the fountain, "she is mine! She will always be mine. Eric, I will not let her marry Kendall."

"There is very little you can do. Unless you can get her to change her mind. I have seen and heard all that I need to, lad. She's got her mind set on marrying Ian. I was hoping you would arrive sooner than this. I am afraid it is too late."

"It is not," his voice was deceptively calm. "Now, Uncle, suppose you tell me about the Grays."

Eric studied his nephew's determined expression. Then he sketchily outlined his encounter with Charles Gray. "I have seen two plates—the very ones from the Philadelphia bank. Gray insisted we buy two now. I am willing to give him some money, although not what he asked.

"Nick, there is something else. I did not have the heart to tell Morgan about those plates. The other eight are buried outside of town. I haven't found the spot yet. I am meeting him tonight. We will discuss the transfer of funds."

"And Andrews?"

"It is the damndest thing, Nick. I haven't heard Gray mention that name. Not once. I wonder if there ever was an Andrews."

"Morgan couldn't have mistaken what her father said. Samuel Rhinehart only mentioned Andrews, not Charles or Jane Gray."

"Well, I can tell you this. Andrews is not in New Orleans."

"When will the Bank of New Orleans 'lose' its currency plates?"

"I think in a few days. I have told Gray that I must leave the city for France in one week. He said not to worry."

"The bank manager has the duplicate set of plates we had made?"

"Yes. That is all arranged too. Now," Eric stood again, "enough of this conversation. If you are calm, I suppose you can come inside and share a drink with me. You will stay in my home tonight?"

"No—I—uh, I have other plans. Sorry," he grinned mischievously. "Come, I promise I will behave. Just keep her away from me."

Ian was waiting for Morgan.

Trying to appear calm she recounted her meeting with Nicholas. It was what she did not say that worried him. When Morgan excused herself to freshen up, Ian frowned, his worried eeys focusing on the entrance to the veranda. Nick was his friend, but Nick would not claim Morgan. Not as long as he could prevent it.

Nicholas calmly walked toward Ian. "Hello Kendall. I suppose I should offer my congratulations. But I won't. It doesn't seem fitting. The first husband wishing the second husband good luck," he sardonically raised an eyebrow. "You work fast, my friend."

"Rhodes, listen to me. I will forget your barging in unannounced, and I will forget your lack of manners. Stay if you like. But if you do anything to upset Morgan, I'll kill you," he pretended to smile, "on the dueling field or on the waterfront. I don't care."

"Neither do I." Nicholas disappeared into the crowd.

The glorious evening was tarnished. But Ian Kendall would not let it show. Knowing Morgan, she would try to put on a bright face for the remainder of the ball. Damn, Ian cursed, if only we were married before that pirate had the audacity to show up in New Orleans.

How much longer could she hide in her bedroom? Morgan had been gone for twenty minutes. Seeing Ian's concerned face and remembering Nick's furious one had forced her to flee the ballroom. Once inside her room, she angrily paced across the carpeted floor.

Why did he come back into her life now? She did not want to see him every again. Why did she let him kiss her? But worse, why did she respond to his kiss like a lovesick schoolgirl?

Trying to recall his words and then Eric's, Morgan realized that something was said about the Grays or the currency plates. But what she vividly recalled were Nick's cruel words and rough embrace.

Carelessly examining her appearance in the cheval glass, Morgan took one deep breath before rejoining the party. Maybe he would be gone. Please be gone, she silently prayed.

But he wasn't. No sooner had she entered the ballroom than her eyes darted about, instinctively honing in on Nicholas. Standing on the side of the room, he appeared to be in animated conversation with a very attractive young blonde. When he threw back his head in loud, pleasant laughter, Morgan fought the temptation to leave.

"Damn him," she muttered under her breath. Not taking the time to study his appearance earlier, Morgan squinted hard to see what he looked like. What a pleasant surprise to see Nick dressed as a gentleman.

Whereas most of the gentlemen wore white or buff-colored jackets and breeches, Nicholas, of course, had to be different and stood out in a metallic gray jacket and black satin breeches. Even the shirt and cravat were not the customary snowy white, but a sky-blue silk. It was strange that even with her poor eyesight Morgan could see his flashing liquid silver eyes, which attracted her like a beacon on a dark night.

Not wishing to be seen staring at him, she headed for the other side of the room to the safety of Ian's arms.

"It is all right, cherie. I know you are upset. It is a shock to see him again after all this time. He will not bother you."

What could she say other than, "I am fine, Ian. I suppose it had to happen some time. At least I don't have to worry about when he will interfere with my life." She brightly smiled, "Dance with me."

The topic was closed for the night—at least between Ian and Morgan. Spinning about the dance floor, she tried to repress any thoughts of Nicholas, but it was like trying not to breathe.

The guests left well after midnight. Once again, Morgan and Ian stood by the front door accepting good wishes as the guests slowly existed.

"I am exhausted. I shall fall asleep in an instant. Do not worry if I sleep the whole day," she said before kissing him good night.

Unfortunately, it was not a deep sleep. By the time the maid helped her out of her dress and brushed out then plainted her long hair, Morgan suddenly felt wide awake. It must be the humid night air or the excitement of the evening finally catching up with her. Wearing a pale pink satin nightdress, Morgan tried to force herself to sleep, twisting to find a comfortable position. Because of the heat, the covers were quickly kicked off. She lay alone in the bed that was surrounded by a soft white netting . . . like a fragile curtain.

At last sleep came and with a wonderful, confusing dream. She was in Halifax, but in a house she had never seen. It was summer, for all the windows were wide open and the bright hot sun beat down on her body. She was running away from the house, holding a straw bonnet in one hand, lifting the white lace dress in the other. But she was laughing; it was such a light, carefree sound as she kept running to a wooded area behind the large house where there was a small thicket surrounding a pond.

Overheated from her brisk run, she could not deny a short swim in the inviting cool pond. Doffing the white lace dress,

358

Morgan reveled in the feel of the satin chemise against her bare skin.

Wanting to dip into the pond, she could not decide if she should remove the chemise. Who would notice? The area was secluded. Why not?

But it wasn't secluded. In fact, the hands that removed the garment did not belong to her. They were Nick's. She knew that without turning around. He was there, standing behind her, raining tiny kisses along the slender column of her neck while his hands slowly raised the satin above her hip then higher, until it was tossed aside.

Leaning into his fully clothed body, Morgan was afraid to speak. If she did, he would go away and the dream would end. One hand held her pliant body against his, and the other . . . the other slowly moved along her derrière then around to rest at the junction between her thighs. Anticipating more, Morgan breathed deeply, waiting, wanting to feel those fingers play with then enter her. The thought made her knees weak and her body tingle.

While he continued to nibble her neck and ear, his warm breath chilled her. Please don't let this end; don't let me wake up—not now.

The sensation did not go away, even as he led her to the ground. Wanting to see, she tried to turn around, but was on one side with her buttocks firmly pushed against his stomach. His hand still toyed with her center and his tongue outlined one ear.

"Oh, please," she could not contain the moan, "I want . . ."

"You want what, Morgan? Do you want to feel me deep inside you—like this?" his finger dipped further, and was joined by another. "Or do you want to feel more, beauty? Tell me," his passion-filled voice seemed so real.

"Yes. Yes I want more."

"You have to beg for it," he suggestively moved against her, making his desire quite obvious.

"Please, oh please Nick. I want all of you."

"Then open your eyes, beauty. Turn around and look at me."

Eagerly complying with the demand, Morgan shifted to face

him. He was tensely poised above her.

"Don't you dare scream, or I swear I will gag you," he threatened. The dream had become real.

Her eyes snapped open. Nicholas was here, in her room . . . in Ian Kendall's home.

"How dare you," she began, but was interrupted.

"I told you I was not through with you," his deep voice still held her mesmerized. Slowly unbuttoning the blue silk shirt, his eyes never left hers. Thinking she might scream, Nicholas lowered his half-clothed body over Morgan, his lips taking hers in a powerful kiss.

It was his way of letting her know that he could not be deceived.

"You want me Morgan. Don't deny it. I can make you beg for it. I can feel it here," his tongue moistened her lips, "and here," his fingers found her aching center. "You are liquid with desire for me, Morgan. For *me*."

The hot rush of desire enveloped her while she felt his fingers, his mouth, his body, moving against her.

"Do you want me to leave, dear wife?" he passionately sneered. "Do you? Answer me Morgan." Nicholas caught her chin, forcing her to look into his sparking silver eyes.

"No." It was a defeated whisper. "No."

He wanted to say more, to hurt her with his scornful words. But as he looked down at her, he saw a face filled with passion and defeat; Nicholas could speak no more words of hate.

"I want you Morgan. For weeks I could think of nothing else. Damn you, woman. You are in my blood, your soul is entwined with mine in an everlasting embrace." Nicholas ground his body and mouth against her yet again.

"Will you watch me undress for you, my love? Promise me you won't scream," his mouth teased hers. "Do you promise?"

"Yes."

Wide-eyed, Morgan remained frozen as Nicholas slowly removed his boots and breeches. With each unfastened button, he would look at her and smile victoriously. He had conquered her this night—perhaps for all time. And they both knew it.

"Touch me, Morgan."

He was ready for her. Tentatively, Morgan reached out, but when she found what was sought they both gasped with remembered pleasure.

"You have not forgotten—have you, my love?" he asked before easing on top of her. Nicholas had no intention of making this a short, quick lesson in lovemaking. Long, lean fingers roamed all over her receptive body. Yet he wanted much more.

"I want you to feel unbridled passion. I want you to always remember this night—with me."

Whatever part of her his fingers left his mouth found. Beginning with her earlobe, then along the exposed neck, Nicholas tormented Morgan's body with knowledge of her desires. He stroked, kissed, suckled, but did not touch her in the place that was nearly erupting with passion.

"Not yet," he murmured when she writhed against his body. "Not yet."

Traveling down her flat tummy to the insides of her thighs, to her ankles, he masterfully dominated the body he knew so well.

Morgan pulled the pillow over her mouth to stifle the loud groans when he finally concentrated on her center . . . on the core of her desire.

"You are not ready yet," he taunted.

While his tongue and finger circled the outer area, one finger, then two slowly eased inside her. Like a succulent peach ripened to perfection, Morgan felt herself open to his hands, and then thankfully to his mouth. Her liquid passion mingled with his saliva as Morgan could not contain the first shudder that transported her to a new level of ecstasy. She was in another time, another place, and did not hear his triumphant chuckle or see the softening in his eyes.

Kissing her, his hands again roamed the contours and hollows of her body. Feeling his manhood powerfully pressed against her stomach, Morgan acknowledged the familiar tingling arousal that began in the inner recesses of her stomach.

"Again, beauty. You need all of me this time. As much as I need to fill you."

"No, not yet. Let me . . . Nick," her eyes opened, "I want to touch and taste you. Lie down."

Suddenly, their roles reversed. Morgan played the same teasing game with Nick's body and would not relent until he too begged for more.

"Loosen your hair, Morgan. I want to see it fall around your body, my body," his eyes bore into hers. "Do it," he softly commanded.

With the same degree of studied control he used to taunt her while undressing, Morgan leaned back on her haunches, slowly unplaiting the long raven locks.

"Now spread it over your shoulders. Here," he helped her, loving the texture of her soft, thick mass of hair in his hands.

"My turn, Nick. No more orders from you," she huskily laughed, noting his delighted, wicked smile.

Although her black hair inhibited his view, Nicholas could feel. And what he felt was a pleasure beyond recounting. She consumed all of him, her hands, mouth, lips, teeth, and tongue finding, stroking, making him as obsessed with passion as she.

Unable to stand it any longer, Nicholas grabbed Morgan's waist, lifting her up and over him.

In calculated slow motion, Morgan eased herself onto him, sheathing his body.

A tiny moan escaped from her sealed lips.

Nicholas securely held her above him, orchestrating their movement. But Morgan wanted complete control, and rode him like a wild stallion free of restraints.

"You are exquisite. You are mine," he fiercely whispered, pulling her down to lie atop him. While hands stroked her breasts he sucked her nipples in a way that Morgan loved.

"Oh God, Nick. I don't want to let go—not yet."

"Then you won't," he quickly replied. Poised above her, Nicholas moved teasingly in then out of her.

"Kiss me, Nick."

As soon as he took her mouth, Morgan's hands locked and pulled him into her. They moved as one, thought as one, and felt the full fury of their united passions. Like a small stone going downhill, gathering speed, their desire erupted into an avalanche of unbounded pleasure.

The sun was high in the New Orleans sky when Morgan finally awoke. Languidly stretching, she thought she had never felt so good. One hand reached to the other side of the bed, but he wasn't there. Quickly sitting up, allowing the sheet to fall over her naked body, Morgan surveyed the scene about her. Had he been in her bed last night or had it only been a glorious dream?

Looking around, she saw the crumpled sheet and the soft indentation in the pillow beside hers. Her pink satin nightdress appeared to be hooked to one of the bed posters like a conquering symbol . . . a symbol of what, she thought. Lying on "his" pillow, Morgan could still smell Nick's scent. The spicy scent that so reminded her of the sea and their happier days brought a muffled curse to her lips.

"Damn him for being in my life again."

Reaching under the pillow, she felt something large and cold. Morgan's fingers traced the outline of what was unmistakably a ring . . . an anchor ring with a jeweled sword in the center.

Why? Why would he part with that ring? To Nick it was a sign of daring, strength, and freedom. Was he trying to tell her something? Did he need her to regain his strength? Or was it because she had left her wedding band in the Rhodes house— on her bed—thrown away in anger and pain. It was the last gesture before storming out of that house. Did someone give it to Nick? Did he carry it with him?

Suddenly his parting words came back to her. Perhaps he had murmured them before surreptitiously leaving this house, or while he was making love to her. She could not tell anymore. Fantasy and reality collided. But yes, she recalled, he did whisper something.

He had said, "You will always be a part of my life—as I am of yours. You are mine, Morgan. No other man can claim you. You know that as well as I do. You are too afraid to admit it. But I will have you again and again."

Those were not exactly words of love. They were spoken as a fervent challenge, almost a threat.

Leaning against the headboard, Morgan unthinkingly slipped the huge anchor ring onto her left hand, bringing it to her mouth. Did it belong there? Did she "belong" to Nick Rhodes?

No! Damn you Nick, no! she raged within. I will not let you march into my life, pretending that you did not betray me. I do not care what you do to me. As she threw an arm over her eyes, Morgan noticed a small bruise on her forearm. A matching bruise was on the other. It could have happened when he held her above him or underneath him or . . . No, don't do that, she scolded herself. Don't think about the ways he ravished your body last night. Pretend it was a dream. And pray that you will not see him again. But she refused to let go of the shining ring, staring at it, oblivious to the tears that clouded her vision.

Chapter 29

"Where have you been, lad?" Eric said from behind Nicholas's desk.

"That, dear Uncle, is none of your concern. I told you I had an appointment." Nicholas angrily slammed his cabin door. Marching over to the washstand, he practically tore the blue silk shirt off his back. "Who let you on my ship anyhow?"

"I believe your crew has seen my face before," Eric snarled. "She must have been some hellcat, son, judging from the marks on your back."

Nick peered over his left shoulder. Not seeing any marks, he looked into the small mirror and saw the uneven scratches in the center of his back.

"I've seen you in those black moods before, lad. You shouldn't have done it to her, Nick. You will only hurt her again."

"Hurt her again," he mocked. "Again you say?" He turned on Eric, slamming the first object in his way crashing to the floor. "What about me? My hurt? What about the pain I suffered because of that black-haired witch?" he thundered.

"I know lad." Eric was genuinely sympathetic. He loved Nick so much. Nick was the son he always wanted . . . the young, defiant boy who had grown into a competent, strong, independent man. Eric proudly claimed some credit for Nick's development. He would not let his nephew fall apart now.

"She will not listen to you, Nick. She says she wants to marry Ian Kendall. He is a good man. He loves her."

"So what? He is not for Morgan. I am. Just because she ripped up that marriage license does not mean we are unwed. She is still my wife."

The early morning raindrops struck against the gallery window. It was the start of a new day, but Nicholas could only view it as another day in a series of endless days and nights without Morgan. But last night, ah, last night . . . he could not and would not stay away from this woman.

Unintentionally, he had actually formulated a plan for seeing her alone again. He left with the other guests, but quickly circled back on foot. The stairwell in back of the Kendall home led to the second floor. He knew precisely where Morgan's room was located, having seen her enter it earlier. It was to the rear; the small balcony was surrounded by a trellis. The window would have to be open in this heat.

Nicholas stopped thinking. In one silent, fluid motion he jumped across the middle balcony onto the trellis leading to her room. No one could have heard him.

Her window was open. When he stood at the side of her bed, Nicholas was momentarily afraid to reach out. He wanted to study, to memorize her as an artist studies his subject. Partially hidden by the gauze netting, he could see her thrashing about in the bed, in the throes of some dream or nightmare. The covers were flung off. The sight of the satin nightdress riding up one side was breathtaking; one long shapely leg that was carelessly flung over the other was exposed. One arm was stretched out, reaching for the other pillow.

Nicholas had to touch her. She was almost within his reach. All that separated them now was the white gauze that made her appear as an enchantress in bed. He paused for another second, then found the opening. She turned away from him, but he saw her hand seductively reach for the satin nightdress, slowly moving it above her legs.

It was more than he could stand. As if he were able to subdue Morgan's mind, Nicholas sensed what sort of dream she was having. He was confident that the dream lover would have his face. His hands quickly joined hers, and the passionate groan that escaped her ripe lips sent him on another of their heaven-bound journeys. He only wanted Morgan to speak his name.

366

And she would; awake or not, she would.

He had wanted to speak to Morgan, but what could he say? This was not the night for heated discussion. Rather, Nicholas decided to remain the phantom lover—for at least this night.

Afterwards, he knew there was something he wanted to give her. Murmuring a few words against her love-bruised lips, Nicholas slipped the ring off his finger. It had never been taken off, but somehow he believed that after this night it belonged to Morgan . . . as she belonged to him.

"Nick. Stop staring out of the window like that. We have to talk," Eric's harsh voice interrupted what now seemed like a fantasy.

"Talk about what, Eric?" He did not bother to look at his uncle. Instead, Nicholas reached for the bottle of Irish whiskey.

"It is barely dawn, lad. Don't you think your drinking can wait?"

"It is still the night to me, Eric. Leave it alone! I don't have the patience to bicker with you. Nor do I think I need a nursemaid," he rudely said.

"You are acting like you could certainly use one. You could also use a solid punch to the jaw."

Eric was angry and frustrated that Nick could not be reached. The cold exterior seemed to be more than a facade. It ran right through him, turning the compassionate man into a heartless and mean-spirted one.

"All right. I'm listening." Leaning against the side of his desk, Nicholas stared at Eric while deliberately gulping the whiskey.

"Why are you here, Nick? Is it to find the currency plates and the murderers, or is it to reclaim Morgan?"

"I told you . . ."

"You told me nothing. Except that you have been hurt too. So now what do you intend to do? You can't very well lure her away from Ian after accusing her of the things you did last night." Eric tried to sound calm and reasonable, but Nick's defiant glare made it nearly impossible.

"She is mine and she knows that now. It is only a matter of time," he smiled sardonically into the glass.

"I will not let you abuse her like some harlot, Nick. If you want her, you had better start courting her right and proper. If you're not inclined to do so, then let Ian have her."

Eric was infuriated. He kicked the glass out of Nick's hand and leapt out of the chair. Roughly grabbing his nephew's shoulder, Eric dared Nicholas to strike him, for at that moment there was nothing he would have liked more than to wipe the smirk off Nick's face.

"I hope your insensitivity is related to your drunken state, lad." Eric's cobalt eyes darkened as they riveted on his nephew. "I am still strong and mad enough to throw you out of the gallery window and watch you drown in the muddy water. Now, if you cannot or will not get a hold on yourself, I will take care of everything without you. I don't want you near me—or Morgan. I love her the same way I love you," he shook Nicholas, wishing he could knock some sense into the stubborn fool. "Although at the moment I don't know what I feel for you," he added. "You will destroy her and yourself. Is that what you want? Tell me. Is it?"

"Hell, I don't know," Nicholas easily twisted out of Eric's hold. "I came to New Orleans because I could not get her out of my mind. She was there all of the damn time, Eric. Bewitching me with her innocent smile. As long as I had the *Anastasia* to worry about, I was partially freed from her hold. Do you know what, Eric?" He bitterly laughed, "I welcomed the damn patrols. I wanted to fight them. I went a little mad then. I wanted to murder them. I didn't care what happened to me. And it is all because of that seductress."

"Do you think you can go on living this way? If you're not shot by the patrols or your crew—for running them ragged with your incessant demands—you will still have me and Ian Kendall to contend with."

"Yes," Nicholas eased himself into the desk chair, crossing booted feet on the desk. "Ian Kendall. My dear friend, sometimes business associate, and now wife stealer."

"He loves her, Nick. He is good to her."

"Tell me, Uncle. Is Kendall better for Morgan than I?" Nicholas calmly studied his uncle's concerned face.

"No. Of course not, you idiot. What do you take me for? But

you cannot expect Morgan to walk out of Ian Kendall's life and into your arms. It is not that simple and you damn well know it!"

Running fingers through his unruly hair, Nicholas sighed. "I suppose that's true. But time will tell, won't it Uncle Eric?"

Eric knew that Nick was being far too stubborn for his own good. Nor could he leave his nephew in this black mood.

"I know you did not leave directly for France, lad. So where did you go?"

"To Boston. I sailed to France from Boston."

"Did you purchase more merchandise to sell?"

"Yes. I also visited with George Taggart. That was where I obtained the description of Charles Gray as well as the confirmation that the Grays had been in Boston. There was a third man with them; I assume it was Andrews. But you say he is not in New Orleans?"

"Damndest thing Nick. No one has seen or heard of Andrews."

"Charlotte thought she could sail with me."

Eric looked twice at his nephew. What was Nicholas talking about now? The whiskey was affecting his good sense; Nick looked perfectly sober.

"Nick, I think you are changing the subject. Who is Charlotte?"

Nicholas immediately lost the faraway look. "Morgan's mother. I saw her and Morgan's sister in Boston too. They are coming to New Orleans for the wedding. I could not wait for them. But they should be here in a few weeks."

Eric now knew the real reason why Nicholas sailed to Boston, but thought better about mentioning it. "What did you tell her?"

"You would have been proud of me, Eric. I did not spare myself. I told Charlotte everything. And she still prefers me as her son-in-law. Of course Kendall hasn't had the opportunity to use his charming southern ways on her. You would like her, Eric. She is a wonderful woman, and Lizzie," he smiled, "well Lizzie reminds me of the hoyden Morgan must have been at that age. Charlotte now has her own house, you know," he said sheepishly.

"Morgan mentioned that. Say, Nick," Eric leaned forward, "did you have anything to do with the new house?"

"I couldn't allow them to live with the Driscolls. You haven't met Alice. She knew I married Morgan, but it did not stop her from trying to lure me into her bed. Alice thought Lizzie was her servant. I found them a proper house with no difficulty. I know they will be happy."

"That was a nice gesture, lad. Perhaps you haven't lost it." Eric smiled.

"It?"

"Compassion. I might also add generosity."

"Charlotte said the same thing," he muttered, incapable of saying much more. His head was heavy with drink; it was an effort to keep his eyes open.

Eric fondly touched his rumpled hair. "You are a fine young man. You need time to get over this pain, lad. I will not leave you," he whispered as he hauled Nick into the empty wood-framed bed that was covered with a feminine-looking rose satin coverlet.

Nicholas awoke with a pounding headache. The sun was high in the afternoon sky as he struggled to sit up in the large bed.

"Christ! What day is this?"

"It is still the same as this morning—Sunday," Eric chuckled.

"You have been watching me sleep the whole time?"

"Snore is a more appropriate word. Do you think you can comprehend what I am about to tell you?"

"Try me." He rubbed each red-rimmed eye with the heel of his palm. "How did you get my boots off?" he looked down, wriggling his toes.

"With great difficulty. Here," Eric handed Nick a hot mug of coffee, "I know you need this."

"Eric," Nick looked up suspiciously, "did I say anything that I am going to be sorry for?"

"I don't believe so."

"I mean about Morgan—as you damn well know."

"Nothing I haven't heard before, lad. Now," Eric stood, "while you were enjoying your nap, I received a message. Mr. Charles Gray would like to see me tonight. Are you able to join me?"

"I wouldn't miss it for the world."

Later that night Mr. Charles Gray met Captain Nicholas Rhodes.

They were seated at a dockside tavern; the light was so dim that Charles could not notice the resemblance between the two men across from him.

"My nephew Nicholas has recently arrived from Paris with a sizable sum of money to pay for the plates."

Nicholas did not speak. From his position in the dark corner of the table, he leisurely smoked a cheroot. Charles Gray could not possibly see the sharp metallic glower aimed at him. However, Charles knew the tall man was waiting for the appropriate moment to talk.

"Monsieur Gray. The emperor is most willing to pay for these plates. My uncle will be returning to France with the plates in two weeks."

"Two weeks?" Charles nearly choked on the whiskey. "I don't know if it is enough time. Your uncle must have told you that I do not have all twelve plates. I must retrieve them from another place. I would need at least one month."

"Sorry. But that's impossible," the younger man said. "I will give you three weeks at most. If you can have all of the plates for my inspection in two weeks or less, there will be a small bonus—for you, monsieur."

A thin blue line of smoke drifted across Charles's face. "I will see what I can do. But I want partial payment. As I have already told your uncle, I want two hundred fifty thousand francs for two plates—by tomorrow evening," his voice hardened.

"Sorry, only one hundred thousand francs," Nick coolly replied, knowing that Gray was trying to play the same game of nerve. "I would say the sum is more than generous. We are taking you at your word. How do I know you truly have twelve

371

plates?" Another puff of smoke was blown in Charles' direction. "And by the way, Gray, something continues to confound me. I do not ever do business with someone without shall we say, doing a little research. A quiet investigation, i you will. So perhaps you can tell me about your third partner" In Philadelphia he used the name Andrews. I have been informed that he killed the man who was arrested for the thef of the plates—Samuel Rhinehart. My uncle tells me you've met his daughter in New Orleans. What a coincidence, isn't it But to get back to my original question, monsieur, where is thi Andrews person?"

"He is no longer working with us. We bought out his share so to speak. Andrews—his real name is Alan Sterling—sailed for Spain two months ago."

"Odd, don't you think so Eric?"

"I would say. Why would he be bought out before selling th plates?"

"Believe me, gentlemen, he was paid quite handsomely Which was what he deserved." Charles mirthlessly smiled. " must be leaving. My sister is waiting for me. Tomorrow then, a the same table?"

Two days later, a counterfeit set of bronze currenc plates were stolen from the U.S. Bank in New Orleans Only a handful of people were aware of the theft of th four plates: the bank manager, his assistant, Ian Kendall and the Rhodeses.

"The plan is working perfectly so far," Eric confided to hi nephew that night aboard the *Anastasia*. "Now I have to fin exactly where the plates are hidden."

"No we don't," Nicholas mysteriously said, enjoying hi uncle's curious expression. "I know where half of them are."

"Nick, how did you discover the spot? That is wonderfu news. What are we waiting for. Let's get them."

"Wait a moment, Uncle. I said half of them. Gray has th other half. You will have to meet him on the day and hou according to his carefully worded instructions.

"Where will you be?"

"In some town not far from Alexandria, about two hundre miles northwest of here. According to Gordon, Gray's hidde the money in some secluded area twenty minutes outside of a trading post called Les Rapides. It is not much of a settlement, but it has a hotel or cantina, a couple of stores, and houses."

"How did you find out?"

"Mr. Charles Gray is not a very cautious man. He has been followed by two of my most trusted sailors for two weeks. He likes to visit the spot, I guess," Nick shrugged. "Eric, there was something else Gordon found—an unmarked shallow grave, not far from the area."

"Was it . . ."

"He had no time to check. But I seriously doubt Andrews is in Spain."

"Odd, isn't it?" Eric sadly smiled. "All this time Morgan has been pinning her hopes and anger on one man—a man with a birthmark. I wonder what she will think when . . ."

"There is no need to tell her any of this yet. And when the time comes, Eric, I will be the one to handle her." His voice was as icy as the wintry look in his eyes.

"Stay away from her Nick," Eric warned.

"I will be leaving tomorrow for Alexandria."

"Nick, I don't know what you are up to. But I suspect that Charles Gray is not the only reason you are taking this trip."

"Stay out of this Eric. You don't want to know. Just meet me according to our plan."

Like the coward she suddenly thought herself, Morgan did not leave her room on Sunday. Ian sent a note requesting her presence for dinner, but Morgan felt she could not feign the exuberance of a bride to be.

It wasn't fair that he had barged back into her life, interfering in her business. She did not want Nick involved with the Grays. Remembering Eric's comments, the "we" he often referred to could only have been Nicholas.

If Ian saw her puffy eyes and troubled expression, he would know that Nick had been with her. She couldn't face Ian's honest, loving face. She couldn't hurt him the way Nick had hurt her. Being a gentleman, Ian would challenge Nick rather than kill him outright. The thought of either man's blood on

373

her hands was revolting. Perhaps she was the harlot Nick had called her. If she couldn't resist his touch, then all she could do was stay out of his sight. Even if it meant staying in her room until the wedding.

Her intentions were honorable. Early the next morning, one of the servants brought in Morgan's breakfast tray. There were two notes under the flowers. Ian again wished to see her, hoping she was feeling well enough to share a quiet, intimate dinner at a restaurant. His sweet words warmed her heart:

> "You left me standing in the rain without your sunny laugh and beautiful face. I miss you, cherie, and long to see you, to know you are real and that you have indeed agreed to make me the happiest man alive.
>
> > All my love,
> > Ian"

What a darling man, she smiled to herself.

Upon seeing the handwriting of the second note, however, she scowled.

> "Meet me at the French Market—at the straw bonnet and ribbon booth. Today, at noon. If you are not there, I will be at the house to collect you at twelve-thirty. Your choice.
>
> > Nick"

"You bastard! I will not see you!" she fiercely vowed, ducking under the bed covers.

At eleven A.M. Morgan was dressed in one of her prettiest day dresses: a pale yellow muslin dress, decorated with bright yellow and white ribbons and sprigged flowers along the hem and short capped sleeves. Her long black hair was fashionably coiled on the crown of her head, a few defiant wisps on her forehead and the back of her neck. On impulse, Morgan snatched her spectacles, stuffing them into the yellow satin reticule that already contained the heavy anchor ring.

The day was hot and humid. She could have walked, but decided to hire a coach. A brief note was left for the Kendalls.

She promised to be back by three and would be joining Ian for dinner that evening.

Finding her way to that particular booth was not easy. There were at least two others like it, but they were close to one another. As usual, the market was crowded; voices of indeterminate accents blended with the hawkers; children begged for money; prospective buyers negotiated for items as if they were more precious than the rarest jewels. Morgan loved it. The marketplace was alive with color, different faces, thousands of things. If it weren't for Nicholas, she would have enjoyed a leisurely stroll through the area.

Standing before the bonnet and ribbon booth, Morgan could not help but wonder if he would be there. Looking across the wide street to the St. Louis Cathedral, she could not see the clock, but heard the loud chimes announcing the noon hour.

"Why don't you wear your glasses?" His voice gave her the shivers.

Pivoting to face him, she snapped, "Why must you sneak up on me. It is a rather annoying habit of yours."

The insufferable brute had the audacity to laugh. "Here Morgan, I will buy you that bonnet you've been ogling. It matches your dress."

It was a wide-brimmed straw bonnet with yellow and white satin ribbons streaming down the back. It perfectly matched her dress. She wanted to refuse and opened her mouth to say something impolite, but Nicholas's warm hand firmly grasped her wrist.

"Not a word, beauty."

She helplessly watched as her heart fluttered erratically. Why did the sight of him do this? And why did he have to look so damn handsome?

"I hate you Nick," she whispered.

"Yes, I know, my love," he smiled in return.

It was odd, she suddenly thought, that Nick was dressed in fawn-colored buckskin breeches, dark mahogany boots, and a long-sleeved white cotton shirt and buckskin vest.

"Aren't you a bit overdressed?" she commented. "Especially in all that leather."

"No, you are," he mysteriously answered. "Here," he

375

shoved the bonnet into her chest, then pulled it back. "Let me." If his voice wasn't irresistible, his hands were. The light, feathery touch reminded Morgan of the numerous intimacies they had shared.

Silver eyes focused on the top of her head. "You should wear your hair loosely bound, my love. At least this hat has a wide crown for your fancy hairstyle."

It must have fit and looked very well on her, for Nicholas continued to hold her shoulders with an admiring gleam in his eye.

"Perfect. I think hats suit you. I rarely see you in hats, but now . . ."

"Thank you for the gift," she said through gritted teeth. "Would you please tell me what is so important about my meeting you here. Ian will . . ."

"Ian is at his plantation today. He will not be back until the evening—in time for your romantic little supper," he cut in. "Come on," he took her elbow, "I have to show you something."

"I will not!" she defiantly stood still. "I will not go anyplace with you, Nicholas, not until you tell me what is going on."

"Do you want to see Andrews?" his lips curled in a sneer. "If you do, then you will follow me now, without asking any more of your stupid questions."

Nicholas was no kinder now than he was the night of her engagement party—the long, passionate night spent entwined in her bed. Well, she decided, if he can so conveniently forget our tryst, so can I!

"You don't have to be so rude, Nicholas. Or mysterious."

"Don't tell me what to do or say." He didn't look down at her, but merely stared straight ahead while practically pulling her along.

They walked to the edge of the market and crossed the busy street.

"Where are . . ."

"Shut up Morgan. I have a brutal headache."

"Drinking again, Nicky?" she taunted, finding great pleasure in the way his back stiffened when she used the name they both loathed.

"It is a short coach ride. See if you can be quiet for twenty minutes."

Deciding that she would rather be anywhere but in this small enclosed coach, Morgan indignantly sat as far from him as possible. No matter how much she squirmed, his powerful thigh pressed against her leg.

"Stop fidgeting. You are annoying me."

"Annoying you!" she flared. "You are taking me on a ride to who knows where, with virtually no explanation. You honestly think I should trust you—accept your word. Hah! I find myself in this unbearably hot, stuffy coach with your huge body so close to mine. And you say that I am annoying you?" She dug into her reticule, "Here, you loathsome bastard. Take this offensive ring back." She threw it in his lap and watched as he calmly put it on his left hand before presenting her with his chiseled profile.

Morgan knew she was losing her composure. When his hateful personality surfaced, it was a mistake to go anywhere with him.

"Nick, I think I would rather not go with you. Why don't you give me the information and I will have Ian or Eric take me." She tried to sound conciliatory.

But there was no response.

Placing one gloved hand on his sleeve, she tried again. "Nick? Please listen to me. I want to go back to the Kendalls. Please ask the driver to turn around." She took one quick look out of the coach. Seeing they were leaving the immediate town limits, Morgan declared, "Nicholas! Where the devil are we going? If you think I will spend one more minute in this coach with you, you are mistaken. Turn this coach around. I demand it."

"Shut up Morgan," he snarled. "Sit still. It will be cooler that way. You will see where we are going soon enough."

She silently fumed for ten more minutes. They were near the large plantations; but it must be in the opposite direction from Ian's home. His home, she remembered, was northeast of New Orleans.

"Are we going north or south?"

"South, then northwest."

"Inland or toward the coast?"

"Inland."

Two more minutes passed. The coach bounded along what must be rough roads. Tiny dots of perspiration formed on her brow and neck. One furtive glance at Nick made her angry once more. He looked cool and totally unruffled.

"Nick," she sounded subdued. "I think I am going to be ill. Please stop the coach," she put one hand to her mouth.

Nicholas turned to face her. "I don't believe you, sweetheart. You look fine."

What he wanted to say was that she looked ravishing, that her sultry looks and fiery expression tempted him to take her right here in the coach.

"Really Nick. I am not well. Oh please," she gagged, "I don't want to soil myself."

With a muttered curse, Nicholas asked the driver to stop. Before the coach came to a complete halt, Morgan deftly jumped out, headed for some bushes, and ran as fast as her dress-impeded legs could move. The new straw bonnet flew off and hair pins scattered, allowing ebony curls to escape down her back. Lifting her skirts, Morgan blindly forged ahead on the dusty path. She did not know when she first heard the crunching of booted feet, but within seconds she fell onto the ground, protectively encircled in Nicholas's arms.

"I should have known you were a lying bitch," he growled in her ear.

Stunned, Morgan lay on the ground while Nicholas stood over her prone body.

"Get up."

There was no tenderness in the fathomless steel eyes. Slowly, she rolled over to face his angry countenance. "Help me up, will you?" She extended an arm.

A gentlemanly reflex prompted Nicholas to reach for her. She was almost erect, when a handful of dirt was ruthlessly flung into his face.

"I hope you are blinded!" she viciously yelled as she once again darted out of his way. Winding in and out of the paths, Morgan hoped to find a spot to hide in or at least be near the grounds of some plantation where surely someone could help her.

Straight ahead there was a copse of feathery green cypress trees. Panting with fear and exertion, she ran on pure impulse. But her eyesight was too poor for her to notice the roots of the trees that stuck out of the earth. One foot twisted as she stumbled. Caught painfully unaware, she tumbled forward, hitting the hard ground.

She was engulfed in blackness and could not see Nicholas's expression alter from fury to concern.

Gently pulling Morgan into his arms and surveying her condition, Nicholas felt the injury was not serious. Perhaps it was all for the best, he thought, for surely he would have hit her if she once again defiantly refused to get into the coach. In her unconscious state, Morgan could not complain, whine, or argue about their destination.

"Is she all right, Captain Rhodes?" Gordon worriedly asked seeing the limp woman securely held in the captain's arms.

"Just a bump on the head. Perhaps we can make up for the lost time now that she cannot struggle. Hopefully, we will reach the farmhouse before dusk."

With Morgan's head resting on his lap, Nicholas settled into the hot coach. Brushing the unruly hair and dirt off his face, he absentmindedly continued to stroke her face.

Closing his eyes for a few minutes, Nicholas wondered if he had made the right decision. He had kidnapped his own wife. How would she react upon learning the truth? Would he have to bind and gag her to keep her subdued? Would she finally give up and stay with him for the next few weeks?

"Morgan, my love, I don't know why you bring out the worst in me. Yet I cannot remember a time in my waking or dreaming life when you weren't ruling my thoughts," he whispered.

Chapter 30

She must have been dreaming. Lying in a narrow bed with a scratchy wool blanket as the only cover over her chemise-clad body, Morgan did not recognize anything in the small, dark room. One candle valiantly glowed off to the right, but the thousands of bright stars she saw from the window made it appear as if it were lighter outside than within.

Afraid to open her eyes to find the dream a nightmare, Morgan turned onto her side. What did she recall? It came back like a splash of cold water on her face.

Nicholas had abducted her! He had taken her—against her will—to some godforsaken place in the wilderness. She remembered tripping over something and hitting her head. But was it really Nick's voice that whispered, "Forgive me, my love," or was it wishful thinking? Was she safely nestled in his strong embrace throughout the coach ride? Did he tenderly place her on this bed, lightly kissing her forehead after he undressed her and attempted to wash the grime off her face?

"Oh no," she moaned aloud.

"Morgan? What is wrong?" he appeared out of nowhere.

"It's all real, isn't it?" She did not turn to face him, but felt the bed sag from his weight.

"Afraid so, beauty. I could think of no other way to get you away from your protective watchdogs."

"Nicholas," she slowly turned, ignoring the dull throb in her head, "this is ridiculous. This is kidnapping!"

"I know," he grinned.

"You must take me back. Ian will be frantic."

She couldn't have chosen more inappropriate words. The previously calm countenance disappeared. "You do not really think I care, do you? The man is a wife stealer and you worry about his being frantic!"

"He is my fiancé," she quietly replied.

"Like hell he is. When this little adventure of ours is over, Morgan, I have every intention of finding your precious, frantic Ian Kendall and beating him senseless—before I kill him."

Trying to sit, she declared, "You wouldn't. You couldn't. Nick, Ian has been wonderful to me. I will not hurt him," her eyes searched his face for understanding but found none. "Ian loves me."

She was thankful for the darkness. Mustering a passionate response, she sighed, "Oh yes, Nick. I love him very much. He is a wonderful love—I mean man." There, she thought triumphantly, I hope you choke on your anger and jealousy.

"I am sorry to hear that. It will be a long time before—or if—you ever see your precious lover again," he said in a controlled but brittle voice.

"Nick. This is absurd. You must let me go. If you won't take me back to New Orleans, then give me a horse and I will find my own way."

"Not with your 'superb' eyesight you won't. Besides, I have a job to do and I want your company. Your body will comfort me on these long, lonely nights."

"I am not comforting you like some common whore," she wiped a loose strand of hair from her eyes.

"You aren't?" he asked. "Why that surprises me. It appears to me as if you offer yourself to anyone who asks."

The words wounded her, but she refused to let it show. "Is that so? I think I would rather have Ian sharing my bed than you. Now, if you will excuse me, Nicholas, I have a dreadful headache."

"Morgan, you think you have won this round. If I were you, I would not be too smug about it. We are going to spend a great deal of time together."

She thought he smiled, but could not tell as he turned and

swiftly stalked out of the room.

By daybreak, he was back.

"Get up, Morgan. Here." A package was dropped on her chest. "Wear these. Be swift; we have a lot of time to make up."

"Nicholas, I told you . . ."

"I recall every word you said. But I am going to warn you this once. If you do not do as I say, I will strip you of what is left of your clothing and dress you myself. Then I intend to bind and gag you."

Taking a menacing step into the room, Morgan thought Nick looked fiendish. He was dressed in buckskin breeches and red shirt, his booted feet parted. He was ready to assault her.

"Well, the choice is yours."

"Thank you for your generous offer. But I think I would prefer to take care of myself. So," she falsely smiled, "keep your filthy hands off me."

"With pleasure." The door slammed after him.

Rummaging through the parcel, Morgan found her old pair of breeches, a new pair of black leather breeches, three white cotton shirts, one silk chemise, and extra underthings.

The temptation to try on the leather breeches was greater than her stubborn impulse to disobey Nick's orders. With no mirror to assist her, Morgan could only assume the breeches fit perfectly. The shirt was large, but comfortable. However, she had no idea what to do with her knotted, unruly hair, or bare feet.

"Nick?" she petulantly stormed out of the room, "what do you expect me to do now?"

Looking up from a map, he felt a white hot flash of desire for the vixen standing in the doorway. The leather breeches were an inspiration, but Nicholas had only imagined how flattering they would look. This surpassed his expectations. Christ, and he swore he would not touch her. The breeches were perfectly molded to her sensuous body, hugging her hips and rounded derrière where his hands would roam, if given a chance. Her ebony hair cascaded about her shoulders.

Knowing Morgan would instantly be aware of his arousal, he schooled his features into a bland expression.

"Do you have a problem, my dear?"

"Yes, I have a problem. Don't be such a fool. You know very well I do not have shoes, unless you return my slippers. I'd also like my dress. Or did you rip that off me last night?" she maliciously added.

"I suppose you would like a bath as well. How about a maid to help you dress and style your hair?"

"That would be wonderful. But even you couldn't produce such a miracle."

"There is another package for you over there," he pointed to a chair, not looking at her but at the map. "I think you will find what you need."

Too angry to gasp at the splendor and workmanship of the knee-high black leather boots, she grabbed them, asking, "Do you have any hose or stockings? And a brush while you are at it?"

"Demanding little wench, aren't you?"

Reaching for a canvas bag beneath his legs, Nicholas searched for the articles.

"Here, you can borrow mine." He tossed the hose and brush at her. "Take this too." She barely caught those things before he tossed a red scarf. "Use that for your unruly hair. And Morgan," his stormy gray eyes looked through her, "don't dawdle."

"Why you . . ."

"No more. I am tired of this."

"You are! How nice. Well I too am tired of this. I want to go back to New Orleans—to Ian."

This time, Nicholas refused to take the bait. "You have exactly two minutes to be ready." He tucked a pistol in the waistband of his breeches, picking up the canvas bag plus a leather saddlebag. "That saddlebag is yours. I suggest you take it. We are traveling on horseback. The terrain is rough."

The door slammed. Morgan was alone with a saddlebag and stray bits of clothing.

"One more minute, Morgan," he shouted from inside. "Then I am coming back inside and heaven help you."

She was outside in forty-five seconds.

Seated on a huge bay stallion, Nicholas glared down at her

while holding the reins of what looked like a packhorse. "You did say you could ride. I fail to recall if I ever saw you astride," he deliberately paused, "a horse, I mean."

"Where is my horse? You don't think I would share anything with you," she fearlessly marched toward him.

"Turn around, Morgan, or are you too blind to see a large horse that is no more than five feet away from you."

The gray mare patiently waited for Morgan to mount. "What about my things?"

"I don't know, what about them?" He placed a wide-brimmed hat over his tawny head.

"I have done everything you commanded me to do. You have kidnapped me, mocked me, threatened me. Is there anything else?" she defiantly tossed her head.

"Yes. Plenty. But I suppose you have had enough shocks for twenty-four hours," he conceded. "I will give you a hand," Nicholas lazily placed one leg over the other and dismounted.

His hands were inches from her legs as he tied the saddlebag. Morgan remained perfectly still, except when he accidentally brushed a hand over her thigh and she experienced a brief, searing shock.

"Something wrong, beauty?" He did not look up.

She kicked him in the chest. "Oh, I am sorry. It was an accident," she brightly smiled.

"Let's go," he slapped the horse's rump.

"Where is Gordon?"

"He went back to the city. Eventually he and Eric will join us. For the time being, however, I would rather be alone with you."

They traveled under the blistering sun for three hours. Morgan did not complain, and Nicholas refused to turn around to check.

Wishing for something to at least cover her head, Morgan wiped her perspiring brow with the back of her gloved hand. "I hate you Nick," she muttered more than once.

Nick had told her they would be traveling northwest. The terrain was typical of this lowland and plains region of the territory. The land changed from swamps, marshes, and cypress trees to more arid land, dotted by bottomland forest and pine trees. In the span of fifty miles, the land became a striking contrast with what she knew in New Orleans. Yet, she was aware that they were following the rivers and bayous as they headed north.

By noon, she was losing her interest in the surroundings. Nicholas, of course, had a different attitude. Sitting erect, he did not seem affected by the heat or the dusty ride. However, Morgan knew that if she did not stop soon, she might fall. But she would rather do that than ask for his help.

"There is a village up ahead. We will stop there. Can you manage?" he asked without turning.

"Yes," she croaked, but seemed unaware that he slowed his horse in order for her to catch up.

"Sure is a hot one," he reached for a canteen, took a long swallow, and handed it to her. "Take some." Seeing the mutinous look that effectively hid her fatigue, he added, "This is not the time for martyrdom."

The cool liquid soothed her parched throat. "Thank you," she managed to say.

"Keep it. But sip it slowly. We'll stop for lunch if we find a clean place. Can you ride?"

That was enough to pull Morgan out of her lethargic state. "I am fine, Nick." She galloped away, missing his low chuckle.

No one was on the street when they trotted through the little village. Nicholas's keen eyes located a sign half hanging from a storefront. Knowing that Morgan needed a brief respite but was too proud to admit it, he decided to stop.

"Wait here," he ordered, and dismounted.

Morgan did not want to remain on the horse any more than she wanted to remain alone on the deserted street. As quickly as her sore muscles allowed, she followed him. After one look inside, she wished she hadn't.

The dark room of the tavern reeked of stale tobacco and liquor. A dozen or so suspicious male eyes focused on the tall stranger wearing a bright red shirt, but immediately shifted to the small black-haired wench in tight leather breeches.

Nicholas stiffened, realizing what was going on.

"I told you to wait outside, Morgan," he growled. "Now you have done it. Come over here," he extended a hand. "And don't say one word."

They sat at a table closest to the entrance. After five minutes, an unkempt, overweight man approached. "Drink?"

"Rum for me and anything cold for her. Got anything edible?"

"What?"

"Food. Got any food?"

"Some bread and cheese."

"Fine. Bring it."

"Um, Nick," she spoke at last. "Where do you think I could wash and . . . well, you know."

"There must be something out back. I'll take you before we leave."

"You will not," she hissed. "I told you I refuse to have you near me."

"Either I escort you to protect your worthless body and nothing more, or you will find yourself escorted by one of these nice looking gentlemen. Any potential beaus here for you, sweetheart?"

They silently ate what the proprietor called food. Morgan drank something cool, but it had an aftertaste.

"Be careful Morgan. It's probably spiked with rum."

"Nick, I have to leave," she squirmed.

"Jesus, Morgan. Come on then," he almost pulled her from the chair, leading her through another doorway.

Standing guard while staring down the leering faces, Nicholas leisurely rested his right hand on the handle of the pistol, his left inching the hat above his brow.

"Morgan, where the devil are you?" he fiercely whispered through the door.

Two minutes later Morgan emerged, her hair neatly plaited in one long braid that hung over one shoulder. Oblivious to what was going on, she smiled brightly at Nicholas. "I am ready now."

"Give me your gun," he ground out the words through a forced smile.

Nicholas thought they would make it out of the door with no difficulty—but he was taking no chances. They were almost there when one squat man then another taller one stood in

387

front of their path.

"Leaving us so soon, fella? We thought to get to know ya better. Your lady friend too."

"Real purty lady too," said the short one.

Morgan took one hesitant step towards Nicholas, then another. But a grimy hand clamped down on her wrist.

"Have a drink with me, lady."

"My *wife* does not want a drink right now."

A third man appeared, standing between Nicholas and Morgan.

"I think she does. Don't ya lady?" He picked up the end of her braid. "Dark, dark hair, soft too. Wonder what your skin feels like?"

Terrified, but unwilling to show it, Morgan took a step back, hoping for a comforting glimpse of Nicholas. As long as he was within her sight, she would not show any fear.

"I already told you my wife . . ."

"I think the lady can answer for herself," the one closest to Nicholas said.

"All right," he calmly said. "Morgan dearest, would you like to join these gentlemen for a drink? Do tell them, honey, how it affects you—being in your third month and all. Yep," he wickedly grinned, "mighty unpleasant sometimes too."

"Oh don't be ridiculous, Nick," Morgan forced a laugh. "I don't get that ill. I only soiled myself once and you once. But if you think I should have a drink with these people—well, fine." She turned to the man who had touched her hair. "You, why don't you sit close to me. I like company when I drink."

Morgan led the way to a table, leaving the three to stare at her back. Let this work, she prayed silently.

Nicholas made his move. It was their only chance. No one saw him draw the gun. But in one motion it was drawn and he shot one of his tormentors in his side.

"Get out of here," he shouted at her.

Another was making a move—for both his weapon and Morgan's hair.

"Move," Nicholas commanded again.

Jolted by his sharp tone, Morgan did jump and only afterwards realized how ominously close the third man was

Instinctively reacting the only way she could, Morgan's booted foot lifted high, squarely hitting his groin.

Nicholas grabbed her arm, shoving her forward. "Run for the horses. I'll follow," he pushed again. "Out now."

Temporarily blinded by the bright sun, Morgan halted then ran for the horses, untying all three. Mounted and waiting, she prayed he would be joining her.

There was one shot followed by another. Morgan did not realize that she was crying. Tears slid down her cheeks and chin. If he doesn't come out now, I am going inside. I will kill every one of them, she decided while rummaging through the saddlebag for a knife or any weapon she could use.

Prepared to dismount, Morgan halted when she saw Nicholas casually sauntering out of the cantina as if he had all the time in the world.

First he looked at her, then up at the hot sun. "Everything is fine. They won't be giving us any trouble. Here, sweet, wear this. The barkeeper thought you might need it." He produced a hat—much like the one he wore.

"Nicholas, did it belong to any of those slime?"

"Nope."

Examining it, she said, "Well, it looks clean. I suppose it will do."

"Wait. You seem to have some dirt streaks on your adorable face. Let me," he took the scarf from around his neck and gently wiped the tear streaks. "Did you have a nice time today, Morgan?"

"Nicholas, either we are both crazy or I am hallucinating. You—you almost died in there and I could have been raped. And now you calmly inquire if I am having fun!" She looked skyward. "Heaven help me from this madman."

"Look at me, Morgan," his deep voice commanded. With one thumb, Nicholas pushed the hat far off his face, exposing his metallic silver eyes. "I wouldn't have let them touch you. Although you sure as hell know how to put us in trouble."

"Me? Trouble? I suppose you just wanted to take me on a short ride—to return me to my fiancé at sunset," she panted.

"Come on. Let's get moving. We lost enough time. Put this hat on and keep this pistol by your side. I've reloaded it."

As he pulled the horses around, Morgan asked, "Nick, when did you learn to shoot like that? Or to ride? I thought sailors don't learn those skills."

"Most don't. I'm not just a sailor, Morgan. You haven't learned very much about me, have you?" he jeered, not waiting for a response.

Three horses were slowly led along the dusty road, heading northwest again toward another unknown, more dangerous adventure.

"I refuse to sleep next to you in that!" she yelled.

"Morgan, see if you can recall that aside from our enjoyable stop this morning in the cantina there was no town, no farmhouse, certainly no hotel or inn to accommodate us this evening." He continued to spread the bedrolls beside the fire.

"I don't care. This is not safe." She dramatically waved her hand at the deserted area.

"Safe? You want safety? Or do you want Andrews?"

"I want," she said evenly, "to be out of your charming company. I want a hot bath, a real bed, and Ian beside me."

"It gets cold at night. Sleeping under the stars can be an interesting experience. But for a pampered bitch like yourself, I guess nothing will do." He remained on his haunches, not looking at her angry face.

"Oh yes, some things do satisfy me. But it is not you—you loathsome creature."

"Please," he held up one hand, "I am tired, Morgan. I do not want to hear another word about Kendall's charms. You will have to dream about him while you sleep next to me."

"I refuse to share that with you," she stubbornly repeated, and kicked some dirt into the fire.

"Suit yourself." Nicholas completed his chores then settled between the bedroll, his back once again toward her. "Good night, Morgan. Sleep well."

Angrily she took a blanket and moved to the horses. Groaning and complaining to herself, she finally thought she might be able to sleep. She barely had one boot removed when she heard strange noises.

"Nick?" she fearfully whispered. "What's that?"

He did not answer. The bastard is probably asleep. Well, if it doesn't bother him it won't bother me, she decided. Under the blanket, punching the saddle beneath her head and pulling another blanket up to her nose, Morgan waited for sleep to come.

It didn't. But she heard something howl, and then it was joined by another. Which could be worse, she wondered, two beasts howling in the night or the beast snoring near the fire?

The sky was barely pale pink when Nicholas awoke from his sleep. He smiled as he noticed Morgan curled against his back, her partially clothed body seeking his warmth and protection. Knowing that this moment would end too quickly, Nicholas decided to lie quietly at her side.

Morgan had no idea how she affected him. Of late, there were too many times when he could not control his anger or jealousy. In fact, that was the only way he could respond to her. She was his, and if kidnapping were the only way to prove it, so be it.

That was why Nicholas left a note for Eric, explaining what he was doing. But Nicholas could not explain why he had taken Morgan—not to himself. So it was impossible to put these thoughts on paper and make them sound logical. Positive that his uncle would be furious, Nicholas was equally sure that Eric would come.

However, in order for the plan to be a success, it was necessary to bring along others. Would Ian Kendall be among them? Probably, Nicholas decided. After all, if the situations were reversed, Nicholas would have been trailing Ian with a vengeance. Hopefully, Eric would explain something to Ian.

Yet none of it mattered, not as long as Morgan sought his protection. For Nicholas firmly believed—despite her harsh words and actions—that she cared for him. Perhaps she no longer loved him, but she could again. He had to believe that Morgan would love him again. Not until the moment she admitted it, though, would Nicholas Rhodes acknowledge that he had never fallen out of love with his wife.

It was better not to think any more about this. Better to act on anger, instinct, and passion, but not love. His resolve stiffened and so did his spine. Morgan must have felt it and moved closer, throwing one leg over his.

"Are you awake, Morgan? It's almost dawn and we must leave now, while it's cool." His tone was almost pleasant.

She was out of the bedroll and on her feet in seconds. "I am sorry Nick. I didn't mean to . . . it's just that . . ." she paused, examining his face. His head rested on one bent elbow as he continued to smirk at her. "It's just that I was a little frightened and you were here. I haven't slept outdoors in years. And damn you, Nicholas Rhodes, since you kidnapped me, the least you could do is protect me."

His bold laughter annoyed her, but not as much as his rakish good looks. Despite having slept barely five hours and not having shaved in two days, he looked wonderful. Tawny sun-streaked hair fell onto his forehead, and his eyes looked brighter than the rising sun. And when he stretched his muscular body, Morgan wanted to kill him for being so attractive—especially since she considered her own appearance so unappealing.

"I hate you Nick!" she vehemently declared. "Stay away from me."

"I am not anywhere near you," he calmly replied. "I take it that your foul disposition must have something to do with the lack of bathing water. If you can keep quiet long enough to listen and pack our gear, I will take you to a stream. It is a two-hour ride from here."

Even after he stood, Nicholas could not look at her. Morgan thought it was because he couldn't stand the sight of her unkempt appearance. Nicholas knew differently.

"Well," he folded the bedroll, "are you interested in a cool bath for your hot temper? Jesus, Morgan," he half turned, "your temper tantrums seem to be worsening with time. What has happened to the sweet-tempered girl I used to know?"

"She married you! That's more than enough," she quickly retorted. "Would you mind turning your back while I . . ."

"Go ahead." He did not want to look at her ripe body. With only the memory of the one passionate night of a week ago, Nicholas was quickly inflamed by anything she did, even if she cursed him, which happened too often lately.

When she returned, he was astride the stallion, hat pulled low on his head, his finger thumping maddeningly against the saddle horn.

"Now Morgan?"

"Yes Nicky, I believe I am ready. Would you like your comb? You look as if you could use some tidying up," she sweetly smiled.

Before she could mount up and follow, Nicholas was trotting away. "I will get even with you yet, Nicky. I swear I will," she growled to herself.

Rather than weakening from the long, hard ride, Morgan surprisingly found that her stamina was increasing. Under any other circumstances, this experience would have been viewed as a great adventure. Out in the wilderness not far from the Spanish Territory, enjoying what there was of the scenery, this was an incredible experience for a young northern woman— for any woman.

When Nick was in one of his rare loquacious moods, he would explain the wildlife; a variety of birds such as woodpeckers, quail, cardinals, mockingbirds abounded. Once she saw a wild turkey. The night sounds of coyotes were usually what kept her close to Nicholas. Thankfully, she did not see any black bear, cougars, or panthers, which were known to be in this wooded area. They were not far from the Red River, which was the second largest waterway after the Mississippi. He had explained to her that the rivers and bayous determined the paths of settlement in the Louisiana Territory. Depending on the settlement or location, the Louisiana Territory had a population as diverse as New York or any other major city or state. There were separate communities of French, Spanish, Indians, and settlers of various other origins.

Morgan also learned how to build a fire and how to look for signs of animal life and water, all of which were fascinating. But she was afraid to tell Nicholas any of this. She was afraid that Nick would think she wanted to stay with him. And for the hundredth time in the last hour, Morgan had told herself that she hated being in his company, that she must return to Ian.

"Nick, how did you know where to stop?" she asked much

later in the day. Following the winding path of a river, he found one of the most inviting streams Morgan had ever seen.

"I can read maps, Morgan, and Gordon had mapped this area for me," he tersely replied while busying himself with the care of the horses.

His mood tarnished her cheerful one. "Don't you think, Nick, that it is time you told me everything?" she inquired irritably.

The stream was only a few feet away. Morgan could almost feel the cool water on her parched skin. But Nick's brusque manner was grating on her nerves. Alone for hours with her thoughts, she could not dismiss or forgive his uncivil behavior. None of this was her fault. It was obvious, too, that he was not telling her everything.

"Where are we going, Nicholas? Since I cannot very well trot back to New Orleans, I would like to know where you are taking me."

Tired of seeing his muscular back, Morgan angrily marched around to face him squarely; her eyes were ablaze with pent-up frustration and fury for the man who was destroying her life.

"You will see soon enough," he quickly answered in an amused voice. She must think she is intimidating me with her holier than thou attitude and defiant stance, he thought. "We have exactly one hour to spare. Do you want to waste it arguing with me? Or would you care to bathe while I nobly keep my back to you?"

"Damn you! That is all you do. I hate seeing your stupid back. I hate hearing your single syllable answers. I hate your voice. I hate you!" she shouted so loudly that her voice reverberated against the trees.

"Morgan, I hate your foolish temper tantrums. Now," he said in a deadly voice, "either you do as I say for once and take your goddamn bath, or so help me, Morgan, I will rip your clothes off and throw you in the water. And I don't care if you drown!"

Nicholas made the mistake of turning away from her.

Morgan ran toward him, fists flailing. "How dare you," she screamed, "you cannot do this to me. I am not your stupid little simpering wife any more." She started to pound his back.

"I don't worship you any longer, Nick Rhodes. I don't grovel at our feet, hang onto every word you utter. In short, *Nicky*," he sneered, "I do not love you!"

"Morgan, cherie," he deliberately mocked Ian's affectionate endearment and jackknifed about to catch her wrists. Painfully, he squeezed them, almost lifting her off the ground to meet his icy stare. "I am glad you don't love me. Because when I take your body, wherever or whenever I please, you will finally understand that all I care about is using you to satisfy my needs. And being the good whore that you have undoubtedly become, you will comply with my demands."

His cruel taunt stung far deeper than she ever imagined. Refusing to show her astonishment, Morgan coldly smiled. "I told you before, Nicky dear, I have had better than you. So if you want to rape me, go ahead. That, my dear, is the only way you will ever have use of my body again."

"I doubt that Morgan." He flung her aside, ignoring the muffled groan when she fell to the hard ground, on top of his saddlebag. Not one muscle moved as he towered over her, saying, "I am not interested in your services at the moment. I have to see to the horses."

Morgan's eyes were riveted on his loathsome face, but her hand instinctively rummaged through his saddlebag, searching for any weapon to use for protection. Remaining in the dirt, a half smile formed on her face when she found the cold handle of his sheathed knife. If he came near her, she would not hesitate to use it in his black heart.

Feeling more secure with the sharp blade, Morgan hid it behind her back, tucking it into the leather waistband of her breeches. Half sitting, she tried to catch her breath and wipe the dust off her clothing. The black braid loosened, but Morgan did not want to be bothered combing her hair at the moment. Instead she shoved it under her hat. Wary amber eyes waited for his return.

"Forget the dip in the stream, Morgan. I don't believe you have earned it. Not yet, that is."

Morgan refused to look up and continued to stare at his black-sooted feet, which took two steps closer to her before spacing slightly apart.

"Take off your clothes, cherie. It is time for you to please me."

Was that harsh, menacing tone really Nick's—or some ruthless stranger's? Believing that the only way to fight back was to hurt him with equally harsh words, she snarled, "I told you, Nicky, you will get nothing from me," and one hand moved behind her back.

"I said," the booted feet moved so close they almost touched her legs, "take off your clothes."

"No." She finally looked up at his stony face.

A stinging slap to her cheek was his response. Her hat fell to the ground as her head reeled from the shock. He is going to beat me, she realized when she saw his raised hand.

"Don't make me do it again," he growled.

"All right. Help me up, Nick," she lifted her left hand to him. Her voice was deceptively calm, her actions calculated.

When Nicholas partially lowered to grab her arm, Morgan made a quick, instinctive move. With incredible speed, she withdrew the knife from its sheath, swinging her right arm high in an arc, imbedding and withdrawing the knife from his left shoulder.

"Ahh," he moaned, kicking the knife out of her hand. Grabbing his bloody, aching shoulder, he snarled, "You devious bitch! I ought to beat you senseless and then, Morgan, then I will take your whore's body in ways you never imagined."

The wound stung and had to be treated immediately. She could have deeply imbedded the blade in his chest—but didn't. Morgan could not know that she had stabbed him in the fleshy part of the shoulder. He would ache for sure but the wound could have been far more serious. Glaring at her once more, Nicholas could not see her lowered face. She was staring at the bloodied knife.

"Get up, Morgan. And for God's sake, don't say one word."

She looked at him then, clutching her throat, her eyes rounded in horror. Tears streamed down her dirty face, hands trembled in her lap. "I—I don't know what, why— Oh my God, Nick! I didn't mean to do it. I just didn't," she cried, her voice raw with pain. "You frightened me to death. I never saw

396

you like that before. I—I'm sorry," she began sobbing.

"Damn you. Don't you dare become hysterical now? You've got to help me cleanse my shoulder."

"Nick, please—please," she wailed. "I don't know what happened."

"I do," he quietly said, standing before her, his right hand still holding the bloody shoulder. "I never thought you would get this angry though," he actually smiled.

It was more than she could bear. "Oh my God. Nick, I will do whatever you want. I swear it!" her eyes flooded with sorrow, tears, and pain. Pain for him . . . for what they once shared together.

Chapter 31

Some semblance of Nicholas's good sense returned. Perhaps it was Morgan's terror-stricken face and sobs that jolted him back into reality. He had pushed her too far. He knew that now. But the need to strike out, to hurt her as he was hurting, to become immune to her beauty and her words, was overpowering. Blood seeped through his hands. Nicholas tore off his bandana, crudely placing it against the wound. Lowering to one knee, he wanted her to look at him, but Morgan recoiled from his proximity.

"Morgan. I will not hurt you. I swear. Look at me," he evenly said.

She didn't, but Nicholas continued to speak. "It is not a serious wound. Perhaps you will help me cleanse and bandage it. I have some items in my saddlebag. Will you help me Morgan?"

The softly spoken words finally penetrated her horror-struck mind. "All right," she whispered. "Nick, how can I explain my insane attack? I don't . . ."

"Stop. You acted in self-defense. You shouldn't accept the blame." He tentatively smiled, but she could not concentrate on anything but the bloodied knife.

"I didn't know you could use a knife."

"Neither did I," she hiccuped.

"Please look at me Morgan." He wanted to touch the tear-stained face, but was afraid of her reaction. "We won't talk about it anymore. I provoked you; I don't know why.

Sometimes you make me so damn furious, I can't think straight. I believe," he gingerly moved his aching shoulder, "I cause the same reaction in you."

"I could have killed you," she choked back a sob.

"No. I don't believe that and neither do you. You could have aimed for my heart or my back—but you didn't. At this close distance, even you can see what you are aiming it. Will you help me?"

Slowly, Morgan raised her head. Despite his words, she saw the pained look in his eyes. Drained of emotion, she wiped her swollen eyes and forced her numb limbs to move. Standing before him, head still lowered in abject misery, she mumbled, "I'll wet a cloth."

It took a great deal of effort not to cry when Nicholas gave her instructions for cleansing and bandaging his wound.

It did pain him a bit, but he was suddenly more concerned about Morgan's defeated spirit than his wound.

"Why don't you take that bath now," he looked at the glaring sun. "It is too hot to travel. We might as well remain for a couple of hours. We have enough time to reach the cabin tonight."

"What cabin?"

"Gordon found it, bless his heart. It is clean, Morgan, and within a three-hour ride from here—where we eventually must be."

"I don't understand," she turned to him.

"I haven't told you everything. But I will. Take that bath, Morgan. I will stay here near the horses, in the shady area beneath those pine trees. When you return, I will tell you all that I know. All right?"

He actually smiled, which made Morgan all the more miserable. Shirtless, the shadows created odd patterns on his tawny-haired chest. With the exception of the ugly knife wound—the area was red and blotchy around the white bandage—Nick's muscular upper torso was bronzed. Her Greek god, she remembered, thinking of him as that so long ago. So long ago, she wearily thought.

"I think you should bathe too. You cannot afford an infection."

"I will. After you've returned."

Long ago they would have eagerly jumped into the cool stream together, laughing at each other's antics. With a heavy heart, Morgan wished her mind could be cleansed as thoroughly as her body.

By the time she returned, Nick was sitting under a pine tree, his back pressed against the trunk, dark blond hair spilling across his brow. His eyes were closed—in pain or slumber, she guiltily wondered.

Her wet black hair was plastered to her skull. Deciding not to disturb him, Morgan searched his bag for a brush. Sitting a few feet from him, she silently brushed her drying hair, her eyes never leaving Nick's face.

After one hour, Morgan faced a dilemma. Should she wake him so they could be on their way? Or should she let him sleep? Twice she wanted to place a blanket over his bare chest and twice she sat on her hands to resist the protective impulse.

One of the horses nickered, startling Nicholas. In seconds he was wide awake, perfectly aware of the surroundings. "Did I sleep long?" he uncrossed his long legs.

"No, an hour or so," she quietly responded.

"Let me take that bath, and I will tell you about this trip of ours." He stood without assistance, relieving Morgan of some worry over his bloodied shoulder.

Only when he was out of her view did he grimace, testing the sore shoulder. The cold water was invigorating. With his right hand Nicholas was able to lather his body and hair.

When he returned, shaking off the water like a large animal who had been drenched, Morgan felt his friendly smile.

"Can I help you?"

"No, I'm fine. Really, Morgan. Hand me a clean shirt."

For one brief second their fingertips touched as Morgan handed over a beige cambric shirt. Managing to get it over his head, he appeared to have some difficulty tying the front laces.

"Let me do it."

Her voice was a husky whisper and it disturbed Nicholas as much as the delicate finger that played with the laces. Her featherlike touch on his chest heated his blood. But Nicholas would not touch her. Perhaps she would never again welcome his touch. Perhaps, he jealously thought, Morgan craved only Ian's touch.

This time they rode side by side, at a slow pace. Morgan anxiously watched Nick's body for signs of fatigue or pain. After the first hour, she noticed the slight droop to his shoulders; he wiped his perspiring brow more than once and the injured left arm limply hung at his side.

Guilt overwhelmed Morgan. He would never admit to needing a rest; if she remembered his words correctly, they would need to travel two additional hours before finding the cabin.

"Nick?" she faintly called. "I am not feeling very well. Could we make camp for the night?"

Lost in his own misery, Nicholas had no idea that Morgan was ill. "It's only a two-hour ride. Can't you make it?" he turned to her, his voice slightly strained.

"No, I am exhausted. I apologize, Nick," she raised the brim of the hat to get a better glimpse of his face. "Please?"

He answered quickly. "Of course. We can camp at the base of those hills up ahead."

He didn't jump out of his saddle the way he normally did. Nicholas slid off the animal, afraid to jar his throbbing shoulder. There was work to be done: unsaddling and feeding the animals, making a fire, searching the area for signs of Indians or marauders. He would simply have to summon the energy.

"Nick?" she stepped near him. "Let me do something this time. I've watched you quite often. It will take some of the strain off your shoulder. I know we have water, but if you bleed again, or worse if you pass out on me, I will have no idea what to do." In a more determined voice she said, "I would rather learn with you to guide me than try to figure it out on my own. It could be a long, cold night," she wryly added.

How could he not smile at her strange logic? "Fine. If it makes you happy, I will show you what to do. But Morgan," he touched her arm, "don't start thinking you can run out on me now that you know how to make camp. It's dangerous out here alone and you know it."

"Don't be ridiculous Nick! I have no intention of going

402

nywhere without you."

"That's not what you previously said." He did not remove
iis hand.

"That was yesterday. We have come this far and you
promised to tell me all you know about Andrews. I am not
;iving up when we are this close to solving this horrible
:rime."

Pleased that she had used "we" instead of "I," Nicholas
could not suppress his smile.

"I assume, madam, that you have given me your word."

"In a way, yes." She returned the smile, all too conscious of
iis penetrating gaze and the hand on her arm. "Well? Are you
;oing to show me or not?" she challenged.

Although his movements were stiff and slow, Morgan
hought she learned and could remember a number of things.
Together, the chores were completed in thirty minutes.
Wearily, Nick sank into the bedroll. "I hope you like beef
erky. It's all we have for dinner tonight."

"How delicious. You don't have any wine hidden, do you?"

"Would tequila do? There is a bottle in my canvas bag."

It would do them both some good to release their tension
through strong whiskey. Perhaps Nicholas would forgive her.
More importantly, perhaps she could forget what she had done,
t least for this night.

They shared the whiskey. Nicholas admired the way Morgan
;amely took the bottle, taking one long swallow of the fiery
iquid and handing it over to him. It was an intimate act—the
only one he would probably be allowed to share with this
trange, beautiful creature.

"I'm ready now."

He choked on the tequila.

"Ready?" he coughed.

"Yes," her golden eyes peeked at him through lowered lids.
'I am ready to hear the sordid details of our trek into this
untamed wilderness." Morgan languidly leaned against the
eather saddle, her hair freshly plaited like an Indian maiden's
with two long braids reaching her lovely breasts.

"Morgan, my love, I'm afraid you will be surprised, no
hocked, to hear what I have to say."

"Nothing could shock me. Not after today," she muttere
more to herself than to him.

"I told you we were going to find Andrews. But that is no
quite true," he began, fortified by the drink that was warmin
his veins and relieving the pressure of the throbbing shoulde

"Nicholas."

"Please, Morgan. Whenever you use that menacing ton
and my whole name, I am almost chary to say anything."

"Don't tell me I frighten you?" she took the bottle out of hi
hand.

"In a way, yes. But that is not what we are talking about, i
it?"

She wasn't sure. Morgan recognized Nick's questioning gaz
and tone, wondering if indeed his words had more than on
meaning. She did not respond.

Nicholas took that as an answer. "As I was going to say,
think whatever we might have thought or imagined Andrews t
be is—well, he isn't. We may have figured this all wrong. I d
not think Andrews—whose real name, by the way, is Ala
Sterling—was ever the mastermind of the thefts. It wa
Charles Gray," he paused, waiting for a reaction.

Morgan stared into the orange glows of the fire. "All th
time, all these months, I could think of only one name—on
face. I honestly believed, Nick, that if we ever came physicall
close to Andrews, I would know him because I would feel h
murderous presence—here," she touched her breast.

"He murdered your father, Morgan. I am not sure if he did
on his own or if it was an order from Gray. Whatever," h
heavily sighed, "I do not think Andrews is alive."

"I know."

The words were spoken so softly that Nick asked her
repeat them.

"I said I know. I thought it odd that after all the time I was i
New Orleans, I would see or hear of the Grays but no one els
At least no one of medium height with a birthmark on h
cheek. Andrews might have been hiding, but I did not think
possible. Isn't it strange, Nick," she looked at his profile, "
think of one person for so long. I gave him a face, a personalit
I thought I knew what he was thinking and feeling. It is as if

404

she searched for the right words, "it's as if I imagined him."

"You are not telling me you want to give up? Even if Andrews is dead or gone, there is still the matter of the currency plates."

"Of course I won't give up," she vehemently answered. "I have to clear my father's name. But how will we ever prove that Andrews or Sterling murdered him?"

"We will. Remember, Morgan, there are Charles and Jane Gray left to consider," he yawned. The firelight caught the gold anchor ring, reminding her of the days past.

"Nick? Why did you give me your ring that night in New Orleans?"

"I don't know. It seemed the right thing at the time." He thought a moment. "It was a gesture."

She was afraid to look at his face, afraid to see something that would melt her determination to leave him and return to Ian. Yet Morgan believed that unless the loose ends of the past were neatly tied, she would not be able to look at the future. Nicholas was the only one who could help her. Silently, she prayed it would not always be this way. In the last nine months, Nicholas had been the center of her life. No matter which way she turned, Nick was there, like the highest peak in a mountain chain that reaches boldly for the sky and gives meaning to the hills around it. Nicholas was her peak. And please, God, let it not be this way forever. She had to know what he was thinking before she could be purged of him.

"A gesture Nick? For what?"

"An apology of sorts—for the way I treated you, or rather the way you thought I treated you," he shifted his weight. She heard one leather boot rub against the other. "I never meant to hurt you, Morgan. Believe what you want about my promise to my father to find you and the plates. But never, ever," he emphasized, "think that my motives were less than honorable toward you. I am many things, beauty, but not a calculating, manipulative bastard who married you for those damn plates.

"When I met you that first time in Boston, I could not believe my luck. It's true that I went to Boston for two reasons—you and the cargo I purchased. But from the moment you opened your tiger eyes and squinted at me, I knew who you were and were not. You were helpessly thrust into a tragic set of circumstances and you needed help, Morgan. I wanted to be the one to help you—nothing more. Think what you want about my word, but I do not dispense promises the way a womanizer dispenses compliments.

"I was captivated by you. It was only after I gave you my word to find the traitors and the plates that I realized my dilemma. It was of my own doing. I know that, and I have been paying for it ever since."

The words were whispered, but Morgan thought they were painful for him. Was it because of his shoulder wound or his heart?

Staring at the black sky dotted with thousands of tiny sparkling stars, Morgan felt a cool breeze blow across their sanctuary. Off in the distance she heard an animal's cry, then an answer—a call to its mate, perhaps—reaching out for another in this vast, lonely land.

"It is hard for me to think clearly, Nick. My life has drastically changed in the months following my father's death. I have changed too."

"I know that. The little girl is no more. You are a mature, independent, and damned headstrong woman," she knew he was smiling to himself. "It was a shock to see the dramatic change. Could it have happened after you walked out on me? Or was I too blind to see it when we were together?"

"Both. You've taught me a number of things, Nick. But most importantly, you taught me not to rely on others," she could not disguise the bitterness.

"I don't know what to say. I am glad you have learned independence, but I did not mean it to happen the way it did. Morgan? Would you sit next to me?"

Without hesitation, Morgan acquiesced. But they did not touch.

"I wanted you to have this ring, no matter what had happened between us." He began to remove it, but Morgan stayed his left hand.

"It is not necessary, Nick. It wouldn't fit on my finger anyhow," she forced a light laugh. "That ring symbolizes your strength, your character. I will not take it from you."

"I know you don't have your wedding ring. Do you still have the repaired locket?" His chin brushed the top of Morgan's head.

"Yes, it's in my jewel case along with the anchor pin."

"I am sorry for that too. Christ!" he snorted. "For a man who has trouble saying 'please,' apologizing is as difficult as having one's teeth pulled. Ah, Morgan, my beauty, you do strange things to me."

Morgan thought he was reaching for her, but it was the almost empty tequila bottle he sought.

"I want to say one more thing, then I will let you go to sleep," he took a deep breath. "I missed you, Morgan. When you left me, I felt as if my world began to unravel. I was drunk for almost two weeks," his hand tunneled through his wavy hair. "I don't remember much. Except that when Eric finally found me, I was in some dockside tavern with a full beard, a black eye, and sore knuckles.

"After that, I became reckless. You see nothing mattered without you. I agreed to make that crazy cargo run to France and another to Halifax before the end of May. Peter is expecting me in July as well. But I had to come here to New Orleans. I had to keep my promise to you, whether you wanted me or not. I wanted to see if you and Ian were together. I wanted to see if you were happy. Are you, Morgan?" he looked down at her. "I mean are you happy with Ian? Is he good to you?"

"Yes. He has been wonderful, as has his family."

She did not mean it to sound that way, as if she were disparaging Nicholas's family. "Nick? How is your family?"

"Angry and upset," he laughed. "I am not sure if anyone is talking to my father—not even Jon. Funny," he smiled in the darkness, "I didn't think Jon would stand up to my father. And for me? My brother truly surprised me. Eric told me that after we both left that night, Jonathan stood up tall and straight, telling my father that if he didn't try to find us to patch things up, to forget about this nonsense, he would not have anything to do with him. Do you know what, Morgan? When I left New York, Jon still hadn't spoken to him. And my mother? Well she feels responsible for what happened. She is madder than a hornet, though, and told my father that he was a stubborn jackass before moving into our—I mean my—house."

"He is a stubborn man—like his son. But to be honest with you, Nick, as Maryann Mackenzie I cared for your father. He seemed gruff on the outside. Inside, though, he was kind."

"I am not so sure I agree but," he yawned again, "at least you won't have to face them again, will you?"

"No, I suppose not."

"I didn't mean to bore you with my talk. Must be the tequila. Morgan?"

"Mmmm?"

"Sleep next to me tonight. I won't touch you, I swear it."

Within seconds, Morgan heard Nick's slow, even breathing. Their backs touched, but that was all. No longer exhausted, her mind whirled with his words, repeating them, wondering if he meant all that was said. Did he care for her? Morgan wanted to ask him if he had ever loved her, not bothering to consider if he loved her now. She didn't have the courage to ask about Margaret Lawson, who was probably waiting ever so patiently for Nick to return to her. Did he return to Margaret's bed after she left New York?

In the darkness, Morgan was not distracted by his ruggedly handsome face. She could not see if his eyes lit up or darkened when he spoke. She could not see if he cynically raised an eyebrow or frowned; smiled with pleasure or scorn. No, she concentrated on his tone, which was nearly impossible to disguise.

He sounded said, wistful, at times angry. To reach out to him would have been a mistake. She would have nestled in his arms, allowing his chin to rest on the crown of her head, letting him kiss her temple, her eyes, and her lips. She would have forgotten his past actions and Ian's kindhearted patience. No, she firmly decided, it was for the best that they did not touch.

With a sharp start and a soft groan, Nicholas awoke before Morgan, who was curled on one side, her head leaning against his right arm. It was not quite what he would have liked, but it would do for the time being. The shoulder ached, but he was

408

confident that in a couple of days he would not feel any pain.

What a hellcat she had become. He shook his head in wonder. It would be a shame to hand her over to Ian Kendall.

"Come on, beauty. Let's finish this journey today."

He loved the way Morgan woke up. In the first few moments her befuddled mind refused to function. Then she would smile, a soft hesitant glow brightening her face, and he believed he could face the worst trial as long as she smiled at him like that.

They broke camp after a quick breakfast of more dried food and water. It was well before noon when Nicholas spotted trouble.

"Morgan," he urgently said above the noise and blowing dirt. "When I give you the signal, I want you to ride as fast as you can. Head straight for those trees up ahead."

"What is wrong?" she turned to face him, keeping up with the quickened pace. "I want to know."

"There is a small group of Indians off to the west. Three. I don't know if they are after us or not. But we won't wait to find out. Come on."

They rode as swiftly as the three horses allowed. Morgan had no time to think about her fear. Blood pounded in her ears as she tried to concentrate on the dusty road ahead. The swampy area to the left became one shade of dull gray-green; the area to the right became undecipherable blotches on the landscape. She thought she smelled pine, but the horses kicked up so much dust she couldn't be sure. The familiar sound of the pounding hooves of their three horses consoled her; for as long as Morgan didn't hear additional hooves, there was some hope.

Suddenly she heard voices, shouting, and at least one new set of hooves. Nicholas, who was riding alongside, turned, nearly losing his leather hat. Pulling the pistol out of his waistband with the hand that held the reins of the third horse, he waited for the Indian to get close, to make a move or gesture that would indicate his intent. But Nicholas was hampered by the packhorse and his sore shoulder.

Perhaps all the Indians wanted were their horses. Or did they want the woman astride the horse? He would not let them touch Morgan, although one look at the golden eyes and long black hair would entice any man. Oh no, he thought, I will not let anything happen to my woman.

Instinct told him to gamble. As soon as one of the Indians caught up with him, Nicholas shouted, "Keep going Morgan and don't look back!"

The Indian was up to Nicholas's leg. That was when he made a move and let go of the reins of the pack horse. His right hand was now free to aim the pistol at the startled Indian. Luckily, the Indian was distracted by the riderless horse and slowed to capture the animal.

Morgan was in front of Nicholas, riding as if her life depended on it. Boldly turning around, Nicholas's face split into a wide grin after seeing the three Indians together, their interest apparently taken up by the animal. A good animal was sacrificed as well as most, if not all, of their supplies. But what did it matter? Not as long as they were alive.

As good a fighter as he was, Nicholas knew he could not deal with three strong braves, especially with his wounded arm. However, once they reached the cabin, they would hopefully find all the supplies they would need. If not, Nicholas believed there was a village a few hours east of the cabin.

"Morgan," he called, "keep riding. We'll be fine."

She nodded, and he laughed at the delightful sight of her pretty backside clad in tight leather breeches, bouncing in the saddle. They would be tired and sweaty by the time they reached the cabin. With more luck, Morgan might be receptive to his comforting embrace—or a kiss. He would settle for one kiss and one beguiling smile.

Nicholas slowed the pace after one hour. As far as he could tell, the Indians were not on their trail. The cabin was less than an hour away. It was close to the Red River and the town of Alexandria and the larger and oldest town in the Louisiana Territory—Natchitoches. If the plan worked on schedule, Eric would be joining them in two days. There should also be another "guest": Charles Gray with the six remaining currency plates.

In one week, Nicholas would either be aboard the *Anastasia* bound for Boston and the cargo that awaited sale in Halifax, or he would be with Morgan, sharing his heart once again. If it made any difference in her feelings for him, Nicholas would gladly wait.

By nightfall, the two nearly exhausted riders reached their destination. Nicholas hurried to Morgan, offering a friendly smile and assistance. Her drawn, pinched face covered with dust revealed how difficult the last few hours had been.

"I never—no I cannot believe we made it. Back there, I was afraid to think, but afterwards, Nick, I could only think that at any moment I'd feel a knife in my back or be pulled off the horse," she said. "Oh God, Nick, I thought so many horrible things." No longer willing to tolerate the distance between them, she pleaded, "Hold me, Nick. Please. I need you."

Instantly, she was in his comforting embrace, her face buried in his shirt, her arms entwined about his neck, accidentally knocking off his hat.

"You rode courageously Morgan. It's all in the past now. Luckily, the Indians were more interested in the horse than us. Let's see what is inside. I only hope that Gordon left us supplies. With the packhorse gone, I may have to ride to a nearby village."

"We'll manage." She thought for a moment, "I suppose."

The one-room cabin could have been worse. It could have had no beds instead of the one in the alcove. It could have had no blankets instead of the one large wool cover on the bed. However, it was clean; there was a window, a fireplace, cooking utensils, food, well water and, miraculously, a small but serviceable tin tub.

"The tub, Nick. You asked Gordon for that, didn't you?" she smiled, pulling out of his arms to look into the amused silver eyes.

"My pleasure, beauty. If you look next to it, you'll find some scented soap. I'll help you heat the water."

It was a delightful treat. While Morgan bathed, Nicholas was busy seeing to the horses. Clad in her last clean shirt, she hummed a tune while brushing her wet hair. Somehow, it did not matter that she would be sharing the bed with Nick tonight. In fact, she considered, it would be a pleasant experience. And if she were honest, an experience that she had been looking forward to for days.

When he finally came back, Nicholas removed his leather

vest, pulled the shirt out of his breeches, and began to unfasten them, hesitating a moment and sheepishly turning to Morgan. "I am sorry Morgan. I forgot. I would like to bathe as well. If you would prefer to wait outside or keep your back to me, I won't be long. Just a quick wash. I've got more dust and grime on my body than barnacles on my ship's hull. Would you mind?"

How could any man look so handsome and boyishly charming at the same time? Was he a chameleon, or did he know how she was affected by him?

"Go ahead. I can manage," she replied in a distracted voice.

They ate a light meal of bread, cheese, and fruit. Morgan was tired, yet did not want to make the first move to bed.

"Why don't you turn in Morgan. I'll sleep in that chair." He made the decision for them.

Suddenly, it struck Morgan that this would be their last time alone in the wilderness—away from society's conventions. She wanted to share this last night with Nicholas beside her. She would not settle for less.

"If that is what you prefer."

"If that's what I . . ." he stupidly repeated, before realizing her meaning. "Morgan, what are you saying?" he stood beside the small wood chair that was to be his bed for the evening. "I assumed that you would like nothing more to do with me. Can you trust me not to touch you if we share the same bed?" He wanted to add that he couldn't trust himself.

"No," she considered. "But Nick, I have a request," she boldly walked over to face him, the long hair fanning her face and upper portion of her body. "I want to share this bed with you tonight. I don't want to think about any of the reasons for or against it. I only know that's what I want. Are you willing to accept my request on my terms?"

She was so damn serious, he fought the urge to laugh. "What a brazen wench you have become," he grinned. "I readily accept your offer, my beauty."

Nicholas blew out the candle on the table and stood in front of Morgan, towering over her much smaller but erect body. With deliberate care, he unbuttoned her shirt. "It looks much better on you than me. But I'm afraid I cannot give it to you—

unless I ride shirtless tomorrow."

"I won't mind," she longingly gazed into his face.

Was it a look of desire or love? Christ, how he wanted to believe the latter. But tonight there were no questions.

As if he had never seen her naked body, Nicholas worshipped her creamy skin, her proud, upturned breasts, her slender but so provocative curves. Only when he had his fill, did hands follow. This would be a night for loving—slow and easy, not out of lust. Yet he would not admit to himself that they might never share another moment like this again.

His left arm swooped under her knees, lifting Morgan into his arms.

"Nick, your shoulder . . ."

"It doesn't bother me, my love. Just relax. Never did I want to take what you wouldn't offer freely."

"Tonight, my captain, I freely offer myself to you," she nuzzled his neck while one hand played with his hair.

The kiss was not passionate but it left them breathless, and a deep sense of yearning filled their bodies and minds.

Carrying her over to the bed, he huskily whispered, "I have missed you in my arms."

"So have I," she looked up at him opening her arms.

They explored, discovered, and rediscovered each other that warm April night. Nicholas touched and kissed every inch of her willing body more than once. Morgan responded by boldly taking him into her hands and mouth.

Neither of them wanted to release the tightly held simmering passion. His soft caress, her responsive body, were touched by the province of heavenly bliss. It was a lovely, bittersweet moment in time. Each one believed that this time together was their last.

And after the lone candle burned out, Morgan fell asleep in his arms; one arm possessively flung across his chest, her long black hair spread behind her. Nicholas's left hand idly roamed along her slender spine and around to her thigh.

"I will miss you, Morgan," he achingly whispered before pulling the blanket over them.

413

Chapter 32

"Nick? Where are you?" she sat upright, wondering if she had dreamt their loving interlude of the previous night. The place beside her was cold and empty. Yet it was only dawn.

Where was he? Could he have left her alone? Scurrying off the bed, she donned his shirt and ran to the window. She saw the rising sun against the dark hills and over the tree tops, slowly brightening all that it touched. But Nicholas was not there.

There was no reason to panic, she decided, not yet. With the lone wool blanket as protection, Morgan pulled open the door and stepped out into the chilly morning air. The dew clung to her face, a refreshing soft breeze ruffled her hair.

"Nick?" she softly called. "Are you out here?" Chilled and barefooted, she stepped further out, toward the horses.

Nick was there. Sitting on a rock clad only in leather breeches, smoking a cheroot, elbows resting on his knees, Nicholas seemed to be staring at the dark side of the sky that had not yet been touched by the sun.

Lost in thought, he did not hear her hesitant approach. "Nicholas?" she called again. "Are you all right?"

Her husky voice startled him. "Yes. I am fine, Morgan. Couldn't sleep, I guess."

Stepping closer, Morgan gingerly sat beside him on the cold rock. "Why couldn't you sleep?"

"I don't know. After the last few nights of sleeping outdoors, I guess I felt closed in. That's all, Morgan. But," he finally noticed her flimsy overgarments, "you shouldn't be out here like that! It's too cold. Why don't you go back inside?"

"What about you?"

"I think I would like a few more minutes alone."

He said it kindly, but with finality. Morgan was not invited to stay outside with him. Last night seemingly hadn't existed. The invitation to share the bed was hers—not Nick's. But she would always have the memory of this night: the slow, intoxicating kisses, the soft exploring caresses—the whispered words of love.

No, she was positive there had not been any whispered words of love. Only her foolish fantasy. She stopped to rack her brain. Did he say anything about love? Well, it no longer mattered. If Nick had said those words, it was because she was soaring alone to the stars and his enjoyment was in seeing her eyes closed in ecstasy, hearing the not-so-soft whimpers of pleasure. He had stroked her wet hair, taken her ripe lips, and moved with tantalizing slowness, bringing them both back to the peak of fulfillment.

Four hours separated Nicholas's ruminations from their ephemeral moment of love. But it was as if an era had passed. Dejected and dispirited, Morgan walked into the cabin and did what she could with her appearance. She wanted to be fully dressed when he returned—ready for whatever new adventure the day would bring.

When he came back, one hour later, Nicholas found Morgan sitting by the wood table, impatiently tapping her fingers against the tin plates.

"Your breakfast is ready Nick. I cooked the last of the bacon. There is a pot of coffee. I didn't know when you'd be back so I couldn't make the eggs. Would you like them now?"

"Fine," he muttered. She tried to remain composed. Her hair was tightly pulled away from her face, secured in back by a silk scarf. Not wanting to watch her movements, Nicholas dressed and shaved the two-day stubble off his face.

He ate in morose silence, mumbling a "thank you" each time she served him. He was almost out of the door when he heard her speak.

"Where are you going? Do you want me to get ready?"

416

"No. We need some wood. There's a pile in the back to be chopped."

He was gone again. Morgan had no idea what she was supposed to do. His shuttered look suggested she keep her distance. It did not comfort her to hear the steady sound of the ax splitting wood. In fact, Morgan was finding it difficult to remain passive and understanding. She thought she had seen all of his moods—even his worst fits of temper—but this sullenness was new to her. And it was irritating.

She opened the door just as he was returning, his arms laden with wood.

"Thanks," he uttered, setting the wood near the fireplace.

"Will you please tell me what you are doing? Rather what we will be doing. I've patiently waited for you to change your mood, but Nick, I've run out of patience."

"I think you should wash what's left of our dirty clothes," he spoke as if he had not heard any of her carefully chosen words.

"Nicholas. I don't want to become angry. I will wash the clothing—after I know what we are doing or where we are going today."

Leaning one arm against the window, he said, "I am going to scout the area. I told you there is a little village where I can purchase our supplies."

"What am I supposed to do while you disappear?"

"Wash the clothes. Jesus, Morgan, didn't I say that!" his temper flared.

"Why can't I go with you?"

"It's too dangerous. I think you should stay here. In fact, the more I think about it, I have decided that you would be better off waiting here for Eric. He knows to come here first before meeting me in Les Rapides. That town is nothing more than a trading post, Morgan. I don't think you'd be comfortable there. Besides, when I meet Charles Gray tomorrow, you can be damn sure I don't want you within fifty miles of that fiend."

"What!" she exploded at last. "This is as much my responsibility as it is yours. Especially after you've abducted me. I will not remain here like a obedient pet. I want to see the

417

plates, see Gray and Andrews's grave. I will not . . ."

"Enough!" he cut off further protest and stiffly stood in front of her, in his usual intimidating way. "I have heard more than once what you will and will not do. And I don't care. You will do as you are told. You listened to me yesterday, didn't you? If you would have decided to ask those Indians what they wanted, or if you would have decided to slow down, we could have been scalped! Why is this any different? Why can't you ever listen to me!" he shouted.

"I have and look what happened. I find myself married to a hypocrite or a liar, then not married. I am dragged from Boston to Halifax to New York because I listened to you, Captain Rhodes!" she yelled back. Pacing across the room, she took a deep breath before continuing her tirade. "Then I stopped listening. I found someone I could trust. And what happens? You come along and ruin my life—again. You start telling me what to do. I will not have it!" she marched to the other end of the cabin, her temper well out of control, her fists clenched in pent-up fury.

"That's too bad, Morgan. You're stuck with me for the time being. But don't worry, my love," he sneered. "You will be safely delivered into Ian's precious arms in a couple of weeks. Then you won't be bothered with the likes of me again. But," he found his hat, pushing it low on his head, "until Eric comes for you, you will stay in this cabin and listen to whatever I tell you." In a deceptively calm and low voice, he added, "I am afraid you have no choice. Be a good girl and stay put."

Nicholas stalked out of the cabin. Before Morgan realized what was happening, he rode off, leaving her alone with her fury and murderous thoughts.

Grabbing her hat, she ran out to her mare, intent on following him. But all she saw was dust, and when she turned to the horse she realized that her saddle was gone!

"Damn you Nicholas Rhodes," she shouted. "Damn you for doing this to me. I hate you! I truly hate you!"

Some time later, she found the saddle by the wood pile, along with a pistol. She could try to find him and run the risk of getting hopelessly lost—or she could wait for his return and then tell him how much she hated him.

By four P.M., Morgan alternated between anger and worry. Was he coming back? Was the village so far away he wouldn't return until tomorrow? Was he hurt along the way? Did the Indians track him and . . . no, she decided not to think about that.

It did not matter if he ever returned, she tried to console herself. Who cared? According to Nick, Eric would be here sometime soon. She would manage somehow. Even if there wasn't enough food. Looking about the sparse cabin, Morgan saw there were plenty of candles and wood; the clothes she had angrily washed earlier in the day were almost dry. Well then, you will be fine, she repeatedly told herself.

Feeling a bit more positive about the situation, Morgan went about her chores. By six P.M. she defiantly fixed dinner for one.

"Let him fix his own meal," she grumbled aloud. "Let him starve." As long as she thought someone—Eric or Ian—would eventually find her, Morgan felt confident. She could manage without him.

Up until the very moment she crawled into the bed—alone—Morgan felt fine. Yet she could not fall asleep. The night sounds suddenly seemed loud. The whinny of the horse made her think that Nick was returning, or that someone or something else was near.

But then there was silence. Tossing to find a comfortable position, Morgan punched the old feather pillow, wishing it were Nick's smug face. After a couple of hours, she felt wide awake. Staying up with only the few candles for light was not an appealing thought. There wasn't a book in sight. But there was, she remembered, a bottle of whiskey.

Padding over to the shelf where the bottle was located, Morgan remembered that she had only tasted this stuff once and hated it. Aside from sherry and wine, brandy was the strongest drink she ever had. Nicholas had introduced her to that, she recalled.

"Well, I will try it," she said aloud, filling a cup with the brew. It was awful. It burned her throat, watered her eyes, and the fumes were as bad as the taste. Not wanting to get drunk, as she would not hear Nick's return, Morgan took a few more sips, not gulps. This would have to do, she decided, replacing the bottle on the shelf while leaving the cup on the table.

Ambling to the bed, she finally sought the most comfortable position and fell into a light sleep.

She dreamed of Nick, his handsome bronzed face split in the familiar rakish grin she so loved, his arms open to her. He told her how much he loved and needed her; that he always loved her and could not live if she left him for Ian Kendall. And then he begged her to forgive him, telling her they would sail far away if that was what she wanted. Anything she wanted, as long as they remained together.

"I love you, my beauty," she actually heard those huskily spoken words. "Say you love me too. Please," he begged.

"Oh I do love you Nick. I do," she whispered back to the phantom.

"Come with me Morgan," his image began to fade and she chased it.

"Don't leave me, Nicholas," she cried in despair.

Her own cries jolted Morgan awake. It was dawn. She was alone in the bed. Nick had not returned. Vividly recalling the dream, she laughed at her stupidity. "You can't love him, silly. Don't ever say you love him."

Dressed in her old breeches and a pale yellow shirt, she braided her hair while racking her brain for something to do. She could feed the horse, clean the tiny cabin, take a walk around the area. She could bathe again.

Yes. She would do all of those things, then save the bath for last—a luxurious treat.

Dragging the buckets of well water inside, heating them as best she could with two pots, Morgan was almost tired by the time the bath was ready. Only twice that day did she allow herself to think of Nick. Each time she felt fear, but forced herself to dismiss the notion.

"Cabin fever," she muttered.

Remaining in the small tub until the water became cold, Morgan checked her pocket watch for the tenth time. It was three P.M. There was still a chance that Nick would return before sunset.

She might as well be dressed and ready. Wishing she had her yellow dress—it had been in the pack on the third horse—

420

Morgan donned her leather breeches, a white shirt, the boots, and a red silk scarf. She didn't look elegant, but she felt clean and wished she could find some adornments for her hair. It occurred to Morgan that her pearl combs were not in the missing pack, but carelessly tucked inside one of her shirts. Most of her things were thrown hastily into Nick's canvas bag.

Rummaging through their things Morgan found the combs, but had only Nick's hairbrush to use. Touching his possessions conjured up strange memories. At times, the smallest item like a watch, a comb, his scented lotion, created images of Nick: screaming, smiling, sleeping, making love. Other objects reminded her of their times together: the happy, laughing moments; the heartbreaking time when she miscarried; the tender times when he presented her with the anchor pin and the locket.

"Get out of my life, Nick Rhodes. I warn you, I will not tolerate your intrusion," she nearly shouted.

Yet she could no longer deny his presence any more than she could deny breathing. Nick was indeliby etched in her memory.

Sitting by the window in case she could hear or see his approach, Morgan absently unbraided her hair, taking her time to brush the tangles. It rippled down her back as she created a rhythmic motion. Staring at nothing, but thinking; thinking about Nick and without realizing it, comparing him to Ian.

Ian Kendall. Sweet, darling Ian who worshipped her. In his way he was as strong and determined as Nick; however, not as stubborn or foolish.

Did she love Ian? Yes, in a way totally different from Nick. "Oh no, Morgan," she corrected herself. "You do not love him. Keep saying it. Maybe you will convince yourself." The words tumbled forth before she could stop them.

No. It could not be that she still loved that rogue. It was Ian. Ian with whom she would spend the rest of her life. Ian who would love and protect her.

"I do love Ian," she said, hitting her thigh with Nick's hairbrush. But she knew it was a love based on gratitude and friendship. If only she had met Ian before *him*. There would have been no one with whom to compare Ian. It wasn't fair.

She could forget Nicholas. It would simply require more effort. Ian would help.

But is it fair to Ian? she wondered. What does Ian deserve? Am I being honest with him and myself?

The answers were obvious. How could she marry a man who deserved a woman's whole heart—not half of one? Why should Ian Kendall be punished for her deficiencies?

Morgan stopped brushing. She knew what she had to do. Ian would have to know the truth. And if she were totally honest, Ian would be released of any and all obligations toward her. Somehow, she must pay him back for his generosity and kindness. Perhaps she could borrow the money from Eric.

Lost in thought, Morgan did not hear or see the two approaching horses. Looking out the window and not seeing anything, she again thought that Nick had returned and was already behind the cabin, caring for his horse.

The surge of excitement she felt was geuine. She did not want to deny it. He was back, and she was glad.

Running outside to the rear of the cabin, Morgan forgot all anger as she gleefully cried, "Well, it is about time you returned! What . . ." She froze in mid sentence. Morgan stood openmouthed, her eyes rounded in disbelief at the two people she never dreamed of seeing here!

"Well, well, Jane dear. It appears as if our contact has a guest," Charles Gray said in an unfriendly tone. "I had heard you disappeared, but this is most interesting."

"What are *you* doing here?" Jane angrily turned on Morgan Rhinehart. "Charles, what is this about?"

Morgan decided not to wait for his answer. Turning about in panic, she ran to the cabin, hoping to lock herself inside against the Grays. It was of no use.

Charles Gray was too close. Morgan was inside, pushing the door against his superior strength, exerting every ounce of courage and power she could summon to prevent his entry.

With one powerful shove, he easily pushed the door open. Morgan fell back, landing on her backside, her eyes widened in fear.

"Get away from me," she crawled backward before scrambling to her feet. Frantically, her mind searched for a weapon—any utensil she could use for protection.

"Come here, Miss Rhinehart," he roughly grabbed her arm. "I think you have a lot to tell me," his pale brown eyes glowed with anger; or was it lust, or murder?

Jane Gray immediately followed. She looked less matronly than the last time Morgan had seen her. Wearing a long black skirt—which hid her wide hips—and a pink blouse, she seemed unaffected by the arduous trip and her new environment. Her pale eyes searched Morgan's appearance.

"I don't understand what she is doing here." Jane removed her black hat, allowing her dull brown hair to fall onto her shoulders. Removing one glove at a time, she surveyed her surroundings. "Very cozy," she dryly said. "Don't you agree, brother dear?"

"Just what I've been thinking. Suppose you tell me what you are doing here, Miss Rhinehart." His grip on her arm was firm but not painful.

Morgan's head was dizzy with possible answers. How much would they believe? How long could she stall for time? She moved out of his reach.

"I am here for the very reason you are, Mr. Gray." She sought the chair by the table, her topaz eyes unflinchingly meeting his. She thought it best not to show any fear or worry; she could not afford to panic or to make an error that could be fatal.

"I think you should explain yourself, dear," Charles persisted. "Where is Captain Rhodes?"

"I am here for the currency plates. I know that you are selling them to Captain Rhodes, and I intend to collect my share of this financial arrangement. That's what he promised me," she stubbornly lifted her chin. "I will not settle for less than my share. Call it blood money, if you will," she mirthlessly laughed. "My father's life for the money received from the sale of the currency plates. I'm afraid I'm in need of some compensation, you see."

"I don't believe a word she is saying," Jane interjected.

"No? Would you prefer to think that Captain Rhodes abducted me? Everyone in New Orleans must think that, you know. He thought the trip might be a lonely one without

423

companionship. I only recently told him who I really am. He doesn't mind, though. I make him very happy," she smiled, her meaning quite clear.

"So I gathered from your greeting," Jane snidely said.

"As you said, the accommodations here are less than spacious. I am simply making the most of it. By the way, how long are you planning to stay?"

"Don't be so coy with me, Missy," Charles took a menacing step closer to Morgan. "I've run out of patience," he rubbed the pearl handle of the pistol. "I want the truth. Where is the captain and what are you doing here?"

Lord, what could she saw now? Her answer would affect Nick's life and hers. She had to protect Nicholas—at all costs.

"All right," she deliberately stalled for time by rising from the chair, trying to display a cool facade. "I met Captain Eric Rhodes in New Orleans. Quite by accident I learned of the reason why he was there. I found out about the currency plates. I never dreamed I would come face to face with the people who stole them. I wanted to forget that part of my life. You made it difficult for me, Charles. May I call you Charles?" she actually smiled before continuing. "When the U.S. Bank in New Orleans was robbed, well, one doesn't need to be a genius to figure it all out," Morgan casually waved her hand and strode over to the window.

"I did not know who had stolen the plates. I didn't care. I wanted my share. I devised my own plan for meeting Captain Nicholas Rhodes. We have developed a—shall I say—certain fondness for one another. I knew he intended to rendezvous with the people who had the plates. So I followed him. Two days out of New Orleans, I surprised him and told him what I wanted. He didn't seem to mind. We've been traveling together ever since then.

"You should have seen the way he reacted to my tears when I told him about the murder in Philadelphia. But he has promised me money. And I do enjoy his company," she winked at Jane, "if you know what I mean."

"Kill her," Jane said. "Do it now before the captain returns."

"Oh, I wouldn't do that if I were you," Morgan ignored her

424

pounding heart. "You see, Nicky is taking me to France with him. He would be very disappointed if he sailed without me or the currency plates. He has a violent temper, you know. Why for no reason at all, he killed two men who said some nasty things about me. You must have passed through the same town, so I am sure you heard the story," she chattered.

"We'll kill him too."

"Oh, but the Emperor Napoleon has such a nasty habit of wanting vengeance—as does Eric Rhodes. I seriously doubt, dear Jane, that you or Charles would find a safe haven anywhere on this continent or in Europe. Of course you could try the Far East."

"Shut up!" Charles ordered. "I have heard enough and I don't know if I believe any of the things you've said. But I am willing to wait for your lover to return. We'll see what he has to say."

"What a wonderful idea!" Morgan gaily said. "I suppose you'll be staying with us tonight?"

"That all depends on your lover."

How was she going to relay this fantastic tale to Nick? He'd walk through the door and then what? There was no telling how the Grays would react—or Nicholas for that matter.

Although the pistol Nick had left Morgan was safely hidden under her pillow, she had no way of retrieving it until later. And how many weapons did the Grays have? she wondered.

"As long as we are forced to spend time together, suppose you tell me who you really are? Who was Alan Sterling?"

Charles warily eyed Morgan. The bitch seemed so confident that he almost accepted her story. Jane was skeptical however.

"What about your fiancé?" Jane asked at last.

"Oh, Ian," she laughed. "He is a dear man, isn't he?" she tossed her head emphatically. "But he wouldn't understand my need for money as Nicky does. Ian is a bit straitlaced."

"Not from what I've heard," Jane added.

"Well, are you asking me if he is a good lover? He is, Jane. Oh I recommend him," she laughed. Her comment lacked sincerity, but Morgan continued, "Please make yourselves comfortable. I'd like to hear about you."

Jane stiffly sat on the edge of the bed—where the gun

was hidden.

"So. Where are you two from? Ohio, you said."

"That's right. Listen, Miss Rhinehart . . ."

"Morgan, please," she almost choked.

"The less you know about us, the happier I will be. My sister and I are not interested in gossip. We are here for business."

"Oh. Well, where are the plates then?"

"Where I hid them. I have two with me now."

"May I see them?"

"No."

Morgan was at a loss. If conversation stopped, she was afraid that Charles and Jane would have the opportunity to examine the flaws in her story.

"I do so love New Orleans. It will be a shame to leave the city. But I am so excited about France. As soon as we arrive, Nicky promised me a new wardrobe. I plan to use my share of the money to buy some jewels," she chattered.

"Who is giving you a share?"

"Why Nicky, of course. Although I am sure you two can spare a little from your tidy little sum—four hundred thousand francs, wasn't it?"

"Who told you that?"

"Why, I overheard it. Eric Rhodes is a very good lover too, Jane. You should add him to the list."

"I am not interested in your wanton words," Jane tartly replied. "I am not interested in men."

"Oh, what a shame. Don't you think so Charles?"

"If the captain didn't have such an awesome temper, I might be tempted to taste what you seem to give away freely. Perhaps we can arrange it," Charles touched her hair.

"For a price? Well, I might consider it, Charles," she forced her facial muscles to smile at him seductively. And then she did something that sickened her. Morgan actually stepped closer to Charles Gray, placing one hand on his shoulder while putting his hand on her hip. She didn't need to stand on her toes to kiss his thin lips. Fighting the nausea that rose in her throat, Morgan pressed her body into his, kissing him fully and passionately on the mouth.

Think of Nick—only of Nick, she squeezed her eyes shut.

426

"What the hell is going on here?" a familiar voice bellowed louder than the slamming door. "I leave you alone for a day and find you in the arms of the first man who comes along?"

"Nick?" she wanted to faint and wake up in three days. "Oh I am so sorry, darling."

Nicholas dropped his saddlebag and grabbed Morgan. His back turned to the shocked Grays, he mouthed two words, "trust me," before slapping Morgan on the cheek.

It sounded worse than it felt. But so much had happened in such a short time that Morgan was tightly wound—about to break. Nicholas sensed as much and roughly pulled her into his arms. "You are mine—remember that. Shall I prove it to you?"

He kissed her soundly, but it was a relief to feel his mouth on hers, his tongue invading her mouth. When he moved to kiss her ear, he whispered, "I heard it all. Courage, my beauty."

She sagged against him.

"There! I believe that proves my point." He confronted a stunned Charles Gray. "What the hell are you doing here? And if you don't keep your hands off my woman, you can forget this whole deal!"

His words were so low, but the menacing tone shook Charles Gray. The man was crazier than his bitch of a girl friend. He would kill me and our deal over this whore, he incredulously thought. "Wait a minute, Captain. Your woman approached me. My sister will concur. I am not interested in her until our arrangements are concluded. I can find my own companion, thank you." A light sheen of perspiration dotted his brow, stringing his brown hair.

"I don't know if I should believe you," Nicholas skeptically said.

"Well you should!" Jane snapped. "Do you know who this woman is? She said she told you she was the daughter of the man who was killed in . . ."

"Please," Nick interrupted her. "I know about it and if I were you, Miss Gray, I wouldn't remind us of it. Terrible thing, you know. Morgan should be compensated in some way."

"Now, Jane. I don't think you should anger the captain," Charles admonished his sister. "Let's start all over, shall we?"

his thin lips lifted into a half smile.

"I don't know if I should let you out of my sight again," Nicholas turned to Morgan who was desperately struggling to regain her composure.

"I told you to take me with you, Nicky. I get so lonely without you." She stepped toward him. "I want to sleep with you tonight under the stars—alone." She pointedly looked at Jane Gray. "After all, how do I know that you wouldn't prefer her in your bed, or both of us."

"Well!" Jane's shocked voice was a breath of fresh air. "I never. Charles and I will stay outside tonight, if you don't mind. I think it is safer that way."

"Why should I trust you or your brother?"

"Because I want that money, Rhodes. And you want all of the plates."

"Well, I don't know where the plates are, and I can assure you, Mr. Gray," he sneered, "the money is not in this cabin or outside. Perhaps it is hidden near your plates?" Nicholas laughed shrilly.

If this performance wasn't his best, Nicholas swore never to sail his ship again. If only he could fake a demonic gleam in his eyes. Glancing at Morgan, he thought she almost looked convinced that he was hot-tempered and a bit deranged.

"Morgan, my darling, where do you want to sleep? I want whatever makes you happy. Inside or outside. No," he tossed his wide-brimmed hat on the table, "I changed my mind. I want the bed tonight. Good night, Mr. Gray, Miss Gray; I am too tired to talk to you any more. We will get better acquainted tomorrow. Do you have bedrolls?"

They nodded and turned to leave. But before they walked out the door, Nicholas cheerfully called, "Oh and Charles, I am a very light sleeper. And sometimes I have this nasty habit of shooting first then asking questions. Sleep well."

Morgan dropped into the bed, one hand covering her eyes. "I don't . . ."

"Shhh. Keep your voice down," he motioned for her to remain silent. Unfastening his red shirt, Nicholas fell beside her.

"We cannot talk too much. They'll be more suspicious than they already are. Damn, I don't know how they found this place."

"Nick, I promise I will do anything you say. I was so afraid that . . ."

"I know, sweetheart. You are a very clever thinker, and a better actress. I had no idea you were so convincing. If I didn't know you better, I would believe it myself. I was damned lucky to see their horses outside before charging into the cabin," he smiled broadly.

"I was so worried for you Nick," she turned her head to see his face.

"Why?"

"I would never want anything to happen to you."

They spoke in such low whispers that Nicholas wondered if he heard correctly. Certainly this was not the night for discussions or revelations.

"Can we forget about the other day?" he asked, his husky voice so close to her ear that Morgan felt goose bumps along her neck and arms.

Quickly nodding, she added, "I don't know how much longer we can keep this charade going. They frighten me, Nick."

"Don't worry. Eric is bound to arrive shortly. I thought he'd be here by now. I don't intend to make a move until then. Besides, we have to go to the spot where the plates are hidden."

"What about the money?"

"I have some of it here. That's all you need to know."

The answer did not satisfy her. "Nicholas," she growled.

"Morgan, my love. Trust me. Please?" he kissed the tip of her nose. "Let's get comfortable," he pulled her legs onto the bed and after removing their boots, joined her. "It's been a big day," he yawned, pushing the hair off his forehead.

"Nick—you can't be going to sleep." She rigidly lay, her eyes wide open.

"Of course I am and so are you. Here," he cradled her head against his shoulder. "Try to relax. I know you left the pistol under the pillow."

Overwhelmed by the day's events, Morgan felt her heart erratically pound and her breathing suddenly come in shallow gasps.

But Nick was here to smooth her hair as he rained kisses on her eyes, cheeks, and lips. "Relax, my beauty. I am here and we will be fine. You'll see. Keep your eyes closed. I'll keep watch over us," he crooned, turning onto his side with Morgan still in his warm embrace. Kissing the top of her head, he whispered, "I missed you Morgan, my love. My only love."

Nick listened to the familiar night sounds and the unfamiliar whisperings of the Grays. Were Charles and Jane desperate enough to kill for the plates and the money?

The answer was yes. But if Nicholas could reinforce the notion that the emperor would seek revenge if his emissaries were murdered, perhaps the Grays would think again. Since Napoleon ruled most of Europe, the Grays would not be safe—unless, of course, they went to England. However, Nicholas would not consider that. Somehow, he would find a way out of this morass—as long as Eric arrived within the next few days. Nicholas hated these odds, spending most of the night trying to improve their chances.

He would not allow Morgan to be hurt. That was what had infuriated him the other day. The thought of Morgan confronting her father's murderers or being placed in a dangerous situation frightened him. How could he think straight if Morgan was constantly on his mind? And she was never far away. If not her image, then her lavender scent, her full mouth, her brilliant or petulant smile. There was always some part of Morgan, something about her, that lingered in his brain.

He had ridden off like a madman. But he was hoping to prove a point: that she could not manage without him; that she needed him—as much as he needed and wanted her. He wanted her to have time alone to think and hopefully realize that she still loved him.

Morgan did not know that her had never been far away. He had made his way to the village quickly, and by two P.M. was headed back for their cabin. The much needed food and supplies were loaded onto a newly purchased horse.

Nicholas had been halfway up the path when a thought occurred to him. Let her stay alone this night. Let her *think* she was staying alone, he corrected. He was close by in case there was any sign of danger. From his position—ten miles away—no one could travel this route without being seen.

But early the next morning, Nicholas had decided to hunt for fresh game and took a different route. It wasn't exactly a trail; rather it was overgrown swampland that he had deftly led the animals through.

It must have been pure instinct that told him to linger until late afternoon before slowly approaching the cabin. He would have burst through the clearing, but stopped when he saw the Grays appear. Deciding to wait and listen, he nevertheless cocked the pistol and had his knife within easy reach. Nothing would happen to Morgan.

At first, amazed at the things Morgan had said, he began to laugh. Under the circumstances, her facile lies were almost believable. Perhaps she deserved a little lesson, he decided, and waited another fifteen minutes. When Nicholas detected the change in her voice—suggesting agitation—he decided it was time to act. He also heard the hesitation in her voice when she walked over to kiss that murdering bastard. Lord—she must have been gagging. Unsure of Charles's response to Morgan's bold act, Nicholas did not think it prudent to wait. He burst through the door.

It would be difficult to travel with the Grays, and even more difficult to exchange the currency plates for the money he supposedly possessed. If the plan failed and the Grays headed for the Spanish Territory—which was not very far from Natchitoches—Nicholas doubted they could be forced back to the American side to stand trial for treason and murder. What would Morgan do then? he wondered. Give up? Go back to Ian or wait for her mother's arrival in New Orleans?

On his long, lonely ride into town, Nicholas had made a promise to himself: He would not let Morgan go away believing that he did not love her. He would tell her that he had never stopped loving her. He would ask for her forgiveness. But he would let her return to Ian Kendall.

Chapter 33

Morgan awoke before Nick. There was a faint touch of pink in the otherwise dark sky. She would have to summon the strength to resume her performance. At least, Morgan happily concluded, Nicholas was here.

Looking down at his peaceful face, she wondered how he could remain so calm, so sure that everything would work out fine. Long tawny lashes almost touched his skin. There wasn't a wrinkle on his face—except when he laughed, she fondly remembered; then tiny lines fanned out from the corners of his eyes. Taking stolen seconds to study his features, she smiled. His aristocratic nose was not really perfectly straight. There was a small bump near the bridge. She never did ask him how he got that small scar above his left eyebrow. For a fair-haired man, the stubble was so apparent, even one day after shaving. She loved watching his mouth—especially when they made love, when Nick was positioned above her, his full lower lip sensuously extended. Many times Morgan could not resist nibbling on those lips before her tongue sought entry into his warm mouth. His cheekbones were more prominent than she remembered. It was probably due to the way he drove himself these last few weeks. He had obviously lost more weight than she originally thought.

"Are you finished, Morgan? I would like to open my eyes now," he softly whispered, but the humor was evident.

"Oh you. How could you let me embarrass myself like this!" she accused.

"I thought you were enjoying yourself. Why should I stop that? Come here," he pulled Morgan into his arms. "Let me taste your luscious lips. I've been hungering for you since I left this place."

The kiss was soft and full of such tenderness, Morgan wished it would never end. Nick broke away first, trying to gauge the odd expression on her face.

"You're not afraid, are you?"

"Of course I am, you idiot."

"Is that why you look so sad?"

"No." She moved her head, splashing his bare torso with her silky black hair.

"What is it then?"

"I don't think I can ever forget you," she looked down into his hypnotic eyes.

"I'm glad. I know I will never forget you," he chuckled, cradling her face with his hands.

"Sometimes I wish we could have met under different circumstances. Would you have courted me?"

It was a strange question to ask—especially today with danger lurking outside the cabin door. What could she possibly be thinking? he asked himself.

"I would have wanted you, beauty. For the very reasons I do now. Isn't it obvious?" he flung back the blanket, showing the evident arousal bulging against his breeches.

"I don't mean that," she tried to pull away.

"I know what you mean, love. Would I have courted you? Yes. Admitting defeat to a raven-haired beauty does not come easily to me. But you know, Morgan, I never seriously considered settling down. I think that with you, I would have done it without any prompting. Well," he smiled at her dubious look, "perhaps a little provocation. What I mean is, child or no child, murder or no murder, family promises or no family promises, I would love you just the same."

Once the words were out, Nicholas wanted to explain. But it was Morgan who prevented further conversation by cupping his rough face in her soft hands. She smiled into his attentive face, kissing his forehead, nose, cheeks, and lips.

"You will always be a part of me," she whispered.

434

"I know," he raised his head to take her freely offered mouth.

"Let's wake them with your groans," he half jested.

But minutes later, Nicholas had to put one hand across her mouth to prevent Morgan's ecstatic moans from echoing outside.

He wanted to tell her he loved her. And he hoped she understood what he'd begun to say. But Nicholas also wanted to tell her when they were truly alone.

She must have dozed, for when Nick's hand gently nudged her shoulder, Morgan saw the morning sun.

"Wake up, beauty. The Grays are mumbling aloud out there. I guess either we woke them or the insects did."

He was fully dressed in black breeches, beige shirt, a white cotton cloth tied loosely around his neck. Holding his hat in one hand, Nicholas tried to straighten himself, but Morgan's slender arms insistently wrapped around him. So touched was he by her clinging arms that he bent down for one more breathless kiss. Only after she could see the passionate glow in his silver eyes did she let go. "I want you to remember that— all day. Call it my brand." She lifted her legs over the side of the bed to stand.

"What happened to my breeches?" she looked about in confusion.

"Over there, where I threw them."

"Oh. Nick? Could you get me some water from the well. I forgot to get it last night."

Impatiently stalking out to the cabin, Nick's loud grumbles could not be ignored by the Grays.

"She wants water. Say, Lady Jane, would you like some too? You can wash yourself in there after the princess finishes."

"Yes, thank you," came the haughty reply.

Morgan heard enough to be dressed and finished before Jane Gray entered the cabin. She could not decide who was more peculiar—Jane or her brother. Jane seemed to have an aversion to all men—except Charles.

The newly formed foursome was ready to leave. Nicholas took command of the departing group, leading them down the narrow, marshy path. Morgan rode last, her pistol never out of

435

reach. She would not give Charles the opportunity to shoot Nick in the back.

As soon as the road widened, Nicholas fell back. Turning to Charles, he said, "I believe I know where we are headed. Since you seem to have been there in the recent past, however, why don't you ride alongside me?"

They did. Morgan remembered Nick telling her that the ride was at least two hours from the cabin. She marveled at his casual attitude. Why, he and Charles seemed to be engrossed in pleasant conversation. Charles laughed—or tried to—a couple of times, and Nick appeared to find great humor in some of Charles's stories.

Nicholas declared it unwise to stop for lunch, after relating the embellished story of the Indian attack. Charles readily agreed. Morgan continued to observe the surroundings.

Nick had explained to Morgan that the Louisiana Territory was huge, much larger than the thirteen original states. But much of the territory which was not yet habitable, he arrogantly declared, would be settled in no time by the newly arrived immigrants and those Americans who wanted to explore the West. There was a great deal of Spanish influence in the area; in some towns anti-American sentiment ran strong, while in others, anti-Spanish. Until the borders were clearly defined, Nick did not think that anything other than forts would be established along the frontier.

There were, she recalled now, great gaps in their travel. When they originally set out from New Orleans there were plantations, farms of various sizes, and small towns along the trail. Of course Nicholas avoided all towns, believing Morgan would try to escape. But the farther they traveled, the settlements became more sparse—as did the land.

Unfortunately, the insects did not. Morgan did not think that there could be so many pesty mosquitoes. She was grateful that Nick had provided her with cotton long-sleeved shirts and gloves, for whenever her arms or neck were exposed a tiny row of itchy red blotches formed.

The slow prancing of the horses lulled Morgan into thoughtful state. It had been a strange two weeks with Nick. Her life would never be the same and her thoughts would never stray far from the man she still loved.

They reached their destination in the early afternoon. The area was very similar to the one where the cabin was located: bushes, copses of pine and oak trees, and bayous that obviously flowed from the Red River. One particular spot was surrounded by overgrown trees, and the area was almost marshy. They were, Morgan now knew, only six miles south from Les Rapides. She grudgingly admired Charles's clever selection of the spot where the plates were hidden.

"How did you expect me to find this place?" Nick asked while dismounting. "Your directions were not as good as you thought. I could have been in Les Rapides."

"That's right," Charles smugly smiled. "I thought it would be safer to meet you where there are witnesses. After our first meeting, Captain, I do not think I would give you my back to aim for."

"Well, I think I can understand. However, it is my sad duty to inform you that we must wait."

"Wait?" the Grays said in unison.

"Why yes, of course. Charles," Nick calmly turned to the man, "do you have all ten of the remaining currency plates in your possession?"

"Why yes," he stammered, "yes I do."

"I am pleased." Nick left the baffled Grays to stare at his back while he sauntered over to Morgan, easily lifting her off the mare. "We have some time to wait, dearest. Care to join me for a stroll?"

"But, Nicky, you promised me a bath."

"So I did. Well, we will have to go into town. I don't see any swimming places in this area. I'd hate to have you bitten by a snake or something," he enjoyed Morgan's fearful expression, then immediately felt guilty and pulled her against him. "I'm only joking, sweetheart," he whispered for her ears only.

"Captain Rhodes," Charles cleared his throat. Jane was anything but pleased. "Would you, uh, could you please tell me what we are waiting for?"

"The money." Nick forced a high-pitched laugh. "You don't believe I would travel two hundred miles with this money-grubbing bitch around? She'd stick a knife in my gut faster than you would, Charles. No, I am playing it safe. Eric will be here tomorrow or the day after." He refused to look at Morgan, knowing exactly what he would see on her face—fury.

"Why, that is impossible," Jane sputtered, still seated on her mare. "We must be in Mexico by the end of the month."

"You will, Jane dear, don't fret. It's only another two days at most. Who knows? Maybe Eric is waiting for us in Les Rapides."

"Nicky," Morgan stomped her foot, "you are a bastard. Why didn't you trust me? I thought you did, and even loved me a little," she pouted.

"Oh I do, angel. I love you very much. I would simply rather not let you near my money until we are at sea. That was our bargain, wasn't it querida?" He gruffly rubbed her cheek. "I think we should all go to town and wait for Eric. I know I could use a bottle of tequila and a good game of cards," his eyes suggestively roamed over Morgan, "and your luscious body. What do you say, Charles? How about that game you promised me?"

"Well," he hesitated, seeing his sister's angry glare. "I don't see why not."

"Don't you dare gamble away our money, Charles—not like the last time. I will not let you play unless you agree on the sum of money to bet."

"Is your sister loco? Hey Janie, you can't tell a man what to do." Nick actually believed what he was saying.

"You, sir, should keep your vile mouth closed. This is between my brother and myself." Jane refused to dismount. "Well, Charles. Do I have your word to be cautious or not?"

"Dammit," he muttered. "I would give anything to have your wench with me instead of my sister."

"Well, if the price is right, I suppose . . ." he actually appeared to consider the proposition.

"Nicky, I will stay with Charles if you keep saying those nasty things about me. After all, he is going to have all the money," she winked at Charles. "You can have Jane."

"Too plain for me. No," he made an elaborate show of roaming his hands along Morgan's curves, "I am not tired of you yet, angel. And I've only just begun to break you in."

Amazingly, she did not cringe or blush. Caught up in their incredible, deathly performance, Morgan almost believed that Nicholas was as calloused and mentally unbalanced as he appeared, and that she was no better than a fancy whore.

Yet there was one thing she needed to know. Remaining in her part, she wrapped both arms around Nick's waist, turned to Charles, and asked, "Where is Alan Sterling's body? I think I would like to see it. Wouldn't that be ironic, Nicky? To see the murdered man who murdered my father?" she looked into his shoulder.

"I never said anything about a grave," he quietly replied. "What kind of fool do you take me for, Gray?" Nicholas angrily began. "Do you think I accepted your story that Sterling or Andrews quietly disappeared? Oh no, I am not easy to mislead. And those who have tried, well I guess they are visiting with Alan Sterling," he laughed. "So if the lady wants to see the grave, tell her where it is."

"Over there, beyond those rocks. It wasn't easy to bury him in this area. Who knows, maybe the alligators found the bastard's body."

"Was he a good friend of yours?" Morgan innocently asked.

"He was my husband!" Jane Gray sneered.

"Your what?" Morgan lost her composure.

"Yes, my husband. The stupid bastard thought he knew everything. Thought he could handle it all, his own way. He never listened to reason. He was such a hot-headed fool, I hated everything about him. Always hated him," she said more to herself than the startled listeners. "But stealing the plates was his idea," her venomous tone did not soften. "Whenever he touched me, I wanted to kill him. I am glad I did it though, very glad," she smiled. "You must realize that he . . ."

"That's quite enough, Jane. There is no need to say anything else to our associates," Charles admonished.

"Wait. I want to know why you killed him," Nicholas persisted, more for Morgan's sake than his own.

"Sterling had been an actor. He knew about disguising oneself. And he did well in Philadelphia, until he decided to return for Rhinehart's trial. Jane and I were waiting for him in Pittsburgh. The fool wanted to stay for the trial, thought it

439

amusing that another man was on trial for our crime. But your father recognized him and Sterling did not want to take any chances, so he killed him."

Morgan was gripping Nick's waist in stunned disbelief and fury. "Why did you kill him? I was hoping for that honor."

"He would have killed you first. That's exactly what he was planning for Jane and me. Sterling couldn't believe that Jane would take me over him. We fought out here—he wanted it all. Before he could slit my throat, Jane shot him between the eyes."

"Morgan, I don't want to see his grave now. I want to ride into that town, have my drink, and have you take care of me. I don't give a damn about Andrews or Sterling. The bastard deserved it."

Morgan did not think that Nick would turn his back on the Grays—not after this confession.

"Yes, he did deserve to die," Jane quietly said. "I am glad he can't touch me anymore. Charles is all I need," she lovingly looked at her brother, but it was not the look of a sister, Morgan noticed, and shivered at the thought.

Their barely clean lodgings were above a cantina. Morgan did not care about the lack of cleanliness. She needed to be away from those awful people—although their rooms were down the hall. She needed time to think about their evil deeds. She did not want to worry, but not for one minute did she believe that she or Nick would be safe once the money was exchanged. If only Eric were here, perhaps she would feel reassured.

After midnight, Nicholas crawled into the narrow bed, reeking of stale smoke, whiskey, and something else.

It was the cheaply scented perfume that awakened Morgan. That, and the clumsy way he lit the candles.

"What is . . . Nicholas, goodness . . . you stink! And if I am not mistaken, there is a distinct—very distinct scent of sweet rosewater all over you. Ooh, that is awful!"

"Please woman, not now." He dropped onto the bed. "That man can drink. I am surprised that he can imbibe so much and still engage in reasonable conversation. But he did, Morgan, and he is downstairs drinking and playing cards at this very moment. Whew!" he rolled his eyes. "I might have underestimated Charles Gray."

"Don't forget, sweet Jane. The woman who murdered her husband. I wonder if I should emulate her," she half seriously commented.

"Try it, my love. And you will never sit again without remembering me."

"You've explained the smoke and, I assume, the whiskey. Where does the perfume come from?"

"Jesus, Morgan, I had to play the part didn't I?" Nicholas looked at her shocked expression. "I didn't bed any of them, if that's what your open mouth means. One or two sat on my lap, that's all." She didn't look convinced. Nicholas held up his let hand, "That is all, Morgan. I give my oath. I have a part to play, you know. Even Charles allowed a friendly hand to roam up his leg."

"'Even' Charles, you say. You allowed some harlot to . . ."

"No, beauty, I did not. But I couldn't tell them to get off my lap, could I? I couldn't say that I am hopelessly devoted to my wife? I mean my former wife," he looked sideways. "What the hell are you, anyhow? Are you my former wife, or my former mate. I mean my former lover?"

"Don't you dare make it sound so sordid," Morgan folded her legs beneath the cotton nightdress.

"I'm not. As far as I am concerned, you were, no I mean you are, my legally wedded wife. You know, Morgan, if you are still planning on marrying Kendall, I think you should annul our marriage—in case it was legal."

From his prone position on the bed, Nicholas could not see her pout. In a small voice, she responded, "I suppose you are right. Should I do it or you?"

"I will do it. But Morgan," Nicholas quickly flipped onto his stomach, able to see her face in the dim light, "are you?"

"Am I what?"

"Are you going to marry Kendall?"

"I am not . . . really—I mean, I don't know what I should do. His family is wonderful, you know . . ."

"I know, I know, you must have said that at least a dozen times."

441

Morgan ignored the mild rebuke. "What I am trying to say is that it wouldn't be fair to Ian. Yet I cannot hurt him or his family—although he deserves better than me. 'A trifle used,' isn't that the expression you have for a woman who has known others?"

"Others? Are there others?" he held her gaze.

"No, oh Nick, you know exactly what I am trying to say." She pulled the sheet high on her chest. "I mean that Ian deserves a young, innocent girl who can worship him the way he deserves to be looked upon."

"Is that what you want Morgan? You do love him, don't you?"

"Well, in a way, yes," she lowered her lashes, refraining from adding, not the way I love you, Nick. "I don't think you would understand," her voice hardened, "nor do I owe you any explanation, Nicky."

"Morgan, you wound me with that horrible name," he cupped her chin, trying not to smile.

"You deserve far worse," she couldn't stop the answering smile.

"Ah, sweetheart, I shall miss you—if you go back to him. I think it's a mistake, though."

"Why?" she leaned close, fighting the urge to run fingers through his messy, but still foul-smelling hair.

"He is not for you. You need a man who will understand you, respect you, cherish you, and harness your stubborn angry nature." He inched closer to her parted lips. "You need me, Morgan. And I am willing to wager the currency plates and the money that you love me," his mouth pressed light kisses on her cheeks before settling on her lips. "Morgan, open your eyes."

She complied with his demand. Nicholas sat on his haunches, staring into her wide eyes. "I want you to know something," he took her hand. "I want you to understand that I have never stopped loving you. I don't know how to say it any clearer Morgan and, no," he cut off her protest, "I am not drunk or drugged or insane. I want you to know how I feel. I want you to know that I would give my soul to have another chance with you—to prove what I failed to do the first time—

and that I will cherish your love, always. That I will protect you with my own life. Morgan . . ."

"No!" she shook her head, placing hands over her ears. "No, I don't want to hear it, not now—not tonight. Nick, we have been acting some absurd role for two days. Or am I wrong? Perhaps we were acting for the last seven months. Please, I am no longer sure of anything—except that Charles and Jane Gray have the currency plates that will clear my father's name. I don't want to think beyond that. I cannot!" she tried to hold back the tears. "It is all too much, Nick. I want to believe you, but I am not sure that I can."

"All right," he took her hands away from her face, "I will not speak about this again until it is all over. When you have handed the currency plates over to the authorities—once you have that precious piece of paper that clears your father's name—I will ask you *once,* only once more, Morgan, to think about a life with me. Not with Ian. I want you back," he took her mouth again, his tongue tracing the outline of her lips.

The kiss was like a refreshing thundershower on a hot, humid day. It told of secrets still deeply buried. But with patience and love, the secrets would be exposed.

"Oh Nick," she clutched his neck, "you are driving me insane."

"No more than I am, beauty," he nibbled one earlobe. "Let me love you tonight."

It was not a question or a statement that needed a response. Forgotten was the cheap scent on his clothing, the smoke in his hair; forgotten were the hurts and pain of the past. Nicholas was holding Morgan in his strong, but tender embrace, kissing every inch of her body, willing her pain away.

In two minutes, the nightdress had parted company with her body. But Nicholas would not release her mouth; with his hands he would explain to Morgan what words failed to accomplish. They made a different kind of love that night. It was soft and tender; Nicholas's hands stroked her, held her. Each time she thought the sky would explode into thousands of tiny stars, he called her back to him, whispering passionate words in her ear.

Morgan felt fragile and cherished. They moved as one heart,

one mind. If each never said a word to the other again, it would not matter. Their bodies spoke of a brighter future—of promises left to keep. It was a night Morgan wished she could have conceived his baby.

Afterwards, Morgan could not explain why she was crying. Nicholas alternately wiped and kissed the salty tears. It was almost dawn, but neither wanted to sleep. Sleep meant the end of this beautiful interlude, of the precious heaven in each other's embrace. Nor did they want to talk about Ian or Nick's family or of the future. It was safe to talk about the present.

"Nick? What will we do if Eric doesn't arrive tomorrow? I mean today."

"I think we have to bluff. We need more time. If that doesn't work, we may steal the plates." He was serious.

"And how do you propose we do that?" she lightly responded.

"I mean it, Morgan," he stared down at her, leaning on one hand. "I have been thinking about this. We are not sure that we are 'negotiating' with normal people. Jane Gray is very strange . . ."

"Strange? I think I'd use a stronger word for someone who murders her husband."

"To protect her beloved brother and their scheme," he added. "They believe our charade, for the time being. How much longer they will believe us could prove dangerous—if not fatal.

"I shouldn't have left Charles alone with his sister at all. But Christ, Morgan, I wanted to be alone with you so badly, I ignored my better instincts. Anyway, the other night I suddenly remembered how much Charles loves to gamble. With luck, he is either still downstairs playing or in a drunken stupor." He idly ran one finger along her arm.

"Did Charles lose money to you?"

"Indeed he did. A very nice sum at that: five thousand dollars."

"My God! How can he do that?"

"It's a sickness, Morgan. He cannot stop even though he is losing. He keeps believing that the next hand or the one after will pay off big. So he bets more money on each successive hand."

444

"Jane would not approve."

"It probably doesn't matter to Charles what anyone thinks. But if he is desperate and if he comes to realize that you and I are imposters, we could have a serious problem. He could shoot me before I find the plates."

"Nick, he could also shoot you while your back is turned."

"I am well aware of that. Which is why I think we have to gamble too. We are evenly matched. I am a hell of a lot stronger than Charles, and Jane, just from her sheer size, is probably stronger than you."

"But I can use a pistol."

"In case you forgot, dear, so can she. But, if you keep a cool head, you can outsmart her."

Morgan thought about his words while snuggling against him. "How can we get him to show us the remaining plates? Ten bronze, possibly buried plates—six of which are genuine. They could be scattered all over this town."

"I doubt that. Charles didn't have the time to bury the plates. He was too busy trying to kill Andrews, remember? No, I'd wager that the plates are in one spot—not far from Andrews's grave," he looked at her lowered head. "Morgan, you are not upset with me because I didn't let you see the grave, are you?"

"No, not really. I simply can't believe that the man—the image I had engraved in my brain—is in a shallow grave. I simply want to make sure he is dead. Does that sound ghoulish?"

"No. It is hard to let go of a perception you've been living with for months. It's the same with love, you know," he cleverly changed the topic. "If you have an image, a perception, it takes a long time to change it—no matter how hard you try."

Morgan ignored the comparison to love. She knew precisely what he meant, but could not address it.

"Try to get some sleep," he stroked her hair. "I think I have some more work to do."

"Nick?"

"Shhh, let me handle this, all right?"

"No, it is not all right. But I will try to sleep. Just come back to me."

Nicholas hugged her inviting body. "I always will, beauty."

While Morgan slept, Nicholas walked outside the cantina and kept walking to the outskirts of town. He needed time alone. A dog barked in the distance, a lone horse trotted down the only street, a baby cried. Watching the town slowly come to life, Nicholas thought about his life—the part he spent without Morgan Rhinehart.

She had refused to believe him. In a dim corner of his brain, Nicholas understood. She had been hurt. She had used the time away from him to pick up the fragmented pieces of her life and start again—this time with Ian Kendall by her side.

Kendall was undoubtedly a good man, and surely loved Morgan almost as much as Nicholas did. Certainly Kendall's family was receptive to her, despite the name. No—he could not blame Ian or Morgan.

There was also something else that Nicholas understood. Morgan had never taken Ian as her lover—despite her words to the contrary. She did not need to admit the truth, he simply knew it. Ian, gentleman that he was, most likely did not press her to become his lover. Perhaps that was a greater sign of his love for Morgan Rhinehart.

Perhaps Nicholas did not deserve a second chance with Morgan. He had caused her nothing but unhappiness: from the vicious Catherine Stevens to the loss of their baby; from their illegal marriage to his mother's request and his father's angry demands. There never was time for trust. The relationship started as a lie.

Could he blame Morgan for not believing in his love? More importantly, Nicholas reached another conclusion: Should he deny Morgan the opportunity to marry a man who could make her deliriously happy, whose family welcomed her? Morgan was content in New Orleans. No one threatened her safety. She was welcome, not as the daughter of a traitor, but as the vivacious young woman whose beauty and wit impressed all who were fortunate enough to meet her.

Was he being fair to take it all away? The question haunted Nicholas for the rest of the day.

Chapter 34

"Where is the money, Rhodes?" a red-eyed Charles confronted him later that morning.

Nicholas laughed. "My dear Charles, after last night's card game I should be asking the same of you. Where is *my* money? You, as I recall, owe me five thousand dollars. Your memory is failing." He casually leaned back in the wood chair, propping his legs onto the table. No one else was in the cantina.

"No, I have not forgotten. I will deduct the money from the francs you are paying me. Let's see. You and your uncle have paid one hundred thousand francs, which of course leaves three hundred thousand francs."

"No Charles—no more conversion. That money is not mine, but the property of the French Government. Five thousand American dollars is mine."

"But . . ."

"But nothing. I think I have been patient with you. I want my money this afternoon." Nicholas glared at Charles, while toying with the same knife Morgan plunged into his shoulder. "I think I am being rather considerate—unless," he paused, "you would care to play another game. Same stakes?" Charles's eager expression amused Nicholas. The man's eyes seemed to glow with anticipation of another game of chance.

"Double them," Charles announced, reaching for the deck of cards.

"Double is fine. That means two thousand dollars per hand. Charles, I am perplexed about this. If you have no money, what do you propose to use as collateral?" he asked, praying to hear the right answer.

"One currency plate," Charles coolly replied.

It was what Nicholas wanted to hear, but he did not look up. Instead he seemed preoccupied with his fingernails. "I accept."

"Done. You know, I too would like you to put up collateral—your pretty little companion. I get her for one night if you lose. Deal?" Charles's sallow face actually brightened.

For a brief moment, Nicholas was unsure if Charles's excitement was due to the game or the opportunity to bed Morgan. Thank goodness she was asleep. He doubted she would ever understand his self-confidence or his next words.

"Agreed. I am tiring of her," he drawled. "I won't miss her tonight."

"Perhaps she wears you out. I have been waiting for a chance with her since the other day," he slapped the deck onto the table. "Yes, I am feeling lucky."

But the feeling didn't translate into results. Nicholas won the currency plate. This was simply too easy, he thought, and wondered if it were possible to win the remaining seven plates.

He almost won a second, when Jane Gray suddenly appeared, wearing a starchy white blouse and long brown skirt.

"I should have known you would be here. And with *him*," she disdainfully curled her lips. "How much did you lose this time, Charles?"

"The game is not over, Miss Gray. Why don't you stroll about this town and come back later? We'll be fine without you," Nicholas continued to study his hand.

"I am sure you will. But I believe I asked my brother a question, Captain. Why don't you find your whore while I try to sober up my brother?"

With supreme effort, Nicholas fought the urge to strike her.

"Jane, I must finish this hand. Don't worry, I will be . . ."

"No!" she shouted. "I have heard this many times before. You will not wager everything we have worked so hard for. Captain," she frowned, "either you stop fleecing my brother of the plates or I swear I will reconsider our deal. The British

448

contact happens to be in Natchitoches. I am confident he will accept our price. What do you say, sir?"

The chair scraped against the wood floor. Nicholas slowly rose from his cramped position to tower above Jane.

"Do not ever threaten me like that, Miss Jane. I do not appreciate your manner," Nick placed the knife on the top button of her blouse. "Perhaps Charles can accept it, but I cannot. I think you should reconsider your position," the knife touched the cameo pin at her neck. "Perhaps if you would like me to accompany you to your room, we can chat about this matter."

She took three steps backward, her eyes frantically beseeching her brother for assistance. But he was smiling. "I don't think so, Captain."

"Jane," Nicholas almost bit his lip, "I think you need a real man." He touched her neck and ear, "I am sure I can tame you."

"Why you vile, disgusting animal! Stay away from me. And that goes for you too," she yelled at Charles. "You are all alike, aren't you? Eager to put your hairy hands on a woman, to take what you think she so eagerly wants to give. Well, I am not like that slut of yours. I hate you! Like I hated Alan," she continued to rave. She unexpectedly found herself staring at Nicholas's back. "How dare you turn you back on me."

"Charles, I think we should continue our game later when we can have some privacy. I'll accept the same terms. But really, Charles, you must do something about your sister. She could use some warming; I thought you've been doing that Charles." Nicholas coolly stared at him, the meaning of his words clear.

He was out of the room before Jane started to scream obscenities at him.

Although Charles appeared spineless, Nicholas knew Jane was dangerous. It was unwise to bait the woman. She was strung so tightly that Nicholas suspected she was about to snap, and he would give anything not to be within fifty feet of her demonic rage.

Nicholas realized he had been overlooking something: If Charles was willing to wager a currency plate, it had to mean

449

that some, if not all of them, were in his possession and not buried somewhere outside of town. Somehow Nicholas had to get into that room to search for the plates. But he couldn't do it without Morgan's help.

She was rising when he slammed the door.

"Thank goodness I'm awake, although I assume you awoke the entire town."

"Morgan, my love, you remind me of another viper with whom I've had recent contact." Stripping himself of his shirt and tossing it across the bed, Nicholas walked over to the washbasin. "I feel dirty, Morgan. You would too if you had to touch Jane Gray."

"Don't tell me you kissed her?" she leaned on her hands and knees to see his face.

"Don't be daft—although it was a close call. Morgan, we have got a few problems and I know of only one way to solve them."

"I don't want to hear it."

After he sketchily outlined the plan, Morgan raised her frightened face. "Nick, it is dangerous. How can I keep both of them out of their rooms? How much time do you need?"

"Charles won't be a problem. It's Jane. You have got to get her out of this," he looked scornfully around the room, "dare I call this place—a hotel?"

Despite the danger, Nicholas had the audacity to smile. Morgan jumped off the bed to dissuade him of this scheme. "It will not work. Why can't we wait for Eric? At least with one more ally, one of us could keep Charles interested in cards while the other could keep Jane occupied." Suddenly she paused then clapped her hands in delight. "Nick, we've been looking at this from the wrong point of view. It's me! I'm the one who should look for the plates—not you. Besides," she rushed on, ignoring his dubious expression, "I would wager every bit of jewelry I own on the probability that the plates are in Jane's possession. Nick," she grabbed his bare forearms, "don't you see? They wouldn't suspect me. You could say I am sleeping or indisposed or bedding every man in this hotel. I could not cover for you as well as you can for me." She brightened, completely taken with this idea, and paced across the room.

"It is perfect Nick. You can keep both of them busy, I know it. And I know I can find the plates—I've seen them too. Think Nick, if we had eight bronze plates, where would we hide them?"

Willing to consider her scheme, he said, "The most obvious place—among the clothes. If the plates are in Jane's room and the Grays are planning on leaving this charming little town quickly, they wouldn't carry much baggage."

"I would search her clothes, especially her underthings."

"Her what?"

"Her underthings. The nightdresses, chemises, you know underthings. It's that or her jewel case, and the plates are too large for it."

"Morgan," Nick put his large hands on her shoulders. Her stubborn chin was lifted high, her eyes filled with determination. "Perhaps you are right. I might be willing to consider this bizarre idea of yours if . . ."

"If what," her heart pounded.

"If you promise two things," he smiled at her wary expression. "One, that you stay in the room for no more than fifteen minutes. I hope I can give you that time," he wrinkled his forehead.

"And the other?"

"That you wear your glasses."

Burying her head in his hairy chest, she held his waist. "How can you possibly engage in humor at a time like this?"

While Nicholas and Morgan were trying to enjoy lunch, the Grays approached.

"Here it goes, Morgan. Good luck, beauty," he muttered.

There was no time to reply. Charles seated himself next to Morgan while Jane sat between the men.

"Listen to me, Rhodes. Jane and I have been discussing our situation; we are not waiting any longer. Either you come up with the money this afternoon, or the deal is cancelled," Charles wiped his perspiring brow. All that remained of his bout with whiskey and cards were some dark smudges under his eyes.

"What about the plate and my five thousand dollars?" Nicholas coolly inquired. One arm was draped over the chair while the other held a fork.

"Here," Jane placed a cloth-wrapped rectangular object in his hands. "Captain Rhodes, why are you so interested in one plate?"

"It was just a notion, Jane. I thought I might win all eight from Charles. I would have paid you some of the money, but not all three hundred thousand francs. Who knows? I thought Morgan and I could make use of the extra money and our private sale of some of the plates. The lady has expensive taste, you know," he openly winked at Morgan, who was clearly confused by the turn in the conversation.

"I suppose that in lieu of your five thousand dollars you will be more than willing to take this plate," Jane handed over another.

Of the eight remaining plates, four were the fakes from New Orleans. There was no time to examine which ones these were. "How very generous of you, Jane," Nicholas laughed. "Hey Charles, even though I won the wager, I think I should keep my part of the bargain. Certainly I don't have to, but you and Jane have been such good sports." Nicholas faced Morgan, his eyes darkened with some hidden meaning, "Morgan love, Charles would like to spend the night with you."

Positive that he was the only one who saw the imperceptible tremor in her shoulders, he continued, "I said it would be all right with you since you were draped over him the day I found you in the cabin. You can have him for this one night only, Morgan. Do you understand?"

"Aren't you thoughtful," she replied in a tone only Nick could understand. "I shall not forget your gesture, Nicky," she sweetly smiled, linking one arm in Charles's. "Isn't he thoughtful, Charlie?"

A lustful gleam in his pale eyes revealed his thoughts. It doesn't matter, Morgan, she told herself. It is all a charade. Remember you are on a stage and this is a performance.

"Just in case you like her, Charles, you should know," Nicholas leaned back in the chair. "Morgan and I are leaving

452

first thing tomorrow morning. I don't want her to see you again."

Jane gasped. Morgan hid her smile behind the napkin. Nicholas was better at this than she. The more he acted, the more believable he became, even to her. Casually attired in a white unlaced cambric shirt and nankeen breeches, he seemed unaware of the danger they were in. No wonder he was a smuggler. He must enjoy every second of the tension, yet there wasn't a gray hair on his sun-streaked head to show for it.

He smiled at the three people. "Morgan, you get yourself nice and pretty for Charles, while I take the Grays on a short ride."

Ride? There was no mention of a ride in their plans. "I think I would like a bath, a scented bath. Could you arrange that for me, Nicky," she batted her dark lashes, "or should I ask Charles? I cannot wait to get out of this warm dress," she touched the pale pink muslin dress.

"I'll do it, honey. Now Charles," Nicholas focused on the man across the table, "since I intend to leave here tomorrow, I want to settle our differences today. The hell with my uncle. We can't wait for him any longer. You were right—I do have the money. I didn't think it smart to let you know about it sooner. I thought it would be fitting to hide the money near Andrews's grave. You and Jane can go with me." Nicholas paused, his eyes never leaving Jane Gray's face. "Perhaps Jane, you would like to ride with me. I'm going to be lonely tonight. I could use a little company."

"Great idea!" Charles exclaimed. "Jane and I can leave this very minute. Can't we, sister? I don't want to waste any time—not when I know who is waiting for me," he leered at Morgan.

"If we ride quickly, we can be back within the hour. I took the liberty of having the horses saddled." Nick shot out of the chair. "Give me a kiss, honey. I'll miss you tonight."

As the three briskly walked out into the hot afternoon, Morgan felt chills along her spine. Nicholas was alone with those two murderers. Suddenly, she realized that Nick was not wearing his pistol; he had left it in their room. Morgan closed her eyes, praying for his safety. Seconds later, she was on her feet heading toward their room. Once there, she peered out the window onto the dusty street below.

When she saw the three horses trot out of town, she quickly headed for Jane Gray's room. The barkeep had graciously given her the key.

After ten minutes, Morgan knew she wouldn't have success finding the plates. They were not where she thought they'd be. Another ten minutes passed and Morgan broke out in a cold sweat. She must have searched everywhere: under the bed and rug, in the chest of drawers, in Jane's portmanteau.

Nick had two plates—both wrapped in what Morgan thought was a piece of brown velvet. Where did that material come from? A dress? Possibly, but there was nothing of the sort in this room. Morgan stood in the center of the small room, turning ever so slowly, making sure she did not overlook any spot.

Brown velvet, she kept thinking, before it dawned on her: a man's jacket, perhaps? The plates must be in Charles's room, she triumphantly thought.

Making sure nothing looked touched, Morgan silently approached the adjoining door, holding her breath until she found it unlocked. Thank God, she whispered silently.

Charles's room looked much the same as the other. Morgan wasted little time examining the neat room. The plates had to be here, they had to be, she told herself. If Charles Gray buried them—as he originally stated—Nicholas would be alone when the Grays realized that there was no money. How would Nick manage, she thought, fighting down the rising panic.

There was nothing under the bed and inside a large canvas bag; again there was nothing other than clothing and some papers. Morgan stood, still frantically trying to wipe the hair out of her face.

That was when she noticed it. A small leather bag, similar to a doctor's satchel, was neatly tucked between a pair of boots and a portmanteau.

Rushing toward it like a magnet to iron, Morgan grabbed the brown leather bag, hastily putting it under her arms. She almost cried with joy with she saw the six remaining currency plates, each individually wrapped in brown velvet.

She couldn't simply take the bag; Charles would undoubtedly check for it. Why hadn't she thought of this sooner?

Morgan stealthily left the room for hers. Nicholas had informed her that four of the plates were counterfeit. Ignoring her trembling fingers and shortened breath, Morgan unwrapped each plate, looking for the ones from the Bank of New Orleans. There were three; one had been given to Nick earlier. Morgan need only be concerned with replacing the weight of three plates.

She rummaged through her things. Her brush seemed to be the only item that would do. But it was not enough.

"Think, Morgan, come on think. Stay calm," she said aloud. She looked through Nick's things. There was nothing in his saddlebag but clothing and a small box. A box? It looked like a jewel box. Curiosity won over panic. Morgan could not resist taking a peak.

It was her wedding ring. Nestled in the dark blue velvet box, the gold shining at her eyes. Where did he find it?

"Oh my God," she moaned. "What does this mean?"

This was certainly not the time to ponder her relationship with Nicholas, nor his professed words of love.

"Not now, Morgan," she said aloud.

Shoving the box into the bag, she searched the room for some other item and reluctantly decided that the pewter candlestick holder would have to do. Wrapping it in some brown velvet, she stuffed it under the New Orleans plates and returned the bag to Charles's room.

Only when she was safely back in her own room with the door firmly locked and supported by a chair did her heartbeat return to normal. Clutching his pillow to her chest, Morgan softly cried, "Oh, Nick. Please come back. I want you to hold me."

The entire escapade took less than fifty minutes. After one hour, she started to tense again. How did Nick manage? she wondered. This morning he had told her not to worry, that he had taken care of everything. Stupidly, she did not ask what that meant.

Now she allowed herself to think about the ring. Nick had taken it—had kept it with him since New York. Did he ever look at it while thinking about her, about their marriage? Was it true he regretted what had happened? Was the ring a reminder of what was or what could be?

Tossing the pillow aside, Morgan's thoughts became clouded by worry. Walking to the dirty window, she tried to conjure his tall form riding along the street. It did not work the first or succeeding three times she stood by the window. It was late: three P.M.

They should have been back by now. She braided and unbraided her hair and changed into riding clothes—a dark blue skirt and silk blouse. She made sure her bags and Nick's were placed near the door. Feeling the security of the pistol in her pocket, she was ready for their quick departure. Perhaps, she decided, she should have her mare saddled. Yes, that's what she would do.

Once downstairs and outside the hotel, Morgan ran to the back of the building.

"What can I do for ya lady?" an old man asked.

"Can you have these two horses saddled?" she pointed to the packhorse and her mare.

"You aren't leaving tonight?"

"I'm not sure. I'm waiting for my husband to return," she stammered.

"Well he didn't return with his two friends. They rode in a few minutes ago."

Those two? Could the Grays have returned without Nicholas?

"No," she whispered, looking about wildly, "that cannot be true."

"Suit yourself, lady. I know what I see," he turned from Morgan's stricken expression.

Climbing the stairs, trying to ignore the feeling of dread that weighed heavily on her small body, Morgan went to her room. Perhaps the old man hadn't seen Nick arrive. Yes, she brightened, that's it. Lifting her skirts, she ran to their room.

"Nick?" she called cheerfully. "Oh Nick, I am so . . ."

"So what, my dear?" Charles held the door open. "So eager for my return?"

"Or mine," Jane added, a slight smile on her otherwise bland face.

"Where is he?" she asked, remaining near the door. "What happened to Nicholas?" she searched their faces.

Charles looked awful. His face was horribly bloodied and bruised and he seemed to be favoring his left side.

"Nicky," she sneered, "could not make the ride back with us."

"Why?"

"He did not feel like traveling."

"Did you know that your lover was double-crossing us?" Charles began. "He had no intention of taking you with him, my dear. Jane and I only have two hundred thousand francs, but I suppose that will have to do," Charles approached her. "Jane and I have to keep a date with a British acquaintance."

"No, that's not . . ."

"How much do you know, Miss Rhinehart?" Jane queried.

"Why, why nothing," one hand rose to her throat. "Nick told me very little. I was hoping for my share of the money . . ." Morgan knew she didn't sound convincing.

"You do not appear dressed for our evening. Rather, it seems to me you are dressed for an outing—or departure?" Charles moved close, almost within touching distance, but Morgan backed up against the door, one hand resting on the knob.

"You are mine for this evening, and each succeeding one if I so desire it," he grinned. "I took quite a beating for you and it had better be worth it."

"Nick already told you, Charles, that I . . ."

"Enough." Jane interrupted. "You can stop playing your little games, dear. The captain is dead."

"What? No, no it isn't true, cannot be. . . . I don't believe you."

"Well, I didn't examine the body. But when we left, he wasn't moving," Charles casually said.

"Or breathing," Jane added. "It was a clean shot."

Refusing to accept their words, Morgan persisted. "Where? Why did you shoot him? He was going to pay you all of the money," she was hysterical.

"No he wasn't. He did not have the money. Besides, we

decided we would rather make a deal with the British. Your lover was expendable." Jane advanced on Morgan, "As are you."

Nick, her mind screamed, you are fine. You must be. Please, I need you. I love you so. Please don't die!

In a flash, Morgan knew what had to be done. She had to escape the Grays and find Nicholas.

"Charles, I thought you and I were to become better acquainted?" she forced a friendly smile. "I don't know what to think any longer."

"Jane," Charles turned to his sister, "you promised I could have her tonight. I won't be denied."

Morgan's eyes darted from one murderer to the other. It was Jane who shot Nicholas—it had to be. The man-hating murderous bitch must have caught him unaware. Think Morgan! You must think, she scolded herself.

"Charles, make her leave. I will stay with you, but I will not share you with her," Morgan said in a voice as firm as Jane's.

"She is mine, Jane. You had your fun, now let me have mine. Wait for me in my room," he instructed.

Morgan feared the worst. Jane would undoubtedly check the bag that held their plates. Would she examine the contents? Did Morgan want to take that chance? Her only chance was to keep the Grays separated. At least until she escaped. And there was only one way to prevent them from coming after her.

Jane reluctantly left. "Watch her, Charles. I don't believe any of her lies. She is in on it I tell you and she wants to save her lover. I'll be waiting up for you Charles," her voice softened.

As soon as the door closed, Morgan casually strode to the bed. "Why don't you get undressed Charles while I pour the drinks. You will share a glass of whiskey with me, won't you? Whiskey always relaxes me. Makes me agreeable too, if you know what I mean." Since her back was turned, Charles could not see her strained expression. "I think you need to clean those horrible cuts and bruises, Charles."

It was evident Charles was ready for her. In a minute, his shirt was off. His breeches were almost undone, when Morgan thought she heard a scratchy sound at the door. Was someone here? Could anyone help her? The barkeep wouldn't, she knew. Perhaps the old man from the stables. She heard it again, but thankfully, Charles did not.

"Are you sure Jane won't come back?" she kept her back to him. "I don't want her in my room."

"You have very little choice, my dear. You are alive because I wish it. So you better be nice to me. I'll see what I can do about my sister." It sounded like he was standing, "Why don't you undress?"

Before Charles could approach, Morgan handed him a drink. "Let's share a couple of drinks first. Then I promise to remove each article of my clothing. Perhaps I will let you assist me. Would you like that, Charles?"

His lascivious grin was sufficient reply. "Come here," he ordered.

He was going to kiss her. She knew it, but wasn't sure how he should respond. She put the drink down. She had to use the pistol; it had better shoot straight. She had only one shot. In that instant Jane would be in the room and Morgan wanted to be on her way out.

"Sit over here," she pointed to the rickety chair. His back was to the door. As Morgan slowly, reluctantly, walked to him, her eyes were on the door.

It was opening—so slowly, it was almost imperceptible. Didn't Charles lock the door? Someone must have a key. No intruder could be worse than what she was about to endure.

Charles's pale eyes were riveted on the silk bodice. To keep him distracted she unfastened the two top buttons. The other hand was inside her skirt pocket, searching for the pistol.

The door opened. A man's ringed hand gripped the side of the door as Morgan almost cried aloud. The anchor ring! It was Nick!

"Charles, tell me what happened. Why did Jane shoot Nicky?"

"How do you know she did it?" he curiously asked.

"She doesn't like men. I think she prefers you to all others. Why should that be Charles?" she reached for the third button.

Nicholas staggered into the room. One look at his bloodied

shoulder—the same shoulder on which she had inflicted a stab
wound—made her sick. The bleeding had not stopped. His
white shirt was almost crimson. He could barely stand.

"Charles, dear. Would you like to make a deal?"

"Don't be idiotic. I don't need to make any deals with you."
He began to rise.

"Yes you do," she allowed a smile, pulling the pistol out of
her pocket, leveling it at his heart. "I think you should remove
your breeches."

"Honey, I was going to . . ."

"Mind if I watch?" Nicholas's voice was a low, pained
sound.

It was all up to Morgan.

"Rhodes!" Charles turned his head, but Morgan would not
let him rise. "What are you . . ."

"Your sister is a poor shot. She missed my heart." Nicholas
leaned against the wall. "You also left my horse. Not very
competent of you, Gray."

"Stay there Nick," Morgan said. "Jane is not here yet."

"Jane won't be joining us Morgan. I saw to her first. I tied
her up," he grinned. "She thought she saw a ghost." He
rasped, "Charles, my wife told you to take off your breeches.
Do it."

"Your wife?" he turned his incredulous eyes to Morgan.

"Love at first sight, Charles. I told you I wanted to propose
deal and I do."

"Why?"

"Because I want you to leave Les Rapides tonight—without
us. But you can have the currency plates." Morgan calmly
stared at Charles, her jaw firmly set.

"I have them."

"No you don't. I do."

"Morgan, what the devil are you saying?" Nick protested.

"Be quiet, Nick. Let me handle this. Keep your gun at his
head please." She found his pistol and handed it to him. Taking
Nick's saddlebag she continued speaking, "The remaining
plates are here. If you want them, I am willing to make a deal."

"What kind of deal?" Charles warily asked.

"A fair one. That must be new to you. I want our money

back. Take the plates and get out of this town. Let me tend to my husband. But you better leave tonight," her voice hardened. "Nick was telling you the truth about his uncle. Eric was here; he'll be back in one hour," she lied smoothly. "If he finds you, Eric won't be as civil or as generous as I am. Jane will be the first one he shoots."

"Morgan, no! Don't give him the plates."

Nick was sagging. His right hand still clutched the bloody shoulder, but it was slipping. Nicholas was losing consciousness. She had to help him; nothing else mattered. Nothing and no one else had ever meant more to her than this golden man, her knight, her husband.

There is only one true overpowering love in a woman's life. Nick was hers. And she could not let him die.

"I will trade you the plates for time. You will get on your horse. When you are ready to ride, I will get Jane. Then and only then will I give you the plates. Take my word, Charles, I do have them. I visited your room today. There were six, neatly wrapped in brown velvet. I guess the British will pay much more than the French. Will you agree to my terms?" she poked the pistol at his bare chest. "I will use this gun, Charles. I will not let my husband die. So," she stood erect, her voice tinged with authority, "what is your decision?"

"Give me the plates. The money is in my room."

"Good. I know the way." Her eyes settled on Nicholas. "Nick? Can you keep an eye on Charles for me?"

"Morgan, you are making a mistake. You want those plates more than . . ."

"No, Nick, I don't. You are wrong. Watch Charles while I ready their horses for their departure." She started for the door, then turned around. "Charles, don't come back. I know you are headed for Natchitoches. I suggest you go there fast. Otherwise, I will tell Eric that you raped me. He is very protective and will definitely seek his own form of vengeance. I don't think you will be pleased with his methods. And after he finishes with you," her smile disappeared, "I will kill you! You are slime, Charles. My father was murdered because of you, my family destroyed.

"But I suppose I should thank you for one thing. I met

461

Nicholas. He promised to help me find you and the plates. And he did. But do you know what?" she shoved the gun deeper into his chest. "It doesn't matter any longer. All I want is for you to be out of our lives." The gun was cocked.

He nervously nodded.

"Morgan, I can handle this scum. I wish he'd give me a reason to shoot him." Nicholas stood without the support of the wall. There was a strange gleam in his eyes. Was it pain or admiration?

Morgan worked faster than she ever thought possible. When both of the Grays were finally mounted—Jane's hands were still bound, her pale eyes alive with hatred—Morgan handed Charles the currency plates.

"It's not over," Jane hissed.

"Oh yes it is. If you value your brother's precious life, believe me it is. I hope you get what you dearly deserve," Morgan looked into the woman's eyes. "I can think of nothing better."

Slapping the horses' rumps, Morgan proudly stood, watching the Grays ride out of her life, hopefully forever.

Racing back to the room, her heart in her throat, she gasped at the sight of Nicholas slumped in the chair. "Nick? Oh my God, Nick? What can I do for you? There is no doctor in town. Tell me what to do," she knelt before him.

A rising fever glazed his eyes. Nicholas whispered, "You shouldn't have done that, Morgan. I know how badly you wanted the plates. Why did you . . ."

This was not the time for confessions. "It doesn't matter," she replied, smoothing the wet hair off his warm brow. "What matters is you. Now tell me, did the bullet pass through your shoulder?"

"No," he grimaced, "that's the problem. It has to come out."

"Let me help you," she struggled under his weight, leading him to the bed.

Moving quickly, Morgan washed the bloody shoulder, sickened by the blackened area, the ugly hole, the blood. But she felt his eyes on her face and would not reveal how scared she was. Gently, she tore the blood-stained shirt, trying not to touch his wound.

"There must be someone who can help. I don't think I can do it. I can't hurt you, Nick!" She bathed his shoulder again, ignoring the soft groan.

"Hold this against your shoulder. I'll be right back."

Morgan found the barkeep, but he was in no position to assist her. It was almost dark. The nearest town, Alexandria, was too far to reach at night. Taking a knife, whiskey, and white linen, she charged back into their room, but stopped short.

Nicholas was unconscious. The blood was still oozing. Think, Morgan, do something. The knife had to be sterilized. Morgan prayed that Nicholas would remain unconscious. She couldn't contend with his struggling body and the knife.

Perspiration soaked her blouse and brow. "Here we go, my love," she whispered, the knife poised for incision.

"Don't do it Morgan! Don't!" a stern voice commanded.

"Eric! Thank God it's you." The knife dropped on the bed. She ran into his arms. "Oh thank God. Please, please Eric. We must save his life!"

Eric, his clothing covered in dust and grime, rushed to the bed. "How long has he been this way?"

"A few hours. He was shot this afternoon. How he managed to ride back here in that condition is beyond me. We must do something, Eric."

Eric kneeled beside his nephew. "I've only done this twice before." His brows furrowed in concentration and pain. He picked up the knife. "Is this all you could find?"

"It's the best I could do."

"I must wash. Morgan, you have no idea what kind of impression you made when I walked in. All I saw was you leaning over his prone body. I thought Nick was sleeping and you were going to stab him. I saw your back and hand raised with the knife and," he laughed, "I jumped to the wrong conclusion. I just didn't think."

"Eric, I should be furious with you, but I won't be—not tonight. Wait until tomorrow. Nick will . . ." she caught herself, realizing how absurd this was.

"Nick will be fine. Watch me, Morgan. I'll need your help."

463

Probing his shoulder, Eric jumped when Nick groaned. "It's deep, but I can get it out."

They worked side by side for at least one hour; Morgan dabbing Nick's brow, Eric probing for one lead bullet. They did not speak or look at one another.

Aside from his moans, Nicholas blessedly did not struggle. However, when the knife dug very deeply into his shoulder, he screamed, "No! No, Morgan." He pleaded to a phantom, his hand moving to thwart the knife.

"Morgan," Eric looked sideways, seeing her horrified expression, "don't pay any attention to him. He's delirious."

"I know. But Eric, I did stab him you know. Not tonight, but nearly two weeks ago. Same spot. Nick must be remembering that day."

"Morgan, you've got to try to hold him down. Talk to him Morgan. Soothe him."

Leaning forward, her mouth touched his temple. "Nick? Please listen to me. I want you to listen. Eric is here, Nick. I am here. We want to help you. More than anything, Nick, we want you to help us. Please lie still. Trust me. Let Eric remove the bullet. We want you to help us." She kept repeating these words.

It seemed to work. Nicholas's head moved toward her calming voice. "We love you Nick. Please, help us." Morgan saw Eric's pursed lips and knew what was about to happen.

"Hold him down, Morgan."

"Nick, I have to hold you. This is going to hurt. Let me hold you." Moving to the opposite side of Eric, she pressed Nick's right shoulder into the bed. "Trust me, Nick."

She might have been roughly tossed across the room, but Nicholas responded as he was instructed.

"A little longer, Morgan," Eric encouraged. "Keep him still."

"I love you, Nicholas. I am sorry for what I put you through. I wish you could hear me," a tear slid onto his warm cheek. "I remember the very first time I saw you. I was lying in your bed in the cabin of the *Anastasia*. I opened my eyes and saw the most handsome man I had ever seen. I think I fell in love with you then," she kissed his face.

Were her eyes blinded by tears, or did she see him smile? Whatever occurred, it did not last long. Eric's final plunge pushed Nicholas into unconsciousness. He did not feel the alcohol burn his skin.

"Ah, it's out. We are lucky Morgan." Eric broadly grinned, tossing the bullet into a can. "So is my nephew. I got the whole bullet. I don't think there is going to be any fatal infection. But from the looks of him, his fever has risen."

"What can we do?" she whispered, her eyes never leaving Nick's face.

"We'll simply have to wait. We must sponge him to get the fever down. We can't move him."

"Should we find a doctor in Alexandria?"

"I don't think it's necessary, but we'll have to wait." Eric noted her pallid face, bloodied hands, and soiled blouse. "Why don't you wash and change your clothes. Perhaps you can order some food. We'll spend this night together and you, young lady," his blue eyes deepened, "have a lot of explaining to do." He took Morgan's trembling hand, "You'll never guess who my newest houseguests are."

"This is not the moment for games, Eric," she sighed dispiritedly.

"Your mother and sister are in New Orleans, in my home. I thought it best—under the circumstances."

"Oh God," she cradled her head, "I completely forgot! Here? They are here for my wedding to Ian."

"I know dear. Please Morgan, you look faint. I cannot take care of both of you. Do as I say and then we'll talk. I wonder if any of this makes sense?"

"I will tell you one thing," Morgan tenderly looked at Nicholas, "it's all his fault."

Chapter 35

It was a long, restless night for the unconscious patient and an even longer night for the two people watching over him.

As calmly and coherently as she could, Morgan told Eric all that had happened since the day Nicholas kidnapped her.

It took some restraint on his part not to interrupt. There were many things he should have said, but Morgan was far too distraught to consider Eric's words or advice seriously. Her eyes and thoughts were riveted on Nicholas. She ate quickly, but immediately returned to Nick's side, sponging his brow, whispering encouraging words.

To Eric's amazement, Nick remained still. Perhaps he did hear Morgan calling to him, comforting him in a way only a woman deeply in love could.

"Eric, I am sure you think I'm out of my mind for letting the Grays leave with the plates. Nick couldn't understand it. But I had to do it. I had nothing more important to bargain with."

She stood by the washstand, rinsing the cloth. Dressed in the same light blue riding skirt and silk blouse she had worn earlier, Morgan looked haggard. Hair fell carelessly around her face, her hands were red and chapped from the cool water, her eyes a dull amber. She had the posture of a defeated woman; Eric knew he could not allow it.

"Morgan, let me tell you what has happened since your hasty' departure. The most pleasant news is that I entertained our mother and sister as best I could; I answered endless questions about you, Nick, and Ian. I even tried to console Ian,

467

who was first frantic then livid when he found out what Nick had done.

"I assume Nick told you I was on the way. I rode two hundred miles to find you—Nick's directions were unclear. But did you know that I sent Gordon and a very expensive Indian tracker into Natchitoches?"

"I don't understand," she began to show interest.

"We rode together but split up in Alexandria. They are probably ahead of the Grays. But I guarantee that the Grays will be found in Natchitoches. The Grays wouldn't consider our being ahead of them. I told you before dear," Eric rose placing a comforting hand on Morgan's arm, "I want to find the traitors as much as I wanted to find your father's murderer. I won't let them go."

"It would be nice to find them," she responded absent mindedly.

Eric could see he was getting nowhere in his efforts to lift her spirits. "Your mother is a very pretty woman."

"She is, isn't she?" Morgan turned to look at Eric.

"And your sister could be you—except for the brown curly hair. Quite an imp," he smiled.

"How I have missed them, Eric. Well, I am glad you like them. I think—at this rate—they will be in your home for a few more weeks. It was so kind of you to invite them."

"I couldn't allow them to stay in a hotel or at the Kendalls. It was no imposition, believe me." He laughed. "I've rather enjoyed it."

She briefly brightened. "Eric, don't tell me . . ."

"Tell you what?"

"Don't feign ignorance with me. Remember, you're very much like our patient over there. You liked them! I mean you really got a taste of family life, didn't you? And it didn't frighten you."

"Well no," he nervously coughed, "it didn't."

"Eric Rhodes," she threw herself into his arms, "I love you."

The laughter suddenly turned to tears when Morgan looked at Nicholas. "Oh Eric. I am so frightened for him. He is so flushed and feverish; I cannot let anything happen to him," she clutched Eric's shirt.

With a knowing smile, he asked, "Will you admit it now?"

Raising her tear-stained face, she nodded and said, "I love him so much." She sniffled, accepting the handkerchief Eric offered. "When he told me about his feelings, his regrets, his love, I refused to accept his words." Her eyes filled again, "Eric, I have not been fair to him at all. I only want to have the chance to tell him."

"You will, my dear. Believe me, you will," he stroked her hair paternally.

Morgan was dozing in the bed beside Nicholas. Eric was sleeping in a chair, his feet propped up on the bed.

Nicholas moved about restlessly. As soon as he did, Morgan's cool hand rested on his hot brow.

"Eric," she cast a worried look, "he's warmer than before. Shouldn't his fever break soon? How much higher can it go before it, I mean he . . ."

"I said not to worry," he tried to sound convincing. "I'm sure his fever will go down."

"I pray that's so." She kept her hand on his cheek, but Nick threw it off when he tossed onto his side.

"Morgan? Morgan, why aren't you . . ." Nicholas began to mumble.

"What? Nicholas, tell me what you want," she kneeled before him.

His head moved from side to side, his eyes opening intermittently.

"I need Morgan. Oh God, why won't you believe me?" he sighed.

"I am here, Nick. I believe you." She smoothed his hair, "I need you too. Can you hear me?"

"Morgan, why?"

"I wish he could understand," she said to Eric.

"Morgan?" it was barely a whisper, "I . . ."

"Nicholas. Please listen to me. I am here. So is Eric. We want to help you. We love you," she motioned to Eric to say something.

"Nick, lad. You've had a nasty wound. You're making Morgan frantic with worry, lad. So why don't you fight this fever and get well."

For the next two hours Morgan alternated between mopping his face and whispering in his ear.

"You must get well. Damn you Nicholas. You must listen to me. I said I love you. But if you don't come out of this, you'll never hear me say these words again." She stopped listening to her absurd words.

"Eric, I think I am going crazy. He's unconscious, raving about who knows what, and I am scolding him for having a fever. I must be the one who is feverish," she mused.

"Whatever it is, my dear, it seems to be having some effect on him. Look," Eric smiled, "he's stopped fighting us."

Not sure of what she was saying or thinking, Morgan looked longingly at the strong man who had gone through such hell— all because of her.

"He did it for me, Eric. All along Nick tried to tell me. No, Nicholas showed me how much he cared. I think I was too selfish and stupid to see the obvious."

"Only naive. My nephew is strong, stubborn, overpowering, and amazingly, hardheaded. You've stood up to him, Morgan. You gave him what he richly deserved. But now, my dear," Eric took her hand, "you must decide what you want, or rather you must decide who you want. Nicholas or Ian. No one can help you make that decision."

"Don't you think I know?" she cried, staring at Nick.

As if sensing her turmoil, Nicholas called out weakly, "Morgan? Are you here?" His right hand moved, "Morgan?"

Taking his hand in both of hers, she kissed his fingers. "I am here, darling. I will not leave you."

Struggling to open his eyes, the first sight that greeted Nicholas was his Morgan, lovingly staring at him, smiling at him—that dazzling smile he loved.

"Ah, my Morgan. You haven't left me yet."

"No, Nick. I'm not leaving. I want to stay with you—always. I love you, Nicholas. Can you understand that now?"

"Mmm," he smiled, closing his eyes once more. "I love you, too, you know. Always have . . . and always . . ."

"Will," she finished for him. Nicholas appeared to be asleep. It was a promising sign. He would get well; she was confident of that.

"Eric, I need a drink. Would you care to join me?" she blew her nose in the soiled handkerchief.

"There's still some whiskey left. It's not very good, but it sure as hell is strong!" he chuckled.

"Perfect. I propose a toast," she grabbed the bottle, not bothering to find a glass. "To Captain Nicholas Rhodes. To his health."

Morgan took a full swig and when she did not cough, she proudly wiped her mouth with the back of her hand—the way Nick often did. "I am beginning to like this brew. Here," she offered Eric the bottle, "please join me."

Nicholas awoke to the noise in the street below. All he could hear was two men arguing over the value of either a horse or a woman. The words were not clear enough for him to decipher. He had no idea of the hour of day, for the sky was a cloudy gray. But Lord from the way his body felt—sore all over, especially his left shoulder—Nicholas felt he must have slept two days.

Gingerly moving his head, he saw Morgan curled in a tight ball on the bed, her head resting on one hand. She was fully clothed, except for boots; her hair was tangled, the silk blouse rumpled. She was breathing heavily, and Nicholas could swear that from this distance he could smell whiskey on her breath.

Looking past Morgan, Nicholas smiled. Eric was uncomfortably slouched in the rickety wooden chair, but his head and arms were on the bed—not far from Morgan's feet.

If they looked that awful, he must look a hell of a lot worse. Stiff and uncomfortable, Nicholas was chary of shifting his body weight. The thick wadding of cloth at his shoulder prevented too much movement. From the looks of things, they sorely needed sleep.

Eyes closing once more, Nicholas forced himself to recall yesterday's events.

After leaving with the Grays, he had been confident that Morgan would find the plates and be ready to depart as soon as he returned.

Perhaps, he realized now, his confidence had been his undoing. It did not occur to him that once the Grays led him to Alan Sterling's grave, they would try to kill him too.

Nicholas had given Charles another one hundred thousand francs. Eric was supposed to bring the balance the following day.

"You'll have to wait for him, Charles. I'm leaving with the plates and my woman."

"I thought you said I can have her for the night?"

"Yes, I did and you can." Nicholas decided that if necessary, he would kill Charles Gray before he touched Morgan. "But I also said she is leaving in the morning, with me."

It was at that moment Nicholas realized his mistake—perhaps a fatal one. In his haste to depart, he had stupidly left his pistol in the hotel room. All he had with him was his knife and a rifle that was on the horse.

"Where are the plates, Charles? I've grown weary of the game. I want to go back to town."

"Why?" Jane had startled him. "Why are you in such a rush? There's nothing there for you." She partially stood behind her brother. "Unless you mean that harlot you conveniently left behind."

"Do you have the plates?" he asked again.

"Yes, I have them. But since you haven't paid me all the money, I don't think I should give you the plates."

Brother and sister continued to stare at Nicholas. There was no point in remaining any longer. He had given Morgan more than enough time to find those plates—if they were in the hotel. Nicholas considered his alternatives.

If he jumped Charles now, what guarantee was there that the plates could be recovered? That left Jane—whose wild-eyed look unnerved him. With only his knife as protection, Nicholas didn't have a way to neutralize a pistol.

Nicholas wanted Charles alive. He wanted Charles arrested, tried, and hung—in Philadelphia. It was the only way to vindicate fully the name of Samuel Rhinehart.

If fighting was ruled out, all that was left was his cunning.

"Listen to me, Charles. I told you I had some of the money.

But it's not my money. I don't give a damn about saving some of Napoleon's francs. I only want my share. The emperor will pay my uncle and me when I hand him all twelve plates." Nicholas inched toward the horse, hoping to even the odds by getting the rifle.

"Don't move, Captain," Jane held a pistol to Nicholas's chest. He could barely see her eyes, which were shaded by a large brown hat.

"You don't think we believe anything you say. But three things are clear," Charles paused for emphasis. "I will have your woman; I will have the money; and last, you are not coming back with us."

Like a panther leaping on its prey, Nicholas suddenly crouched low then sprang on Charles Gray.

Surprised, unarmed, and far less strong than Nicholas, Charles knew he had no chance.

"Shoot Jane!" he yelled, rolling on the dirt. Nicholas's fists pummeled his stomach and face.

Nicholas heard the command but knew his chances were better if he tried to subdue Charles. Jane could not shoot her brother—not as long as he struggled with Nicholas.

But Jane was not in control of her emotions. All she saw was this giant man, hell bent on murdering her brother. A red haze filled her brain and clouded her eyes.

"Stop it," she shouted, "get off my brother!" The gun was pointed at the men. She leaned forward, waiting until Nicholas hauled the barely conscious Charles onto his feet.

Nicholas was standing, clasping Charles's shirt at the neck, his right hand pulled back for the final blow.

"No!" she stepped closer, aimed at Nicholas's heart, and pulled the trigger.

It all happened within seconds; Morgan's smiling face flashed before his eyes. Nicholas sank onto the hard ground, barely conscious, clutching his left shoulder. He did see the two people stand over him and he heard their grating voices. They said he would die, and for a moment, he was sure they were right. The bullet was lodged high in his left shoulder—almost exactly where Morgan had stabbed him.

Charles's swift kick to his side made Nicholas groan. "Sorry,

473

Captain. But I don't think I want to deal with you any longer. I think I will take what's left though," Charles held the leather bag with the money, "including your woman."

"It shouldn't be a slow death," Jane laughed. "Should I shoot him again Charles?"

"No. Let him think about his life. I hate to kill in cold blood." He wiped his bleeding lip.

They rode off, leaving Nicholas to die. So confident were they of his fate that they stupidly left Nicholas's stallion.

Only one thought registered in his pain-filled mind. Morgan would be at the mercy of those two murderers. There was little hope she could survive. Jane Gray would not let her remain alive.

Nicholas clawed his way to his horse, then tore the bottom of his shirt and placed it over the wound. Above all, he could not allow the blackness to claim him. "You must stay alert," he mumbled.

He kept talking to himself, willing himself not to succumb to the pain.

How he managed to get onto the stallion he did not know. But he slowly made his way back to town. He must have blacked out several times, but tenaciously clung to the horse's neck. If he let go, Morgan would be at their mercy. He could not let go. It was that simple.

Amazingly, he made it. Staggering into the cantina, he found Jane Gray first, wanting to kill her with his bloody hands. Stunned, she did not move as Nicholas advanced menacingly.

"You are insane. I believe I will kill you. If not today, then soon enough. Always watch your back," he vowed, his voice barely audible. Despite his failing strength, Nicholas had to refrain from breaking Jane's neck and be satisfied with a forceful clip to her jaw. He left her sprawled on the floor of the room, her hands and feet neatly bound.

When he had found Morgan trapped by Charles's odious voice and sexual demands, he fought to stay alert. So far, she was unharmed. Somewhat relieved, Nicholas leaned against the wall.

When she noticed him, Nicholas felt a renewed surge of strength. Did she see him wink encouragingly at her? She faced

Charles with a steely determination. All Nicholas needed was time to gather his strength and to dispatch Charles. But he was stunned by her next words. Why would she make a deal with Gray? Why?

Who did she think she was bargaining for? Certainly not for me, he thought. He may not have been thinking clearly, but he objected to Morgan's words.

Ignoring his protest, Morgan continued to negotiate with Charles Gray. Why? Why would she give up those precious plates that meant everything to her?

There was no time for talk. Nicholas was too weak for further protest. Left alone with Gray, he pretended to be strong. As long as he had the wall for support, he could manage.

"Charles, if I were you I would leave this town," he said, pointing the pistol at his head. "I would love to kill you," he paused for breath. "But this is my wife's decision. However, I will find you and the plates. You can count on that."

"Not in your condition you won't," Charles sneered, rising out of the chair.

The pistol was cocked and Nicholas stood unaided. Damn Morgan's deals, he should kill the bastard now, keep the plates, and wait for Eric.

It finally dawned on Charles that Nicholas had every intention of killing him. "Don't do it Rhodes. Please," he begged.

Nicholas was beyond reasoning. Luckily for Charles, Morgan bustled into the room to dissuade Nicholas.

"Come on Charles. I think it's time for you to leave," she said, none too kindly.

Charles and Jane Gray rode out of Les Rapides with the currency plates, Morgan's only hope for vindication of her name. Nicholas's last conscious thought was that she had been magnificent.

Much later he had heard words, soothing, loving words, a few harsh commands. There was Eric's voice, and Morgan's soft kisses. Somehow, he knew it wasn't a fevered dream. Her cool hand on his temple soothed him more than laudanum could.

She had told him she loved him. But Nick, he asked himself do you love Morgan enough to give her the life and peace she deserves, the kind of life only Ian Kendall could provide?

These thoughts kept him awake and saddened him. As soon as he was able to ride, Nicholas would find the plates. He knew now that Morgan had given up the plates for him. To buy insurance on his life. It was a selfless gesture, an act of love.

When he retrieved the plates, he would let Morgan go.

"Damn," he cursed aloud.

"Nick? Nick, what's wrong? Oh thank God you're awake Eric," she called joyously, "he's awake."

Morgan kneeled before him, checking his brow and shoulder, fighting the urge to throw herself into his arms.

"You're still feverish. But," she grinned, "I believe you will live to scold me. I am so glad," she smiled.

"Seems like she said it all, lad." Eric also grinned.

"If I look half as bad as you two, I know I'll be fine. Uncle Eric," he rasped, "you've got great timing."

"I know."

Nicholas did not know that he held Morgan's hand. "Will you answer a question?" His eyes focused on Eric.

"Of course."

"When can we get out of this town?"

"Whenever I think you can ride, my love," Morgan answered for Eric.

Less than two days later, Nicholas was out of bed and prepared to go after the Grays—although his left shoulder and arm would remain bandaged and in a sling for a few more weeks. He had had a lot of time in that bed, time to think about Morgan's sacrifice.

"What are you doing, lad?" Eric found Nicholas testing his sore muscles.

"I'm ready to leave, Eric, as I assume you and Morgan are." Nicholas was dressed in nankeen breeches, but the blue cotton shirt was half on. Eric had to assist him with the left sleeve.

"Yes, of course. But don't you think it's too soon for you? We're talking about an arduous trip, lad. You know how difficult the roads are. Perhaps you need . . ."

"No, I don't," he interrupted in a clear, strong voice. "I've been in this bed long enough. I am going to Natchitoches."

"You are not!" Morgan joined the conversation.

She had taken over his life, feeding him, bathing him, sitting with him while he dozed. They had spoken of superficial things. Nicholas knew Morgan was waiting for him to talk about their future—together. Somehow he could not summon the courage to say what was best for her. Once he did, she would be out of his life—forever.

How can a person let go of something or someone that has become an integral part of his life? It had to be done; yet each day he postponed the inevitable.

Morgan, however, would not be put off. Perhaps they knew each other too well. "Nicholas, I would like to speak to you alone."

Knowing what was about to happen, Eric hastily made an excuse to leave the room.

Nicholas stiffly sat on the edge of the bed. Morgan stood near the bureau. Her hair was neatly pulled back, secured by tortoiseshell combs. She was wearing the familiar black breeches and pink silk blouse—an odd combination, he thought. Each was poised and ready for verbal conflict.

"Why won't you talk to me Nicholas? For two days you have avoided what is uppermost on our minds."

Why did she have to be so damn beautiful, he thought. And defiant.

"You are right, Morgan. I've been avoiding the subject," he looked into her puzzled face.

"Why?"

"For two days I have thought of nothing else but you. You and me. You and Ian. I think you know that I love you." He saw her nod. "I love you more than my life, Morgan. And because I feel this strongly, I know I must do something for you."

Morgan's spirits lifted. He was going to propose again. No longer speaking in delirium, anger, or passion, Nick was going to explain how they were destined to be together. She couldn't contain her buoyancy.

It almost broke his resolve. "Morgan, you deserve happiness, security, and love with a man who can give it all to

477

you. You made a tremendous sacrifice for me—after all I have done to you. I still can't really understand," he paused, his eyes turning to dark gray. "You amaze me, woman. You have changed so much in one year and I love you more each day."

"Oh, Nick," she started toward him, expecting to be taken into his arms, but he motioned her to stop.

"Let me finish. What I am trying to say is this. You deserve better than me. Marry Ian Kendall," he rushed on, ignoring her gasp of surprise. "He will take care of you, cherish you. I think you love him in a way. I know it differs from your feelings for me. But I believe that Ian will make you happier than I can."

"How can you say such nonsense!" she heatedly replied. "No one can make me happier than you. I only want your love. What I sacrificed was meaningless compared to all you have given and done for me." Morgan tried to catch her breath, but could not contain her anger. She stood before him. "I should be begging you for forgiveness, Nick. I was wrong," she patted her chest. "You never used me, yet I accused you of doing so many things. I was wrong, don't you see?" she pleaded.

"No. I have made up my mind," his right hand clutched the mattress. He sounded less sure of himself than before.

"Nicholas, I love you. I have always loved you. I can't stop loving you because you say so—because you think I belong with Ian. I know where I belong, Nick. It's with you. I won't let you walk out on me. And don't for one minute think I am walking away from you because you demand it. You're a fool!" she panted.

"Wait one minute." Nicholas suddenly stopped feeling sorry for himself and found that he was angry with this minx.

"No, you wait one minute," she advanced, raising one fist before him. "You are going to marry me. The only choice you have is where. In Alexandria, Natchitoches, or New Orleans. I will not go back to New York or Boston unless I am legally your wife!" She stomped across the room and returned to glare at him.

"Morgan, you are unreasonable. Think. What about Ian?"

"I know Nick. But should I marry Ian and make him unhappy because I don't love him the way I love you? Should

478

I? Is that fair to Ian? Doesn't he deserve a love like ours?"

"Well," he hesitated, and at that moment Morgan knew it was a matter of time before Nicholas completely gave in. Trying to hide her smile, she said, "Nick, why don't we walk outside. I think you could use some exercise."

"There you go again," he flared. "Listen to me, woman. Stop telling me what to do." He rose to stand before her menacingly.

She was unfazed. "Yes, Nicholas."

Lifting her chin with one finger, he saw the amber eyes beseeching him. "You don't fool me for a moment, madam."

His loving expression sent a longing tremor through her.

"Will you please give up, Nick? I am not leaving you." Morgan wrapped her arms around his waist, careful not to jar his shoulder.

"Not ever, huh?" he spoke into her hair, inhaling the jasmine scent that was so much a part of her.

"You still haven't answered my question," she said.

"Which question? You've said so many things, how can I recall which question was left unanswered?"

Not flinching, Morgan boldly met his eyes. "Where are we getting married, here or in New Orleans?"

They clung to one another for a long time. Neither wanted to let go of the complete joy they were sharing.

"Morgan, my love, I swear I will never hurt or mislead you again. But I want to know that you trust me." He held her at arm's length.

She looked in his glistening eyes. There was a hint of a tear or two, but Morgan could not believe it was possible. "I trust you Nicholas. And I love you too."

"I can't make you promise to obey me though, can I?"

"No. Can I ask the same of you?"

"No. But you know, Morgan, if you were a man you would make a superb lawyer," he chuckled. "You could don those breeches and use that artificial bass voice of yours."

A soft knock on the door reminded them that Eric was still in the hotel.

"Well, is it safe to come in?" Since he hadn't heard any shouting, he immediately thought that they were either making love or one had left in anger. Hearing softly spoken words through the door prompted him to act. Perhaps Morgan needed his help in convincing Nick that she had no intention of leaving without him.

"Ah hah!" he beamed. "She finally got you to see what is right. You've had her on pins and needles for the last two days, lad, with your sullen moods. I thought it would take a lot longer to make you see the light of day."

"Have you been scheming with this, this meddling, crusty old sailor, Morgan? Has he been telling you lies?" Nicholas's exuberance was contagious.

"He told me I would be a fool not to see how much you love me. He told me we would both be—if you pardon the expression—jackasses if we didn't marry again. Is that meddling?" she innocently asked.

"Yes. But I am grateful for everything, Uncle Eric," Nicholas's eyes brightened again. "Damn, it must be the fever."

Morgan hugged him. "Nick? You are wonderful. But since you haven't answered my original question, I will answer it for us. Let's marry in New Orleans. I think I can trust you long enough to remain unwed for two more weeks. Can't I?"

"I suppose it would be nice to have your mother and sister joining Eric and us for the second wedding. You will join us, Eric?" he laughed.

"I must. Someone has to make sure everything is legal and binding this time."

Chapter 36

LATE APRIL, 1809

All that remained of the early morning rainstorm was a light drizzle. Moisture glistened on the magnolia trees, while the light breeze rustled the scented flowers.

Morgan awoke to featherlike kisses raining along her neck and bare chest.

"Come on, beauty, today's your second or third wedding day. Don't forget this day, Saturday, April 22." His rakish smile reminded Morgan of the last few nights together.

Although they were to be married again, they could not tolerate the idea of sleeping apart. Nicholas had given Eric a choice: Either he and Morgan stayed in Eric's home or aboard the *Anastasia*. Eric willingly offered his large master bedsuite and would have gladly left them locked in there until the day of the wedding.

Unfortunately, there were too many things to do. Ian Kendall was the first person Morgan sought out as soon as they had returned from Les Rapides.

Morgan knew she had to see Ian soon. They had arrived in New Orleans late Monday night. Lizzie was asleep. Charlotte greeted her daughter with tears, laughter, and one brief lecture. At that moment, Morgan finally discovered who had purchased the house in Boston, and she cried all over again in tender love. Exhausted but ready to face the next day's problems, Morgan begged Nick to let her face Ian—alone.

Agreeing reluctantly, Nicholas went with Eric to see Governor Claiborne. While there, he discussed the fate of the Grays, who were returned to Philadelphia from Natchitoches after being apprehended. Under arrest and facing charges of treason, the couple remained under heavy guard. They were to be tried in Philadelphia, in the same courtroom in which Samuel Rhinehart had been tried. Nicholas briefly pondered the fate of the Grays, hoping their trial would bring peace to the three Rhinehart women.

He believed this could be accomplished if he obtained the stolen currency plates. He convinced the governor to grant him the privilege of returning the eight authentic currency plates to Secretary of State Albert Gallatin. Since the New Orleans plates were counterfeit, Governor Claiborne had no cause to keep them.

Nicholas had specific plans for those plates. Only after the wedding, after they were safely aboard the *Anastasia* bound for New York, would he tell Morgan about them. She seemed to have forgotten the whole episode. As far as Morgan was concerned, the Grays and the currency plates were a closed chapter. Her family and her man were all she needed. The courts could handle the rest. Nicholas was willing to take Morgan to Philadelphia for the trial, but she quietly refused.

"It's all over, Nick," she said. "I want to put the whole thing behind us now," she wound her arms around his neck. "I want to plan for the future with you. That's what matters to me now."

How could he argue with that logic? Perhaps she was right. It was time to bury the past. Eric had told him the same thing the other day when they talked about Warren Rhodes.

"It's time, lad. You have another chance with Morgan. No more grudges—no more anger. Make peace with your father, Nicholas."

Should he? Could he forget that disastrous January night in New York? Yes, he could, provided that Morgan was accepted. He would settle for little else, although Nicholas doubted that Warren Rhodes would receive Morgan with enthusiasm. As long as she was not hurt again. Above all else, Morgan would be protected, loved, and cherished.

For both Morgan and Nicholas there was unfinished business to attend to before they could marry. Morgan had to see Ian Kendall. Nicholas could never understand how much Ian and his family had done for her. But Morgan deeply appreciated their generosity.

Morgan had requested a private meeting with Ian at his home. Afterwards she wanted to speak with the Kendalls. Ian greeted her at the door. As always, his dark hair was neatly combed, his clothing perfectly tailored. His hazel eyes glowed with warmth, but Morgan sensed the pain in his facial expression and she fought the urge to cry.

"Ian, I am here for many reasons, among them to beg for your forgiveness," she sat primly on the gold settee, in the same room where Ian had proposed to her. Morgan took extra time to remove her gloves.

"I was wrong, cherie. I was wrong to think you could ever forget him. Nick knew it, he told me so. I did not want to believe him."

"I think I should explain everything," she nervously slapped the gloves against her pink muslin dress.

"Morgan," Ian took her cold hand, "I could make it hard for you, but there is no reason. You know how deeply I care. Yet you were honest about your feelings for me. My love for you does not disappear overnight, nor did it in the four weeks you were gone. But I think I know what happened between you and Nick."

"Ian, I never wanted to go with him."

"I know that too. You fought your feelings for him. You did it for me. I think, cherie," he softly smiled, "you did care for me a little."

"Ian, I care for you a lot," she squeezed his hand. "I never wanted to hurt you. I shall never forgive myself, Ian. This is my pain. I had no right . . ."

"Please, Morgan. It is I who had no right. Nick never wanted you to leave him. My friend is very tough, very stubborn, and very much in love with you. I took the last opportunity left to me by offering you my home at a time when you had none. I thought you could forget him."

"He's not easy to forget," she felt the color rise in her face.

483

"I would like to give this to you, Ian. I have no way of paying you for all that you and your family have done for me. Don't say it," she placed two fingers on his mouth before he could protest, "let me finish. I cannot keep these magnificent jewels," she took the topaz and diamond necklace and ear bobs from her reticule. "Please, give them to the right woman." Morgan put the jewels in his hand.

"I did. Morgan, I bought those jewels for you, with your face in mind. Until I find another golden-eyed, black-haired siren, I want you to keep them. Think of me with affection whenever you wear them."

"I don't need jewelry to remember you, Ian," her eyes glistened with unshed tears. "I have nothing to give you in return."

"You have, cherie, believe me."

She had broken his heart, broken her vow to him, yet he sat calmly before her, smiling. "Please know that I will always be there for you, Morgan, as a friend."

"I don't deserve your friendship. I do love you Ian." Her voice filled with emotion, Morgan tried to smile.

"I know. It's not the same feeling you have for your fearless pirate."

She reached for him, embracing Ian not in passion but in love and friendship. "Promise me, Ian Kendall, that if you ever need or want me for anything, you will have no qualms about contacting me. Do you promise?" she searched his face.

"Yes, cherie. He is a damn lucky man, you know."

Morgan remained in his fond embrace, wondering if any woman was as fortunate as she to have known a man like Ian Kendall.

The interview with the family was equally painful.

Morgan solemnly stood before Marie and Paul Kendall, explaining as much as she could about her marriage to Nicholas Rhodes. She tried to explain what she barely understood; their lives were intricately woven together.

"You have been my family when I needed one most. I hope you can forgive me someday."

She did not ask for more than that. Shoulders slumped in regret, Morgan left the Kendall home.

484

When she returned to Eric's house, she headed directly for the bedroom.

Tiptoeing into the room, Nicholas saw her lying perfectly still on the bed, staring at the white-beamed ceiling. "Morgan, my love," he sat beside her, "I know it was hard. Do you want to talk about it?" He rubbed her arm comfortingly.

"No, no. I don't think I should. I've done a terrible deed. I shall have to live with that guilt, Nick. It wouldn't be fair to ask you to share it," she focused on his concerned face. "It was all my doing."

"Not quite, beauty. I have something to do with this. So, by the way, does Ian. You can claim some responsibility but not all." He kissed her hands. "I will be downstairs when you are ready to join me," he said before leaving the room quietly.

Nicholas understood her pain but could not take it away. With time, Morgan would forgive herself.

Her melancholy lessened as the days passed. There was a wedding to prepare for. There was the man of her dreams, waiting for her again. They would let nothing stand in the way of their happiness.

Although Nicholas's shoulder was still bandaged, he discarded the sling on the day of his wedding.

On Saturday morning, April 22, 1809, Nicholas and Morgan were joined in marriage. Witnessing the event were Eric, Lizzie, and Charlotte.

Nicholas had insisted she have a new gown made for the occasion, no matter the cost. It was worth it. Seeing her in a gown of pale yellow silk with white lace trimming, wearing a matching hat on top of her loosely bound ebony hair, Nicholas knew he would never grow tired of living with and loving this woman. When he lifted the white lace veil from her face and proudly kissed her soft lips, he wished the moment would last forever.

But Lizzie would not be denied her congratulations. She was ecstatic. In her child's mind, no man could ever match Captain Nick—except, of course, Captain Eric. Of late, Eric Rhodes had been spending a good deal of time with Charlotte.

"I haven't seen my mother this happy in so long, Nick, it makes me want to cry," Morgan said after the ceremony. Eric

485

was holding Charlotte's arm while Lizzie clung to his other outstretched hand.

Morgan and Nicholas Rhodes did not stay in Eric's house that night. Instead, Nicholas gave the entire crew of the *Anastasia* shore leave. He and Morgan would share this night in their cabin with the lace-curtained window.

"I love this ship, Nick."

"No more than I. Someday soon, I hope she can sail proudly on the open seas, without the American patrols to avoid. However, Eric and I plan on building more ships. The Embargo Act will not last much longer. I want to be prepared. With Peter Mackenzie and Eric Rhodes as partners, I believe I will have an advantage over every merchant in the United States."

It was the first of many conversations they would share. To Morgan, her husband seemed at peace with himself. Of course the reckless rogue and fearless smuggler were a part of his personality, but so were the tender lover and compassionate man. He had become the dear friend who could listen, laugh, and discuss the trivial and important things with her. He had become the man she could trust; her lover, her friend, her hero—her husband.

It was with renewed spirit and confidence that the *Anastasia* boldly sailed into New York Harbor on April 29.

"Nick, don't you think this is a little dangerous?" she asked, standing by his side on the quarterdeck. "I mean aren't you carrying some French items in the hold?"

"I sold most of them in New Orleans. The cargo I am carrying will not cause any trouble. I purchased most of it in New Orleans. Besides, the patrols are not expecting us in New York."

"Why?"

"Because the *Christine* will be making the run to Halifax. And, well," he grinned down at her, pressing Morgan against him, "since the *Christine* and the *Anastasia* look identical, I've allowed some to think this ship is halfway to Halifax. By the time the patrols realize what is happening, we will be at sea again—with cargo, of course."

"Nicholas," she looked mutinous, "I don't understand. And

I think you want it that way. Are you sailing to Halifax without me?"

"Never," he squeezed her waist. "In fact, I've thought about letting McNeil take the *Anastasia* on the next run. But never fear," he kissed her neck, causing some of the crew to stop and stare at the captain and his wife, "I will keep my word. I will not sail without you."

"Good." She turned to face him.

"Married less than a week and I am already henpecked," he chuckled. "But I give you fair warning, madam. You are not going on every run with me. I will not put you in a dangerous situation again."

"Yes dear," she meekly complied, resting her head on his shoulder. Unfortunately, Nicholas missed the wicked grin.

They were heading toward the gangplank when a rider galloped to the dock.

"That's Jon. What the devil is he doing here?"

Jonathan Rhodes sauntered up the plank to greet his brother and Morgan. "I will not say one word to you, brother, if this woman is not your American wife!" Jon kissed Morgan's cheek.

"Wait a minute, Jon," Nicholas coughed.

"No. I have no time for your stern lectures. I've heard quite a few and given some of my own in the last few months." Jonathan turned to Morgan. "Did you marry him or do you intend to act as if you don't love one another?"

"Oh yes, Jon," she flashed her wedding ring. "I think it is legal this time. My mother and Uncle Eric would not leave the church until they certified that all was correctly signed and sealed.

"Good. It's about time you both came to your senses," Jon slapped his brother's back.

Nicholas was startled. Who was this buoyant, outspoken man? Surely not the Jonathan Rhodes he had known; the man who looked more like Nicholas's father than brother.

"I've been looking out for the *Anastasia* for weeks. Peter Mackenzie had written to tell us when you might be in New York. And Eric sent one letter, explaining as much as he could

487

about your hasty departure."

"Then you don't know?" Nicholas suspiciously asked, his arm securely resting on Morgan's shoulder.

"Know what?" Jon tried to shade his blue eyes with his hand.

"About the currency plates?"

"Nick, I don't give a damn about those plates. Father never should have made you promise to find them or Morgan. Although I'm pleased you found Morgan," he happily announced. His grin was infectious. Morgan could not help but smile in return.

"Poor Father," he continued, "I haven't spoken a civil word to him in months. I doubt that Mother has yet. She moved back into their house last week."

"Wait." Nicholas lifted one hand. "What the devil are you chattering about?" he impatiently demanded.

"I don't know what you see in him, Morgan. Such a fierce temper. Now I am not like that. I can be . . ."

"Jonathan, so help me, I'll . . ." Nicholas's mottled expression amused Jon and Morgan.

"Why don't we go to your house? I had it readied for your return."

"You did?"

"Of course, brother. I was sure you would be back within the month. So I took the liberty of rehiring the Carltons."

"Why?"

"What a stupid question, Nick. You are my brother, aren't you? I wanted to be of assistance." Jon was offended.

"I will not budge until you tell me why you are here, why you haven't spoken to Father, why Morgan . . ."

"The southern sun must have addled his wits, Morgan. Nick, you don't think that any one of us wanted to see you or Morgan hurt. It was all wrong. It was wrong of Mother to ask you to play that stupid charade. It was wrong of Father to accuse Morgan of those dreadful things. Who would believe such nonsense?" he asked rhetorically. "It was wrong of you, Morgan, to pay attention to Father's nonsense, and *you* Nick, to go off in the middle of the night half-cocked." Jon paused to catch his breath.

"I don't believe this, Morgan," Nicholas scratched his head. "What is so funny?"

"You. Can't you understand what Jonathan is trying to say. He's telling you that he has—and I would venture to say always will stand up for you. You simply have to open your eyes, Nicholas Rhodes. Pay attention," she scolded mildly, but the mirth was in her golden eyes.

"Dammit, I'm trying."

"Nick, my man. It's really quite simple. After you left, I did a lot of thinking about Father, you, and me; about standing up for what one believes to be right. You were wrong about me. But I harbor no resentment. Neither does Sally. You and I are different, I suppose. But not as different as you think."

"I need a drink," Nicholas muttered.

"So do I," Jon laughed. "Morgan, why don't you keep Mr. McNeil company?"

Morgan dared not disturb the brothers. Surprised and pleased by Jon's bold actions, she hoped that Nick would be impressed. If nothing else, he would hopefully conquer the ambivalent feelings he had toward his brother. Jon cared for him, and had stood up to Warren because of him. What else did Jonathan need to do to prove that he too was independent? Christine Rhodes knew that. Morgan had suspected it. What would Nicholas think?

Enjoying herself above deck, Morgan watched the unloading of the cargo. How Nick had found the time to purchase items in New Orleans she did not know. Nevertheless, there were crates and barrels of sugar, corn, tobacco, lumber, cotton, a variety of spices and food, and other products from the western and southwestern sections of the Louisiana Territory.

Morgan suspected that some of the unmarked barrels might appear to have been purchased in New Orleans but originated in France or the Spanish Territory. No wonder Nick was interested in going back to New Orleans, she mused. He could make as much money in less time with less danger than sailing in and out of Halifax or across the Atlantic.

A cool breeze ruffled her skirts and hair, but Morgan seemed unaffected. She smelled the air, which was a mixture of the pungent sea and the land. It had become a familiar scent to her.

Although the crew was busy finishing their chores and preparing for shore leave, no one left the ship without bidding farewell to the captain's wife.

"Ye better be sailin' with us again, Mrs. The captain's a might nicer with you aboard. Sure is a pleasure," said one.

"He was real cross when we sailed to France. He was pining for ye, Mrs. That's what we all figured. Kidnapped ye, we heard. Well he sure as hell goes after what he wants."

The crew probably knew the whole story of their stormy relationship, but seemed genuinely pleased that the captain found his wife. The mysterious but ever-present Gordon had become Morgan's unofficial protector. The big man who rarely spoke remained tight-lipped about their trek across the Lousiana Territory. Morgan leaned over the rail of the quarterdeck to plant a chaste kiss on his cheek.

"You are a good man, Mr. Gordon. Thank you for everything."

The man blushed to the roots of his red hair and quickly disembarked.

"My goodness, Morgan, you have the entire crew eating out of your hand. I wonder who they will listen to in the future, you or me?" Nicholas's broad grin was infectious. "What do you think, Jon?"

"I think you will have a problem if she keeps wearing breeches."

"How did you know?" She turned to Nicholas. "You told him?"

"Not everything. But I believe we will have the time for another conversation."

Nicholas and Jonathan stood side by side. Jon was beaming his arm affectionately patting Nick's shoulders.

"I might sign up on your next voyage, if you'll take a landlubber." His laugh was similar to his brother's.

"With or without Sally?" Morgan innocently inquired.

"Definitely without. Speaking of wives, I must be off. See you at dinner tonight."

"What dinner?" she suspiciously asked after Jon left.

"We, my lovely wife, are going to visit my parents tonight. I have a surprise for my father."

490

"You're giving him the plates tonight?"

"I no longer wish to have those bronze items in my possession. As you have said," he tweaked her pert nose, "they are part of our past."

Morgan could say no more, for he quickly returned to ordering the crew about.

One moment they were aboard the *Anastasia*, the next in their Greenwich Street town house, and the next approaching the Rhodes home on Broadway. Nervous, but filled with determination, Morgan stepped elegantly out of the coach, assisted by her handsome husband. Not completely willing to yield to convention, Nicholas wore a snow-white silk shirt and dark blue breeches. The jacket was held in one hand.

They were barely at the front door when it was wrenched open by a very robust-looking Warren Rhodes.

"You're back! You're both back. What took you so long?" he bellowed. Warren fired so many questions that neither Nicholas nor Morgan could summon an adequate response.

"It's good to see you in such good health, Father," Nicholas cautiously said. They stood awkwardly in the marble foyer.

"No thanks to my wife or elder son. I tell you they haven't said a decent word since you left. Now that you've returned, perhaps I'll have peace in my home once more."

Nicholas extended his right hand, but Warren would have none of it. Grasping his son's shoulders, he pulled him into a warm embrace. "I've missed you son."

Morgan did not see Nick's face, but she saw Warren's. He was flushed with excitement and his blue eyes were bright with unshed tears.

"You too Morgan," he extended an arm to her. "I haven't had a book or legal document without remembering the sound of your pretty voice."

It was more than she could take. Morgan openly wept on Warren's shoulder. From the sound and feel of his heaving chest, Warren was moved. Nicholas looked on bemusedly.

Wondering what was taking so long, Christine Rhodes found her son, husband, and daughter-in-law shuffling their feet and

491

wiping their eyes.

"It's all right to come in. I wasn't the one who was : stubborn and foolish."

"Ah Chrissie, how much longer will you go on punishing m for my mistake," Warren blew his nose.

"Long enough for you to tell your son and his wife how sorr you are."

"Can we do it in the library?" Warren sheepishly asked

Nicholas leaned against the teakwood desk in a familia casual stance. Morgan and Christine were seated in th Sheraton armchairs to his left. Warren paced, pausing befo each of the family portraits along the panelled walls.

"I do owe you an apology. Especially you, Morgan. I wond if you can ever forgive a foolish old man. I committed a crim you see. One of the most unreasonable acts a law-abidi American can commit. I tried and judged you unfairly. I d not want to hear or see the evidence that undoubtedly prov your father's innocence. I was, as my wife has reminded me hundreds of occasions, stubborn and prejudiced. But I ho you can forgive me," he paused to clear his throat. "I understand if you don't; certainly Christine and Jon haven But I want you to know I will do everything in my power help you clear your father's name."

"That won't be necessary, Father." Nicholas broke in, l voice tempered by emotion. "We have something for you Nicholas excused himself and went out to their carriag quickly returning with a leather satchel.

"They are all in here. The eight genuine bronze curren plates. Morgan and I want you to have them. You can retu them to the secretary of the treasury. I guess it is what y wanted from the outset," he boldly met Warren's surpris gaze.

"Yes, it was. But it was a terrible price I had to pay. More f you, dear, than any of us." Warren approached Morgan.

Moved by his words and genuine sorrow, Morgan knew s could forgive him. "It's all over, Mr. Rhodes. It was the wor and best year of my life. I had a mission to accomplish. In doing, I experienced pain and sorrow, but also more love a happiness than any woman could find in a lifetime." She ro to stand beside her husband. "I found Nick, or rather," she laughed, "he found me. But I am so glad. For that you see, Mr. Rhodes, I really should thank you. If you hadn't made him promise to help you . . ."

"Stupid and foolish on my part."

"And mine," Nicholas added.

"Yes but I never would have met you, now would I?" she linked one arm through his. "I do believe we owe your father our thanks," she winked at Christine.

"My wife has the strangest logic I have ever heard. You should hear some of her comments," Nicholas chuckled, but his eyes softened as he looked upon his lovely wife.

"You haven't heard your mother's way of reasoning, son."

"But I am often right. Isn't that true Warren?"

Standing behind his wife, Warren said, "I'll have those plates delivered to Mr. Gallatin tomorrow. And hopefully he will remember what I have done, especially if I need his assistance."

"Assistance for what, Father?"

"If you are ever arrested for smuggling, someone will have to free you. It might as well be me," he said gruffly.

Nicholas stared at his sleeping wife, nestled as usual in the crook of his arm, her black hair splayed in tangles behind her. He closed his eyes and held his love tightly.

They had finally come home.

I hope you enjoyed reading about the adventures of Morgan and Nicholas. I would love to hear from my readers. I will personally answer all my mail. Please write to me at:

P. O. Box #1
Bay Station
Brooklyn, N.Y. 11235

Victoria London

CAPTIVATING ROMANCE FROM ZEBRA

MIDNIGHT DESIRE   (1573, $3.50)
by Linda Benjamin

Looking into the handsome gunslinger's blazing blue eyes, innocent Kate felt dizzy. His husky voice, so warm and inviting, sent a river of fire cascading through her flesh. But she knew she'd never willingly give her heart to the arrogant rogue!

PASSION'S GAMBLE   (1477, $3.50)
by Linda Benjamin

Jade-eyed Jessica was too shocked to protest when the riverboat cardsharp offered *her* as the stakes in a poker game. Then she met the smouldering glance of his opponent as he stared at her satiny cheeks and the tantalizing fullness of her bodice—and she found herself hoping he would hold the winning hand!

FORBIDDEN FIRES   (1295, $3.50)
by Bobbi Smith

When Ellyn Douglas rescued the handsome Union officer from the raging river, she had no choice but to surrender to the sensuous stranger as he pulled her against his hard muscular body. Forgetting they were enemies in a senseless war, they were destined to share a life of unbridled ecstasy and glorious love!

WANTON SPLENDOR   (1461, $3.50)
by Bobbi Smith

Kathleen had every intention of keeping her distance from Christopher Fletcher. But in the midst of a devastating hurricane, she crept into his arms. As she felt the heat of his lean body pressed against hers, she wondered breathlessly what it would be like to kiss those cynical lips—to turn that cool arrogance to fiery passion!

Available wherever paperbacks are sold, or order direct from the Publisher. Send cover price plus 50¢ per copy for mailing and handling to Zebra Books, Dept. 1787, 475 Park Avenue South, New York, N.Y. 10016. DO NOT SEND CASH.